OPERATION CACTUS BLOSSOM

A PRICKLY PEN INVESTIGATION

Books by Stacy Lee

Prickly Pen Investigations Series
Operation Superglue
Operation Cactus Blossom

Coming Soon!
Operation Desert Blues

For more information
visit: www.SpeakingVolumes.us

OPERATION CACTUS BLOSSOM

A PRICKLY PEN INVESTIGATION

Stacy Lee

SPEAKING VOLUMES, LLC
NAPLES, FLORIDA
2025

Operation Cactus Blossom

Copyright © 2025 by Stacy Lee

All rights reserved. No part of this book may be reproduced or transmitted in any form or by any means without written permission.

ISBN 979-8-89022-299-2

For Ryan Lewis, your kindness, dedication, and passion
for helping others—especially your advocacy for those with mental illness—
make the world a better place. I'm grateful for your guidance, your work, and
your invaluable insight into private investigation.

Acknowledgments

I am truly blessed to be living my dream as a full-time author, and I am overcome with gratitude for the many incredible individuals I have been blessed with along the way. A gigantic thank you to my agent, Nancy Rosenfeld of AAA Books Unlimited, Kurt and Erica of Speaking Volumes, Kris from the Talking Book, Allen Redwing of Story Genius, and Lynn and her team at Red Adept Editing. I appreciate all of you!

To my husband, Paul Barbagallo, thank you for believing in me, encouraging me, and loving me unconditionally. You truly are the "Jon" to my "Lina." Thank you to my children, Paul and Lucy. Paul, you are crushing your third year of high school. We love watching you play football and supporting you in all your sports. I can't believe we are looking at colleges! Lucy, we are so proud of you for discovering your love of running through cross country and even prouder that you have tried something new. You are crushing your first year of high school, and we can't wait for your first songs to be released. We are so incredibly proud of you both. We will always have your backs, and we will always be your biggest fans.

I am incredibly grateful to Jaclyn Hannan for her constant guidance and support and for helping me discover who I am as my authentic self. To Rob Hulse, my deepest thanks for going above and beyond and for helping me to stay on track with my goals. We are so proud of where your DJ career is taking you—we're just getting started.

Thank you to my parents, Karen and Dan DeBruyckere; sister, Kate Giglio, and her husband, Joe; my sister-in-law, Cheri Grassi, and her husband, Mike; my father-in-law, Paul Barbagallo; my aunt, Pat Fishwick; and my brother, Dan DeBruyckere Jr. Thank you to my friends Kara Holloway, Leigh Anne Hulse, and Jessica Delano. Thank you to everyone who has been a part of this journey, and to those I've lost along the way, there will always be a place for you in my heart.

Of course, I need to thank you, the reader! May you continue to love without hesitation and dream the biggest dreams. Remember, nothing is impossible. You are stronger than you think, and there is always a way if you follow your heart. Never give up, even in the stickiest of situations, and remember—love is a chance worth taking; you can't win if you never play the game.

Content Advisory

Operation Cactus Blossom is a private investigator romance suspense novel. Although the underlying themes are lighthearted and uplifting and we have grown to love our witty characters, the comedic banter, and "sticky" situations Jon and Lina experience throughout the story, this book does contain content that may be sensitive to some. *Please stop reading this advisory if you wish to avoid spoilers.*

This book includes sensitive themes, such as teenage-kidnapping, organ trafficking, infidelity, mental illness, gambling, theft, and gang activity that may be distressing to some readers. Please proceed only if you are comfortable with these subjects. Your well-being is important to the author, so please read with care.

Prologue

The Midst of the Storm

Within the thirsty sea of sands,
A cactus blossom in cruel hands.
Resilient, strong, she never bends,
But with his touch, her spirit mends.

In the darkest night, in fear's tight hold,
The truth unknown, each promise gold.
Threatened by hope, longing to shine
In the midst of storm, their hearts align.

Love blooms in places unexpected,
A heart once guarded, now connected.
In desert winds, he finds her way,
A silver line on the darkest day.

The fading sunset calls to all,
In calm or rage, we rise, we fall.
But can we see, in tempest's might,
The beauty in each other's light?

She rises tall, with gratitude,
Appreciating life's vastitude.
For every mistake, a new life's begun,
Love is a gamble—this time they've won.

Chapter One

Then (October 2023) Alanna

Growing up, I had the most overprotective and predictable parents imaginable. Of course, they were great humans, and I was truly blessed to have them in my life, blah blah blah . . . but man oh man, were they over the top. Picture it—Dad, living his best life on the daily as a park ranger at Cave Creek Regional Park, working the practical hours of 10:00 a.m. to 4:00 p.m., allowing him ample time to get settled back home at the head of our rectangular oak dining room table in his knee-length brown khaki shorts and matching Boy Scout-wannabe shirt just in time to sink his teeth into Mom's homemade meatloaf, green bean casserole, or the bane of my existence, her roasted-chicken-and-brussels-sprout special, with a genuine sense of gratitude and a boyish grin as he stated with admiration, "Thank you, dear. This is delicious." Every. Freaking. Day.

It wasn't that I didn't appreciate them. Honestly, my dad was my hero. Not only had he figured out a way to stomach my mother's overcooked, rubbery, tasteless chicken for over twenty years of marriage, but his performance was Oscar worthy, and if we're being honest, I often wondered if my mother saw through his faux love for her culinary ability or if she truly believed him. Of course, we appreciated the lengths she went to cook for us, as she had a career of her own as a flight attendant for Jet Blue. Although she only flew east to Boston and back to Phoenix on a schedule that was considered breezy compared to her co-workers, Mom never missed a Sunday dinner at our home. The single-family ranch had been in our family for years. Also, over her dead body would she miss a parent-teacher conference, school play, or cheerleading competition. As a matter a fact, both my parents would be found front row at these Emerson Academy events with painted faces and the most obnoxious noisemakers you can imagine. You think I'm exaggerating? Consider me ungrateful? My cheerleading team received a two-point deduction my sophomore year because my dad made a sign that read My Daughter Is a Better Cheerleader Than Yours and jogged past the judges' panel, flashing it with pride as they announced my team onto the mat. We missed first place by two points.

I'd been told my parents were protective because I was the oldest of three siblings, and another popular opinion was that I should have *appreciated* what they did for me. And trust me, I was *not* a spoiled brat. I loved Patrick and Laura—really, I did—but they embarrassed me on a level that I can't quite put into words. And when my younger siblings, Christopher and Eliza, bitched and moaned about them, I *did* have their backs. I reinforced the positives like an older sibling should to a fourteen-year-old brother and nine-year-old sister, especially because I realized how impressionable and immature they still were, unlike myself, a seventeen-year-old senior who would graduate Emerson the following year with honors and an early acceptance to UCLA's nursing program on a partial scholarship.

I should also mention that I was a fantastic daughter. Seriously, I made their lives easy, compared to some of my peers. The lowest grade I'd ever received at Emerson was an A-, I helped around the house, I volunteered at the local shelter, and I carted my younger siblings around to activities without even a simple complaint. So, why, then, couldn't they even partake in a single negotiation about my curfew being extended past nine-thirty at night? I would be eighteen soon, and I had no social life because, apparently, that was not essential to my well-being. And I think they liked it that way.

So, as I gathered my blonde hair over one shoulder and squeezed my boobs together inside my sports bra, creating a decent amount of impressive cleavage, I puckered my thick lips, smiling up provocatively at my flawlessly angled cell phone for the perfect selfie. In the back of my mind, I thought about my crush and the excitement that would rush through him when he received my selfie in Snap, and I couldn't help but think I was sticking it to my perfect parents and their nine-thirty curfew, and they could kiss my ass.

They didn't know about my crush, and I would rather die a slow and painful death than tell them—not because they wouldn't be open to meeting a guy I was seeing but because I've only ever talked to Lincoln over Snap. If they ever found out about him, I would lose Snapchat, my phone, and any sense of freedom I did have. But I didn't care because my crush, Lincoln Stone, was the best thing to happen to me since my favorite books were adapted into a show, *The Summer I Turned Pretty*, and my celebrity crush, Christopher Briney, was announced as the lead role. If you'd known me back then, you would've realized what a big deal that was, because Christopher Briney is *electric*.

It wasn't that Lincoln didn't want to meet in person. He did, and I was counting down the seconds until I could meet him in real life, to touch his golden skin and run my fingers through his thick, shaggy blond tresses. I often fantasized about his crystal baby blues and what they would look like as he leaned toward me in anticipation of our first kiss. But with my curfew being so early, it just hadn't happened yet. Lincoln went to a public school in Scottsdale and between work and sports would only be able to meet me after ten in the evening, which did not bode well for my nine-thirty curfew.

I tugged my T-shirt over my head and smiled to the sound of my phone buzzing, knowing without even looking that Lincoln had snapped me back. We had a Snap streak of ninety-two days, and I knew he wouldn't miss a beat. I reached for my cell and swiped open our chat to find that Lincoln had responded with a photo of only his side abs. His sculpted abdominal contour and V-shaped torso machine-gunned flashes of electricity from my phone's screen to my eyeballs and into the depths of my soul. Heat immediately flushed through my face and chest as I wiped the dripping beads of sweat from the base of my neck with my palm. I glanced around the locker room to see if any of my fellow athletes were still there, because I knew what was coming next. The last time Lincoln had sent me a Snap of a body part, he asked for one of mine in return. Honestly, I didn't love doing it, but I did love what I had going with Lincoln, so I had indeed sent him photos before. Before you panic or feel the need to report me to Laura and Patrick, you can rest assured that the photos were very PG-13, nothing I would make any money for on Only Fans. However, pervs pay money to see feet, so if my nursing career fell short, that was always a possibility. I did have nice feet.

My concentration shattered as my phone lit up with a text from my friend, Hank. I ignored it at first, hyper focused on Lincoln and our chat, but Hank texted three more times, so I flopped down on the locker room bench, my sweaty legs sticking to the wood as I scrolled through my friend's texts.

Hank: *Yo*
Hank: *You still at school?*
Hank: *Chill tonight? Bill and his crew scored beers.*

I rolled my eyes, knowing damn well that I wouldn't be able to hang with Hank and his twin brother, Bill, as it was my night to volunteer at the shelter until nine, and that wouldn't leave time for partying of any kind. Also, if I was going to do anything, it would have been with Lincoln, but that was beside the point.

Alanna: *Hi, sorry just finished practice. OMW to the shelter. TTYL*
Hank: *Dude, WTF*
Alanna: *???*
Hank: *You ghosting?*
Alanna: *Nah, just swamped.*
Hank: *Who's the dude? You back with Zack?*

I rolled my eyes and shook my head as my fingers pressed briskly against the phone's surface. I didn't keep much from Hank, but Lincoln was the first guy I'd liked since I broke it off with Zack, the football team's starting quarterback, who was also one of Hank's best friends. I wasn't sure how he would react. I mean, I knew Hank and I were just friends, but talking about Lincoln out loud just felt like that might make it go away or something. Thoughts of Lincoln had consumed me. My friendship with Hank was more like a sibling relationship, and I didn't need my big bro knowing about my interactions with someone I'd met over Snapchat. Every part of me knew he would never understand. My snaps and messages with Lincoln were more than just flirty and fun, they were *real*. I was starting to fall for Lincoln, and I wanted to keep him to myself.

Alanna: *Let's hang Saturday. K?*
Hank: *FML*

I breathed a heavy sigh and swiped out of my text with Hank, hopped up from the bench, and packed the remainder of my things just as my phone buzzed again with a message from Lincoln. My cheeks flushed in embarrassment at his request, and I glanced around the locker room again before removing my T-shirt and sliding down my black Under Armour sports bra just enough to give Lincoln what he asked for. A satisfied smile formed as I sent the photo, and to my relief he sent a chat.

Lincoln: *Baby when can I see U? CU2N?*

My cheeks flushed and I shook my head no as though he could see me. I let out a frustrated groan. I would have loved to see him that night, but again, that wasn't in the cards.

Alanna: *Not tonight. But soon. I'm sorry.*
Lincoln: *How soon? No cap.*
Alanna: *Soon.*

I tucked the phone into my shorts pocket and draped my backpack over my shoulder, heading out of the locker room and into the hallways of Emerson Academy, wondering how and when I would be able to pull off meeting Lincoln Stone.

My phone buzzed again, and without looking, I knew it was Lincoln. I continued down the deserted hallway, reaching into my pocket and retrieving my cell. I stopped in my tracks as my eyes landed on his photo. His blue eyes were sad and longing, and his lips formed a tiny pout.

Lincoln: *Pleaze, Baby.*

I let out a frustrated moan and studied the tall ceiling and its intricate molding and ornate details, searching for answers. I was tired of being treated like a child, and it was time I put my foot down. There had to be a way to convince my parents to let me stay out just a tiny bit later than curfew. My parents were logical, reasonable human beings at least fifty percent of the time. So, I took a deep breath and dialed my mother, hoping and praying that maybe, just maybe, that would be the day she budged just a tiny bit and I might just get to meet my crush, Lincoln. I was convinced he could be way more than just a sneaky link, someone I was seeing in private but also someone who would sweep me off my feet and love me the way I'd always wanted to be loved. I wanted so badly to hear his voice, to learn his laugh, to uncover his thoughts by gazing into his eyes, to hear him call me Baby—amongst other words he'd typed—to touch him in ways I'd fantasized about but had never spoken of. Lincoln could be the *one*—the one who would see me the way I'd always wanted to be seen. I'd been waiting for a guy like him, and I was so glad I'd waited. Because Lincoln would be my first. And I was ready. I was ready for him. And if that meant breaking the rules, disappointing my parents, and shutting out my friends, then so be it.

If only I'd known then what I know now.

Chapter Two

Now (March 2025) Lina

I fiddle with the magenta stone of Jon's promise ring and exhale longer and louder than I intend, my blank laptop screen taunting me in ways that just don't seem fair. I've experienced writer's block before, but this most definitely is *not* that. With writing, I have skills and strategies for pushing through and being productive. For example, if I'm having a bad writing day, I can skip ahead in the story's timeline and revisit it later—or even better, I can take a coffee break and start fresh when I'm ready. But this is different. Being overly puzzled and dumbfounded about how to solve a case or even how to find one measly lead is an entirely new annoyance for me. My stories are fiction, but in this case, lives are at stake. No, really—a life is at stake. You don't believe me? Ask Alanna Foster. That's right, you *can't* because she's been missing for over a year. And although I came close to bringing her home to her family, I fell short. I could've saved her during Operation Superglue, but we were just too late. And I get to live with that for the rest of my life.

    The truth is I've been an author for decades longer than I've been a private investigator. Yes, you heard me correctly. I, Lina Rivera, mother of two from Scottsdale, Arizona, am a licensed private eye. How badass does that sound? Admit it. It's hardcore—little ol' me, fighting crime and saving lives. You think I'm kidding? Man oh man, do I have stories that would blow your mind. And since I'm stumped—like, legit mentally blocked on where to go from here on this case—I will take a moment to fill you in. Grab a Starbucks, ladies and gentlemen. We are going to be here a while.

    It all started last August when, for the first time in my writing career, a novel in my series fell flat. You see, I write young adult crime and suspense novels. My reviewers accused me of being out of touch with my target audience, teenagers. That was somewhat humorous, considering I *have* twin teenagers. One of the reviews stated, "Who is the author of these books, anyways?

How old is she? Like, eighty? Her protagonist is a sixteen-year-old female with the soul of a woman in her mid-forties." As it turned out, the reviews couldn't have been more accurate. Being a teenager in 2024 was a lifetime of difference from when I graduated from high school in the late nineties. And to say I found this out the hard way is an understatement to say the least.

I'd been meeting my ex-husband at the Starbucks in Tempe monthly since we divorced over ten years prior. We'd used our meetings to brief one another on our cherubs, mostly talking about our daughter Lucy and her latest friend drama or schoolgirl crush, along with our son Max and his ADHD diagnosis and challenges in school. Ironically enough, this meeting was not only the same day I received the negative book reviews. It was also the morning I caught our fifteen-year-old Lucy in bed with her boyfriend, Oliver, and I was painfully contemplating whether or not to bring this issue to the attention of my ex-husband, knowing he would not only emotionally overreact but would also gut Oliver from the inside out with his bare hands.

So, on that insanely hot desert morning as I sat across from Jon Cote, I used my book reviews as a shield for my daughter and her idiotic boyfriend, and as I did, Jon formulated an idea that would change everything. You see, Jon is a private investigator and had been working an assignment since the previous March. Three high school students had "run away" from Emerson Academy, and the dean of the school, Dean Elizabeth Downing, was convinced the students had been kidnapped. Jon got hired as the school's substitute art teacher, hoping he could locate the missing girls. Alanna Foster had been the first to run away. She disappeared in October of 2023 after having an argument with her mother about her curfew. The Tempe police were convinced Alanna had run away based on the circumstances at home and missing items from her bedroom. But then, Chloe and Teresa, two more girls from Emerson, went missing in late fall and early winter of the same school year.

So, you can imagine Jon's frustration when I sat with him that late August morning. After being undercover at the school since that previous March, he didn't have one single lead. When he learned that I needed to be in touch with my target audience, he couldn't resist. He spilled the tea about Operation Superglue and asked me to go undercover as Gemma Mendoza, an eighteen-year-old transfer student from Jupiter, Florida. And because of my extremely solid genes—my mom has great skin—and because I've always taken such great care of myself with top-notch skincare and Botox injections for migraines, I look younger than my mid-thirties, so much so that I can't even buy a scratch ticket without being carded. For these reasons alone, Jon insisted I go undercover to help him find the missing girls.

I hadn't agreed to it right away. My marriage with Jon had ended in the most devastating way possible. He had an affair with a college student while undercover. My best friend and former college roommate, Daphne, found a post on social media that insinuated Jon's infidelity, but it wasn't until I barged in on him myself and found him smack dab on top of the woman did I believe it for myself. As if that wasn't bad enough, in order to preserve his cover and prevent the drug-dealing frat boys from murdering all of us, Jon pretended he didn't know me, leaving Owen, the frat boy in charge, to beat me to a pulp just so Jon could prove his loyalty.

If it hadn't been for our children, Max and Lucy, I would've broken all ties with him completely. But when my editor threatened to cut my best-selling series short by one book and encouraged me to write women's *divorce* fiction, I knew I had no choice. So off I went, undercover as Gemma Mendoza as a high-school senior. And although it wasn't pretty—I've been in counseling weekly for the past six months—I did it. I, Lina Rivera, with the help of Jon Cote, solved Operation Superglue. We found *most* of the missing girls—all but one, Alanna Foster.

But Operation Superglue wasn't a complete bust. We reunited fifteen teenage girls total with their families, and somehow, I found my way back to Jon, and he found his way back to me. And being undercover and forced to lie to everyone in sight, I gained something of an appreciation for what Jon went through while undercover. It didn't happen overnight, and we're in no way back to where we started, but just one week ago, at Prickly Pen Investigations, he got down on one knee and offered me a promise ring, along with the promise that he would always be honest with me from there on out. That is that happiest ending I can think of, and trust me—I am good at happy endings.

And although I can pillow my head at night, knowing I've done so much good, I still can't shake the fact that we never saved Alanna. Aside from that, the trauma I experienced in the process of rescuing the other teens is something I struggle with every day. Not only have I been diagnosed with PTSD for the second time in my adult life, but the multiple concussions sustained during the undercover operation have contributed to the worsening of my migraines, and lately, I've had more headache days than not. And even though we haven't been officially rehired onto Alanna's case, against Jon's advice, I have continued digging because no matter how hard I try, I can't get the image of Alanna Foster out of my mind. Her wide sea-green eyes were stunning against the contrast of her tanned skin and light blonde hair in the school photo Jon and I referenced for Operation Superglue. She was due to leave for college that fall to pursue a career in nursing, and she had a heart for helping the homeless and mentally ill. It just didn't seem fair that she was taken, probably in a similar way to how I'd been kidnapped. And I won't rest until we find her, no matter how many times Jon asks me to stop.

I tap my fingers against the glass surface of my desk and stare blankly at the ceiling, hoping beyond hope for some kind of idea, any idea as to where Alanna might be. Just one month ago, we had a lead, the Super Scorpion Pest Removal van. Yes, you're hearing me correctly—a pest control van. It showed up at my house prior to my involvement with Operation Superglue. The driver was allegedly soliciting new clients in my neighborhood but took an exceptionally odd interest in my age. Then that same company's van transported me from where I was being held underground with other kidnapping victims to an abandoned warehouse in Tempe. Last week, I followed the van with Jon and my ex-boyfriend Travis—that's a story for another day—and ran its plates, only to find that it checked out. Super Scorpion Pest Removal was not our guy.

That leaves me with this: absolutely freaking nothing. Sure, I rescued the other girls, and I am proud of that. I discovered a lot about myself during my experience undercover, gained a friend in Molly, one of the students I met during my time at Emerson, and found my way back to Jon. Those are all positives, right? So then why, at the end of the day, when I close my eyes and drift off to sleep, do I feel like a failure? I'll tell you why: because somewhere across town is a family missing their daughter. And instead of being safe and sound in a dorm room at UCLA, living it up as a college student, she is God knows where—if she's even still alive—all because I couldn't get to her in time.

My thoughts are interrupted by the sound of the front door of PPI, and Jon enters, Starbucks in hand.

"My hero," I sigh before the door closes behind him.

"For you," he says, passing me a somewhat melted Frappuccino and kissing my forehead.

"You're a lifesaver," I say, soaking in the warm sensation of his lips against my skin on the exact spot where my head has been pounding for what feels like eternity. "I needed that."

"The kiss or the coffee?" he challenges, one eyebrow raised.

"Both, I confess." I pierce my straw through the whipped cream and suck in the frosty beverage. "But please don't make me choose."

Jon smiles with the boyish grin I can't resist and runs his thumb and index finger over his beard's scruff. Jon stands tall at six feet two inches and seems to be skyrocketing over me as I sit in my office chair. I cover my eyes from the sun's glare, and I beam up at him, smile wide. He is so incredibly handsome, and it's times like these, when he shows up unexpectedly and surprises me with coffee, that I find myself letting my guard down and optimistically looking forward instead of back.

"I would hope you would choose me," he scoffs. "But then again, *coffee* has never let you down." His smile says he is goofing, but his eyes contradict this.

So I rise from my chair and stand on my tiptoes, reaching my arms around his neck, and bury my face against it. "Stop that," I whisper. "We aren't looking back, remember?"

Jon remains silent but squeezes me more tightly. I inhale his sweet, spicy scent and feel the tension and my neck and shoulders release. "Maybe I just need a real kiss," I boldly suggest.

Jon pulls back, eyebrows raised. "Oh yeah?"

I smirk, gently guiding his chin toward me, holding my gaze on his baby blues until my mouth presses against his, and he releases a deep and gravelly moan, and I part his lips with my tongue, reaching my hands behind his head and yanking him as close as I can to me.

I pull back only to whisper, "Better than coffee," before kissing him again, this time tracing my fingers under the back of his shirt, his skin warm against my hands.

Jon glides down onto my chair and pulls me on top of him, gripping my legs on either side of his torso, sliding my pencil skirt up just enough for me to move freely, and clasping his hands around my lower back, our kiss becoming more intense by the second.

"Jon," I moan unintentionally but unapologetically, completely and utterly lost in a simple kiss.

But that is how this has been, kissing Jon Cote. Yes, I've known him since my college years, but we've started over, which means acting like horny teenagers sometimes—like now. I, a thirty-six-year-old mother of two kids—*his* two kids, to be exact—am acting like some sort of wild savage, pressing his jeans-covered bulge between my thighs and thrusting myself against him like I've never been with a man before, let alone this man.

"We should lock the door," I whisper between breaths while biting on his earlobe.

As if on cue, the office door swings open, and I leap off Jon's package like I've spontaneously caught fire.

Jon bolts upright, adjusting the waistband of his jeans with a muffled, "Sorry, Travis."

I do my best to straighten my disheveled brunette tresses, tuck my blouse back into my skirt, and mutter a quiet, "Sorry, Travis . . . again," without looking Travis, my ex-boyfriend, in the eye.

Yes, my life is that ass backwards. My ex-boyfriend, the guy I was dating while undercover during Operation Superglue, is now an employee and partner at Prickly Pen Investigations with Jon and me. Cause why not?

"Why in the actual hell is it too much to ask for you two fools to get a room? I've seen you humping like rabbits at least five times in the past six months."

"My place, tonight?" Jon says more than asks, and I nod, wondering how I'll be able to wait that long to finish what we just started and trying with all my might to compose myself.

Jon and I ignore Travis. Since this has turned into his standard greeting because Jon and I haven't been able to keep our hands off each other, there's really nothing left to say. Also, my relationship with Travis is overly complicated for more reasons than I can count because when I was under with Operation Superglue and keeping it from Travis, he was simultaneously being blackmailed by Dean Turner and, without knowing what he was getting himself into, was responsible for some of the kidnappings, including my own. Of course, mine was orchestrated by Jon and me in an effort to find the missing girls. We'd been stuck without any leads until I received a Snapchat message from a hot blond stud muffin named Lincoln Stone. I realized immediately that his profile was fake, and when I agreed to meet him at a bus stop in downtown Tempe, it was obvious I was attending the event as nothing but bait. And after being smashed in the side of the head with a baseball bat and stuffed in the trunk of a car, I arrived at my destination only to find Travis Mullins on the other side. Yes, you heard that right. Travis, my boyfriend at the time, not only helped to kidnap me but—wait for it—also unintentionally broke my arm during my attempt to escape and contributed to one of my concussions. My arm has since healed, but my head is another story, in both a physical and emotional sense, that is.

But when Travis approached us about working together to find Alanna, we couldn't say no. Sure, he'd been involved with the kidnappings, but he only did what he did because he was being blackmailed. We'd learned that Dean Orson Turner handed the girls over in exchange for his own son's freedom from an underground gang. Travis, a pharmacist, was illegally prescribing medication for the dean's son, Emmett, which was going well until he threatened to turn Travis in if he didn't help with the kidnappings. And Travis is more dedicated to finding Alanna than anyone else. His guilt has been devouring him from the inside out, and not only that, he was also living in fear that Dean Turner would throw him under the bus at any given moment. For whatever reason, even though he was behind bars for what he did, Dean Turner wasn't speaking about Travis to the cops. This is a relief to Travis but serves as a huge red flag. If Dean Orson Turner hasn't been telling the cops about Travis, he's been keeping other things from them, too, and preventing us from finding Alanna. That's becoming more and more problematic as time ticks away and Alanna is still unaccounted for.

I plop back down on my office chair and study Travis out of the corner of my eye. I fan myself with a folded-up piece of notebook paper, sure that my cheeks are flushed, and the rise and fall of my chest reveals my rapid heart rate. Travis's eyes meet mine, and I mouth a humiliated "sorry" with my lips, and he shrugs and snaps open his laptop, his fingers briskly meeting the computer's keys in his usual no-nonsense manner when it comes to the investigation.

"I can't believe the plate numbers check out," I say to change the subject but also hoping that collaborating with Travis might spark a lead or an idea as to where Alanna might be. "What program did you run them through?" I ask Travis, hoping maybe we missed something.

"TLO, LexisNexis, and Tracers," Jon answers for him as he straightens up his desk and sorts through paperwork.

"I guess we were thorough, then," I say. "It just *doesn't* make sense. What are the odds that the same van that showed up randomly at my house was the same one that transported me as part of human trafficking?" I remove a scrunchy from my wrist and gather my hair into a messy bun atop my head, still somewhat shocked that scrunchies have made a comeback—not just for sleeping or working out reasons, but as an actual fashion statement. I chew on my lower lip and shake my head in frustration over our lost lead. "I just don't get it. The Super Scorpion Pest Removal van . . . It was there that day. That can't be nothing."

"I agree. It's messed up," Travis concurs. "We should check it out even though the plates match the registration. Just because it checks out doesn't mean a thing."

It doesn't take a detective to notice that this aggravates Jon. His cheeks flush, and he flings his paperwork onto the glass coffee table with unnecessary force. He sinks down on the white leather sofa and runs his fingers over his beard's scruff, clearly distressed. "I think we should find another angle," Jon grunts, allowing the words to slowly trail off.

"Why?" Travis and I ask in unison.

Jon shrugs. "Because it checks out. Could have been any van."

"No." I chuckle a bit. "It was the Super Scorpion Pest Removal van."

"Sure was, man," Travis confirms.

"I don't want to get into this right now," Jon sighs. "I have a meeting in five."

Then it hits me like a ton of bricks. Jon doesn't believe Travis and me. He must be starting to wonder if we were hallucinating. But we didn't make it up. I saw it with my own two eyes. Sure, I was concussed, traumatized, and starving to death, but I know what I saw. And even though June, one of the kidnapping victims, hadn't seen it, Travis had.

"You don't believe us?" I ask, eyes wide and my frustration not going unnoticed.

"How's the headache?" Jon asks from the white leather couch, clearly changing the subject. He rests his drink on the coffee table and spreads papers in front of himself as he usually does when preparing to meet with a client.

"The same," I say even though it's gotten worse. And now that I'm tackling the embarrassment of Travis barging in on us and still stifling the desire to rip my ex-husband's clothes off and tackle him on the couch—mixed with anger and annoyance that he might not believe me—my heart is pounding even harder. "Who are you meeting with?" I ask, running through a mental list of our current cases and trying to take my mind off my current situation. I sip my coffee and allow the thickness of the frosty beverage to trickle down to the depths of my soul.

"Patrick and Laura Foster," Jon says nonchalantly.

Travis leaps to his feet as I choke on my coffee. "Alanna's parents?" Travis asks for me.

"Alanna's parents," Jon confirms.

"Why didn't you tell us?" I ask, clearing my throat, eyes wide.

"Yeah, what she said," Travis says.

"Because," Jon says, his tone even-keeled as he runs a hand through his blond hair, "the two of you are preoccupied enough with the Foster case. They haven't officially hired us back. I need you to focus on the other important things we have going on." He motions toward the whiteboard behind his desk. "Travis, where are you on the wedding-crasher case? Any new leads?"

I sit up a bit straighter in my seat, intrigued by the idea of hunting down real-life wedding crashers, something I've only read about in books and watched in movies. But yes, believe it or not, wedding crashing has become a problem for CEO Tanner Navarro and Navarro Dreams Hotels, a four-hotel franchise in the state of Arizona. Apparently, after multiple crashed weddings in a short amount of time, Mr. Navarro hired us—Prickly Pen Investigations—to put a stop to these crimes while keeping a low profile and to take the suckers down.

"Yes, where are we with that?" I ask in my new and well-versed PI voice.

Travis shakes his head. "Three venues hit in two months, and nothing. Whoever this is knows what they are doing, man. They've even figured out how to cut the security cameras."

"Did any of the suspects' descriptions match up?" Jon asks Travis, his tone hopeful.

"Consistently across all crime scenes, witnesses have reported sightings of an unidentified male and female presence, neither of whom were accounted for on the official guest list."

"Physical descriptions are inconsistent?"

Travis opens a folder and scans a document with his large, dark eyes. He blinks a few times and reaches in his desk for a pair of dark-rimmed reading glasses before reading aloud from his paperwork like a student being called on by his professor. "The descriptions of the female subject vary significantly across reports, ranging from a white Caucasian female with long, curly black hair to a short-haired individual with a black bob. Notably, in one instance, she was described as a wedding guest sporting a blond updo. These discrepancies suggest a deliberate effort to disguise her appearance, indicating a level of sophistication in her approach to infiltrating the events. Also, some witnesses report the couple look to be in their early twenties, while others claim they could be in their thirties, forties, and in some instances even fifties."

"Well, that's going to make this harder," Jon sighs. "Nice work, Travis. What about the male?"

"Thanks, boss. The male suspect has been consistently reported as approximately six feet tall and weighing around two hundred pounds. However, witness descriptions of his appearance vary significantly, with some depicting him as a white Caucasian male with dark-brown hair, others noting blond hair, and even instances where he's described as having salt-and-pepper hair."

"Salt and pepper?" Jon asks, scrunching his nose.

"Yes," Travis states with confidence.

"It means specks of white and gray," I explain. "It's actually sort of hot . . . you know . . . depending on the man . . ." My voice trails off as my ex-husband and ex-boyfriend shoot daggers at me with their eyes. "Knock it off." I chuckle. "If a hot chick walked in here, the two of you would be drooling, and you know it."

"Check in with Mr. Navarro for lists of upcoming events. I also recommend reviewing the inventory of stolen property once more, paying close attention to potential patterns that may have eluded us thus far. Notably, the stolen items include gifts, cards, guest pocketbooks and wallets, and in one instance, even wedding bands were reported missing. Identifying any consistent themes or targets among these stolen items could provide valuable insight into the perpetrators' motives and methods."

"Copy that," Travis says, making his voice deeper than necessary and scribbling something on a notepad. "I've been working with his son, TJ, and his daughter, Beatriz. It's Beatriz who manages the functions. I'll follow up with her right away."

"What about me?" I whine. "I'm not on a case. I have time to work on Alanna's," I suggest, sounding more hopeful than ever.

"When's your manuscript due?" Jon asks without looking up from his notes.

"I have time," I insist, ignoring his question entirely.

Jon shakes his head and continues sifting through the paperwork. I sigh, frustrated with him. Sure, he's looking out for me. He wants me to take care of myself, and a huge part of him blames himself for the decline in both my physical and mental health since the events that unfolded during Operation Superglue. But does that give him the right to keep me off cases? Especially Alanna's? I decide I'll talk to him about it tonight, away from Travis and his curious gaze. Travis all but proposed to me last year, convinced I was not only the love of his life but the woman he was destined to start a new family with. Travis was, without a doubt, the best sex of my life because I hadn't realized until I was with him that men could move their bodies in the way he was able to. This, let's be real, makes my work environment hostile and confusing enough, and I don't need a boss using what he knows about my personal life against me. So instead of arguing, I huff a quiet "Okay, Dad," which is a dig at Jon but also a playful inside joke between the two of us.

"Still not funny," Jon says, his eyes steady on his paperwork.

I roll my eyes and stretch my arms over my head. "Can I help Travis on the wedding-crasher case, then?" I ask. "I'll make you a margarita tonight... or three." I wink.

"You know you can't drink until your headaches get better," he reminds me. "You should probably also lay off the caffeine, but we all know there's a greater chance that hell will freeze over."

"Please? The wedding-crasher case?" I ask, ignoring his valid buzzkill of a reality check.

"That's up to Travis," Jon says, sipping his coffee and scribbling something in his notes.

But our conversation is interrupted because the door to PPI swings open, and I squint through the glare of the setting sun to find Laura and Patrick Foster, Alanna's parents, standing before me.

"Come in," Jon says, rising from the couch and shaking Patrick's hand.

Patrick reciprocates Jon's handshake and says a soft "Hello." He brushes his hands along the front of his tan park ranger attire, and guides in his wife, Laura, a petite blonde with hair in a slicked-back bun and bags underneath her eyes the size of entire continents.

"Would you like to meet out here where we typically sit, or would you prefer our newly renovated conference room?"

"Here is fine. I don't want to take up any more of your time than necessary."

Jon gestures for the couple to have a seat adjacent to him on the white sectional, and I make an awkward attempt to act as if I'm working diligently on something of the utmost significance to keep myself from staring.

"Patrick and Laura, this is my business partner, Travis," Jon says in a voice deeper than his typical gravelly tone. "And this is Lina . . ." he continues, but his voice travels off into another dimension as he clearly has no idea what to label me.

"I'm his ex-wife," I say with a cheerful smile, clearly taking both off guard. "Ex-wife and business partner," I add, nodding my head in a way that either makes me seem overly sure of myself or like I'm actually not sure which I am. And since I apparently have made it my life's goal to completely humiliate myself in front of the entire office, I choose to awkwardly add, "I mean, if you want to get technical, I'm not *just* his ex-wife. We are sort of dating . . . or *talking* . . . whatever the kids are calling it these days." I laugh nervously.

"She's always struggled with labels," Travis adds from his desk, just loud enough for only me to hear him.

I shoot daggers at him from the corner of my eye and fix my gaze back to the sofa, where Jon, Patrick, and Laura study me, somewhat confused and maybe a bit concerned. Sure, I was madly in love with Travis when we dated, but I had trust issues upon trust issues because of my failed marriage, and I wasn't emotionally available enough to commit to him. When will the guy let that go?

"Lina worked with me on Operation Superglue," Jon explains with a confident nod of the head, like a proud parent. "She helped retrieve the other missing girls."

"Oh, Lina," Laura says, leaping to her feet and clasping her hands at her chest in gratitude. "You're a hero, my dear."

"Oh," I say, shaking my head and unintentionally rolling my chair away from Laura. "I'm . . . I'm far from a hero . . ." I stumble over my words, my voice trailing off as Laura makes her way toward me and extends her arms out for what looks to be a hug.

"What a wonderful thing you did," she exclaims, wiping a tear from her eye and continuing forward.

I rise from my seat and follow Laura's lead, allowing her to scoop me up in a motherly embrace. "You *are* a hero," she repeats. "Those girls are alive because of your bravery."

I resist the urge to pull back and allow Laura to squeeze me close. "Thank you," I whisper. "I . . . I only wish I could—"

"She's your typical Wonder Woman," Jon interrupts, eyebrows raised, and I can see he immediately regrets drawing attention to me. "When you're ready, Mrs. Foster, we can get started with our meeting."

Laura releases me, and I drop onto my chair and immediately reach into my pocketbook, scoop up four Advil, and pop them into my mouth in hopes of some headache relief. However, barely after I swallow the medication, the door to PPI is flung open, and in rushes a very familiar face. Her ginger hair is pulled up into a high ponytail, and she stands tall with her perfect posture, dressed in a light cream-colored blouse and a high-waisted tweed skirt and leather loafers, perfectly embodying the light academia aesthetic with her vintage-inspired ensemble.

Penelope Gallagher.

"Penelope," I gasp, choking on my ibuprofen.

"Lina." She nods sternly, dabbing the corner of her eye with a tissue. "Is there somewhere we can talk in private?"

"Of course."

I glance over my shoulder at Jon, who's having an in-depth conversation with Patrick and Laura. Travis is eagerly typing away on his laptop, and if he's noticed Penelope's swift entrance, he doesn't seem to care enough to stop what he's working on.

"I'll be right back," I say to anyone who might be listening.

I gather my belongings and gather my long brunette tresses over one shoulder as I lead Penelope Gallagher out our back door and into our conference room. A sense of pride washes over me as Jon and I have recently completed these renovations together, and we couldn't be more pleased with our results. The room is bathed in a warm and natural light that streams through the floor-to-ceiling windows, the space exuding an air of professionalism and sophistication. Overhead, contemporary pendant lights cast a warm glow, creating an atmosphere conducive to speaking with clients, and state-of-the-art audiovisual equipment lines the walls, including a high-definition projector and a large flat-screen television.

"Have a seat," I instruct Penelope, gesturing toward a black leather office chair at the head of a large, polished oak table.

She does and immediately bursts into tears.

I pass her a box of tissues and gently ask if she would like a bottle of water. She silently nods, and I grab one from our fridge. As I pass it to her and she sips gratefully, I realize that Penelope looks like she hasn't slept in days, and I can't help but worry about what might be wrong. *Why might she need me?*

I met Penelope at Lucy and Max's first Mommy and Me swim class. She was with her twins, William and Henry, who were a couple of years older than my children. At the time, Jon had been working, and my mother, Celeste, attended swim with me that day. Her husband had been with her, and I'd been so incredibly disappointed that Jon hadn't been there to meet him because he was working overtime as a rookie police officer for the Tempe Police Department. It was fine because it turned out that other than having children the same age, we really didn't have much in common. I know this because Penelope and I had done the playdate thing from time to time, and even though she was only older than me by a few years, our conversations didn't go too far past naps, diapers, nursing, and spit up, so much so that we didn't stay in touch at all, not even on social media.

That was until I ran into her smack dab in the middle of Operation Superglue and realized that the eighteen-year-old boy I had recently hit on in hopes of finding the missing girls was her son, Hank. Yup, that's right. I put the moves on a teenager who was once a squirmy and energetic two-year-old boy in tropical swim trunks and bright orange swim floaties in my Mommy and Me swim class. And if that wasn't bad enough, Penelope almost blew my cover. I ran into her at Emerson's main office, and she recognized me immediately. If not for Dean Elizabeth, Operation Superglue would have been a bust, and I hadn't laid eyes on her since. So, to say this is a bit awkward is quite the understatement.

I put a calming hand on her shoulder, waiting intensely for a pause in her gut-wrenching sobs, and when that doesn't happen, I ask, "What can I do for you, Penelope?"

She dabs her eyes with her tissue, takes a sip of water, and sighs a defeated sigh. "First of all," she chokes, "I want to tell you how sorry I am about what happened at Emerson. If I had known you were undercover, Lina—"

"No," I smile reassuringly. "I'm the one who is sorry. I hated lying to you, and Dean Elizabeth really nailed you to the wall over your interrogation." I laugh.

Penelope's lips curl into a soft side smile. "That woman is ruthless."

"I wouldn't want to meet her in a dark alley." I chuckle.

"But seriously, Lina. When I saw on the news and all over social media what you and Jon did, I was so grateful, and I couldn't believe I almost blew your cover."

"It's water under the bridge," I say, sounding more like my mother than ever.

"Thank you," she says, her tears slowing for a beat.

"What's really going on?" I ask in my mom voice.

"It's Jasper," she says, her words catching in the back of her throat. "My husband."

"Oh no," I whisper. "Is he okay? Did something happen?"

"He's fine," she hisses. "That is, if I don't kill him myself."

My heart sinks to the pit of my soul. Evidently, Penelope is here because she believes her husband may be having an affair, and I try to stay composed because infidelity is not something I take lightly.

"What happened?" I ask.

"Oh, he's having an affair, I just know it."

I reach toward the center of the conference table and grab a legal pad to take notes. "Is this an assumption you are making? Or did you find evidence?" I ask, choosing my words as carefully as I can in these new and uncharted waters.

"I don't have evidence," she says, becoming defensive. "That's why I came to you."

"Okay." I nod reassuringly. "Let's start from the beginning. Tell me what you know."

Penelope rolls her green eyes and stares up at the ceiling as if looking for answers, and my heart breaks for her. "He's been distant," she starts. Then she stops and starts again. "I assumed it could be, you know, like an empty nest thing since the boys are nineteen now and heading off to college. I've read that couples need to sort of rebuild their lives and start over when that happens, you know?"

"Yes," I agree, even though I don't know. My teenagers are sixteen, and I love them to death, but I am ready to kill them on the daily, and if we're being honest, an empty nest sounds a bit enticing to me right now. "Is that it? He is just acting weird? Any change in his routine?"

"Well, he hasn't initiated sex in, like, months," she huffs. "He even turned me down last week."

"Is he staying out late or anything like that?"

"No. But he is spending more time at the gym, a gym that's an hour away. It is on the way to his office, but do you think it's necessary to drive twenty-five minutes out of the way for a gym? And he turns his Life360 notifications off midafternoon. That's a new thing."

I stop myself from cringing because it doesn't take a private investigator to know that's a red flag. "Did you ask him about it?"

"He blames the Wi-Fi connection," she says, slamming her palm down on the table, startling us both. "Sorry," she whispers then cries harder. "This sounds bad, huh?"

"Let's take this one day at a time, okay?"

"Okay." She nods. "But I want to hire you, Lina. I know you will get to the bottom of it. I read what you did for those girls, and this will be nothing for you. I just . . . I need to know."

"I understand," I say because I do. "But Penelope, I've been where you are. And maybe take a day or two and really make sure this is what you want. Because once you know," I say, squinting my eyes for a bit and grasping my aching belly, "you can't unknow it. Once you know, you can't go back." I wipe an unexpected tear from the corner of my own eye.

"Lina," she says, reassuring me, "the difference here . . . is I *do* know. It's written all over his face. The signs are all there. I just need you to catch the bastard for me. Can you do that, Lina? Catch the bastard?" Her words are harsh, but her tone is calm and proper, like she's having martinis with a girlfriend and exchanging pleasantries.

"Okay," I agree with a heavy sigh. "I'll catch the bastard."

"Excellent," she says like I've agreed to cohost a charity event, and she gathers her belongings. "What are my next steps?"

"I just need to clear everything with Jon," I say with a smile. "It's just typical process and procedure," I lie, knowing full well that the last thing Jon Cote wants me doing is hyper focusing on an infidelity case, dragging me down a road so dark that I might be unable to find my way back.

Chapter Three

Then (October 2023) Alanna

I was cursing my mother under my breath when a tray of shepherd's pie smashed to the ground, scalding my legs as bits of ground beef and gravy smeared the laces of my favorite Converse sneakers and caused the line of incoming guests to gape at me in horror. "Sorry," I mumbled under my breath, partly to them and somewhat to Georgia, my supervisor.

"Not to worry, dear," she said, reaching for a nearby mop. "There's more where that came from. Did you hurt yourself?"

"No," I replied, the word catching in my throat because I wasn't sure. I trailed through the mess, nearly slipping in the mixture of mashed potatoes, meat, and corn as it smeared across the eggshell-colored tile floor until I reached the sink. I grabbed a clean rag and ran it under cool water before wiping my legs down and attempting to salvage my shoes. "It's just been a day," I admitted, "I'm really sorry, again, for dropping the food."

"Don't even give it a second thought, Alanna," she reassured me. "Just happy to have your help."

I nodded, shaking off my frustration, but my cheeks still burned from embarrassment. I'd been serving at Harmony House Soup Kitchen since freshman year, and I'd never made an error that substantial. Of course, I'd been frazzled since arriving at my shift because my mother and I had yet to resolve an earlier argument. And by *resolve*, I mean she won't change her mind. Bottom line: curfew would not be extended, and I was expected to be home by nine-thirty.

Lincoln had been disappointed, to say the least. He urged me to meet up with him anyway, insisting that even an hour with him would be worth the consequences. I laughed at that because he didn't know Patrick and Laura. If he did, he would understand that an hour with anyone, even Lincoln Stone, wasn't worth breaking their trust.

"Those are ready to serve, when you are ready," Georgia said, motioning toward the rows of trays that lined the metal counters, each containing multiple paper plates with generous servings of shepherd's pie, glasses of milk, and prewrapped Hostess Cupcakes.

"Got it," I replied, wiping my hands on my jean shorts and adjusting my ponytail. I turned and collided with my friend and coworker, Chloe May.

She leapt back in surprise, catching herself against the counter and sliding in the mashed potatoes I had yet to mop up.

"Oh God," I moaned. "Chloe, I am *so* sorry. I should go home before I hurt someone."

"You're fine." Chloe chuckled. "Volleyball ran late, and Hunter needed a ride to therapy, so I was running in hot. Totally *not* your fault."

"Gotcha," I said, glancing over my shoulder to see a custodian cleaning up the mess. I thanked him as I reached for two trays then made my way toward the round tables that lined the church basement, Chloe trailing alongside me.

"How is Hunter?" I asked, remembering Chloe mentioned she had a younger brother with special needs who relied heavily on her. She'd also mentioned that she loved helping with him and the Special Olympics so much that she'd decided she would like to become a special education teacher one day.

"He's great," she said with a smile. "He's starting to show some interest in basketball, and there's a program at the YMCA that will be perfect for him." She lit up when she talked about Hunter. "Here you go," she said to the guests as she placed paper plates in front of each with a genuine smile. "Enjoy!"

Chloe and I served over sixty plates of shepherd's pie before pausing to take a break. "Such a big turnout," I sighed, removing the latex gloves as Chloe did the same. "Lots of new faces today," I said with another sigh.

Serving the homeless always felt so rewarding, but at the same time, it was always alarming to see how many people weren't able to afford food and shelter. I just never felt okay that so many people needed so much help.

"I was thinking the same thing," Chloe agreed, removing her hair elastic and readjusting her dark, curly tresses into a low bun. "The regulars are here," she said, motioning toward the center of the room. "But I don't recognize *them*," she added.

I followed her gaze to a corner table occupied by a cluster of men who appeared to be in their forties or fifties. Most of them sported buzz cuts or completely bald heads and wore sleeveless shirts that revealed tattooed arms that were so thin and lanky that I swore I would've been able to see their bones if not for their sun-scorched tans and sunburns.

"Word must've gotten out that it is shepherd's pie day," I said with a shrug.

"Must have," Chloe agreed, a spark of sorrow in her eyes. "Do you think . . . Do you think they're in a gang?"

"Possibly," I shrugged, a bit embarrassed by the mere fact I wouldn't even begin to know what being in any kind of gang would entail, as my sheltered upper-class suburban life left a lot to be desired in the "worldly experience" department. And honestly, the only time I'd ever felt any sort of hunger pain lasted minutes at the most, forget hours or days.

We waited until everyone appeared to be finished eating before clearing tables. Chloe started at the center of the room, and I worked my way around the outskirts, forcing myself to smile as my heart shattered for the guests who didn't have homes, beds, or home-cooked meals waiting for them, and like clockwork, I appreciated my home and my overprotective parents as I usually did when serving at the soup kitchen.

"Thank you, Alanna," a man hissed from behind me, interrupting my thoughts and shocking me for a moment, as maintaining our anonymity was a strict policy at Harmony House. As I spun around to face the table of men who made up Chloe's alleged "gang," I half expected to recognize someone, but I didn't. Instead, I scanned the blameless faces of the men and tried my best not to ogle as one of them licked his paper plate in an attempt to slurp up every drop of food.

"Did . . . Did one of you just say something to me?" I asked, trying to shake the uneasy pit forming in my gut and the unexpected chill radiating down my spine, When nobody replied, I assumed I was hearing things and continued clearing plates, suddenly eager to move on.

"What time's the pickup tonight, Ace?" a scrawny bald man asked another man with a shaved head and more piercings than I could count, catching me off guard for a moment.

"No pickup tonight," the younger man with a shaved head hissed, and I assumed that was Ace. For a moment, I was sure he was the same man who'd said my name just moments earlier. But that couldn't have been, because these men didn't know my name unless they'd overheard Chloe talking with me, which I doubted was the case. They didn't know who I was.

"What the hell, man? You promised you would deliver, and now my ass is on the line too."

"Shut the hell up, Slinky," Ace barked as I cleared their last plate and eagerly left.

But as I turned to walk away, it was nearly impossible to ignore Ace and Slinky and their creepy banter because I was almost positive that Ace, under his foul-smelling breath, mumbled just low enough for me to hear, "Don't stay out too late tonight, babe."

Chapter Four

Now (March 2025) Lina

"What did you tell Travis?" Jon asks between heavy breaths. We'd barely kept our hands off each other in the fully occupied elevator, and the door to his two-bedroom Tempe apartment wasn't even fully closed behind us before he pinned me against the wall of his entryway, compressing my wrists over my head and against the wall with one strong hand, his other unbuttoning the buttons of my fuchsia blouse, his kisses as powerful as fireworks on July Fourth and toastier than the scalding Arizona midsummer sun.

"Parent-teacher conferences," I pant as Jon slides one hand under my skirt while keeping the other wrapped around my wrists, causing my cheeks to flush and my heart rate to increase tremendously. Waves of electricity shoot through me as Jon presses against me right where I want him.

"It's almost April," he snickers, pulling his lips from mine just long enough for his mouth to curl into a playful grin. "Parent-teacher conferences are in the fall."

"I don't care about Travis," I gasp as Jon releases his grip on my wrists and slides his hands down my lower back, unzipping my skirt and watching with wide eyes as it falls to the floor, leaving me standing before him in an unbuttoned blouse, revealing my favorite black Victoria's Secret lace push-up bra and matching thong. "I just . . . I needed to be with you," I say softly, kicking off my strappy heels and reaching my hands under his t-shirt, feeling his body pleasantly warm and firm against my shaky fingers. "Besides, he *told* us to get a room."

"Shit, Lina. You are effing sexy as hell," he says, his voice both gravelly and hoarse. It's highly unlikely he's still thinking of Travis, considering the fact that both of us bolted from Prickly Pen Investigations just moments after our meetings concluded, eager to finish what we'd started just an hour prior on my office chair.

"No, I'm not," I argue between breaths. "That's quite the compliment, Jon Cote, but I'm not feeling so *effing sexy as hell* these days."

Jon gently presses a finger to my lips and whispers, "Stop talking about my girl like that."

I breathe a relieved sigh, grateful that my insecurities hadn't spoiled the moment, because that hadn't been my intent. "I like when you call me your girl," I admit, tugging his T-shirt over his head and pressing my lips to the American flag tattoo over his pectoral muscle, my favorite spot to kiss, then I trace a pointer finger over the four eagles, an addition to the tattoo Jon had designed after we were separated, the birds representing Max, Lucy, Jon, and me. "I love this tattoo," I sigh as I slide my fingers down his chiseled abs and to the V his hips form just above his belt buckle.

Jon's teeth trace over his lower lip, and his eyes radiate down on me, and I can't help myself—I wrap my hands behind his head and tug him toward me into a deep and passionate kiss. With one push of his fingers, my blouse slides down off my shoulders, leaving me breathing heavily against the apartment wall, longing for him in just my underwear—that is until Jon unclips my bra, and that, too, slides to the floor.

"I want you, Lina," Jon coos. "I want *all* of you."

I squint my eyes, trying with all my might to calm my pounding head, and I shake away the negative thoughts that oftentimes sneak up on me when Jon and I are intimate. Sure, we've slept together many times, recently, even. But in some instances, moments like this when I just wish I could let my guard down and completely lose myself with my ex-husband, it doesn't come easy. The emotional wall I've constructed because of our history looms over a decade strong, and it constantly takes effort and vigor to shove the negativity away, but with every touch and every kiss, every beat of his heart as he presses his chest to mine, the feelings of doubt softly subside.

"I want you too," I whisper, biting his earlobe, a spot I know he can't resist.

Jon coils my arms around his neck and with one swift motion has my legs entwined around his waist and has positioned himself against me, ready to give me what I've asked for. He shifts forward, pressing my head against the wall, his eyes inches from mine, and as I lose myself in his deep ocean-blue eyes, I can forget, even if only for a moment—forget the years of misery and angst that followed the destruction of our marriage. I am twenty-year-old Lina Rivera, falling for Officer Jon Cote for the first time again, and I hungrily anticipate him, ready to feel him as close to me as possible.

"I don't want to move," I whine.

"Then don't," Jon says, gently poking my nose with a pointer finger.

"You know I can't lie on your apartment floor naked all day," I sigh. "I've got a *lot* going on."

Jon rolls me on top of himself and positions me so our faces are inches apart. "I know that. I just don't want you to leave. Is that such a crime? Besides, I have another meeting at the office soon, so the truth is, I'm the one that needs to leave."

I kiss his nose and consider this for a beat. "Wanting me to stay isn't a crime," I admit. "But speaking of crimes . . ." I raise my eyebrows and smile like I'm up to no good because I am. I had yet to fill Jon in regarding my meeting with Penelope, and I was desperate to know how his meeting went with Patrick and Laura Foster.

"Oh no," he sighs, kissing one cheek then the other. "No shop talk. Not here, not like this."

"I *need* to know. Did they rehire us?"

"They rehired us," Jon says, sitting upright, and tucking a strand of hair behind my ear. "But I'm worried about you, Lina. I don't want you to get sucked in again."

Again? I think. Why can't this man understand that Alanna's case is the only thing I can think about? I rub my hands over my eyes before hauling myself to my feet and gathering my clothes. I slip each garment back on, one at a time, hoping that Jon can't see the tears threatening to leak out of my eyeballs at any given moment.

"Lina?" he asks.

The lump that forms in the back of my throat prevents me from speaking actual words. "Lina?" Jon asks again, buckling his belt and reaching for his shirt. "Talk to me."

Jon motions toward the couch, and when all I have left to do is button my blouse, I follow him over and take a seat.

"I'm fine," I say because I don't know what else to say.

"Well, that's a lie," he says, half smiling, half not.

I grab a throw pillow and hug it to my chest. "So, they rehired us . . . but you don't want *me* working the case? You don't think I'm ready," I say, wiping my tears with the back of my hand. "You don't think I can do it?"

"Oh, I *know* you can do it," he snickers, taking my hands in his and fiddling with my promise ring. "If anyone can do it, you can. I'm just worried about you—that's all. You went through a lot with Operation Superglue—"

"And I am okay," I say like I've repeated myself a hundred times already.

"Lina," Jon huffs, leaping to his feet. "Just a little over six months ago, your life was not only turned completely upside down, but you were assaulted, beaten to a pulp. Multiple concussions, a broken arm, and you . . . you were *traumatized*, Lina."

I roll my eyes and shake my head. The last thing I need is for Jon to remind me of what I went through with Operation Superglue. My life wasn't just turned upside down. It was ripped to shreds. Hell, I almost didn't even make it out alive. Of course, Jon is sweet to worry about me, but I don't know how he doesn't see how important it is for me to find Alanna. Without finding Alanna, Operation Superglue just feels very unfinished.

"Jon," I start but stop then start again, struggling to find the words. "I really appreciate you worrying about me—"

"Worrying?" Jon asks, the volume of his voice increasing as he hops up and paces in front of the sofa. "Worrying?" he asks again, eyes wide, running a finger over his beard's scruff before stopping in his tracks and kneeling at my feet, the color draining from his face and his eyes welling with tears. He places his hands on my bare knees and squints his eyes shut, shaking his head from side to side.

I study him, this man who can bring me such joy but who has also proven capable of causing me so much pain, and I want more than anything for him to move on from Operation Superglue. Yes, what we went through was a nightmare, and I know Jon well enough to understand that he blames himself for getting me into it in the first place. But when he welcomed me into PPI and encouraged me to go for my private investigator's license, he should've known that I would want to actually solve some cases. So far, my meeting with Penelope was the only action I'd seen independently since the start of my career, and that was only because she barged into the office asking for me when Jon was preoccupied with the Fosters. Jon should know me well enough by now to understand that I need to help Alanna. But as I watch him and realize just how broken he is over this, I decide to bite my tongue and let the man talk, at least for a few seconds.

"Lina, do you have any idea what it was like for me? Once you were kidnapped?"

I stare at him blankly because up until now, I hadn't considered what it must've been like for Jon once I was abducted from the bus stop that night in Tempe. "I'm sure it must have been awful," I say, biting on my lower lip.

Jon runs his hands through his hair and sniffs back his tears. "Awful." He chuckles. "Yeah, Lina, that's one word for it."

"Terrible?" I try again. "Devastating? I mean, I can use the online thesaurus," I joke.

"Stop," he grunts, gazing up at me with tired eyes. "One minute you were there . . . and then you were just . . . gone," he says and clears his throat. "I . . . I didn't think I was ever going to see you again. And that . . . It was the worst pain I'd ever felt in my entire life. The thought of having to tell the kids, needing to face Daphne and Ryker . . . I just . . . I felt so *responsible*."

"I knew what I was getting into—"

"Stop," he begs, resting his head on my knees. "You can say that all you want. That you knew what you were getting yourself into, that you signed up for it . . . but the truth is Lina, I was supposed to protect you . . . and I failed. I failed you, Lina."

Based on the number of tears falling freely between my knees, I have the feeling that Jon isn't beating himself up over just Operation Superglue, but also our failed marriage, which both breaks my heart for him but also pisses me off on a new level. Yes, the destruction of our marriage was entirely Jon's doing, but if I can get over it, he should be able to as well.

"Come here," I say, reaching for his hands and guiding him onto the sofa next to me. "Jon, I need to know. Are you talking about Operation Superglue? Or are you talking about . . . all of it?"

"I don't know anymore," he admits.

I think about this for a beat and decide to leave that conversation for another day. Jon is clearly struggling with something, and even though we will need to get to the bottom of it, we need to stay focused. We have cases to solve, and maybe at some point soon, he can join me for couples counseling, and we can unpack our nightmare of a past, but for now, we just had the best sex since . . . well . . . ever, and I really like where we are right now. No use ripping open old wounds. No, for now, I need to convince Jon that I am okay enough to join Alanna's case.

"Jon," I say, sitting a bit straighter, my voice firm. "I went through a lot. And I'm sure it was scary as hell for you when I was kidnapped from that bus stop. But you need to know that I am doing everything that my therapist and doctors have told me to do. And Jon, I am *stronger* because of Operation Superglue, and I don't have any regrets. And sure, I have horrible migraines, and I'm not sleeping, and I've been through it . . . but none of that will be worth it for me if I don't at least have the chance to help find Alanna. Hell, maybe if we can find Alanna, I might actually start feeling better. I just . . . I want the chance to try."

Jon stares into my eyes, and I can tell he's trying to decide if I'm being completely honest with him. "You just want the chance to try?"

"Yes. Jon, I wasn't born yesterday. I know the odds are against us."

"Because there is a chance, Lina, that . . ."

"That we might not find her alive," I say, bolder than I intend.

Jon nods. "Or we might not find her at all," he whispers like he doesn't want anyone hearing him say this out loud. "You need to know that we might fail."

"I know that," I agree. "But the only thing worse than not finding her . . . is giving up. And I can't give up. Not yet. Please, Jon. Please let me join the case."

Jon stares up at the ceiling like he's searching for answers. "Okay," he finally says. "You can join the case."

I lean over and kiss the top of his head. "I won't let you down. I promise. I won't stop until we bring her back."

"I know," he exhales. "That's what I'm worried about."

I smile and run my hand through his blond hair. "You don't have to worry about me," I reassure him. "Wait right here." I kiss his head once more and squirm away from him, scurrying over to my purse to grab my phone.

"Do I even want to know what you're doing?" He smiles.

"Oh yes." I grin. "I've brainstormed a list of possible names for our case."

"That doesn't surprise me," he says, staring up at me from the floor. "And I want to hear them as we walk back to PPI. I have a meeting in five minutes."

"Sure," I say, waving him off. "And I have to tell you about my case with Penelope. But that can wait because I've already narrowed the names down to one, and I think you'll like it."

"I'm sorry, your case with who?"

"Don't worry about it," I say, leaping to my feet, excitement rushing through my veins for the first time in months—so much so, the pounding of my head feels as though it's easing.

"Oh, I'm worried about it." He laughs. "But go on. I have a feeling I have absolutely zero say in this, so lay it on me. What exactly is the new code name for Alanna's case, Lina Rivera?"

I clear my throat and smile a playful smile, gesturing for Jon to continue, and when he doesn't get my hint, I say, "Lina Rivera . . ."

"Seriously?"

"Seriously."

Jon shrugs and throws his arms up in exaggerated defeat. "What exactly is the new code name for Alanna's case, Lina Rivera, *private eye?*"

"I will never stop loving the sound of that," I confess with an overly dramatic exhalation.

"If we were to find Alanna alive," I say in my detective voice, "she would need to have certain characteristics to ensure her survival. Along with bravery, courage, resilience, and tenacity, she will need to be strong. She will need to stay rooted firmly, and she will need to persevere like no one else."

"Meeting is in two minutes," Jon says, nodding toward the door. "Out with it."

"You're taking the fun out of this," I whine.

"One minute and thirty seconds," he says, playfully.

I hold my hand out like a stop sign and ignore him as I read from my notes. "The cactus blossom," I say like a teacher reading to her class. "A symbol of strength and resilience due to the harsh environments in which cacti typically thrive in any environment, as cacti are known for their ability to survive and even thrive in arid desert conditions where other plants struggle to grow. Despite the extreme heat, limited water, and harsh sunlight, cacti can bloom and produce flowers, symbolizing resilience in the face of adversity." I pause for dramatic effect before continuing, "The vibrant and delicate flowers that bloom on cacti provide a stark contrast to the harsh and unforgiving desert landscape. This juxtaposition highlights the resilience of the cactus and serves as a reminder that beauty can be found even in the most challenging of circumstances."

"Wow," Jon says from the doorway, "those are some big-ass words."

I can't tell if he's impressed with me or simply annoyed, so I cross my arms over my chest and raise my brow. "That's it?"

"Impressive research. And . . . you are *such* an author."

This makes me smile. "So therefore," I sing in my teacher voice, "the name of our case is?"

Jon takes two steps toward me and plants a soft kiss on my lips. He gently tucks a strand of hair behind my ear before saying, "Operation Cactus Blossom."

"Operation Cactus Blossom," I repeat.

"It's perfect. Excellent job."

"Thanks," I say with a soft smile.

Just then my cell phone rings, and Lucy's name flashes across the screen. Jon gestures me to follow him out into the hallway, and as I do, I accept our daughter's phone call.

"Hey, Luce," I sing.

"Hi, Mom," she says. "Where are you? I swung by the office, and Mr. Mullins said you and Dad had parent-teacher conferences. You do realize those are in the fall, right?"

I slap my palm to my forehead and cringe. "Yeah . . . it was a meeting . . . for Max's IEP," I lie.

"Oh, that makes more sense," she says.

"Yes, we are on our way back now. Everything okay?"

"Oh, more than okay!" she squeals. "Guess who's coming to Phoenix soon? On tour?"

"No way!" I squeal, knowing that my daughter could only be talking about her favorite country artist, Darcy Blaze, or Darcy "Blue Boots," a singer who's gone viral and is popularly known for her thigh-high blue suede boots.

"Darcy Blue!" she shrieks, completely in fangirl mode.

"That's amazing." I smile. "We can talk about it at home tonight?"

"Yup. See you at home."

"Love you, Lucy."

"Love you too. And Mom?"

"Yeah."

"I know that Dad is your sneaky link." She chuckles before abruptly hanging up, leaving me gaping wide-eyed, jaw open, and speechless, wondering how on earth Jon and I should address this with our children when we haven't even defined it ourselves.

"What is it?" Jon asks, rubbing the small of my back with his open palm.

"What in the actual hell is a sneaky link?" I ask, typing it into Urban Dictionary. "'A sneaky link is a slang term that refers to a secret or discreet meeting between two people who are interested in each other,'" I read aloud, my voice increasing in volume with each word.

"So, we're busted?" Jon asks, his tone playful as he pulls me against himself in a warm embrace.

"Apparently," I sigh. "I just don't know if I want to dig a hole and bury myself in it out of pure embarrassment or write down 'sneaky link' in my notes for book research."

"Definitely research," he says, planting a soft kiss on my forehead and squeezing me more tightly. "You and me, we have nothing to be embarrassed about."

"Oh, I know that," I say, my words coming out more quickly than intended. "I'm not embarrassed to be with *you*... I guess I'm just a little thrown off," I admit. "I kind of liked that we had some time to figure things out without worrying about the kids and how it impacts them."

"Valid," Jon agrees before releasing his grip on me and tilting my chin toward him with a pointer finger. "It's been over six months," he says gently. "I mean, don't get me wrong—the sneaking around is kind of hot. But if the kids know, we need to address it," he says firmly.

And even though I know Jon's right, I can't shake the dreadful feeling that forms in my gut as I anticipate our conversation with our children, and I fight off the overwhelming fear and the heaviness of our situation, hoping beyond hope that by getting back together with Jon Cote, I'm not doing anything not in the best interest of our children—or myself for that matter.

Chapter Five

Then (October 2023) Alanna

I squeezed one fist tight against my body and bit down on my lower lip hard enough to draw blood, my other hand pressing my phone to the side of my tear-streaked face. "Mom!" I wailed. "You aren't being fair!"

"*I'm* not being fair?" she asked, her tone growing louder and angrier. "*I'm* not being fair? I'm ten minutes away from boarding passengers onto my flight, and my daughter chooses this moment to pick another fight with me about a curfew she has had for four years, and I'm the one not being fair?"

"I'm sorry!" I hollered, louder than intended as I flopped forward onto my bed, landing on my stomach. "I'm just asking for this one night, Mom. It's Friday night, and I'm a *senior*. I'm just asking to stay out one extra hour. Why is that such a big ask?"

The line is silent before Mom replies, "The answer is no, Alanna. We will talk about this when I get home."

I squeezed my eyes shut and tried to calm my racing heart, but it was no use because the blood charging through my veins was beginning to boil over like molten lava threatening to erupt from an active volcano, and I wasn't used to the sensation, the feeling of knowing what I wanted, knowing what I *needed*, and not having the ability to go after it. I wanted to meet Lincoln. I was desperate to meet him. But I also loved my mother more than anyone on the planet, which made this so much harder than it needed to be.

Although my mom was Mom, she also felt like my friend at times. My mother's closest friends often referred to us as Lorelai and Rory Gilmore from *Gilmore Girls* because the dynamic was eerily parallel, other than the fact that my mom hadn't had me when she was sixteen as Lorelai had with Rory. My mother insisted that was due to the fact that her friends had only sons and only wished they could have a daughter like me, or they were jealous that their own daughters were not as fabulous as me. I cringed at that thought because up until that point, I had done nothing but follow the directives asked of me. I'd been nothing but the perfect child. But once she began being so incredibly unreasonable, no words could describe how crushed I felt in that moment.

"Mom," I pleaded one last time, "I understand that you worry, but I promise you, Mom. If you just let me stay out one hour later tonight, I will be *fine*. Nothing bad is going to happen. Why can't you trust me?"

"Ask again," she said, "and you will be grounded for a week."

"This is so unfair," I sniffed. "I'm the only senior with a curfew."

"As long as you are under our roof," she reminded me, "you will have a curfew."

"But I'm almost eighteen!" I wailed, taking myself by surprise with the way the words roared out of me unintentionally. "You're acting like such a bitch!" I slapped my palm to my forehead, regretting the words as soon as they rolled off my tongue. Ladies and gentlemen, brace for impact.

"That's it, Alanna Nicole Foster. You, young lady, are grounded for a week. No, make that a *month*."

"Mom—"

"Mom *nothing*. You thought nine-thirty was bad? For the next month, you will go to school, sports, and volunteer. Nothing else. We will talk about this when I get home."

"Mom . . ." I started again, but my voice trailed off. I wanted desperately for her to know I was sorry. I hadn't meant to call her a bitch. I hadn't meant to get so worked up. But it was Lincoln. The need and the desire to meet him face-to-face had taken over my mind and transformed me into an absolute monster. What was going on with me? Sure, senior year was stressful, and meeting Lincoln was important on a level I couldn't put into words, but I'd always been respectful to my parents, especially Mom.

"Mom, I'm—"

"Alanna," she started but paused, then spoke again. "I'm just . . . I am so incredibly disappointed in you."

Disappointed in me. Those words had never been spoken to me because up until that point, I hadn't deserved it.

"Mom, please—"

"Nope. This conversation is finished. I'll see you when I get home."

I hadn't realized that silence had a sound, but it did. The actual sound of the line going quiet hit me like a kick to the gut. It knocked the wind out of me with such impact that I was sure I would stop breathing right there and then. So, as I curled up in a ball in the center of my twin bed, I pulled my favorite satin pillow over my face and howled into it as loud as humanly possible, overcome with anger and rage. Who did she think she was, hanging up on me? I was her *daughter,* for heaven's sake. Until then, I'd been nothing but the perfect child, and she hadn't even let me apologize. She just hung up on me, just like that. I would never hang up on her. But then again, I never would have thought calling her a bitch was within the realm of possibility.

"I'm sorry, Mom," I whimpered to my empty bedroom, staring up at the ceiling and tracing my fingers over my heart, flabbergasted at the intensity of its aching, but my thoughts were interrupted by a Snap message notification from Lincoln.

Lincoln: *Counting down the seconds, baby. We good?*

I smooshed the pillow to my face once more, soaking the pastel fabric with my tears, which overflowed from my eyeballs like rapids releasing from a dam as my heart broke into at least a million pieces. Lincoln sent me the address of a bus stop in Tempe, and my head pounded harder, and anger continued to rage within me. I prepared to text Lincoln back, to let him know that tonight wasn't going to work at all since I was grounded. Then the thought of being grounded for an entire month hit me like a freight train. Who did my mother think she was? Clearly, she didn't love me and appreciate me like I had thought she did. She obviously didn't understand what it was like to be a teenager. She would never understand what it was like to be me.

Bitterness and fury raged through me as I crafted my hand into a fist and pounded it repeatedly on my mattress, resentful thoughts flooding my mind at lightning speed. I realized this was a turning point for me. I was finished letting my parents dictate my happiness. I, Alanna Foster, was better than that. The time had come to take matters into my own hands. I was too old to be treated that way. I was finished being told what to do. I was going to that bus stop, and I was going to meet Lincoln. Screw my parents and their stupid curfew. I had reached my limit, and they could do nothing about it.

I glanced at the time on my cell, which read 8:45 p.m. Normally, my father would've been home by that time, but he was out with friends, watching the Cardinals game at a local bar. My brother and sister were both sleeping over at friends' houses, and if I played this right, I could get away with sneaking out and getting home in time without anyone even noticing. But would it be worth it? Both of my parents tracked me on the Life360 app, and I would have to shut off my location, which would be an entirely different punishment on top of my one month of house arrest. At that point, I was allowed to go to school and sports and come home. She also hadn't mentioned taking my phone or my car, which would without a doubt be her next move. So, I decided to call her back, and as my anxiety increased with each unanswered ring, I silently begged her to pick up. But she never did. The sound of her automated voice mail shot daggers through my heart because I knew I effed up. I contemplated leaving her a message—honestly, I did—but there was nothing left to say.

I clung to my phone like a lifeline, holding it to my chest for what felt like dear life. Already, my attempts to see Lincoln were having a negative effect on everything. Sure, my parents were impossible at times, but I did love them. And eventually, I would have to look my father in the eye and own up to whatever devious plan I was concocting. So as I squeezed my eyes shut, tears flooding my pillowcase, I knew what I had to do. And if Lincoln was the guy I hoped he would be, surely he would understand. Right?

Alanna: *I just had a fight with my mom, Lincoln. I just don't think I can come.*

As I typed back to him, the tears started flowing even more freely, and the pain in my stomach became too much to bear, causing me to keel over and want to puke. Why couldn't my mom understand me? Why couldn't she just listen and try to see where I was coming from? And why did I have to lose my cool and call her a bitch?

Lincoln: *Do you even want to see me? If you're seeing someone else just say it.*

His words cut through my heart like a knife. *No . . . no . . . no . . . This isn't happening.* I was about to blow it with a guy I was positive could be the love of my life, all because my parents sucked.

Alanna: *That isn't it at all Lincoln. My parents are being assholes. Like legit assholes. They just grounded me for a month. Please believe me.*

I waited in anticipation for Lincoln to write back, and when he didn't respond immediately, I began a downward spiral. I was going to lose Lincoln before even meeting him, and it was all *their* fault. Why didn't they want me to be happy? Was this how it was going to be for the rest of my life? I leapt to my feet and paced around my room, wishing I had someone to talk to about this. I could text Zack or Hank, but neither of them would understand. I considered reaching out to Zack's older sister, Nadia, who had served as somewhat of a big sister to me over the years, but honestly, I didn't even know what I would be trying to accomplish. She would warn me not to date a guy I knew only from Snap. And Nadia would surely report me to my parents and agree with them that I was acting like a spoiled brat, because everyone in my friend group loved Laura and Patrick. That's right, my parents were *those* parents: cool to everyone else but embarrassing to me by simply existing. But I was constantly torn in that department. I didn't have any close girlfriends because, well, my Mom was my best friend. I would just talk to her about all the hard stuff—my mom, whom I'd just referred to as a bitch before she boarded her flight across the country to Boston. *Who am I turning into?* That wasn't me.

I paused for a minute, studying my reflection in my vanity's mirror. My newly spray-tanned complexion was streaked with red, my tired blue eyes swollen and puffy, and I gathered my long blonde hair into a low ponytail as I studied my pathetic shell of my former self. I grabbed my phone, eager to text my mother, hopeful that I still had time to apologize before her departure. I feared something might go wrong on her flight, and the last words I said to her before her plane crashed would be *You're such a bitch*. But as I swiped open my text messages and began typing to my mother, a Snap from Lincoln came through, and I eagerly swiped it open.

Lincoln: *This is messed up. If you can't meet me tonight, then we are OVER.*

My heart stopped beating as I gaped in shock at his ultimatum, the frustration from earlier hammering down on me like the weight of the world on my shoulders, shattering any sense of remorse I had over my fight with Mom. My fingers shook as I whispered, "No, no, no," into my empty bedroom.

Alanna: *I want to see you. You need to believe me. I'm grounded.*
Lincoln: *I love you, Alanna. I need to see you. I can't wait. This is torture.*
He loves me? I thought, my heart pounding in my chest, pushing my fight with my mother even further from my mind.
Alanna: *You love me, Lincoln?*
Lincoln: *Yes. Don't you love me?*

With wide eyes and shaky fingers, I typed my reply, wondering how I'd gotten so lucky. I'd found a guy who not only was able to open up to me, to get to know me, but was eager to meet me and express his love. And Lincoln wanted to meet me just as badly as I wanted to meet him.

Alanna: *Yes. Lincoln. I love you.*
Lincoln: *Then prove it. Screw your parents. Meet me at the bus stop, and let's get the hell out of Tempe.*

I'm pretty sure my heart stopped beating at the thought of leaving my former life to be with someone I'd never actually met face-to-face. But the idea of being grounded for a month, never meeting Lincoln, and living with people who I thought understood me but clearly didn't hung over me like a gigantic storm cloud, dark and angry.

"Maybe getting out of here for a bit is what I need," I said to nobody. "Maybe if they miss me, they will appreciate me when I am gone."

I thought about that for a beat and sighed, knowing that I needed to stand up for myself. I was almost an adult, after all. I would meet Lincoln, and if he proved to be the person I was hoping for, I would go away with him for a bit. Then, when I returned, they would have missed me so much that they would have no choice but to hear me, to see me, to understand that I needed the freedom they had failed to grant me. The idea of my family missing me and learning to appreciate me sent pulses of electricity through my veins, and I hopped to my feet, the tears coming to a stop as quickly as they'd started as I envisioned my family learning to appreciate me, begging me to come home.

Alanna: *Where will we go?*

I didn't even wait for his response before scurrying around my bedroom, the hardwood floor cool against my bare feet, opening the drawers to my oak dresser, gathering only what I couldn't live without: two pairs of my favorite Lululemon leggings, three pairs of my Nike Pro shorts, two sports bras, underwear, and fuzzy socks—couldn't sleep without them even in the summer—and my favorite Luke Bryan T-shirt from his 2021 tour, which was once a bright magenta but had faded to pastel pink because of so many trips through the washer. I smiled for a second, recalling how my sister liked to steal my favorite shirt and thought back to the day I wrote my name on the tag in Sharpie and threatened her life if she tried to take it again. For a second, I started to worry about my brother and sister, wondering how they were going to feel when they realized their big sister ran away from home.

Lincoln: *My uncle has a vacation rental in Sedona. We can go there until we figure things out.*

I screeched with glee because in my opinion, Sedona was one of the most beautiful places on the planet and well out of my father's jurisdiction, and the thought of being cooped up with Lincoln Stone at his uncle's vacation rental sent my imagination on a rollercoaster ride of anticipation and hope. I pictured Lincoln and myself curled up together in bed, my eyes locked on his baby blues, and I added a lacy bralette and matching thong into the pile of clothes I'd set on my bed, along with my favorite perfume, my cosmetic bag, and two favorite books that I don't travel without: *Anne of Green Gables*—Mom's favorite—and *The Sisterhood of the Traveling Pants*.

Alanna: *Okay. Sounds like a plan. Should I pack a swimsuit?*
Lincoln: *Yes, baby. Pool and hot tub. And stop teasing me.*

Blood flushed to my cheeks as I adjusted to my shift in mood, transitioning from completely devastated to incredibly hopeful and optimistic as I pictured Lincoln holding me against himself in the hot tub, whispering how much he loved me and appreciated me. I grabbed my favorite red string bikini and added it to my pile before making my way toward the bathroom I shared with my siblings to retrieve my toothbrush, toothpaste, razor, hairbrush, and face wash, realizing my shampoo would be too bulky to take and assuming I could use his. The thought of sharing a shower with Lincoln caused the sides of my mouth to form a smile that I hadn't even seen coming.

Lincoln: *You make me the happiest guy in the world. I can't wait to see you, baby. Don't forget phone chargers, and if you have an iPad or a laptop, bring that so we can do our homework.*

His message sent ripples of joy through my veins as I flew around my bedroom, stuffing the pile of clothes and items necessary for this getaway with my new boyfriend into my Emerson Academy cheerleading duffel bag.

I added my allergy medication to the side pocket and smooshed everything down in order to add Patches, my favorite teddy bear, which was so well loved that my grandmother had sewn patches over his missing eyeball and other seams that had opened over the years. I smiled at the thought of introducing Lincoln to Patches and sharing my childhood stories with him.

I reached for my backpack that contained my electronics and some schoolwork, and as I glanced around my bedroom for the last time, I slipped into my favorite Vans. I reached for my favorite black Hollister zip-up sweatshirt and turned off my notifications on Life360. I wasn't scared—I was ecstatic, knowing I was about to meet the love of my life, Lincoln Stone, a guy who appreciated me for *me*. And even though everything I ever knew, loved, and appreciated was slipping through my fingers at lightning speed, I didn't care because I, Alanna Foster, was taking my destiny into my own hands for the first time in my life. The idea of that was enough to stifle the feeling of dread, the warning calls, and the fear forming in the pit of my stomach, leaving me with only the hopeful anticipation of meeting Lincoln Stone, the love of my life.

I fidgeted with my sweatshirt zipper and rubbed my bare legs, cursing myself for choosing denim shorts for that time of night and deciding that as soon as Lincoln and I were tucked away at his uncle's place in Sedona, I would change into my leggings.

Alanna: *I'm here. Where are you? I parked down the street like you said, and now I'm at the bus stop. It's cold out here.*

I double-checked the time on my phone, which read 10:42 p.m. and confirmed that Lincoln was in fact late. I gathered my long tresses over one shoulder and stared up at the night sky, wondering where up there Mom was and what time she would land in Boston. I was also growing concerned that my father was most definitely home from watching the game, and he had surely noticed that my notifications were turned off and I was not home. I shook away the pit in my gut, the guilt threatening to cripple my good mood with every minute that ticked by. *Where are you, Lincoln?* I thought as I adjusted my duffel bag and backpack beside me, hoping that Lincoln's parents hadn't stopped him on his way out.

But just as soon as the doubt washed over me, it diminished because a gray sedan pulled up to the bus stop, and my heart skipped a beat, knowing this was it, the moment I would meet Lincoln. But as I squinted my eyes to see through the car's lights, I didn't see Lincoln. I made eye contact with the driver, whom I recognized instantly from the soup kitchen: the scrawny, bald, tattoo-covered man. *What is his name? Slinky? Ace?* It hit me in that moment, as the back driver's side door opened and a figure emerged from the darkness, that I'd made an incredibly big mistake. The guy heading toward me at an overly aggressive pace wasn't Lincoln, or at least, it didn't look like his pictures. He was taller than I'd expected, and his muscular frame was intimidating as he towered over me. He looked to be at least in his mid-twenties, and although he looked as though he could have once been attractive, that man was anything but. He smelled as though he hadn't bathed in months; stains covered his white T-shirt, and traces of dirt were smeared on his face, and I decided that if this was a nightmare, he would be a monster.

"Lincoln?" I asked, my lips trembling and my legs beginning to shake involuntarily beneath me. But even as I said his name out loud, I knew it wasn't Lincoln.

"Hey, baby," the man purred, causing me to want to vomit. "Ready to hit the hot tub?"

"Who are you?" I snapped. "Where is Lincoln?"

"Lincoln? Oh, baby, there *is* no Lincoln. I'm sorry to break the news like this."

I leaped to my feet, one hand on my duffel and the other on my backpack. "What do you mean there is no Lincoln? What did you do to him?" I demanded, taking a step closer to the impostor, locking eyes with him. "Where is he?"

"Do what we say," the monster before me demanded, "and you won't get hurt."

I lowered my belongings back down on the bench and presented my empty hands. "I just want to see Lincoln," I said. "Please."

"Oh, Alanna," he cackled in a tone that could pass for a Disney villain's. "You don't get it, do you? *I'm* Lincoln."

"No," I replied, shaking my head in disbelief.

"Get her in the car, man," the driver called, "before someone sees us."

Imposter Lincoln gripped my shoulders and squeezed harder than necessary. "Like I said," he warned, "listen to me, and nobody gets hurt."

I thought about my parents, especially my mother. These men, these criminals, had set me up perfectly. If what he was saying was true, and Lincoln didn't exist, that meant that not only had I been Snapping a stranger all these months, but also, nobody would know where to find me—not after I turned off my location settings and packed my things the way I did. If all of that was true, it would look like I simply ran away. *Will anyone even look for me? Where would they even start?* My car was parked down the street. I took all my favorite things. Nobody, not one person, knew what I'd been up to. How could I have been so stupid?

"Take what you want," I said. "Please. You can have my laptop and my iPad. My debit card is here . . . Really, it's all yours." My eyes welled up with tears as I reached for all my important belongings, my eyes welling up with tears at the thought of handing over Patches the Bear to these assholes, but if that's what I needed to do to get out of there, then that is what I would do.

"Oh, we're taking *everything*," he said, squeezing my shoulders even more tightly and looking me up and down like a lion preparing to devour its prey. "And we are taking *you* too." He smiled.

"Help!" I screamed. "Someone help!" I gripped the front of his T-shirt, yanking him toward me as I thrust a knee into his crotch, spinning around as he fell forward in agony. "Help!" I yelled again, leaping over the bus stop's bench and landing on my hands and knees behind it. I pushed myself up off the ground and sprinted away, only to be wrestled back down to the ground by another.

"Got her," he hissed as I struggled to break free. "Get her car keys, too."

"Nice one, Ace," one of the men said as he approached, stepping on my knee with his sneaker-covered foot.

"Thanks, Slinky," he replied, his breath tickling my ear as I jammed an elbow into his rib cage.

Slinky leaned forward and pressed a piece of duct tape over my mouth as Ace gripped my wrists behind my back, gasping to catch his breath.

"I told you to listen!" the monster bellowed as he approached me. "But you don't like to listen, do you, Alanna?" I gaped up at him, eyes wide, trembling on the cold, gravelly ground in the arms of Ace and under the weight of Slinky's foot. "What do you want me to do with her, boss?" he asked Ace.

"Get her in the trunk," Ace hissed. "If she gives you any trouble, get the bat."

The monster bent down and scooped me up with one arm, flopping me over his shoulder and into the car's trunk. "Oh, Alanna," he said softly, tracing one finger over my jawline as one of the men forcefully tied my hands behind my back. "You should've listened to your mother."

Chapter Six

Now (March 2025) Lina

"It's hard to believe that our kids are driving themselves here," Jon says, clinking his sparkling water against my glass.

"It's terrifying," I admit, the pit in my stomach filling with dread at the thought of my children together in a car, left to their own devices. "And this sparkling water really should be a margarita."

"Doctor's orders," Jon says with a shrug. He sips his own water and places it back on the table. "You okay?"

I nod with a smile, but the truth is that I don't really know how I'm feeling. "I guess I'm nervous," I admit. "You know, to tell the kids about . . . *us*."

"It's Max and Lucy," Jon smiles. "They'll be fine. What else is going on with you?"

I curse the fact that my ex-husband is a private investigator, which means he can privately investigate *me*. "My sleep sucked last night," I admit, swirling the lime in my sparkling water with my straw.

"Nightmares?"

"Of the worst kind," I sigh, finally making eye contact. "It's fine, though. It's under control."

"You can talk to me," Jon says, squeezing my knee.

"Yeah," I huff. "Until you take me off Operation Cactus Blossom."

"I'm not taking you off the case. Talk to me."

"I get nightmares," I confess, unsure of how much I should reveal. "It's really not a big deal."

"About Operation Superglue?"

I study his baby blues for answers, wondering if he really wants to know or if he's looking for reasons to bench me. "About being undercover," I admit.

Jon nods his head and thinks about this for a moment, clearly connecting to this concept. "That's normal," he reassures me. "Are they about the kidnapping?"

I cringe as images of the metal baseball bat crashing against the side of my head and memories of being stuffed into the car's trunk flood me like water cascading from an opening dam. But my nightmares hadn't been about the kidnapping. They were more about my time undercover at Emerson and how dirty it felt lying to my family and my friends, Molly in particular.

I met Molly on my first day at Emerson when I was undercover as Gemma, and we hit it off as best friends immediately. The guilt that had consumed me—*all* of me—had come from all the lying, but especially lying to Molly, as she hadn't had many friends because her father was Dean Turner, and aside from spending our days together, we spent our nights texting and talking about things you only talk with a best friend about. After we solved our case and our cover had been blown, my friendship with Molly was what I'd been most concerned about. But because I saved her sister's life and help bring back Chloe and Teresa, it was difficult for her to be angry with me. In fact, we'd stayed friends just as I'd promised, and ironically enough, she had become friends with both of my kids.

"Lina?" Jon asked, his words demolishing my thoughts like a glass window shattering into millions of minuscule pieces.

"Huh?" I canvassed my memory for any hint of what Jon had asked me just moments earlier.

"Sorry," I sighed. "Spacing it again."

"It's okay," he said, pressing his lips to my cheek. "That's normal with concussions."

"Memory loss . . . If that's not attractive, then I don't know what is," I chuckle, faking a smile and tracing my pointer finger over the scar on my temple.

"You're attractive, and you know it," he whispers into my ear, barely skimming his teeth against my earlobe, just enough to send shivers of electricity to my core. "You're the sexiest woman I know."

"Flattery will get you anywhere," I admit, struggling to keep my eyes open because Jon's lips have traveled to my neck, and I like it—a lot.

"Hey!" Jon exclaims, pulling away and leaping to his feet.

I snap my eyes open just in time to see Max and Lucy making their way toward the corner table of our favorite Italian restaurant, a place that holds many significant memories for both Jon and me.

"Hi!" I exclaim, my voice louder than intended. "You made it!"

"Of course we made it," Max snickers as he plants a kiss on my cheek and plops down in the seat across from me. "Have a little faith, bruh."

"It's Mom," Jon corrects him.

"It's fine," I say, waving off Jon's redirection. "Hey, girlie," I tell Lucy, who's greeted her father with a kiss and blows one at me before taking the chair across from Jon.

"Max is a great driver, Mom," she says, gathering her long blond hair over one shoulder, making me wonder if it's possible for her to get even prettier than she was yesterday, as she inherited traces of my Mexican-American skin tone and petite figure along with Jon's perfectly structured cheekbones and ocean-blue eyes. "Unlike me," she sighs with a roll of her eyes.

"It takes practice, baby," Jon reassures her.

"Not for Max," Lucy argues. "He just got behind the wheel and, like . . . knew what to do."

"Driving is dope," Max admits, running his fingers through his shaggy brown hair, which desperately needs taming or washing. I would settle for either. "No cap . . . and I am the *goat*."

"Max, can you speak English, please?" Jon asks, raising his brows in frustration but also smiling fondly at his son.

"He means 'no bullshit,'" I clarify.

"It is bullshit," Lucy argues, ignoring us both. "Because *you* didn't almost crash into the side of the building in driver's ed," she reminds him.

"Goat," Max repeats, clearly proud of himself.

"You're such a jerk," Lucy whines, punching her brother in the arm.

"Don't come at me because you suck at driving, Pookie."

"Mom? Dad? Tell him to shut up," she begs.

"Just got to get back in that saddle," Jon says.

"Saddle?" They ask in unison, staring at him blankly.

"Hey there," our waitress sings. "Can I grab you guys something to drink?"

A margarita, I silently beg. *I really need a prickly pear margarita.* "We will take more sparkling water," I say with a fake smile, knowing that's the right thing to do post concussion. "Kids?"

"I'll take a root beer, please," Max says.

"Water is fine, thank you," Lucy says with a smile.

I gleam with mom pride because my teenagers, although they can be a unique breed at times, are consistent with their manners in public, which makes me proud.

"My name is Mia, and I'll be your server tonight," she says, cracking open a box of crayons and writing her name on the table's paper covering. She writes her name upside down so that it's facing our direction, and I silently wonder if she doesn't have a more complicated name, one that might be harder to write upside down, like Guinevere or Persephone, but has declared herself Mia simply because it's easier to write.

Mia leaves the table, promising to bring extra bread for my son, who has already retrieved the blue crayon from the box and started sketching his name in true wall-graffiti fashion, like one might illegally decorate a brick building or an underpass, and I glance from Max to Lucy and Jon and back again, an unexpected sense of joy flooding through me as I wonder just how long it has been since the four of us had dinner together at a restaurant.

As if reading my mind, Jon winks at me out of the corner of his eye. "Do you guys want to put in some apps?" Jon asks them. "The mozzarella sticks here are great."

"I was thinking fried calamari," Lucy says, "but I would have a few bites of those if Max ordered them."

"Mozzarella sticks are lit," Max says, not looking up from his masterpiece.

"Calamari and mozzarella it is," Jon says, closing his menu and catching my eye. "Anything else?" he asks me. *A margarita*, I think. "Nope, that sounds great," I say with a smile. "Although everything here is . . . lit," I smile at Max, who raises his eyebrows, clearly not impressed with my attempt at speaking his language.

"This is where your mother and I had our first date," Jon says with a smile.

When Lucy pulls out her cell phone and begins texting at lightning speed and Max reaches for the orange crayon, I realize this isn't going to be as easy as I originally thought. "It was," I chime in. "I . . . I wasn't even old enough to order a drink," I remember fondly, picturing Jon, five years my senior, sitting at this exact table, already sipping a beer upon my arrival, not even stopping for a hot minute to realize I was underaged. "That was the perfect night," I add, my tone soft and sincere.

"Oh yeah, your first date," Max chimes in. "Didn't you meet here, stay for twenty minutes before you got drunk AF on prickly pear margaritas, get matching tattoos, and then have unprotected sex resulting in . . . well . . . us? Actually, I take back my earlier comments. *Dad* is the real goat."

"Maximus Jonathan Cote—" Jon declares, his light skin turning multiple shades of pink.

"Well, it's true, isn't it?" Lucy asks innocently.

Heat rises to my cheeks, and I remove my cardigan, fanning myself, desperate for relief just as a pounding starts in the base of my neck and creeps up the back of my head. "Shit," I mumble, rubbing my temples with my pointer fingers.

"You okay?" Jon asks.

"I'm fine," I say, reaching for my purse and retrieving my medication.

Max sinks lower in his chair, and Lucy sips her water.

Jon looks at our son. "Your mother deserves respect, Max."

Max nods and reaches for the red crayon just as Mia returns with our drinks and takes our appetizer orders. Jon blots beads of sweat with his dinner napkin, and I realize that it's probably been years since my children have witnessed any sort of interaction like this between Jon and me, and I wonder what this must feel like for them.

"Max?" I ask, placing a gentle hand on his. "Where did you hear that?"

"Hear what?"

"About our first date. Was it Aunt Daphne? Uncle Ryker?"

Lucy shifts uncomfortably in her seat, and I start to understand what's happening. Jon and I are not the only ones keeping secrets. Max has something to hide, and he's doing everything in his power to avoid the topic.

"So, you and Dad . . . Are you talking? Are you a thing? Exclusive? Out with it," Lucy demands boldly.

"We're—"

"Don't change the subject," Jon says. "Where did you hear that, Max?"

Max releases the crayon and drops it to the table, stretching his arms overhead before running his fingers over his chin just as Jon does when he's either deep in thought or preparing to deliver unexpected news to a client. He shifts awkwardly in his seat before chewing on the strings of his emerald-green hoodie. "Molly," he mumbles under his breath, almost too quietly.

"Molly?" I ask, confusion evident in my voice.

"Did you tell Molly about our first date?" Jon asks with a smile.

I retrieve a scrunchie from my purse and pull my hair back into a low bun, wondering when it got so hot in here, knowing that yes, I most definitely told Molly about conceiving the twins on my first date. During one of our mall outings, she'd confided in me about wanting to sleep with her boyfriend at the time.

"Yes," I said, sitting up straighter. "Molly is a friend of mine, and I told her about the night I got pregnant so she wouldn't make the same mistake I did."

"So now we're a *mistake*?" Lucy asks, narrowing her eyes in my direction.

"Luciana Francesca—"

"That's what you just said," Max interrupts. "Don't get mad at *her*."

"Listen," I say, but I'm interrupted by a smiley Mia, who has returned with our apps. She politely places them in the center of our rectangular table and passes around small circular plates.

"Have you had a chance to look at the menu?"

I glance at the expressions of my family members, resisting the urge to ask for the check and get the hell out of this uncomfortable situation, but I'm stronger than that, and I know without a doubt that I can handle them. "We will need a minute." I smile.

"Sure thing. No rush," she says before turning around and leaving us to face a difficult conversation.

"Max, crayon down. Lucy, phone away," I demand in my no-nonsense mom voice.

As if on cue, my cherubs sit upright with their hands on their laps like Jane and Michael Banks standing in front of Mary Poppins for the first time, and I can see the admiration in Jon's eyes.

"The night I met your father," I start but stop and sip my sparkling water, praying that by some small miracle it might possibly have turned into a margarita, but when I find it hasn't, I continue anyway. "The night I met your father, I made some poor choices—choices that I've warned you *both* about," I whisper, my eyes landing on Lucy for longer than she probably appreciates. Lucy knows damn well that I could bring up the fact that I caught her in bed with her ex-boyfriend Oliver and didn't tell her father about it. "But more importantly than the mistakes we made that night, we fell in love. And even though my pregnancy was not planned, we wouldn't trade the two of you for anything."

Max and Lucy nod, and as far as I can tell, they seem remorseful.

"Sorry," Max mumbles under his breath.

"Yeah, I'm sorry," Lucy agrees. "This is just weird, you guys. We know you're back together. Why can't you just be honest with us? Other than when you lost your mind and went undercover as a freaking teenager, this is the only time you haven't been honest with us."

Guilt consumes me because she's right, and for a moment, I'm at a loss for words.

"Your mother . . . We . . . We didn't want to confuse you guys," Jon says for me. "We've been trying to figure things out. You were so young when we divorced, and we didn't want to cause you any pain by getting your hopes up . . . if . . ." Jon's voice trails off as he can't quite figure out how to say what he means.

"We were trying to figure it out," I finish for him.

"So, are you exclusive or not?" Lucy asks, crossing her arms over her chest.

I think about that, trying to recall everything I've learned about the teenage language and decided to throw it all out the window. "Some things can't be defined like that, Lucy. Sometimes, you can't just check relationships in a perfectly marked box."

"Well, are you seeing anyone else?" she asks, looking from Jon to me and back again.

"No!" We both recite in unison, suddenly feeling like we're the teenagers and she's the mother.

"Then you're exclusive," she shrugs.

"I guess we are," Jon agrees, taking my hand in his. "Your mother and I are *exclusive*."

I meet Max's stare and study him like a case I need to crack. "How are you feeling about that?"

Max bites into a mozzarella stick and, with his mouth full, mumbles, "That's sick." He says it with a nod before meeting Jon's stare and sitting up a bit straighter, with authority. "Try not to screw it up," he tells Jon.

"Max!" I exclaim, eyes wide and slamming my fists on the table.

"No," Jon says calmly before meeting Max's gaze. "You have my word, Max. I won't screw it up. I promise."

I rub my fingers over my forehead, eager for my migraine medication to kick in. "He shouldn't talk to you like that," I say to my family with my eyes closed.

"Sorry," Max huffs.

"I think this is a good thing," Lucy chimes in. "I'm happy for you."

"Thank you," I say, reaching for the fried calamari. "So, what's new with you guys?" I ask with a lighthearted laugh, praying that we can change the subject.

"Actually," Max says, running his hands through his hair and dipping his mozzarella stick in the marinara. "I've been talking with someone for a couple weeks, and I really like her."

My breath catches in the back of my throat, and the piece of calamari I'm eating somehow lodges in my airpipe, and I begin choking. Well, maybe it's not technically choking, but it's stuck enough that my coughing fit draws attention to our table. Jon offers me a glass of water and rubs my back until I can regain my composure.

"Sorry," I say, not sounding like myself at all but like an eighty-year-old chain smoker. "Sorry, Max. It's just . . . you've never mentioned girls before, so it took me by surprise."

"Anyone we know?" Jon asks, somehow managing to keep his tone and facial expression even-keeled, like a pro.

But judging by Lucy's expression and the way she's holding her breath, Max doesn't need to say anything because I just know. "It's Molly, isn't it?" I ask, clearing my throat one more time.

"Wow, you really are a private eye." Max snickers. "Yup. Molly and I are a *thing*. I'm asking her to be exclusive tomorrow, so I figured I'd tell you so you wouldn't get surprised and all weird and shit."

I nod, dismissing the notion that my son thinks I'm weird because, to him, I'm always weird. "Thank you for telling us," I say with a smile. "We're happy for you."

Jon squeezes my knee under the table, and I grab his hand in mine, an uneasy feeling washing over me. When I was undercover as Gemma, Molly was my best friend. And although I'm old enough to be her mother, I still sought comfort in the fact we were friends. *How will this change our dynamic? Shouldn't Molly have told me? What other secrets have I shared with Molly that might now get back to Max or vice versa?* This is a lot to process, and when the conversation changes from Max and Molly to Lucy's role as Little Red in the upcoming school production of *Into the Woods*, I decide to let it go and attempt to salvage what's left of our first family dinner in years.

When Max makes a political joke that's so out of pocket it sends Jon and Lucy into hysterics, and my headache begins to subside, I say a silent prayer that this will be the first of many times together, hoping that things will only go up from here. Because really, that's the only direction we can go at this point. *Right?*

"So, the cat's outta the bag?" Travis asks with a smirk.

"Well, if the cat you are referring to is my relationship with Lina and the bag means we talked to the kids about it, then yes, sir. Cat is most definitely outta the bag," Jon says.

I chew on my bottom lip and study the whiteboard behind Jon's desk, their chatter muffled in the distance as I study the photographs, notes, and clues regarding Alanna's disappearance. After meeting with Laura and Patrick, Jon gained some insight into her case and was hopeful that we might have some potential leads, but I can't stop staring at Alanna's picture, fear and dread washing over me at the possibility that this beautiful blond, blue-eyed teen might already be long gone.

"Can I see your notes from the Foster meeting?" I ask Jon. I just want to make sure we didn't miss anything.

Jon slips me a red binder with the words Operation Cactus Blossom scribbled on the cover in black Sharpie as he kisses me on the cheek and whispers, "My place tonight?"

"Maybe." I smirk, wanting nothing more than to spend the night with Jon but still feeling a bit uneasy about Max and Lucy's reaction to our exclusivity. I open the binder and read Jon's highlighted notes as he kisses the back of my neck. "Stop," I warn him. "I'm working."

"You're working *now*," he says. "But what about tonight?" He raises his eyebrows.

"Talk later," I insist as I scroll through Jon's bulleted list of notes from the meeting, most of which seems to be old information. "I want to spend time with you . . . I just . . . I need to keep an eye on Max too. Now that he and Molly are together . . . which is still a hard pill to swallow."

"I get it," Jon says with a sigh. "Let me know if anything in there sticks out to you," he says, motioning toward the binder of notes. "I want you to catch me up on Penelope's case when you're finished. And Travis, I need you to brief me on the wedding-crasher case."

"That case needs a name," I sing as I continue scanning Jon's notes.

"What did you have in mind?" Jon asks, rolling his chair beside Travis, whose eyes haven't left his laptop's screen in what feels like hours.

"Project I Do," I say without looking up from my notes, my lips curling into a side smile in satisfaction.

"Man, it's refreshing to have an author on board," Jon says with a clap of his hands. He stands and writes Project I Do in blue dry-erase marker in all caps. "All right, Travis, fill me in," he says like a coach addressing his star quarterback.

Travis reaches into his desk drawer to retrieve his reading glasses. I cast a side-glance at him as he tips them up on his nose, and for a moment, I'm reminded of why I found him attractive when we dated. I squeeze my eyes closed and shake away the memories of him moving beneath me in the smoothest but strongest way possible and of how secure I felt in his strong, athletic embrace.

"Are these all the notes we have?" I ask, my words jumbling together as I fan my face with my free hand. "I'd like to see the notes from the Tempe Police Department if you have them."

"Feel free to use my computer," he says, nodding toward the PC on his desk.

"I can't use PCs," I whimper like a child avoiding her homework. "Can't you email the file?"

"Nope. You've got this," he says and enters his password and motions at the computer's mouse.

"Fine," I say with a roll of my eyes as I make my way to Jon's ancient computer to search the database he's pulled up. "I still think we need to go to the Maricopa County Jail and question Dean Turner ourselves. If he hasn't turned in Travis, he's holding back in other ways."

"I'll take that as a positive, I suppose," Travis mumbles under his breath.

"Well, it's true."

"One thing at a time," Jon reminds me. "We just got rehired. These things can take time. We don't want to burn any bridges."

"I get that," I sigh. "But *I* was kidnapped by the same people. We need to get our hands on her Snapchat. Remember that dude, Lincoln Stone? She *had* to have been lured in by him."

"True," Jon agrees. "But there is really no way of knowing if it went down that way for her."

"Well, it went down that way for Chloe and Teresa too. And where is Dean Turner's son now?"

"Locked facility."

"Well, I think we need to question him too. How can you be so calm?"

"I want to find her too, Lina, but we need to keep our heads clear. We need to do this right."

"Okay, boss," Travis says, "Ready when you are."

I scroll through police reports and documented interviews for Alanna's case as Travis briefs Jon on Project I Do. "We've got the green light to hit up three weddings this summer: one at Sunset Vista Vineyards, another at the Mesa Mirage Manor, and the third at the Arizona Sutherland. Seems like we've got a hot lead at the Arizona Sutherland Resort, where the latest wedding was infiltrated. Beatriz has been blowing up my phone about it."

"I'm sure she's eager to put this behind her," Jon agrees. "Nice work. What else have you got?"

"I've reached out to the business managers at all three venues for guest lists to track down anyone with stolen credit cards. Unfortunately, most guests caught wind of the thefts early on and deactivated their cards or had their banks flag the charges as fraud before we could nab a lead. Looks like the thieves made off with mostly gifts and cash."

I sigh, wondering how on earth we're going to stop whoever is doing this. *Who in their right mind would break into someone's wedding and steal their wedding bands?* "These people sound nuts," I huff, continuing to read Jon's notes for Operation Cactus Blossom.

"Nuts or desperate," Jon agrees.

Travis clears his throat before continuing, "Did some digging on social media and found that every wedding that got crashed had their event promoted on theknot.com. Seems like that's where our culprits are scouting their targets—"

"I love The Knot!" I exclaim. "We used theknot.com for our wedding."

Both men look at me like I have ten heads.

"What?"

"What is it?" Jon asks, one brow raised.

"It's a web site," I explain. "It lists event details like time, place, after-parties, and stories about how the bride and groom met, where they are registered, et cetera."

"Sounds like a recipe for disaster to me." Travis scowls. "You mean to tell me that by accessing a couple's site, I can view the logistics for their wedding *and* what gifts they are getting?"

I think about that for a beat. "No, not really. Typically, you need a password or a QR code to enter a couple's site. I remember it being secure . . . so much so that my father couldn't even figure out how to log in."

Jon runs his fingers through his beard's scruff. "How do attendees receive that information?"

"Ours was on the back of our formal invitation with a QR code . . . but now I think it's done more over email."

"Interesting," Jon says. "So, the crashers would need to either intercept a paper invite, hack an email, or gain access to the website itself. Make a note that whoever we are dealing with is extremely technically savvy."

"Or . . ." I say, my voice trailing off due to a lack of confidence that I don't feel until I speak up.

"Or what?" Travis asks, peering at me over his reading glasses.

"It's just a thought," I start, rubbing the base of my neck. "But is it possible the crashers could have access to venue employees? Like a mole?"

Jon chews on the top of his pen and stares into the distance, considering that for a beat. "I wouldn't count it out." He nods. "I think it would do us some good to get to know the staff at all three venues. Travis, start with the Arizona Biltmore . . . It is a resort, after all. Lots of employees could have access to that sort of information. I think that's a great place to start."

"Copy that," Travis states in his private investigator voice. "Heading out for coffee. I'll call Beatriz on the way. You two want something?"

"Do you really need to ask?" I say with a wink.

"I got you," Travis says with a smile. "Jon?"

"I'm good, thanks. Keep me posted, and nice work."

The door to PPI is barely closed behind Travis before Jon is standing behind me with his hands on my shoulders, and I assume he's rereading his notes, but his warm palms slide down my sides and under my cotton shirt, up and over the lace of my bra, and pause, pressing against my abdomen. He kisses my neck. I realize he's looking for more than an update on the case.

"Okay, you win. Tonight," I say firmly. Removing his hands from beneath my shirt then fanning my cheeks with the binder.

"Oh yeah?" he asks, his smile wide.

"Yeah. I'll have Ryker go to the house and watch the kids," I say, my voice unsteady and my cheeks flushed. *He basically lives there anyway*, I think, reaching behind his neck and pulling Jon's face toward mine until our lips meet in a passionate kiss.

"Tonight," Jon repeats.

"But for now, we work. I need to brief you on Penelope's case, and we need to make some sort of progress on Alanna's."

"Okay, Lina Rivera, private eye. I like when you take control. It's hot."

"Save it," I say. "For tonight."

"Fine. You win."

The corners of my lips fold into a mischievous smile as I spin Jon's chair around and run my hand over the crotch of his jeans. "I *always* win. Now, pull up a chair, we have work to do."

Chapter Seven

Then (October 2023) Alanna

When I was younger, I was deathly afraid of the dark. My parents would tuck me into bed with Patches the Bear, I would say my prayers, and they would wish me sweet dreams. They would joke about not letting the bedbugs bite, something I never quite understood until I got older. But only moments after they turned on my night light and switched on my noise machine, I would call for them to come back because the idea of staying in my room all night, alone in my bed, was just too much to bear.

My dad was the first to appear in my doorway, ready to search under my bed and in the closet for the monsters, and he would reassure me that nobody was there and monsters didn't exist anyway. And after one more lullaby or one more bedtime story, I would drift away to sleep, secure in the knowledge that if there had been any bad guys, my dad would've gotten them. My tall, strong, park ranger father would strangle any wild animal, monster, or anyone who threatened his baby girl.

That continued until middle school, when it suddenly became uncool to be seen with your parents, and over time, after random sleepovers at friends' houses, I needed to be strong for my brother and sister. Suddenly, the idea of angry beasts or evil demons, home invaders and criminals just . . . subsided. Maybe I was stronger or just more mature. Or perhaps I felt secure, knowing my parents would never let anything bad happen to me.

So, as I slipped in and out of consciousness, the back of my head throbbing from the impact of the metal baseball bat, hunger pains piercing my gut like thousands of knives, I pictured my father. Of course, I was far from the comfort of my childhood home and the luxury of my bedroom. That had been replaced by a minuscule two-person tent and an overwhelmingly filthy sleeping bag that smelled of stale sweat, body odor, smoke, and urine. And honestly, some of those scents might've been *me*. Even still, I used my imagination and transported myself back to my bedroom. I pretended to snuggle with Patches as Dad leaned forward and kissed the injured spot on the back of my head before checking for monsters and telling me I was good to go to sleep and that I was safe.

But as a tear trickled down my cheek and I squeezed myself tightly, hugging my knees to my chest, I knew my dad couldn't save me. Only I could save myself. After all, I was the one who'd gotten myself into this. I was the one who'd *needed* to meet Lincoln. Lincoln, a guy I was ready to leave everything behind for, wasn't even real. I'd fallen in love with a fictional character, a fake Snapchat imposter created just to lure me out in the middle of the night. And the worst part was that, based on the things I took with me, it *did* look like I ran away. Those jerks orchestrated it perfectly. My parents, my siblings, my teachers, my friends—they would all believe I ran away from home. Nobody would know where to even begin to look for me. Hell, I didn't even know where I was, and I had nothing. They took *everything* before dropping me in a stinky old tent. And even though they at least had the decency to let me be, to rot away like an abandoned puppy in the middle of nowhere, they stood guard right outside the zippered entrance, and they did so in shifts.

I didn't know how much time had passed since my abduction from the bus stop, but I did know it was at least two nights, which I knew because I'd been conscious for two of them. But the truth was I didn't know how long I'd been out cold, as the last thing I did remember was the metal bat smashing against the side of my head, then I woke to the voices of Slinky and Ace as they paced outside my new home, the sounds of their shoes clacking against the concrete ground, worsening my headache and causing me to vomit over and over again until nothing was left to throw up.

As if on cue, their sinister voices shook me to my core as they congratulated themselves on my abduction, mumbling something about me being their *first* as they applauded each other with what sounded like celebratory high fives and pats on the back, and I wondered how, in such a short amount of time, I went from Alanna Foster, Emerson Academy senior, to Ace and Slinky's pathetic excuse for a trophy, and my stomach ached even harder as I pictured them stuffing me like a moose on a cabin wall, or gutting me and sticking me to a wooden plaque like a fisherman's first catch. That thought angered me so much that I met my limit and snapped. *Who do they think they are?* They lured me with Lincoln Stone bait, beat me to a pulp, and tossed me away like week-old leftovers, which reminded me of my last day serving at the shelter on Shepherd's Pie Day, and I remembered the creepy way one of them whispered my name, and I hated myself for not figuring out then what was happening.

"Transport is tomorrow," Ace huffed. "Just before sunrise."

Transport? The knot in my stomach grew even tighter, taking my breath away.

"We can't screw this up," he continued. "And by me, I mean *you*."

"Knock it off," Slinky snapped. "I got her down here, didn't I?"

"You didn't do shit, moron," Ace said. "Emmett was the muscle."

"Emmett was the muscle, but I was the brains."

"Keep telling yourself that. I've met cactuses with more brains than you."

"You mean 'cacti'—"

"What I mean is shut the—"

"Will Emmett be here for transport?" Slinky asked, ignoring Ace's jabs.

"Damn straight. I'm not trusting myself with this package. Too much at stake."

I thought about that, picturing the two men with their scrawny arms and lanky bodies and agreeing with them. They couldn't catch and restrain a stray kitten, let alone a person, especially a person young and fit like me. Of course, I would need to consider the fact that I was weak. I hadn't had anything to eat or drink in days, and I most definitely had a concussion. *But still . . . isn't it worth trying?* The man they were referring to, Emmett, was the one who tackled me to the ground, shoved me in the car's trunk, and beat me with the bat. He must have also been the one who carried me to wherever I was being held. Ace and Slinky were simple bystanders.

I resisted the urge to close my eyes and supported myself with my elbows as my head continued spinning, and I realized I needed to get the hell out of there. The problem was I didn't fully know where *there* was. Based on the concrete surface beneath me, I knew I wasn't outside. Maybe I was in someone's house. There was a stench I'd never smelled before, like rotten eggs. Maybe I was in some sort of factory. *Would it make more sense to try to escape now or wait until sunrise?*

"Heading to grab dinner," Ace barked. "I'll be back in an hour. Don't do anything stupid."

My pulse quickened, and sweat formed at the base of my neck as I positioned myself in a seated position, testing my strength. I wondered if I had the energy to run from Slinky. I felt around my sleeping bag for something, anything I could use for a weapon but came up empty. If I was going to flee, I would have to be smart. My timing would need to be right, and I would need to defeat them both physically and mentally. I would also need to be brave. And the truth was that even though I could tolerate the dark more now than I could as a child, it was still scary. But scary enough to wait for Emmett's transport? Hell. No.

"What do I do?" I whispered to nobody, startled by the dryness of my mouth and throat and realizing I was even weaker than I'd anticipated.

I listened for the sound of Ace's or Slinky's voice, and after what felt like years, I decided I was not going to give up. Sure, I didn't know what was on the other side of the tent, but staying inside and waiting for yet another kidnapping sounded like a bigger risk. I shimmied over to the tent flap, only knowing its whereabouts because both Slinky and Ace had entered from time to time. I explored the darkness for the zipper, fear rippling through me as I swiped my trembling fingers against the nylon fabric, excitement shooting through me as I felt the metal zipper. Pinching it between my fingers, I pulled it open only to find Slinky seated on the ground, leaning his bony body against a cement wall. His eyes closed, he was fast asleep.

With eyes wide, I glanced around the darkness of my surroundings, realizing I was in some sort of parking garage or abandoned warehouse, but the rotten-egg smell was worse outside, causing me to involuntarily gag then cough and gag again. Slinky's eyes shot open, making direct eye contact with mine, and I froze, trying with all my might to think on my feet, but my head pounded, and my mind was foggy, and all I could muster was a weak "Hi."

"What the hell do you think you're doing?" Slinky roared, rising to his feet, eyes narrowed, spit shooting out the sides of his foul-smelling mouth as he lunged toward me. "Get back inside. Now!"

Slinky approached me in what felt like slow motion. He reached toward my shoulders, ready to shove me back inside the tent. But I channeled my anger and rage and mustered up enough adrenaline to push him away, back against the wall, then drove my knee directly into his groin.

"Bitch!" he yowled. "Get back here!"

I traced my fingers against the concrete wall as I ran, my legs weak and unsteady beneath me. The foul smell grew stronger the farther I ran from my tent, but the sound of Slinky's voice becoming softer kept me going, and I ran until I couldn't run any more. *Where the hell am I? Why doesn't this building have any doors or exits? Why can't I find my way out?*

I clutched my aching stomach with one hand and pressed my hand against my pounding head with the other, determined to break free from that hellhole. I couldn't run anymore, but I could walk, one foot in front of the other, until I found myself inside what appeared to be a tunnel. The realization that I was underground was enough to send even more waves of fear rippling through me at lightning speed. *Run, Alanna!* I silently scolded myself, and I continued stumbling and tripping over my own feet until a small speck of light broke through the wall's side in the distance.

"A door!" I exclaimed, unable to contain my excitement.

I made my way to the tunnel's door, clutched the handle, and shoved it open. A bright, painful light pierced my eyes, but at the same time, an intense relief washed over me.

But just as quickly as the glimmer of hope appeared in the darkness of my soul, it was zapped away. Standing before me were Ace and his sidekick Emmett, their arms crossed over their chests and their nasty faces mocking me. Emmett clutched the baseball bat with one hand and flipped open a pocketknife with the other while Ace pressed a cell phone to his ear, telling whoever was on the other end of the line not to worry—the package had been accounted for and transport was happening sooner than expected—and I knew in that moment that my dad had been horribly wrong. There were such things as monsters, and he couldn't take them all away, no matter how hard he tried.

Chapter Eight

Now (April 2025) Lina

The Arizona Sutherland Resort and Hotel is one of the most prestigious wedding venues in Scottsdale. And on this seemingly perfect April evening, I—Lina Rivera, private eye—am not only officially undercover as a guest for the wedding of Phoenix and Esteban, an adorable young couple who met in college at the University of Miami, but I'm also getting to spend some needed quality time with Ryker, my best guy friend. Ironically, this brings things full circle since the first time we met was at Daphne's wedding, when I fell head over heels for the former Division I college football player who often passed as Tom Brady, only to immediately discover that we would never be a *thing* because Ryker preferred men to women. That came as a shock at first, but in the long run, having Ryker as a friend has been everything I needed and more.

 Of course, attending this wedding with Jon would also have been enjoyable, but he and Travis are monitoring all venue entryways and parking lots and surveying security footage, while Ryker and I get to enjoy the festivities undercover, which is something we discussed after we had the pleasure of meeting with Phoenix and Esteban last week, only days after our dinner with Lucy and Max. It had been my idea to include the bride and groom in our investigation. Beatriz, the wedding and function coordinator of Navarro Hotels, had spoken with them previously regarding our undercover invite, but meeting the couple in person gave us a chance to ask specific questions about their wedding details and inquire about the guest list, friends and family, et cetera. Phoenix, a desert girl through and through, was born and raised in Arizona, and Esteban, a young drop-dead-gorgeous Marc Anthony lookalike, came to the United States from Puerto Rico, seeking only an undergraduate degree in business, but met his bride the first day of freshman orientation. It was love at first sight, and although I have and will always appreciate a solid love story, I've found myself still somewhat skeptical of marriage and "happily ever after," which is honestly both frustrating and discouraging because Jon and I have come so far since those days, and I'm becoming more and more infuriated with myself for not being able to just move on from the past.

The ceremony was exquisite. It took place in the gardens of the resort, just as Phoenix had discussed with us during our meeting. She had her brunette hair up in a stunning updo, wore an ivory mermaid-style wedding gown, and carried a gorgeous succulent bouquet, looking picturesque, like a Disney princess living out a true fairy tale. And as the couple exchanged vows and tears flooded from Esteban's wide, dark eyes, Ryker gently placed his hand on mine and squeezed it reassuringly, knowing that even after all these years, weddings can be hard for me. Sure, Jon and I are rekindling our marriage *now*, but for years, I carried around the burden of his infidelity, and at times, especially during vulnerable moments like these, my wounds tend to open a bit, the heartfelt and innocent vows of a young bride and groom emotional salt to an open abrasion.

But I'm here on business, so I have no choice but to stay focused on the job at hand: Project I Do. So far, Ryker and I have not spotted any unusual or suspicious behaviors or activity, which is our main assignment. If we notice someone who doesn't quite belong at the wedding, we'll send pictures of them to Travis, who will run their photo through a list of wedding guests and their descriptions, a database we put together from Phoenix and Esteban's social media accounts. That was easier than we'd expected, as most of the wedding guests are friends and family of Phoenix because, unfortunately, most of Esteban's family didn't make the trip from Puerto Rico.

I adjust the top of my burgundy halter dress and attempt to reposition my updo's bobby pin as it pokes into my scalp in a way that could very well trigger a headache, which is the last thing I need tonight. We sit at a table of the couple's college friends, taking on the role of friends from Phoenix's student teaching internship, trusting her advice that this would be a valid cover and nobody would question us—and she was correct. Not only have her friends taken full advantage of open bar, but the group has also been so happy to see each other that they weren't paying much attention to us at all, which was fine with both Ryker and me.

"Almost time for the toast," Ryker says as he slides his champagne glass closer to his place setting. "Jon mentioned that we should keep an extra eye out at that point," he reminds me.

I nod. "Yes, times when all the attention is on the bride and groom. We made it past the vows, so that leaves toasts, dances, and cake cutting," I murmur under my breath as I reach for my champagne glass, only to have Ryker intercept it and replace it with his water. "Dude!" I whine. "It's just one glass."

"I kinda like your brain, Lina," he says, kissing my cheek lightly. "It needs to heal."

"You just want my champagne," I say, punching him playfully in the gut, the firmness of his midsection surprising me a bit. "Hello, abs," I joke, gesturing toward his abdomen. "Someone's been hitting the gym hard."

"Wish we could say the same for you," he says, nudging me playfully.

I roll my eyes, knowing Ryker is only giving me a hard time because he is not only my best friend but also my personal trainer, and working out hasn't been on the top of my priority list or on any list, for that matter, since the start of Operation Superglue. "My arm is still healing," I say, cringing at the memory of my bones breaking in multiple places when Travis tackled me to the ground during my attempted escape from the homeless camp in Tempe.

"That's bullshit, and you know it."

"Concussion? Is that a good enough excuse?"

"I know you're under a lot of stress, Lina. I'm just teasing you. You look . . ." He scans me up and down, the heat from his stare making my cheeks flush. "You look amazing. I just worry about you." Ryker, who knows me better than I know myself, is one of the only people on the planet I allow to peek into my life, and he knows it. "I think getting some exercise in could help, though."

"Yeah, I've got a lot going on," I sigh.

"You still freaking over Molly dating Max?" he asks, his tone tender and empathetic.

"So, about those abs," I say, completely changing the subject. "You trying to get Alex back? Or are they for someone new?"

"Nice try," he smiles and sips his champagne.

"For real. You promised you would give him a second chance."

"I know I did. We're keeping it casual."

"You're sleeping with him?" I shriek, louder than intended.

"I don't think they heard you in the back of the room," he says.

"Like you care. Seriously, though, Alex is a good man. Sure, he made a mistake . . ." I say, my voice trailing off because discussing infidelity is not territory I'm eager to explore. "He loves you."

"Here, take a selfie!" one of my tablemates instructs, passing me a disposable camera.

"Haven't seen one of these in a while," I say as I reverse the camera toward Ryker and myself, and we snap a selfie for the bride and groom and pass it on to the couple across from us.

"The toast is starting," Ryker says, gesturing to the bride and groom's sweetheart table.

I nod, scanning the reception hall with wide eyes. So far, nobody looks out of place or unfamiliar. I'd taken a picture of an older couple prior to the ceremony who didn't appear to resemble anyone on our guest list, but the bride confirmed they were her great aunt and uncle. And one gentleman dressed in all black seemed to be wandering around aimlessly but ended up being the photographer's assistant. Otherwise, everything has been normal. I survey the room with my eyes again, landing on the servers and bartenders as they work efficiently, pouring champagne and mixed drinks. I study the DJ as he smiles at the bride's maid of honor, who talks about the day Phoenix met Esteban for the first time.

"I wonder if all the weddings had the same DJ," I whisper to Ryker.

"It's worth looking into," he agrees.

I open the notes app in my phone and type, *DJ?* as the wedding guests raise their glasses and toast Phoenix and Esteban and the DJ calls the minister up to bless the food. "I can't accuse a minister . . . can I?" I ask my best friend, who just shrugs and shoots back my champagne. I decide that if the minister is the one behind all this, I don't even want to know. Instead, I decide to check in with Jon via text.

Lina: *How's it going?*

Jon: *Good here. Anything sus?*

Lina: *Everything seems to be going as planned. Nobody looks like they don't belong. Security cameras still intact?*

Jon:

Lina: *I was thinking we could investigate the vendors. Maybe there is a common denominator there? Specifically, the DJ.*

Jon: *Good thinking.*

My texting is interrupted because a server plops the best-looking steak I've ever seen on my plate, and my mouth begins to water, but I don't let it distract me. Instead, I scan the room one more time before confirming that everything seems to be okay. I cut into my steak and take my first bite. "This is so good," I moan to Ryker.

"I can't believe I chose chicken," Ryker sighs. "That is one good cut of meat." When I raise my eyebrows, Ryker shakes his head. "Your mind is always in the gutter."

"Here," I say, cutting my steak in half, piercing half the steak with my fork, and setting it on Ryker's plate like I might serve Max or Lucy. He cuts his chicken into two pieces and reciprocates.

"Thank you," he says, between bites. "Always choose steak at a wedding. Rookie move."

"It's fine—" I start, but my words are interrupted by the DJ's voice in the mic.

"Ladies and gentlemen, we have a guest that can't seem to locate her wallet. If you happen to find it, you can bring it right up here to the DJ booth."

Ryker's eyes meet mine as chills run through my spine. "Could be a coincidence."

"I don't believe in coincidence," Ryker says. "We need to look harder."

I know he's right, but I'm out of ideas. For the most part, everyone looks like they belong here. But that could be said about Ryker and me. I poke at my dry, undercooked carrots and sigh. *What are we missing? Are we playing this right?* I mean, sure, blending in as wedding guests is critical for this operation, but sitting here at this table, joking around with Ry and eating semi-delicious food is not going to solve Project I Do. And I desperately need to solve this case, as I need to prove to Jon that I can do this. If I can show him I'm strong enough to handle this pressure, then maybe he'll stop coddling me with Operation Cactus Blossom.

"I'm going to run to the restroom," I say, standing from my chair and pushing it in. "Save me some steak, or I'll kick your ass."

I slide my phone into my clutch and head in the direction of the ladies' room, searching my brain for answers. *Wouldn't the bride and groom notice if any of these guests didn't belong?* I shake my head in frustration as I push open the door and prepare to enter a bathroom stall, but I come face-to-face with a woman who looks to be roughly my age or maybe a bit younger but much, much taller than I am. She wears a short black strapless cocktail dress with strappy black high heels. She smiles at me for a beat before reapplying a shade of red lipstick so bright against her pale skin that her lips almost look like they're bleeding.

"Beautiful night, huh?" I ask, situating my clutch on the counter. I wash my hands, deciding I could bypass the toilet for now because I most definitely have not seen this woman at the wedding tonight, and she's carrying a purse so large that it could easily fit multiple bags or wallets. Excitement makes my heart pound because for the first time all night, I may have a lead.

"Yes, a perfect night," she agrees, adjusting her dark black bob in the mirror.

Could that be a wig? Oh, yes. That, ladies, and gentlemen could most definitely be a wig. It's almost comical how synthetic it looks, reminding me of Lucy's American Girl Doll hair and how disheveled, frizzy, and tangled it would become over time. We would try to brush it with our hairbrushes, but it was never quite right after that. And aside from the sorry excuse for a hairdo, her eyebrows are light, but that doesn't mean much as she could very well just be a woman who colors her hair or sucks at cosmetology. But every piece of my entire being, every instinct in my body is screaming that this could be our wedding crasher. *Don't blow this!* I scream silently. *Think, Lina!* I take a deep breath and count to five, parachuting back to my Gemma days. *What would*

Gemma do? Surely, this woman has already noticed me gawking at her. For the love of God, I've been washing my hands like a doctor scrubbing in for major surgery, and I probably haven't even blinked once.

Trying my best to improvise on the spot, I angle my phone at eye level and flip the camera around so that it faces me in full selfie mode, and I open my mouth wide like I'm at the dentist, picking at my tooth with my fingernail. "Ugh," I moan. "Would you happen to have a toothpick?"

"Excuse me?" she asks, her attention turning to the sight of my tooth magnified on the phone's camera screen.

"I have steak in my tooth," I say with my mouth wide open. "Do you have a toothpick?"

The mystery women unzips her large red Coach purse and rummages through it, and I quickly swap my phone's camera out of selfie mode to snap the perfect photo of her, my heart pounding so hard in my chest that I think it might explode as she continues to search through her purse, obviously pretending to look for a toothpick when she clearly could care less.

"I'm sorry. I don't," she says.

"Oh, would you . . . uh . . . Would you look at that? I totally got it out. Phew. That would, uh . . . That would've been so embarrassing. Who wants to be the girl with steak in her teeth? I mean, my date's gay, so not like it matters, but still, it *sort* of does, you know?" I ask, aware that I am rambling on like a lunatic.

"Very well, then," she says, eyebrows raised, turning toward the door as I snap her photo once more.

"How do you . . . uh . . . know the bride and groom?" I ask, my words jumbling together, forming more gibberish than an actual sentence.

She places her hand on the doorknob and pauses briefly before turning in my direction, twirling a piece of black faux hair around her finger before scratching the back of her head with her manicured fingernails. Then, in slow motion, a long, wavy clump of bleached blonde tendrils scape from the wig's restraints and gather at the base of her neck. *It's a wig! It's a wig!* I resist the urge to tackle her to the ground screaming, "Got her!" Instead, I stand up straighter, locking eyes with her, somehow not even batting an eyelash and keeping my composure.

"I'm with the bride," she says with a genuine smile. "I was Phoenix's nanny. Goodness, the thought that she is old enough to get married just sends goosebumps through me, you know?"

Nanny? Nanny? No . . . no . . . no . . . There was no mention of any nanny on the guest list. This woman is for *sure* the wedding crasher. *But what am I supposed to do now?* I don't know if I should call her on it or club her over the head with my purse. No, that won't solve anything. For all I know, she may have a gun or a knife or pepper spray in that big red bag of hers. I have her photo, and that's a start. So instead of assaulting her, I decide that two can play this game.

"That's so nice!" I sing. "I remember Phoenix talking about her nanny."

"You do?"

"Oh, yes. We worked together for months during our student teaching. Oh, man," I say through squinted eyes, jamming my palm to my forehead as if I am trying to remember her name. "Remind me of your name again? I can't wait to tell her that I met you."

She stands like a statue in the bathroom's doorway, and her pale skin turns red and blotchy. "Jenny," she says through her red lipstick smile.

I grin, picking up my clutch and sliding into a stall, locking the door behind myself. "It was so nice to meet you. Hopefully, I'll catch you on the dance floor," I say, frantically preparing to text Jon her photo. But just as I finish my text and prepare to hit Send, Jon's comes through first.

Jon: *Security cameras cut. What's your twenty?*

I gasp, covering my mouth with my hand. "Nice to meet you too," she sings before closing the door behind herself, and I hit send on my text to Jon with trembling fingers.

Lina: *Bathroom! Fake black wig, red lipstick, black dress, red bag. It's SO her!*

Jon: *We will keep an eye out for her. Be careful.*

I hurriedly finish up in the restroom and wash my hands, suddenly aware of the racing of my heart and the beads of sweat that have formed on my forehead and the back of my neck. *That was so . . . Wow, so nerve-wracking and completely terrifying.* But I loved it. It felt both empowering and validating that I not only was able to find her, but I got her picture and heard her voice. And now, Ryker, Jon, and Travis can all be on the lookout for a tall woman in black heels, in a black dress, with a short black bob.

I do a quick little happy dance before smiling at my reflection in the mirror then whisper, "You've still got it!" with a wink before reaching for the paper towels, drying my hands, and tossing them into the trash can. But my heart sinks. There, in the wastebasket in the ladies' room of the Arizona Sutherland, is Jenny the nanny's fake hair, and before I can even fathom what in the actual hell is happening, the lights go out, and I'm standing alone in complete darkness.

Chapter Nine

Then (November 2023) Alanna

One time, when I was roughly ten years old, my father had decided the time had come to renovate my bedroom, starting with painting my walls. Apparently, the thumbtacks and putty I'd used to hang my dozens of One Direction posters had done some damage, and he was eager to correct the destruction. That was a special day for him and me, as we spent the afternoon at Home Depot, choosing ballet-slipper pink in eggshell for the trim and ceiling, and when we got home, we worked together to remove each poster, one at a time, careful to keep them from ripping or wrinkling, before spackling each hole, sanding the surface, and eventually priming and painting. I can remember, even at such a young age, being very impatient between each step. Waiting for the spackle and the primer to dry before we could move onto the next step was tedious, to say the least.

"Why do we have to wait for it to dry?" I whined. "I just want it to be done already."

"Because," he gently explained, "painting your room is a process. We do one thing at a time, in the right sequence, and we will see the best results. Some things in life just can't be rushed."

"Well, what can we do while we wait?" I asked, knowing full well that Mom was on a flight to Boston.

I remembered him biting down on the side of his lip, like it was yesterday. He studied the ceiling as if the answers were written there before an invisible lightbulb went off over his head, and his eyes lit up like a child's on Christmas day.

"Blackjack and root beers," he said with a confident nod. He lifted me up onto the counter, dropping me with a soft plop, and reached into the junk drawer for a deck of cards, then the fridge for two root beers.

"You like root beer, right?" he had asked, like he was up to no good.

"Yes, but Dad, what in the actual heck is blackjack?"

I would never forget the passion in Dad's voice as he explained the rules of his favorite card game—the importance of standing on a twelve if the dealer is showing a four through a six, and staying on thirteen through sixteen if the dealer showed a two through a six. But his most important rule of all was to always, *always* double down when you have an eleven and the dealer is showing a sixteen. Apparently, his own father stopped speaking to him for an entire week because he broke this sacred rule during a bachelor party at a table with a minimum bet of fifty dollars—a detail that was somewhat confusing to me at the time, but I got the gist.

I would later come to realize that playing blackjack while drinking root beer was a tradition that went all the way back three generations. Playing cards while completing home improvement projects was quite the bonding experience for the men on my dad's side, and I took great pride in knowing I was the first girl in the family to be included in the tradition. Of course, root beer had been a supplement for actual beer, and the fact that Dad never spoiled things with this detail until I was old enough to understand made it more special.

As I lay on the battered mattress of the top bunk in my unknown location, fading in and out of a drugged sleep, staring aimlessly at the peeling white ceiling, I couldn't help but remember that weekend with my father. The memories flooded over me in waves as I drifted in and out of consciousness, one minute desperate to know where I was, how long I had been there, and what was in store for me, and the next, too foggy and discombobulated to even care. I knew for sure at least two weeks had passed because, after a while, I began scratching marks on the bedpost each night at the same time another kidnapping victim would arrive. The first time a new girl arrived, I tended to her as best as I could, comforting her to the best of my ability like a nurse in the ER. But I learned during my time there that it was better to not get attached. The room—correction—the jail cell seemed to have a revolving door. Girls were tossed in like animals and removed on a continuous basis—going where, I didn't know, but what I did know is that I was not like them. Most of them stayed one or two nights before being transported elsewhere, but I didn't leave. For whatever reason unbeknownst to me, I was stuck there—drug injections against my will, bathroom trips when the guards felt like it, and peanut butter sandwiches with glasses of dirty lukewarm water on a good day. So, the easiest thing for me to do was just lie and wait. *Some things just take time.*

The peeling ceiling was in desperate need of repair, and I knew for sure that my dad and I would do one hell of a job fixing it. I imagined him and me peeling off the limp and lifeless flapping pieces and sanding them down with ease. Surely, it would look as good as new by the time we were finished, and I couldn't help but wonder, *If I make it out of this alive and in one piece, will I be fixable? Will my repairs be as simple as my bedroom renovation? Could my wounds be fixed by a trip to Home Depot, some handiwork, sugary soda, and a simple deck of cards?* I traced my teeth over my cracked lips and shut my eyes tight, knowing that if I were to survive this, if I were to somehow make it out alive, it was going to take more than some putty and paint to put me back together. My life, as I knew it, would never be the same.

But the thought of living long enough to legally sit in a casino with my father, drinking an actual beer while gambling in a real-life game of blackjack kept me hopeful. And I couldn't help but wonder if what I was experiencing could be thought of like one of our projects, and maybe, just maybe we were just waiting for the paint to dry before moving on to our next step. *Sorry, Daddy,* I silently said, realizing then that I'd chosen to double down on Lincoln Stone when I should have walked away altogether. And because of one error in judgement, my life as I knew it might come to an end way too soon.

Chapter Ten

Now (April 2025) Lina

"These never get old." Jon's voice is muffled between bites of his taco.

"Pepito's secret sauce recipe for the win," I say.

"Your father is a freaking genius," he says, swallowing the last bite with a smile and taking my hand in his. He presses it gently to his lips before lowering it back to his kitchen table.

"When it comes to tacos, yes." I grin, setting down my seltzer and clearing my throat. "Man, I could use a prickly pear margarita, though. The tacos aren't the same without it."

"No homemade margaritas for you, no matter how cute you are when you pout like that. You have a concussion, and honestly, nothing good comes out of drinking those."

"Hey," I say, "you have two kids because of those prickly pear margaritas. Don't knock 'em."

"*That* was a good night," he says fondly, clearly thinking back to our first date when we drunkenly got tattoos and conceived the twins. Then on our second date, roughly one month later, when I whipped up some of my father's homemade tacos from scratch, we made love on his living room couch, and I proceeded to puke my guts out in his toilet, only to then test positive on a pregnancy test.

"Yeah, you knocking me up was fantastic." I wink sarcastically, wondering if he's aware of how bittersweet it is for me to reopen that file in the Jon and Lina saga. Thinking back to our first date fondly wasn't something I ever thought I would bring myself to do again, but here we are, roughly eighteen years after the fact, full circle.

Jon leans forward and wipes the corner of my mouth with an index finger before gently pressing his lips to my forehead. "Things are going to be different," he insists, the ocean blue of his eyes never having looked so genuine. "I promise."

"Oh," I say, reaching for my water and purposefully changing the subject. My emotional mental block takes full control as I consciously choose flight over fight. "I have an idea regarding Alanna's case. I did some digging into her car, which was never recovered by the way and I found that to be somewhat of a dead end. But . . .I think I may be onto something else."

"We *said* no shop talk on date night," he reminded me with a raise of his brow, crossing his arms over his chest, one bicep poking out the sleeve of his navy-blue T-shirt. I run my hand over his arm, his skin warm to the touch against my fingers.

"I know." I shrug. "It's just that I thought of something we hadn't tried yet. And plus," I say, motioning toward Jon's kitchen sink, "we still need to clean up dinner. Can we say no shop talk once the dishes are done?"

"Okay," he agrees, standing from his chair and heading toward the kitchen. "But I can't help but feel like you might be trying to change the subject on me. I'm running out of ideas."

"Never, officer," I sing innocently, wishing I could lie to this man without him being so sharp and intuitive. I roll up my sleeves and reach for a clean dish towel, ready to dry the dishes after Jon scrubs and rinses them.

"Just promise me you won't shut me out," he begs, his words heavy but his tone gentle and sincere. "You're the only one I want, Lina. I have zero interest in doing this life without you ever again."

"I promise," I say, wrapping my pinky around his just as Max used to do as a child. "Pinky swear," I sing, hoping that having the right intentions behind this promise is enough. Both Ryker and Daphne have suggested bringing Jon to therapy with me, and I'm just not ready to do that yet. I want more than anything to just be able to pick up where we left off over a decade ago. I just wish it was that easy. So, for now, avoidance for the win. I mean, can you blame me?

"Okay, then. Out with it."

"So," I begin after clearing my throat, "I was thinking back to my time undercover in the pest control van . . . you know, when I was transported from the underground homeless camp to the warehouse where you found me? And I remembered the driver speaking Spanish . . . but it wasn't the kind of Spanish I learned in high school. No matter how hard I tried, I couldn't figure out what they were saying."

"Well," Jon grunts, "You had multiple concussions at the time," he reminds me as he scrubs the grease harder than necessary, his jaw visibly tightening.

I playfully whack him in the arm with the dish towel. "You aren't even taking me seriously."

"You're right," he sighs. "Sorry."

"I just really think I'm on to something with this. Please pay attention," I say in my mom tone. "Lucy had shown some interest in going on her school's mission trip to Mexico," I explain, choosing my words carefully.

"*Lucy*? A mission trip? It's likely she'll spontaneously combust without Starbucks and Lululemon, let alone cell service."

"Some guy she had a crush on suggested it. She's *so* not going." I chuckle with a wave of my hand. "But I checked into it on the school's website, and in the recorded Zoom presentation, they made it a point to warn parents that even though their child might have learned Spanish, it doesn't mean they will be fluent in that specific part of the country's native language. They speak Spanish, but Mexican Spanish can be different . . . You know, sort of like how our language can vary in different parts of our country."

Jon hands me the freshly scrubbed pan and pauses, eyebrows raised. "You think Alanna is in Mexico?"

"Honestly, Jon, I wouldn't count it out. After what I learned, I began researching Spanish in Mexico, and it sounds so much like what I heard in that van. Concussion or not."

"Wow, Lina, you might really have something here."

Excitement shoots through my veins at lightning speed.

"But let's say that Alanna was taken to Mexico. How should we proceed? She's not just a needle in a haystack; she's a needle in a country of haystacks."

"True," I say, pausing for a moment. "But when the police sent out the Amber Alert for her, I don't think it included other countries, right?"

"I'll need to confirm it," he says in his private investigator voice. "But I doubt the Tempe Police would have reached outside the country. It was very much assumed she had run away. Patrick and Laura struggled *big time* getting the cops in our county to even consider the possibility she had been kidnapped. I think you may be on to something, babe . . . but we don't have jurisdiction in other countries. You remember that, right? From your exams?"

"Obvi," I say in my Gemma voice. "But we have social media."

Jon leans back against the counter and runs his hands through his chin's scruff. "Go on."

"It's so easy to utilize social media for promo. For example, even though I have a publisher for my books, a lot of what I do is on my own for self-promotion. There are algorithms to Facebook and Instagram. For example, if I am advertising a romance novel about the beach, I can include specific key words to my boosted post. You know, phrases like beach read, east coast, New England, stuff like that—"

"You want to boost a Facebook post and target Mexico."

"Yes!" I cheer, pumping a fist into the air, so relieved that he's following. "It literally costs like five bucks. Cheaper than a Starbucks latte," I wink.

"You're something else," he says, wrapping his arm around my lower back and pulling me close.

"So we can try it?"

"I don't see why not." He tucks a strand of hair behind my ear with his free hand. "It's the best idea we've had in months. Can you handle making that post on top of working your other cases and your book deadlines?"

"Don't worry about me, *Dad*," I sing in my best Gemma voice. "Lina Rivera, private eye is on the case."

Later that evening, Jon and I have successfully released and boosted a missing persons post on social media, and Jon and I are snuggled up on his plush burgundy sectional watching reruns of my new favorite show, *The Resident*. After I openly admitted the celeb crush I have on Dr. Conrad Hawkins and whined once again about the network ending the show after season six, convinced they could've pulled off another successful season, Jon heads over to the fridge in search of dessert, only to return empty-handed.

"Not even ice cream? What kind of restaurant is this?" I groan.

"Sorry." Jon shrugs. "Haven't been grocery shopping in weeks."

"It's okay," I say, digging through my purse and pulling out an opened bag of peanut butter M&Ms. "I've got it," I say, pouring the M&Ms into Jon's open palm.

"You know," Jon says, keeping his eyes glued to the TV screen while I lay my head back on his lap and stare up at him. "I could just move back home . . . you know, with you."

My heart stops beating momentarily because I'm pretty sure Jon just asked to move back home. Actually, I *know* Jon just asked to move back home, and my head pounds at the base of my neck as my jaw tightens. *How in the hell do I tell this man I don't want him to move in with us yet? And even more importantly, why* don't *I want him to move back in with us?* I've considered the possibility, but there's so much to think about. For the love of God, we're just starting to figure things out. *What if it doesn't work out? Where will that leave Max and Lucy?* Of course, we all joked about it from time to time, but this is the first time Jon is suggesting this for *real*. Having another solid set of eyes on the teenagers would be helpful, as Molly and Max have gotten way too close for my liking. Just earlier this week, I walked in on them making out on the couch, and to be honest, I really don't think I could handle another adjustment in the moment, especially one that involves sharing my living space with a man, as it has been so long, even if that man is my ex-husband-slash-boyfriend. So, with my eyes locked on Conrad and Nurse Nevin determined to locate an emergency stash of blood for a patient bleeding out on the operating table, I clear my throat and say, "Want to DoorDash ice cream? I would kill for some double chocolate Oreo."

Jon hesitates for a beat before finishing the last of my M&Ms. "Sounds perfect," he says, crunching the candy between his teeth and reaching for his phone. "You get that, and I'll get cookie dough, and between the two of us, we will be good to go."

I breathe a relieved sigh and silently thank him for letting this go—for now. "Has Travis heard anything about the wedding crashers?" I ask, eager to change the subject once again.

"Nothing," he admits, sounding slightly annoyed. "I still can't believe those assholes cut the power and managed to pick the pockets of six guests. There *has* to be more than just one or two of them."

"Well, I had that chick cornered," I sighed. "Next time, I'm bringing pepper spray. I totally could have pepper sprayed her."

"You can't just go around spraying people with mace, Lina."

"Well, if I had, then we would at least have a lead." I rub the base of my neck with my fingers, determined to get rid of my headache without taking more Advil.

"Well, thanks to you, we have her description," he says, reaching for my head and taking over, his warm, strong hands pressing firmly into my tense muscles, providing me with much-needed relief. "And we have that wig."

"Can't we get DNA off it? You know, like on TV?"

"Well, a wig is a tricky thing. Testing for DNA would be challenging, but we did send it to the lab. We found a tiny piece of adhesive inside the wig, and we tried to pull prints from there, and we also ran a fiber test rather than DNA."

"Sounds complicated," I admit. "How long does that take?"

"It's never as quick as it happens on TV." Jon winks. "With AFIS's backlog, we could know in a few days . . . but it could also be a few weeks. And even then, we won't know for sure if it's our suspect's prints—"

"Or mine."

"Right. You *were* the last person to touch it when you pulled it out of the trash."

"Ugh. Rookie move."

"You're fine." He chuckled. "If it wasn't for you, we wouldn't even have the wig."

"Thank you for rubbing my neck," I moan, relaxing my head on his lap and closing my eyes, so grateful for Jon and internally beating myself up for not acknowledging his request to move back in.

"You don't have to thank me," Jon whispers, bending down to kiss my cheek while massaging my neck.

Then he lifts my face to his, and when his lips meet mine and I lose myself in our connection, I'm comforted by the realization that Jon gets it. He gets me, and there really isn't a reason to stress over our separate living situations.

"I love you Lina," he says, his voice confident but a bit unsteady, revealing a bit of vulnerability with a touch of angst.

No, no, no, I silently scold myself. This isn't what I want, not at all. I don't *want* to make Jon feel this way. I don't want to hurt or punish him. But that is exactly what I am doing, and if I'm not careful, I am going to push him away.

He kisses me again, this time deeper, and I cocoon my hands around the back of his head and tug him down toward me, kissing him back even harder, thankful that we can communicate like this, without words. *Can my kiss be enough of an explanation for him? Or does he need to hear actual words?*

"I don't want you to leave," he admits, rolling me on top of him and enveloping my waist with his sturdy arms. "I want to hold you all night. I can't remember the last time we did that."

"I know," I agree. "It's been too long."

Jon kisses my nose then my forehead. He traces his fingers over my collarbone and my neck and stops when my chin is resting perfectly in his hand. "I don't want to move too fast," he says, his tone careful but firm. "I know you have a lot to sort through emotionally, and I also realize that none of it is your fault."

"Jon, I—"

"Shh," he says, placing a gentle finger to my lips. "I'll wait for you," he says as a single tear escapes one eye. "We don't need to live together . . . yet."

Chapter Eleven

Then (December 2023) Alanna

I never liked going to the doctor's office. The last time I was hospitalized was when I was bitten by an unknown insect on my ankle, camping with my parents when I was six years old. At first, my parents treated it with an over-the-counter antibiotic cream and watched it carefully until one morning, upon removing the bandage, my father noticed a red line coming from the wound and moving up my leg, and they brought me to the hospital immediately, where they admitted me and treated me with various IV antibiotics. I remember being so confused. Not only had I not felt ill, but I didn't even realize I'd been bitten. My parents stayed by my side for my entire hospital stay, and I was spoiled with an unlimited supply of popsicles and ice cream and, of course, a brand-new teddy bear from the hospital's gift shop.

My parents were like that—they knew just how to turn a negative situation into a positive one. If only they could have helped me when I was lying handcuffed to a bed, wearing a puce hospital gown, being treated like someone with a severe illness. I didn't know where I was or why I was there. The only thing I knew for sure was that I'd been there for at least a month, and I knew that only because I had mentally tracked my cycle and my new roommates had done the same. Maria, a seventeen-year-old girl who'd been abducted from a rest stop in New Mexico, had arrived at the mystery hospital one month prior, and Carmen, a twenty-year-old female, was lured into this horrific situation by a modeling-and-acting scam on Instagram. They were able to offer some, but not a lot of insight as to where we were and what we were doing there.

Based on the language being spoken and phrases they'd picked up from the nurses, Maria and Carmen believed we were somewhere in Mexico, and although I'd assumed I had been kidnapped for some sort of human trafficking ring, my roommates had reason to believe we were being held for medical reasons, and after a month at the facility, I realized they were correct. We were nothing more than lab rats. When I became extremely ill from what I assumed was from drinking the tap water, a doctor was at my side in seconds, adding an antinausea medication to an IV that had been inserted into the top of my hand upon my arrival. And when I woke up screaming from an intensely bad dream and my bleeding wrists were throbbing from yanking at my handcuffs, a nurse appeared from thin air, ready to bandage my wrists and add even more drugs to my IV, knocking me out before I could even ask his name.

Our days were consistent if nothing else. We were served oatmeal for breakfast, which didn't settle well either, probably because my stomach had forgotten how to digest actual food. Then, following breakfast, we were escorted to the bathrooms and showers, where we cleaned up in front of the nurses who were mostly male—something I'd been shy about at first but began to care about less and less as the days went on. We ate rice and beans for lunch and dinner and on some occasions were allowed to walk up and down the hallway, hands cuffed behind our backs and escorted like prisoners, my bare feet chilled by the concrete floor.

I got used to my new routine quickly, dreading only the moments when I was poked and prodded like a child dissecting a frog in science class. Most days, the nurses drew multiple vials of blood, and other times, they injected us with needles and IV medication. Sometimes, we would feel sleepy and drowsy, and other times we would feel nothing. Honestly, I stopped questioning it because even though my new reality was terrifying, my circumstances were better than they were when I was at the warehouse and in the underground homeless camp.

My dreams were the weirdest of all. Sometimes, the nightmares were about Ace and Slinky, and others were of my former life, which were the hardest to endure because waking up at the hospital in my new life was only devastating when I remembered where I'd come from and what I'd left. On those days, I would sink into a deep depression because in a way, the situation was my fault. In a way, I *chose* this. I left the comfort of my home in Arizona. I left my family, my two parents that had loved me unconditionally, who took such great care of me, who only wanted to protect me—for a guy I'd never even met.

Thinking back to my life back home was hard, for sure, but not as difficult as the days I would start to give up. The days when the structure of my routine was comforting, when I started to look forward to my dinner and the company of Maria and Carmen—those days were the scariest. Because *that* was becoming my new life. It was becoming my new normal. And each day that I was jabbed and swabbed and rewarded with a walk down the hallway was another day I was forgetting who I was, where I'd come from, and a new reality was setting in. Nobody, and I mean *nobody*, was coming to find me. And that is scarier than even the worst nightmare imaginable.

Chapter Twelve

Now (April 2025) Lina

I hold my breath as I shimmy my house key into the brass doorknob, still in yesterday's clothes. My night with Jon had been truly incredible, and I know beyond a doubt that the giddy schoolgirl smile plastered on my face will not go unnoticed by Ryker and my children. So, as I turn the doorknob and prepare to face the firing squad, I straighten my back and shoulders and enter my house confidently, prepared to not take any crap from my teenagers or my best friend.

"And where were *you* last night, young lady?" my daughter demands, arms crossed, perched at the kitchen island with a mouthful of bagel and Ryker by her side, coffee mug pressed to his lips. "Nice walk of shame, Mom."

"Skibidi, Ma," Max adds as he scurries down the stairs with his hat backwards, a new look for him. "Hopefully, you were *at least* with Dad."

"It's not her fault." Lucy smirks. "She just *found* herself in his bedroom, tripped over his lame ab roller, and fell onto his bed," she says, cracking herself up. "Oops, it just . . . had to happen." She holds up her hands as though to say *Why not?* eyes wide, her mouth twisting into a goofy grin.

"Stop," I beg, biting down on my lip to keep from laughing. "Your father does *not* keep an ab roller in his bedroom. And they aren't lame. They actually hurt . . . a lot," I say, gripping my lower abdomen and cringing.

"Yeah, 'cause, like, that's the important deet." Max snickers.

"You're wearing your hat differently, Max," I say, ignoring their previous jabs.

"You're dodging the subject." Max smirks before planting a kiss on my cheek, and I wonder if he's grown an entire foot since the day before.

When did you start looking like a man? I silently scream, cursing time and its ability to morph my adorable baby boy into a deep-voiced, hairy stranger doused in Axe body spray.

"There's nothing to dodge." I shrug, resting my purse on the counter before hugging and kissing Ryker and Lucy.

"I told you guys," Ryker says between sips and running his fingers through his light brunette tresses. "Your mom and dad worked late on a case. Cut her some slack."

"At least *someone* has my back around here," I declare with a thankful wink. "I appreciate you staying, Ry."

"No offense to Uncle Ryker," Max interjects, grabbing his backpack and stuffing three bags of Takis inside. "But why do we still need a babysitter?"

"Maybe because you would eat chips for breakfast, lunch, and dinner if left to your own devices," Lucy says.

I reach for my favorite coffee mug and slide it under my Keurig, thankful that the spotlight is off me and my walk of shame but hesitant to answer his question. The truth was I didn't trust him and Molly home alone together, just as I hadn't trusted Lucy and Oliver when they dated. But when it comes to Max and Molly, there's just more to consider, multiple layers of emotional baggage that I need to unpack, as technically Molly was my friend first. I know her well enough to know she has the best intentions when it comes to my son, but I also know she's already slept with her ex-boyfriend, Bill, who also happens to be one of Penelope's twins. Honestly, I'm just glad my life hasn't been overcomplicated by Operation Superglue. *Insert sarcasm.*

"Until you're eighteen . . ." I start, but my words fade into the distance because Ryker has already changed the subject with Max.

They're shooting off stats and final scores and other sports-related jargon I can never wrap my mind around, so instead, I take a seat on the barstool next to my daughter and sip my coffee, noticing that her light blond hair is pulled into two French braids and she's dressed in her favorite Lululemon shorts and matching hot-pink top, an outfit I once borrowed when I was undercover as Gemma Mendoza.

"Your hair looks adorable," I declare, rubbing the side of my temple with my index finger.

"Today is field day," she whines. "I hate field day."

"Cause you suck at sports, Luce," Max says with a goofy laugh.

"I hate you," she snaps with a shake of her head. "I don't suck at *all* sports."

"Sorry," he says with a playful and gentle punch to her shoulder. "You suck at all *ball* sports."

"You're such a—"

"Wait, it's field day?" I shriek, slapping my palm to my forehead. "As in the last day of school before spring break field day?"

"Bet," Max says, giving me knuckles. "Vacation time, bruh."

I reciprocate knuckles with Max then rub my eyes and groan in frustration, remembering that I sold my soul to the Parent Teacher Association at the twins' high school during Operation Superglue when I inquired about a student, Lincoln Stone, who had friended me on Snapchat. I had schmoozed the PTA president, who'd been subbing as the school secretary, and she'd agreed to look up Lincoln's name in exchange for my involvement as president for the next year. When Lincoln wasn't in the computer system, that confirmed what Jon and I had predicted. Lincoln's Snapchat account was fake and used to lure the missing girls out for abduction. I thought I'd been off the hook with the PTA until the next school year, but as it turns out, she also talked me into sending in supplies for the last-day-of-school cookout.

"What did you forget?" Ryker asks, reading my mind, as always.

"It's nothing." I cringe. "I'm just tired . . . didn't sleep much last night. Jon and I were up *all* night," I say with a smile. I pause, realizing the three of them are staring at me awkwardly. "Working! Jon and I were up all night *working*. I'm literally working three cases at once right now, and I have a meeting with my publisher today. I also . . . I also forgot about field day."

"You don't need to go to field day, Mom. Unless you're undercover as a sixteen-year-old again," Lucy says, and I can't tell if she's reassuring me or still angry with me for lying to her.

"I'm not lying. And Gemma was eighteen, not sixteen. I know I don't *need* to be at field day. It's just . . . I promised the PTA I would cut up some fruit for the cookout, and I do like to be involved at your school."

"No big deal," Ryker says, rubbing my shoulders like a coach sending in his star quarterback. "Just Instacart some fruit salad to the school and call it a day."

"I can't," I groan, throwing my hands above my head in defeat. "Haven't you heard? Pinterest took over the planet, and now the only acceptable way to send fruit to a school function is to arrange it in the shape of a rainbow or jab it onto wooden skewers organized by shape and color."

"She's not wrong," Lucy agrees. "Melanie Harris's mom made a fruit charcuterie board for Halloween with eyeball grapes and marshmallow ghosts."

"What is wrong with people? Didn't you graduate from fifth grade, like, a million years ago?" I ask, resting my head on Lucy's shoulder. "What time is the cookout?"

"After field day," she says. "Around one o'clock."

I take a deep breath and relax my shoulders, realizing that bringing the fruit to the cookout isn't what has me on the verge of a nervous breakdown. It's simply the straw that broke the camel's back, and I can't help but wonder if Jon was right. *Am I overdoing it? Was taking on Penelope's case a mistake? Am I too emotionally involved in finding Alanna to focus on her and everything else? Hell, when was the last time I even texted Daphne, let alone met up with her for drinks?* That was probably before Operation Superglue ended because that's really the last time I was able to have a drink, at least according to the doctor.

"Time to bounce," Max tells Lucy. "I won't get a parking spot if we don't leave now."

"Translation," she says with an overly dramatic roll of the eyes, "someone needs a good parking spot so we can beat traffic after school and pick up *Molly*."

"Speaking of Molly—"

"Gotta go, Mom. Love you," Max says, kissing my cheek then slapping Ryker five. "Oh, and just bring fruit. They banned fruit skewers after teacher appreciation week because Dillon Jorgenson stuck one up his nose and caused some serious damage to his sinuses. Dude needed surgery."

"Well . . . too bad for Dillon . . . but at least I can just swing by the store and grab some fruit, and I won't be excommunicated for lack of creativity." I wince, wondering how I'm going to add this errand to my already packed day, as I need to be at Desert Fit Performance—a gym in Prescott, Arizona—sooner than later. Getting there will take me roughly an hour, and I'm due to meet with their membership department and tour the facility. This will mark the start of my first day on Penelope's case, one I've cleverly titled Operation Treadmill Temptation, a mission to verify Penelope's husband's infidelity.

The kids have no sooner closed the door behind themselves than Ryker pulls up the barstool and leans close to me, eyebrows raised. "Spill the tea." He grins. "How was last night?"

"Huh?" I ask, clearly dodging his question as images of Jon jumble together in my brain like a prismatic kaleidoscope: the memory of his eyes locked on mine, visions of his jaw tightening and his body gliding beneath me smoothly as he called my name loud enough for his entire apartment complex to hear, my heart full of satisfaction that I could have that effect on him, that I had the power to make another human being feel that good. And that person being Jon was the icing on the cake. It had been an absolutely perfect night. And I wanted to do it repeatedly, every night for the rest of my life.

"Um, Earth to Lina?" Ryker snorts.

"Sorry." I blush. "What time is it? I've got to get in the shower," I say, knowing damn well Ryker isn't going to let me off the hook. "And I need to take some Advil. My head won't stop pounding. Does anyone else think it's just so not fair that I stop drinking and still wake up feeling hungover?"

My phone buzzes in my back pocket, and I swipe the screen to find a text from Molly.

Molly: *Hey, girl. Can we talk later?*

I turn my phone over on the table and shake my head, unable to deal with Molly right now. Surely, she wants to discuss her relationship with Max. Knowing Molly, she's worried that I don't approve of their relationship, and I'm just not ready to wrap my mind around that yet.

"Who was that?" Ryker asks from over my shoulder.

"It's Molly. She wants to talk. I just can't right now."

Ryker reaches into my medicine drawer, retrieves my Advil, and drops two pills into my open palm. "Here you go."

"Cute." I snicker. "Two won't even put a dent in this beast. Hand over two more."

Ryker complies but shakes his head, concern in his eyes. "I'm worried about you."

"Don't be," I say before swallowing the pills and chasing them with the rest of my coffee.

"When's your next head CT? Did you get the MRI?"

"Uh . . . the MRI is coming up, I think." As I say this to Ryker, I realize I missed my appointment the week before, as Jon, Travis, and I were working on Alanna's case and we lost track of time. "Come on," I say, gesturing for him to follow me up the stairs, where Ryker gives me the privacy I need to get into the shower, and I close the curtain behind myself as he shuts the toilet lid and gets comfy because this is a place where we have had some of our hardest and best conversations. As I rinse the shampoo then conditioner out of my hair, shave, and allow the warmth of the water to cleanse my soul, I share *almost* all the details from the night before. I lie a little bit when he asks if the sex with Jon beats sex with Travis, and he tells me about his last date with Alex. As he tells me about their weekend together, stepping just a tad bit into TMI territory without actually being TMI, I smile, overcome with joy that I have a friend like Ryker but also aware of a pit forming in my gut. I realize that if and when Jon moves back home, which he most likely will, things with Ryker will need to change. Surely, Jon won't be okay with another man joining me in the bathroom while I shower, regardless of his sexual orientation. And with Jon home, I wouldn't need Ry to supervise the kids as much, either, which feels so incredibly wrong that I shut my thoughts down as quickly as they appear because surely there is a way for me to have both Ryker and Jon in my life. *Right?*

Thankfully, my publisher agreed to call me on the way to the gym, which will free me up for field day. The purpose of the meeting is to touch base about the cover for the first book in my new series, *Izzy Undercover*, a proposed three-book series about seventeen-year-old protagonist Isabella Monroe, a high school junior who, unbeknownst to her, was secretly trained as an FBI operative as a child by her parents, who were killed in active duty when she was ten years old. After becoming an orphan, she was taken in by her uncle, a private investigator in Tempe, Arizona. On Izzy's sixteenth birthday, during an attempted mugging, her training subconsciously resurfaced, and her attacker ended up hospitalized, nearly paralyzed from the waist down. Izzy and her uncle discover her unique skill set, and he invites her to work for him at his agency as his apprentice, sort of like the show *Veronica Mars* meets *Alias*. It's genius, I know, and the release date can't come soon enough.

My editor and agent raved over my sample chapters, along with my completed manuscript, complimenting me on my ability to stay current with my young adult audience. We are, however, struggling to find the right concept for the cover. Our meeting went wonderfully, but apparently my need to micromanage the cover of this book has not only held up the release date but also left me with more homework, which I really don't have time for. I would need to submit a detailed description and breakdown to the designer by midnight tonight, and for the life of me, I can't figure out where to start. Book covers have always come so easy to me, but something about this series is very special, and it doesn't take a detective to deduce the fact that these stories are very personal and reflect my journey with Jon during Operation Superglue, and I can't help wonder if solving Alanna's case or at least making some sort of headway on it would also help me creatively.

Alanna's missing persons campaign on Facebook and Instagram was successful, according to my social media marketing data. But unfortunately, we still didn't have a single lead. *Discouraging* is an understatement, as I want nothing more than to have good news for Patrick and Laura, who have no doubt in their minds that their daughter is alive out there and have not stopped looking for a single second. As I pull up to Desert Fit Performance and study the cacti that flank the entrance to the parking lot, I can't help but notice the radiant blossoms decorating the slender, spiky, succulent plants, and I consider it a sign from Alanna. She *is* out there somewhere, and I won't stop until I find her.

But for now, I need to focus on the task at hand. After I park my car, ditch my ID, and swap it out for the fake one Travis made me, I head into a building that in no way resembles a gym, but more like a swanky New York City night club. I am no longer Lina Rivera. I am Emery Shaw, a twenty-year-old college student home for break, looking to work out on my parent's dime, and I can only hope that an hour outside my hometown is far enough away to keep my cover. Either way, just to be safe, I adjust the Arizona Diamondbacks baseball cap I stole from Max's bedroom and tug my ponytail through the back. I considered wearing a wig, but the thought of taking a spin or yoga class was overwhelming enough. Add a wig to that nonsense, and it was surely a recipe for disaster.

"Hey," I sing in my best college-kid voice. "My dad called earlier and set up a tour." I smile, thinking about Jon calling the gym and pretending to be my dad, and how I'd teased him endlessly, reminding him of Molly's drunken declaration that he was old as shit but still a DILF.

"Emery?" she asks after a few clicks of her mouse.

"That's me." I smile. "You can call me Em."

"Hi, Em, nice to meet you. I'm Colleen. You're looking to work out while you're home on spring break?"

"That's right. But I'd like the whole membership package. School's almost out, and I'll be coming for the summer too."

"Perfect. I'll be giving you a tour today. After that, if you want to sign up, I'll just need your ID and a card to put on file."

"Cool," I say, resisting the urge to sign my membership paperwork, cancel the tour, and head to the Starbucks I passed on the way here, fighting away the possibilities of everything I could be getting done in this moment on my book cover and Alanna's case.

But as I follow Colleen through the sleek glass doors and hear the pulsating beat of electronic dance music, I'm instantly overwhelmed and feel like a lost child in an enormous shopping mall. *Relax and focus, Lina,* I silently scold myself. If I'm going to solve this case, I'm going to need to know my way around. Besides, Penelope claims that her husband works out at this time every day, so if I'm lucky, I may spot him right away, which will also save time in the long run.

Natural light floods the building from the floor-to-ceiling windows, and somewhere between the heated spin room and the yoga sanctuary, my head begins pounding, and I reach into my purse for some Advil but realize it's too soon to take more.

I'm grateful when we finally arrive in the locker room and my tour commences with an explanation of locker rentals and shower amenities. Colleen explains that my membership allows for full access to spa and recovery perks like the heated jacuzzi, sauna, steam room, and cold tank, and I resist the urge to ask why anyone would want to relax in something called a cold tank. Instead, I thank Colleen for the tour and follow her to her office, where I sign my life away as Emery Shaw before heading back to the locker room to use the restroom. But just as I turn the corner, I stop short, as Dean Elizabeth Downing, the dean of Emerson Academy, is removing a purple yoga mat from a locker and turning in my direction. I don't recognize her at first, as her skirt suit and sleek, slicked, perfect bun has been replaced by yoga pants, an athletic top, and a high ponytail.

"Dean Elizabeth," I whisper from under my cap.

She pauses for a beat before turning in my direction, standing a bit straighter than she had just moments earlier.

"It's me, Lina. I'm undercover," I mouth, peeking around the corner to see if anyone is listening.

"So nice to see you, dear!" she says, pulling me in for a tight embrace.

"Never thought I'd see you here," I say, regretting my choice of words because I sound rude. My face flushes a bright red because I'm sure I've offended her. "You know," I say, choosing my words carefully then clearing my throat. "It's so far from Tempe . . . and it's a school day," I add, hopeful that my explanation overcame my initial *You are the least athletic person I've met in my life, so why in the actual hell would you be at the gym*? reaction.

"We've been on spring break since last week." She grins. "This gym is just far enough away that I'm not getting poked at for an impromptu parent-teacher conference during savasana."

"I get it." I laugh. "I won't keep you, then."

Dean Elizabeth places a caring hand on my shoulder. "You aren't keeping me at all. I assume you're working a case?" she asks, gesturing to my baseball cap. "A cheating-spouse case, I would imagine."

"Yes . . . that's exactly what it is," I whisper, wondering how on earth she could possibly know this information.

"This place is a cesspool," she hisses, scrunching her nose in disgust.

"How so?"

"I'll text you some intel." She winks.

The fact that Dean Elizabeth Downing has *intel* on cheating spouses at Desert Fit Performance is a little too much to process, but I will never turn down anything that will help me solve a case. "Thank you so much, Dean."

"You can drop the *Dean*. Just call me Elizabeth. You and I are friends, now. In fact, we should have dinner."

"I would love that, Dean—Elizabeth," I correct myself. "Old habits die hard."

"Sounds good, dear. I wasn't going to mention it, you know, due to confidentiality and all, but I heard through the grapevine you and Jon are back on Alanna's case?" she says, keeping her voice low.

"We are . . ." My voice fades off because I don't know what else to say.

"Not making any progress?"

"No," I admit. "I wish I had better news."

"If you want my advice," she says, looking over both of her shoulders before making eye contact with me again. "You need to talk to that lowlife scumbag Dean Turner. You know, Molly's dad."

"Last I heard, he was over at the Maricopa County Prison. The cops said they've questioned him thoroughly." But as the words leave my lips, I know I can't say that with enough confidence to convince myself Dean Turner is being honest. Because if he was telling the full truth, Travis wouldn't be the free man he is, because he was very much involved in Turner's last kidnapping attempt: mine. *So, if Turner isn't turning over Travis, who else is he covering for, and what else does he know?* "What do you suggest I do?"

"You didn't hear this from me," she says, choosing her words carefully. "You get that scrawny ass of yours down to that jail, and you do what you need to do to get him to talk. There is no doubt in my mind that that sorry excuse for a human knows exactly where Alanna is. I would bet my *life* on it."

Chapter Thirteen

Then (January 2024) Alanna

Clouds—one of my favorite things to study in science, my go-to setting for any kind of painting class, and the absolute best things to gaze at on lazy days. I could vaguely recall a time I was lying on the grass, staring up at the pale blue sky, but I couldn't recall where I was or how old I was at the time. I just remember big puffy white clouds drifting slowly across the sky, and I couldn't figure out if the clouds were moving or if Earth was doing the moving. Either way, trying to remember any part of my former life felt like this—once beautiful, full of potential, and now drifting.

The nightmare of my new life had gone on for so long that I'd officially started to lose hope of going back to my old reality. But, in the same breath, it felt like just seconds ago that my future was only beginning. I'd worked very hard academically at Emerson to get into nursing school, and not only had I accomplished that, but I was also finishing at the top of my class. I'd always been a great student, just as I had been the perfect daughter. Sure, I'd stretched the boundaries, exceeded limits, and tested my parents at times, but all teenagers do that. *Shouldn't I have been given the chance to make a mistake and learn from it?* It was my first big mistake. I didn't think the punishment really fit the crime.

Jeremy was a boy who lived in my neighborhood. We weren't besties or anything like that, but we rode the bus together and shared the same homeroom throughout elementary school and shared the same classmates until after middle school, when I started attending private school. Jeremy was a great kid. He was polite when he addressed adults and checked the necessary boxes to classify himself as just that, a good kid. He was wholesome and sweet. He was the captain of the wrestling team but never ashamed to take a lead in the school musical. Everything in his life was perfect—until it wasn't. One day, Jeremy was overloaded with academics, work, sports, and girl-related drama, and he needed help staying awake to study. His buddy offered him some of his ADHD medication and told him it was game-changing. What Jeremy didn't know was that his friend's medication hadn't been prescribed by a doctor but was something he scored after soccer practice in the locker room. The ADHD medication had been laced with fentanyl and killed him instantly.

I can remember my mother comforting Jeremy's mother at his funeral: "Kids today aren't even allowed to learn from their mistakes. In our day, we were able to try something and learn our lesson. Today, kids try things . . . and they die."

My mother hadn't been wrong. We'd heard endless stories about teenagers in Tempe and the surrounding areas experimenting with drugs laced with *poison*. My mother made me promise I would never do anything that dumb, and I vowed to talk with her immediately if I ever wanted to experiment with drugs or alcohol, and I couldn't help but wonder if her heart was breaking because she failed to mention that running away with a boy I met on Snapchat was off limits. In a way, I was just like Jeremy. Lincoln Stone had been my drug of choice, and I only tried him one damn time.

If I strained my thoughts hard enough, I could visualize my house and my family, but I was losing the ability to picture their faces. That felt both weird but also somewhat of a relief because it was becoming clear to me that my past existence was becoming more and more nonexistent. Listening to Maria and Carmen carry on about their possible rescues was becoming redundant. Maria, who had been the captain of her high school soccer team, was convinced that her parents and her best friend would find her. She compared her father to Liam Neeson in the movie *Taken* or Jack Bauer in the TV show *24*. Carmen, who had the same boyfriend freshman year through senior year, could feel it in the deepest parts of her soul that they were working with the FBI to determine her whereabouts and would stop at nothing to find her. Carmen's parents were also apparently very wealthy, which in some twisted way was still a comfort for her, and I had to constantly bite my tongue in an effort to avoid raining on her parade. From what I had experienced since my abduction at the bus stop, no amount of money was going to help any of us.

I was somewhat jealous of Maria and Carmen, though, because they had something I would never have: hope. Hope can be a great thing, but it can also be dangerous. Without hope, I had nothing to lose. I don't think I was being unrealistically pessimistic. I mean, Maria was kidnapped from a rest stop. Surely, her parents knew her last known location, and the police were involved. Carmen was part of an unfortunate Hollywood Instagram scam, and honestly, it probably could have been avoided if she'd researched the program better. But I couldn't judge. I fell in love with a boy who didn't exist. And because of my own stupidity and vulnerability, I staged my own runaway. My parents *didn't even know I was kidnapped.* Why would anyone come looking for me? Hell, *I* wouldn't go looking for me. I'd acted like a spoiled brat. I had the world at my fingertips, and I ruined everything—over stupid Lincoln Stone. I'd punch him in the face myself if he actually existed.

"We should be eating lunch soon," Carmen said from her bed, like she did every day. We didn't have a clock or windows in our room, so it was impossible to know what time it was. But Carmen's stomach never lied. She could always tell what time of day it was based on her hunger pains. I nodded, remaining silent like I always did when Carmen and Maria spoke, and continued staring up at the ceiling, picturing clouds—puffy white cumulus clouds that formed funny cartoon shapes, along with thin and wispy cirrus clouds that oftentimes painted the sky. But my thoughts were interrupted by the sound of the doorknob jingling and the overly loud creak our door made upon opening.

"See," Carmen declared. "Told ya."

But it wasn't our nurse, and it wasn't time for lunch. Instead, a new and unfamiliar face was escorted into our room by a security guard. He was younger than our usual staff. A long white lab coat hung over his black button-down shirt and dark washed jeans. He was on the taller side, roughly about five nine or six feet, even, if I had to guess. He carried a clipboard under one well-defined athletic bicep, and as he moved about the room picking up bottles of pills, IV bags, and other supplies, I concluded that he wasn't a doctor or nurse but most likely in charge of medical supplies.

The stranger spoke Spanish in the same way the other employees had. I could pick up bits and pieces of what they were saying from my four years of the language at Emerson, but it hadn't made sense. And as he approached my bed and continued taking notes, he paused for a beat, his eyes locking on mine, his medium-length dark hair grazing the tip of one well-defined cheekbone. His eyes, probably the darkest and most mysterious eyes I'd ever seen, were serious but also intriguing. He finished scribbling on his clipboard before reaching for my wrist to copy the eight-digit number I'd forgotten was even there, printed on my faded hospital bracelet—my new identity. I'd stopped looking at it one day because the moment I realized I was no longer Alanna Foster but 16282422, I'd fallen into a deep panic and needed sedation.

"Eduardo," the security guard said then continued with more Spanish, gesturing toward the shelves adjacent to Carmen's bed.

"*Sí, señor. Por favor espere un momento.*"

Eduardo's skin felt warm against mine, and he placed my wrist down on my bedsheet tenderly, unlike any way I'd been treated since my arrival. Then he pressed a gentle hand on my shoulder before doing the worst thing humanly possible. He smiled at me with his eyes, awakening a part of me I'd wanted to let go. Without realizing it, this man, this stranger, this inventory-taking lab guy had done the unforgiveable. He'd given me someone to take interest in, someone to become curious about. And even worse . . . someone to *hope* for.

Chapter Fourteen

Now (April 2025) Lina

"I still can't believe that inmates get iPads," I say, chewing my Frappuccino straw.

"I still can't believe you call frozen whipped sugar coffee," Travis says with a wink. It might fall into the flirting category, a vibe I hadn't sensed from him since before my organized kidnapping, and I quickly glance from Travis to Jon and back again to see if either of them has found this inappropriate. Jon is focusing intensely on setting up our conference room's camera for our video call with Dean Turner, and Travis has scooped up the legal pad from the center of the table, presumably to jot down another question to ask, so I chalk it up to playful banter.

"Well, I still can't believe . . ." I start but stop because I've got nothing. "But really . . . inmates get iPads?"

"It's not so much an iPad as it is a tablet," Jon explains. "And not all inmates get them. It needs to be set up by their families through an account called Getting Out."

"Dude won't be getting out anytime soon," I say, sounding like my son more than I intend.

"*Dude* has a court date set for one month from today," Jon says. "Don't underestimate the abilities of a powerful man like Turner."

"There is *no way* he's getting out," I proclaim, choking on my drink. "Last I heard, he was looking at a class-two felony between his child abduction and kidnapping charges, let alone unlawful use of electronic communication."

"That's what we hope for," Jon says, placing a reassuring hand on my shoulder before taking a seat next to me at the table, both of us now sitting across from Travis and positioning ourselves to face our large flatscreen TV, ready for our at-home visitation with Dean Turner. "Remember," Jon reminds me. "Turner gets to go before the judge in a pretrial. But don't worry, you will get your trial. It will *all* come out."

Travis shifts uncomfortably in his seat, and it's no secret why. When Turner's case goes to trial, it's highly likely that Travis's involvement with *my* kidnapping will surface, as will the illegal prescriptions he wrote for Turner's son, Emmett, whose involvement with Ace, Slinky, and the underground gang initiated the kidnappings in the first place. Ironically enough, after we solved Operation Superglue and most of the missing girls had been reunited with their families, the police were unable to locate Ace and Slinky. That is shocking, considering they were living in an underground community and had nothing to their names except the clothes on their backs.

"We're on in two minutes," Travis says, the edge in his voice obvious. "Don't forget: he thinks he's just meeting with me. He will be surprised to see the two of you. Are you sure you don't want me to take the call?"

"No," Jon says, for what must feel like the hundredth time. "I want this prick to know who he's dealing with. Nothing wrong with a bit of intimidation."

I slurp my Frappuccino and spin in my chair, tapping nervously to the beat of Lucy's favorite country song, and I pause when I realize both men are staring at me awkwardly. "Sorry," I say, tossing my cup in the trash and sitting up a bit straighter. "This better?"

"That will have to do," Travis mumbles under his breath.

Jon takes my hand in his under the table and squeezes it reassuringly. "Don't change a thing. But remember what we talked about. Travis is taking the lead on the interview. He will ask our questions, being sure to stick to the list. Remember, we have only thirty minutes, and the visit is being recorded by the prison. Turner is smart. He won't say anything that will work against him in trial."

"Oh, and you need to put that on," Travis says, gesturing toward the long-sleeved zip-up sweater I've draped over the back of my chair.

"You're joking, right?"

"Nope," Travis asserts, straight-faced. "Rules are listed here," he says, turning his laptop screen toward me. "No see-through blouses, tank tops, halter tops, or any shirt revealing . . . um . . . cleavage," he says then clears his throat, closes his laptop, and tucks it away.

"I'm not showing cleavage!" I exclaim, tilting my chin toward my chest and squeezing my boobs together, poking my index finger between them to show Travis that the girls are very much covered up, right as our video call begins. "Fine," I huff, sliding my arms into my sweater one at a time before zipping it up to the top in an overly dramatic fashion.

But any thoughts about my wardrobe quickly evaporate from my mind as Dean Turner's face flashes across the width of our conference room TV and I grip Jon's hand for dear life because I suddenly feel like I'm going to be sick. The man staring back at us is *not* Dean Orson Turner, dean of admissions at Emerson Academy. It can't be. Certainly, they must have put the wrong prisoner on our call. I hadn't met Dean Turner too many times, just once or twice during my undercover time at Emerson. He once stood tall and dignified in his tailored suits, was clean cut, and had the same composure as the presidents I'd studied in American government class. This man, this *criminal*, couldn't be Dean Turner.

"Orson," Travis says, his tone one of authority and business.

The man stares from me to Jon then to Travis, and for a moment, I can see beyond his buzz cut, full beard, and freshly stitched cut over his right eye. When he doesn't reply, Travis continues. "Orson," Travis says again, "we are going to cut to the chase. We were able to locate most of the missing girls—all but one, Alanna Foster—and we need your help."

After what feels like an intimidating and awkward ten years, Orson finally mumbles a weak, "Some art substitute you turned out to be."

"Yes sir, I was undercover," Jon says, not missing a beat. "As was she," he says, nodding toward me. "We were both undercover at Emerson, hired by Dean Elizabeth. But you know that already, Orson. So why the BS?"

"No BS."

"Good," Travis says. "Because we have some questions, and we don't have a lot of time."

Dean Turner holds up a hand to stop Travis from continuing. "I'll answer your questions, Travis. Of course I want every victim returned to their families. This was never about them. It was about my son, Emmett."

"Good to hear—" Travis starts.

"But first, I would like a visit with my daughter, Molly."

I feel the heat rise to my cheeks as my heart rate increases and I grow overwhelmingly protective of Molly in a surprisingly maternal way. "What do you want with Molly?" I shout. "She doesn't want to see you."

Jon squeezes my hand as Travis shoots daggers across the table.

"What?" I snap. "She doesn't."

"Well then, you don't have my cooperation," Turner sighs. "You see, my wife and my other children have forgiven me. They understand that I was just trying to protect them."

"Are you kidding me?" I ask, standing to my feet, but when Jon tugs at my arm, I sit back down.

"You have to excuse her," Jon says calmly. "She went through a lot when she was undercover. She was purposefully kidnapped. You know, the abduction *you* organized in an effort to get your other daughter, June, back? Lina here saved June's life. You have her to thank for that, by the way."

Dean Turner's eyes lock on mine and even through the distance of our virtual call I can sense the gratitude in the stillness of his eyes. "*You* found June?"

"Yes," I say. "After I served as *literal* bait, I rescued your daughter. And your *other* daughter, Molly, is dating my son, Max."

Turner scrunches his nose and raises his eyebrows. "You expect me to believe you have a son old enough to date my Molly? Aren't you just a child yourself?"

I resist the urge to smile, because I secretly enjoy the fact that I look younger than I am. But this is about finding Alanna, not about my ego, so I straighten my shoulders, sit up a bit straighter, and clear my throat. "I was undercover as a teenager. I'm a single mother in my mid-thirties," I say as Jon shifts uncomfortably in his seat at the mention of the word *single,* and I make a mental note to apologize later, knowing full well he'll understand—I hope. "My son is Molly's age. They have been dating for about a month."

"My Molly," he says, wiping a tear from the corner of his eye. "How is she?"

"Answer our questions, Orson, and we will ask Molly to visit with you," Travis says.

I bite my lip as Jon places a hand on my skirt-covered thigh and whispers, "Say nothing, Lina," loud enough for only me to hear. *Over my dead body will I force her to talk to this man,* I scream silently. Her own father used her Snapchat account to hack her friends, then he created a fictional character named Lincoln Stone to lure them in, all to cover up his own son's indiscretions. I'd tried to help Molly work through this trauma, but she'd sworn she would never forgive him, ever.

"Will you talk to her for me?" he asks, looking directly at me.

Jon squeezes my leg and nods encouragingly at me, and I have no choice. "Of course," I say. "Answer our questions, and I will talk to Molly about having a virtual visit."

"Orson," Travis says again, "what do you know about where Ace and Slinky may have sent Alanna?"

He takes a breath and considers for a moment. "The two gang members, Ace and Slinky, had Alanna transported to the same warehouse as the other girls. I honestly don't know where they took them after that."

"No," I interject, "the other girls were there, at the warehouse; girls who were taken long before Alanna. Those girls were there, and Alanna was not. The cops arrested multiple people at the scene, people who were able to tell us that the next group of girls, the group I was in, was set to be transported to a human trafficking ring . . . but not Alanna. She was different for some reason, and nobody knows why."

"And neither do I," he shrugs. "I'm sorry, but I just don't have any more information for you."

"Then no visit," I state boldly, crossing my arms over my chest. *"No Molly."*

The room is silent, and I fear that both Jon and Travis may kill me. But Dean Orson Turner licks his lips and leans forward so that his dark eyes connect with mine.

"She's in Mexico, isn't she?" I demand. "And there is something special about her, isn't there? After all, she was *first*. Tell me, Dean . . . how *do* you sleep at night, knowing that Alanna Foster, someone's *daughter*, may never return home again because of you?"

Travis holds a hand up and stops me. "Sorry, Orson. Lina is too emotionally connected to this case—"

"Like hell I am!" I shout, standing to my feet and marching over to the conference room's camera. Surely, our entire video shot is just my face, and for a hot minute, I worry everyone can see up my nose, so I take step back. I place one hand on my hip and point the other directly at the camera, and I speak to Dean Orson Turner like he is a teenager in trouble. "Since you're so good at making deals, Turner, I've got one for you. It's Molly for Alanna. You want a visit with your daughter, tell us where Alanna is. And never mind visitation . . . If you don't start talking, and I mean start talking *now*, I'm not going to allow *my* son to date your daughter. That's right, I'm shutting it down. And then I'm going to tell her it's because *you* said she can't date him."

"Dear Lord," Travis mutters under his breath. "She's lost her freaking mind."

"Give it a minute," Jon whispers behind me. "I think she's got him."

"Well, aren't you a force to be reckoned with," Orson says, crossing his arms over his navy jumpsuit and leaning in so we're face-to-face.

"You have *no* idea what I'm capable of," I say, raising one eyebrow. "I'm also PTA president next year, and I have connections to the bitchiest, snobbiest, most superficial women in your wife's social circle. Does your wife's reputation mean anything to you, Orson? Because if you don't hand over Alanna Foster, she's next. Because I know things, Dean Turner. I know *everything*."

"Make her stop," Travis begs. "We are running out of time, and she's making a mockery of our entire operation."

I tuck my hands behind my back and flip Travis my middle finger before taking one step closer to the camera and staring Turner dead in the eye.

He leans back in his chair and runs his fingers through his ragged beard. "What do you think you know, young lady?"

"Everything," I sigh. "I know all about that summer you spent 'golfing' in Tampa when you were really having an affair with your dental hygienist, which, by the way, is gross on a level I can't comprehend. And oh, I also know that your youngest son, Gavin, can't possibly be yours."

"That's quite the accusation," he counters. "You have no way of proving that."

I smile because I know damn well that I can. "Actually, I do. You see, when I was undercover as Gemma Mendoza, Molly confided in me as her friend. When she referred to Gavin as 'the broken condom baby,' something didn't sit well. Of course, accidental pregnancies happen all the time. But the age gap between your teenage daughter and your infant son is significant. I thought to myself, *How would a couple like Orson and Christine make it sixteen years using birth control correctly, and then, out of nowhere, a broken condom?* Really? So I did some digging, and my friend Ryker's ex-boyfriend—well, sort of ex-boyfriend—Alex is a hairstylist for a living, and as it turns out, your urologist, Dr. Stone was in for his usual appointment with Alex the week you were the hot topic on *every* news channel in our country, and the two of them got to talking, and guess who had a vasectomy back in 2010? You. And yes, I know that vasectomies aren't always one hundred-percent effective—"

"She's in Mexico! The girl is in Mexico. Just, please, leave my family alone. They've been through enough."

"*Where* in Mexico?" I demand, not budging an inch.

"I don't know for sure—possibly Tijuana, but I can't be sure."

"Well, you'd better *get* sure because I'm ready to talk to anyone who will listen."

"I told you. I don't know."

"Molly is sending nudes to Max," I lie. "I found them on his cell, and I have copies. Would you like to see them? I'm sure your wife, Christine, would like to know."

"Tijuana, Mexico. From what I know about this organization, I would start checking hospitals. She will be at a hospital in Tijuana. Now, please, for the love of God. Shut. Up."

Our call ended soon after Turner's confession, and Travis was not only furious with me for taking over but also convinced that the dean had been lying just to get me to cease fire. Regardless, Jon ordered all other cases on a temporary pause and sent Travis back to his desk to begin researching hospitals in Tijuana, Mexico and to start looking into flights. Travis insisted that Jon talk with me about my behavior on the call. "She can't just go rogue like that. Things could have ended differently. And she threatened his entire family on a video call. That could come back to bite her in the ass if this case goes to trial. There needs to be some sort of consequence, man."

"I'll handle it," Jon said. "Everyone is doing the best we can under the circumstances."

That was just moments ago, and as Travis exits the conference room and my ex-husband locks and deadbolts the door, I cross my arms over my chest and lean against the wooden table with eyes squinted, convinced he's going to lay into me and possibly even fire me. Sure, I know I shouldn't have been that aggressive with our only connection to Alanna. And I shouldn't have threatened him like that, but the truth is that he deserved it. Molly trusted me with piles and piles of dirt she had on her father. Hell, she even considered taking him down herself. I couldn't have that ammunition and not use it. It will be worth it if it brings us even the slightest bit closer to solving Operation Cactus Blossom.

Jon storms toward me, his chest rising and falling at rapid speed beneath the tightness of his black T-shirt. His face is fire-engine red, and beads of sweat form above his brow as I silently scold myself for my idiotic actions. Of course he's upset with me. He asked me to listen to Travis, to let him take the lead. And now, because of my stupidity and my emotional involvement with Operation Superglue, my private investigation days will be over just as quickly as they began.

"Lina—" Jon huffs between breaths, but I stop him.

I hold up my hands in surrender and shake my head apologetically. "I'm sorry. My behavior was totally out of line. Fire me. I deserve it," I say as he inches closer, and I can truly see how angry he is because I've never seen this face on him before, and I realize that's because I've never given him a reason to be this mad. Up until now, my record has been clean for the most part. "I suck, and I'm sorry. Just fire me. But don't break up with me. I love you—"

"Lina," Jon says again, reaching his hands toward me, and I stand there stunned that he's actually *this* mad, because he's kicked my chair out of his way and has pressed me against the table rather forcefully, one hand on each side of my waist. "Lina," he repeats, as his jaw tightens and his eyes narrow, meeting my stare with an emotion I've never seen from him in the entire time I've known him. "That was freaking *hot*."

Chapter Fifteen

Then (February 2024) Alanna

Back when I was a student at Emerson Academy, I learned about a study conducted by a man by the name of Dr. Curt Richter back in the 1950s. The objective of Dr. Richter's experiment was to understand the impact of psychological factors, particularly *hope*, on physical endurance and survival. In his experiment, he basically drowned rats. At first, this hadn't bothered me because, quite frankly, I'm terrified of rats. But after learning about Dr. Richter's findings, I quickly changed my perspective.

You see, the rats were dropped in buckets of water, and he timed them to see how long they would take to drown. Initially, it took the rats roughly fifteen minutes to give up. But then, a specific modification was made. Just before the rats were expected to drown, they were removed from the water periodically, dried off, allowed to rest, then put back again. After this modification was made, the rats lasted much longer before drowning—some of them swam up to sixty hours. The study suggested that psychological factors like hope and the belief in a possibility of rescue could drastically improve physical endurance and the will to survive in impossible situations. *Bottom line? Hope floats.*

So, as I rinsed the shampoo out of my hair and tried my best to ignore the guard who stood at the door, a man who had seen me naked so many times that it didn't seem to faze either of us anymore, I tilted my head back and allowed the warmth of the water to trickle down my body, appreciating the way my wrists felt uncuffed, and thought about Dr. Richter's study and its outcome. Since a rat could survive that much longer because of hope, I wondered if that meant a human could too. If that was the case, maybe I shouldn't continue to block out Maria and Carmen and their fantasies about rescue. Maybe I should embrace it. And if I couldn't muster up enough belief in the fact that my family would figure out that I hadn't run away but had been abducted, I wasn't sure I had anything else to believe in. But I knew the answer as soon as I formulated a question about it. *Eduardo*. Perhaps Eduardo was my hope.

"Time," the guard spat like he did every time I showered, but I chose to ignore him.

I'd felt differently since that first day I met Eduardo, a tall, dark, and handsome stranger who popped into our room from time to time, each visit jotting notes on a clipboard, studying our vitals, and inspecting medical equipment. We never spoke to each other with our words, but it was with our eyes instead. It was in his touch. Just being near him physically triggered something in me. Something prevented me from giving up. I was at ease when I was in his presence. I was—I was okay. Maybe I was the rat and Eduardo was Dr. Richter. Maybe he was coming to my rescue right before I was due to drown, picking me up out of the water and allowing me time to rest before dropping me back in again. Or perhaps I'd completely lost my mind. If Eduardo was on my side, he would never leave me in that room. If he was a good person, wouldn't *he* come to my rescue?

"Now," the guard demanded once more, and that time, I turned off the water, dried myself off, and slipped into a clean hospital gown. I paused for a beat and noticed that I'd lost quite a bit of weight since my arrival, and I grimaced at the brown and yellow bruises on my scrawny, pale arms from the various needles that I'd been poked and prodded with throughout the day. *Stop looking*, I scolded myself as I wrung the water out of my hair and did my best to get the tangles out with my fingers. Then I followed the guard down the long, musty hall and back to my room before allowing him to handcuff me back to my bed.

"Shower," he said to Maria as he unlocked her cuffs and guided her toward the door.

"Later, gators," she sang as she exited the room with our guard, leaving Carmen and I together, and I winced, noting that I was finding comfort in this routine, which felt bittersweet, to say the least.

"So, we need to talk," Carmen said, running her fingers through wet, tangled blond tresses.

"About what?" I asked, adjusting myself on my side.

"Getting the hell out of here."

"I'm sorry, what?" I laughed. "Now you're telling jokes."

"I'm serious."

I sat up as straight as I could, restricted by my cuffs and gestured to them, wide-eyed. "I'd love to join you, but I'm a little stuck here, Carmen. My left hand is cuffed to my bed."

"Listen," she whispered. "That quiet guy, you know, the one who comes in with the lab coat and the clipboard—"

"Eduardo?"

"Is that his name?" she shrugged. "Anyways, he was here in our room when you were showering." My heart sank at the realization I'd missed his visit. Maybe if I had showered faster, I would've seen him. I fiddled with my handcuff, keeping my face neutral as I wasn't looking for anyone to gossip with about my crush. "When he was here, he tucked a ring of keys under Maria's pillow."

"He what?" I blurted louder than intended. *Why in the actual hell would one of them leave us a set of keys?*

"Shh," she said. "We think one of the keys is to our cuffs." Hope shot through me like a strike of lightning as multiple emotions flew through me like a tornado. "Are you okay? What are you thinking?"

I'm currently thinking the lab guy has a nice ass, and judging by his biceps his abs are probably to die for, and even though I'm a virgin and have never even kissed a boy, I'd like to see him naked. But I couldn't say that—not to Carmen and not under these circumstances. So instead, I asked, "Are you sure it's the right key?"

"I'm not positive," she admitted. "But we're going to mess with it when Maria comes back. I wish we knew what time it is," she groaned. "There's no way of telling who's on the other side of that door."

"The guards change shifts around ten o'clock," I said surprising myself.

Carmen stared at me, wide-eyed. "And how do you know that?"

I stared at her, stunned, wondering the same thing. *How do I know that?* Then I thought back to a day when the guard brought me back to bed after my shower. I'd caught a glimpse of his watch, and it had read 9:00 p.m. I remember that moment clearly. Just to know the time was a luxury, and that was the night I began counting the seconds, which had turned into minutes, and before long, I'd become an expert at guessing the time.

"I think I started counting in my mind at one point," I confess. "And as I started figuring out the time, I also discovered that the hallways went quiet between ten and ten fifteen."

Carmen nodded enthusiastically. "That would make sense. Because after we shower, we aren't checked on for a while, and when someone does come in, it's a new guard altogether."

"If we're going to break out of here, it will need to be between ten and ten fifteen. And that's probably why Eduardo left us the keys *now*."

"Do you . . ." she starts but stops and starts again. "Do you think we can trust him?"

"Eduardo?" I asked, like I'd known him for years.

"Yeah. The lab guy."

"Yes," I said, without hesitation. "Without a doubt."

"How do you know?"

"I'm not sure," I admitted. "I can just tell . . . you know . . . that he cares. He's not like the others."

"I agree," she nodded. "Once Maria comes back, we'll talk about a plan. But you're in, right?"

"Of course. What do I have to lose?" I asked, thinking of the rats paddling away in buckets of water. *Would the rats turn down an opportunity to escape? Nope. No way in hell.*

"Good. Rest up. We've got work to do."

Later that evening, after the guard brought Maria back from her shower, we worked together, counting the minutes and timing out what we assumed to be at least 10:00 pm, a time we all agreed would be late enough to start messing with Eduardo's keys. I held my breath, shutting my eyes, unable to watch her as she shimmied each key into her cuffs, and when one finally popped them open, I bit down on my lip so hard to refrain from cheering that I drew blood.

"Game on!" she whispered as she made her way to Carmen's bed. "I hope it's the same key." Sure enough, Maria removed Carmen's cuffs with ease before making her way to mine.

"I can't believe this is working," I confessed, my heart beating so loudly that I was sure I was going to blow our cover with the thumping of my beating heart.

Hope shot through my veins like a wildfire, and I envisioned myself breaking free from this hellhole, finding the nearest phone, and dialing my parents' phone number. But something wasn't right, because Carmen's cuffs had popped right off, and Maria was taking too long on mine.

"What is it? What's wrong?"

"Yours must have a different key. None of them are working."

"No!" Carmen wailed. "Are you sure? Maybe you missed one?"

"I've tried them all."

"Shit!" Carmen wailed, trying harder than ever to unlock my cuffs.

"Wait!" Maria proclaimed. "Did you hear that?"

The three of us froze like statues as my knees began to tremble involuntarily, and my stomach flipped once again.

"Footsteps. Someone's coming," Maria said.

We waited for what felt like years upon years for the sound of footsteps to pass as Maria worked tediously to unlock my cuffs. Carmen was frozen, completely paralyzed by fear, and I thought back to psychology class when we learned about fight, flight, or freeze. Clearly, Carmen was choosing the freeze option, while personally, I had enough adrenaline flowing through my body to run through a wall. But considering I remained handcuffed to my bed, I wouldn't be running anywhere, not if Maria couldn't successfully remove my handcuffs.

"The key isn't here. I can't undo them."

I wiped a tear from my eye with my free hand, my stomach twisting in knots as I realized the inevitable. I wasn't leaving this room, not tonight anyway. But if Maria and Carmen escaped, they could send help. "Go!" I shouted through my tears.

"We aren't leaving you, Alanna," Carmen argued.

"She's right," Maria countered. "If we make it out, we can come back for her," she agreed, tugging Carmen toward the door.

"No!" Carmen insisted, louder that time. "I'm not leaving her."

"Go!" I demanded. My words caught in the back of my throat because I didn't want her to leave. I didn't want to be alone again. But I needed to be strong. If I was right, and this was the time of night when our guards switched shifts, we were losing valuable seconds arguing. "Maria is right. Just promise me you'll come back for me."

"I—I promise," she sniffed between tears before freeing herself from Maria's grip and throwing her arms around my neck, our first embrace ever and possibly our last. "I love you, Alanna."

"I . . . I love you too. This isn't goodbye, okay?"

My tears were falling freely as Maria lowered my handcuffed wrist beside me, but to my surprise, she began studying the metal bed frame, brows furrowed with determination. She exhaled deeply while gripping the frame and shaking it with all her might.

"No!" she grunted before falling lifelessly on top of my legs. "Maybe if I—"

"Please . . . just go!" I begged. "You are running out of time." I threw my head back against my pillow in defeat. "Please, guys."

"I'll be back for you," Maria whispers, planting a kiss on my cheek and taking Carmen by the hand.

We stare at each other for a beat, remaining speechless, before Maria grips the doorknob and turns it. She glances down the hallway first to the left then to the right before tugging Carmen out the door. And then there was *one*.

When they were gone, I sobbed the biggest tears I'd cried since my kidnapping. Months and months of emotions poured out of my eyeballs like raindrops the size of golf balls. Carmen and Maria had become my family, and now they were gone, abandoning me just like I did my former family. I wondered how I'd become such a spoiled brat. I'd been blessed with the best parents anyone could ask for. This was my punishment. I was alone again. I had nobody.

"Damn you, hope!" I screamed at the top of my lungs as I punched my pillow with my free hand. "Screw you!" I screamed again, throwing my arms over my head and frantically kicking my legs. "I hate you!" I yelled at the top of my lungs to anyone who could hear me as I continued to sob.

At that point, I realized I had no choice but to give up. Maria and Carmen weren't going to get out of the building in one piece. Nobody was coming for us. And as I lay back on my pillow and squinted my eyes, I pictured myself as a rat, treading water in a bucket, deciding that sure, hope was real, but I didn't know if it was real enough to keep me going forever. Or maybe it was time to surrender. Everyone had a limit, and perhaps I had met mine.

"Hey."

I was so deep in thought, so emotionally defeated, that I hadn't even heard the door to my room open. I hadn't even heard him come in.

"Foster," he whispered in his thick Mexican accent.

Am I dreaming? When I finally snapped my eyes open, there, standing over me, was my *hope*. "Eduardo?"

"Yes," he said, smiling softly. "My name. You remembered."

"You speak English?" I asked, annoyed with myself for focusing on such a minuscule detail at such an integral moment.

"I do," he said, placing a caring hand on my shoulder.

"Am I dreaming?"

"No, Foster, you aren't dreaming."

Foster. I was most definitely dreaming. But then again . . . I didn't recall falling asleep. "You left my friends a key," I whispered, my throat dry from my outburst. I peered over his shoulder to be sure we were really alone. "Why?"

"That's a discussion for another day," he said, holding my hand. "But I need you to promise me, when they question you about this, can you leave me out of it?"

I searched his eyes for answers, something I had done dozens of times over the past months, but came up short. "Who *are* you? Why are you helping us?"

"That doesn't matter."

"If that doesn't matter," I huffed, "nothing does."

"You need to stay positive, Foster. You must promise me that you won't give up."

"My friends are gone," I cry, laying my head back against my pillow and wiping my tears with my bedsheet. "I'm alone again. I'm going to be alone *forever*."

"You are *not* alone," he promised, pressing my hand to his chest with so much passion in his voice that it caught me off guard, and just as I'd expected, his pectoral muscles were solid. *Stop it!* I silently scolded myself. *There is a time and a place for this, and this is not the time or the place.*

"How can you say that? I'm *so* alone."

Eduardo reached into his lab coat and removed a black Sharpie. He rotated my free hand so that my palm was facing him, and he smiled softly as he drew the tiniest heart on the inside of my wrist with the marker. "There," he said, satisfied. "You are never alone, because you have *my* heart."

What in the actual hell? Who is this guy? "I . . . I don't know what to say . . ." But my words became lost because we were interrupted by the sound of a deafening, ear-piercing alarm, and I gripped Eduardo's hand harder than I intended, fear racing through me. "What's that?" I shouted, my terrified eyes locked on his. "Did they catch them? What are they going to do to them?" I asked, eyes wide. "I need to know. Tell me what's happening. Tell me who you are. Why are you helping me?"

"Time to go."

"Eduardo? Please don't leave," I begged.

"I'm going to check on your friends. Stay positive, Foster. Have *hope*."

I squinted my eyes to focus on his dark eyes. I didn't know if he was real, if I was dreaming, or where he was going. "Please," I said. "Please don't leave, Eduardo."

"Call me Eddie," he said with a wink before turning and exiting the room, leaving me scared and alone, just as I had been on the first day I'd arrived.

But just as the tears started to fall again, I remembered Eddie's advice, to stay positive and never give up hope. I studied the heart that he sketched on my wrist, and without thinking twice, I pressed it to my lips, relief and comfort flowing over me like rainfall on a hot, summer day.

"I'm never alone," I said, sniffing back the tears and inhaling deeply, pressing my lips to my wrist once more. "Never. Alone."

The alarm ceased, and I sighed with relief although I wasn't sure why. *Did they find Carmen and Maria? Have they escaped? What is going to happen to them?* I shut my eyes and silently prayed that they were safe, that Eddie was able to help them to escape, that they'd made their way out of this hellhole and were sending help. Really, I had nothing left. The only thing left to do was hope. And after what felt like hours later, but was probably just minutes, I closed my eyes and drifted to sleep, knowing deep down that whatever happened next, I had someone on my side. My new friend, Eddie, was a man I hoped I could trust, a man I wanted to trust more than anything. Because if Eddie really was there to help me, I might have a reason to hope.

Chapter Sixteen

Now (May 2025) Lina

"So let me get this straight," Daphne says, mouth gaping open and eyes wide. "Your *boss* ex-husband bent you over the conference room table and mounted you from behind like a mallard duck during mating season with your *coworker* ex-boyfriend in the next room?" she repeats for the third time, only this time louder than intended.

"Shhh," I say between sips of my nonalcoholic Corona. "There are other people in this restaurant. And they can *hear you*. And seriously, Daph. Mallard ducks? What is wrong with you?"

Daphne tightens her blonde ponytail and waves me off, sucking down the last of her margarita. "I saw it on Animal Planet. Anyways, tell me more about the spanking. That's PornHub material."

"I'm *not* a porn star!" I wail, looking to Ryker for reinforcement.

"Don't look at *me*," he counters, hands in surrender. "I'm not the one getting busy in the workplace. My grandfather always said, 'Don't shit where you eat.'"

"*You* own a gym, and your boyfriend is a hairdresser," I argue. "I don't expect you to understand what it's like working with your significant other."

"He's not my boyfriend . . . *yet*. And he's a *stylist*. There's a difference."

"She makes a good point," Daphne mumbles, biting into her taco. "When *did* your sex life get better than mine?" she asks through her mouthful of food.

"Things not good with Mal?" I ask in an effort to change the subject, but I'm also legitimately concerned. Daphne and her husband Mal were married in 2012, but he never seemed to be around. He traveled a lot for work, but that never seemed to bother her, and until now, I've believed her, as Daphne is the most functionally independent female I know.

"Things are fine," she says so quickly that her words jumble together to form something which is more one word than a sentence. "So," she says, clearly to change the subject, "tell me about this dating app you need help with."

"Dating app?" Ryker asks, eyes wide. "What the hell did I miss?"

"It's for Penelope," I explain, realizing that I've been so consumed with Alanna's case that I left Ryker out of the loop regarding my mission to reveal Jasper as the evil, cheating spouse. "It's no big deal," I say, moving my guacamole around on my plate with my fork. "I ran into Dean Elizabeth in the locker room, and she gave me some intel on a dating app used at some gyms, mainly at Desert Fit Performance."

"A gym dating app? Man, these kids don't realize how lucky they have it." He sighs. "I used to have to, you know . . . go out and *meet* people."

"Well," I exhale. "Not really. It's an app that members use to *hook up*."

"*And* cheat," Daphne chimes in.

"And cheat." I sigh, feeling an uncomfortable pit forming in the depths of my gut, and pain jabs through my stomach as my head begins to pound. "Mostly married people."

"How's that going for ya?" Ryker asks with a smirk.

"Awful," I answer, not missing a beat. "Things are going *so* great with Jon. But every time I listen to Penelope go on and on about Jasper and sift through his obvious indiscretions, I feel like I might puke." As I say this, my stomach turns again, and I rub the base of my neck. "Uh," I groan. "I'm not feeling that great."

"Come here," Ryker says, wrapping his arm around my shoulder and tugging me close. I inhale the familiar scent of his sandalwood cologne and nuzzle into his neck. "Take a breath, girl."

I inhale deeply, followed by a deep exhalation, a technique Ryker and I worked on during a training session after nearly killing me on an air bike. "You smell so good," I sigh. "Remind me again why you have to be gay? Are you sure I can't change your mind?" I ask, batting my eyelashes flirtatiously then busting out in a fit of laughter, unable to keep a straight face.

"You have a better chance of getting with *me*," Daph jokes.

"We've been over this." Ryker chuckles, kissing the top of my head. "Besides, you don't need *me*. You're getting more action than Aubrey Kate *and*

Bridgette B.," he states, squeezing me tightly. "If you need help setting up an Only Fans account, you might get a good number of followers—"

"Stop!" I say, making eye contact with a woman seated across from a little boy who looks to be about ten years old, and I mouth a silent "Sorry."

Daphne places a hand on my wrist. "Jon loves you," she says. "I know it's hard, but in my opinion, you need to let the cheating thing go. It was a *long* time ago, and he was *undercover*."

I sip the last of my fake beer and shake away the pestering voice inside my head that accuses Daphne of gaslighting me, and instead of confronting her about that, I decide to check my texts, only to find that I have four unread messages from Penelope Gallagher and one from Jon.

Penelope: *Any dirt on him yet?*
Penelope: *Bastard never came home last night.*
Penelope: *Lina?*
Penelope: *????*
Lina: *Yes, I have made progress on your case. I have a lead on a dating app used by members at his gym. Do you have access to his phone at all?*

I silently curse myself for taking Penelope's case and swipe open Jon's text.

Jon: *Heading to bed. Wish I could hold you.*

I feel my cheeks flush, hoping I can sneak past Ryker and Daphne, who would have a field day teasing Jon if they laid eyes on his sappy message. I think for a beat before replying to Jon.

Lina: *Ditto. Miss you too.*
Jon: *I can smell you on my sheets, and it's driving me crazy. Come over?*
Lina: *I'm out with Ry and Daphne. She's helping me set up the dating app for Emery. I'll see you tomorrow though, first thing.*

"I'm going to need to get on that app," I groan with a heavy sigh. "Penelope is losing her mind. And honestly, I don't blame her."

"Did you download it?"

"Yes," I answer, sliding my phone across the table. "It's the profile I need help with. I'm going on as Emery Shaw, and I need help making a dating profile. The thing is Emery is a college student, and I'm trying to get Jasper to take the bait and connect with her. Do you think he would stoop that low?"

"And you're asking *her*?" Ryker gasps, clearly offended. "What about me?"

"You can't *always* have her to yourself," Daphne insists with a shrug, slapping Ryker's shoulder with an open palm.

I smile at Daphne, hoping she can't see through my faux exterior. The truth is I have been spending a lot of time with Ryker and not enough with Daphne. I'd intentionally gone out of my way to give her this project. I had every intention to explain this to Ry because the reality of the situation was that Ryker probably would do a better job setting me up on the app, but I couldn't risk leaving Daphne in the dust.

"You can help," I say with a wink, only hoping that he knows me well enough to understand my predicament. "But Daphne is taking the lead on this one. Besides, you're the one helping me with Project I Do."

"How's that going, anyways?" Ryker asks. "Did you ever get any prints on that wig?"

"Yeah, inquiring minds want to know," Daphne agrees. "I have a client getting married this summer, and it would be nice if I don't get mugged while I'm in attendance."

"It's not like that," I say, nudging her playfully. "There were prints on the wig, but they were mine because I didn't think to wear gloves. Anyways, is your client's wedding at a Navarro Hotel?"

"Sure is. The Mesa Mirage."

I bite my lip and nod. "Yeah, don't bring any valuables."

"How do people sleep at night, taking other people's shit?" Ryker asks, shaking his head. "I'm super jealous that you get to work with Tanner

Navarro's son, though," he says, licking his lips like he's talking about his favorite dessert.

"Tanner, Junior?" I ask, shocked because TJ isn't Ryker's usual type.

"What?" Ryker asks, crossing his arms over his chest. "What's wrong with TJ?"

I shake my head and press my lips together, not wanting to touch this one with a ten-foot pole, but I don't have to worry because Daphne has it covered. "He's, like, half your age, for starters."

"That's my cue." Ryker sighs, rising to his feet and dropping two twenty-dollar bills on the table.

"Don't go," Daphne says between laughs. "You know I'm joking."

"No offense taken. I've got places to be."

"Hot date?" I ask.

"Something like that," he says, his lips curling into a soft smile.

"Tell Alex I said hi," I say, standing from my seat and pulling him close. "Next time I need an undercover profile on a gym dating app, you're my guy," I whisper in his ear.

"Damn straight," he replies, holding me for a moment longer than usual. "Love you, girl. You sure you're good?"

"Love you more," I say, pulling back with a smile. "And I'm not just good . . . I'm great. Tell that boyfriend of yours that next time he steals you from me on our night out, he's going to have to go through me first."

"Done," he says, then fist-bumps Daphne and exits the restaurant.

"Okay," Daphne begins, not missing a beat. "Get ready to make the skankiest dating profile of your life."

"Hell yeah," I sing with a smile. But as Daphne begins firing questions at me like an eager reporter at a press conference, the knot in my stomach grows tighter. I'm starting to realize now, more than ever, that I *do* want Jon to move back home. But even though I've been trying to convince myself that things won't change with Ryker, I'm concluding that when that happens, things with Ryker will never quite be the same. And somehow, some way . . . that just needs to be okay.

Chapter Seventeen

Then (March 2024) Alanna

A month had passed since Eddie sketched a heart on my wrist, and I was gratefully relieved that his visit hadn't been a dream. I would have been even more at ease, however, if Maria and Carmen had returned to our room after their escape attempt, but that wasn't the case at all. According to Eddie, their prison break had been a failure, to say the least, which had been devastating to process. I would be forever grateful for Eddie, my new friend, who had vowed to check on them and their more "secure location" and had been true to his word. Being alone in my own room had been a tough adjustment, which made my visits with him even more impactful to my survival.

Eddie's role in this whole operation was confusing, and when I tried to wrap my mind around it, I became overwhelmed and anxious, growing frustrated with myself for needing to analyze why someone with his job would care enough to help *me*. And when I questioned him about his involvement and asked him any questions that moved beyond his role, he would reiterate that he oversaw logistics and coordination of medical supplies, training, and supervision of specific devices, as well as the collection and reporting of data. When I asked him, "Why *me*? What do these people want with *me*? What makes me so special?" he would simply shake his head and shrug or change the subject, which I would fall for every time because having someone to talk to was *everything*.

I missed Maria and Carmen so much. I missed their positive attitudes about the future and their daydreams of rescue and freedom. Living in isolation had started taking a toll on me, and it was Eddie's daily visits that were keeping me from completely losing it. Not only had he been making time to sit at my bedside and listen to me talk about my former life, but he'd also been sneaking in some necessary personal items I had gone without since my abduction. When he asked if he could do anything for me, my eyes lit up like a

Christmas tree. "Deodorant," I begged. "I don't even care if it's women's. I miss deodorant."

He laughed at that, but when I remained straight-faced, he nodded and said, "I got you."

The following day, Eddie returned with men's Arm & Hammer unscented aerosol deodorant, explaining that the only reason he was able to get it past security was by claiming it was his. I scolded him for being sorry and sprayed my pits with it immediately, relishing in the fact that I would no longer be stuck smelling myself all day, and I smiled with satisfaction, tucking it into the side of my mattress for safekeeping.

"I would have paid a million dollars for this," I said with a laugh, but the truth was I hadn't been joking.

That had been at least two weeks ago, and since then, Eddie also smuggled in a small plastic comb, chewing gum, and a mini chocolate bar. I couldn't help but wonder, if I started to gain Eddie's trust, if that could be my ticket to freedom, and as I traced over the Sharpie mark on my wrist, a comforting wave of peace washed over me. *Could Eddie be my hope? Or am I falling for some sort of evil scheme? What if the hospital planted Eddie by my bedside to detour me from finding my own way out?* I mean, the guy *worked* with the very people who were holding me against my will. *Why am I being so trusting? What would I tell Carmen or Maria?* I would tell them to be more careful—that's what I would do. *Didn't I learn anything when I fell for Lincoln Stone?* Not like I was falling for Eddie or anything, but *still*. I'd learned the hard way that people couldn't be trusted. Even nice, gentle, kind medical supply specialists like Eddie, who brought me chocolate and Doublemint gum, could be the enemy.

My thoughts were interrupted when the door to my room creaked open, and like clockwork, there was Eddie. He wore his usual dark-washed jeans with a navy-blue T-shirt and white lab coat—same hair, same smile—and wouldn't you know it, he provided the same relief. I felt the tension in my shoulders release instantly at the sight of him, and for the smallest of moments, I felt like I could breathe and that things were going to be okay. Even if only for a second, I felt it—hope.

"Funny meeting you here," Eddie joked, the same way he did every time he entered.

"Still not funny," I replied with a wink, pulling the bedsheet over my legs. I hadn't had the luxury of shaving any part of my body since I arrived, and my hairy legs were not only itchy and bothersome but becoming embarrassing. "What'd you bring me?"

"Hi, Eddie . . . How are you?" he sang jokingly.

"Hi, Eddie . . . How are you? What'd you bring me?"

"I feel so underappreciated." He sighed dramatically.

I crossed my arms over my chest and waited patiently, biting my lower lip.

"Fine." He chuckled, reaching into the inside pocket of his lab coat and retrieving a pack of playing cards. "I brought you these."

Several moments in my previous life had included what my mother referred to as grand gestures. My prom date, for example, invited me to junior prom by interrupting the PSATs over the intercom. That was the epitome of a grand gesture. But since my kidnapping, my focus had been solely on *survival*, so Eddie's grand gesture shook me to the core. He wasn't just looking to play a game of Go Fish or War. Eddie understood how important playing cards with my father had been. One night, when I was at my lowest, I'd told him I would give anything for five minutes with my dad, a deck of playing cards, and a root beer. I told Eddie that one of the things I missed most about my life prior to my abduction was the relationship I had with my father. My biggest regret had been leaving him behind, and I would give anything, I mean anything, to play a few hands of blackjack with him.

"I . . . I don't know what to say."

"Well, that's easy, Foster," he said, locking my door and sliding a table between himself and my bedside. "I'm the dealer. You just need to say *hit* or *stay*," he said with a smile, shuffling the deck before dealing me a ten and his two cards then turning one over to reveal an ace.

"You know what I mean."

"I know," he said, dealing me a six. "You don't have to say anything. Just enjoy."

"Does the dealer have blackjack?"

Eddie peeked underneath his card and shook his head. "Nope, it's your lucky day."

"Good, because my father told me never to ask for insurance or even money."

I looked at my sixteen and his ace, knowing I should hit instead of stay. My father's least favorite part of the game was hitting on a sixteen, because most of the time, it was a bust. "Book says hit," I said, just as my dad used to.

Eddie dealt my next card, a two, and I breathed a relieved sigh that I didn't bust, while Eddie revealed his next few cards—twenty-three.

"Yes!" I cheered, pumping my fists in the air, but immediately lowered my arms again, feeling overly self-conscious about my hairy armpits.

"Nicely done," Eddie said with approval.

"Thanks," I said with a smile. "I learned from the best." I pictured my father's loving smile, trying to choke back my tears, which slid freely down my cheeks against my will.

"Hey," he said, placing a gentle hand on my trembling shoulder. "It's okay."

"Is it?" I snapped. "I'm still handcuffed to this bed, Eddie. I don't even know what day it is, let alone what month. You're all I have, and you tell me *nothing* about yourself."

Eddie collected the cards and dealt our next hand. "What do you want to know?"

"Come on," I sighed, wiping my tears with the back of my free hand. "This is where I ask you questions about yourself, and you basically tell me it's none of my business."

"Try me." He smirked, dealing me a five and himself a four.

"Okay, then. Why are you here?"

"I work here," he said, dealing me a ten and himself a two.

"Stay," I said, and sure enough, he busted again. "I *know* you work here," I said, rolling my eyes overdramatically. "But if you're one of *them* . . . why are you being so nice to me?"

Eddie collected my cards and prepared for the next round. "I told you. I can't talk about that."

"See." I sighed. "Told you."

"Ask me anything else."

I studied him for a beat, wondering what his deal was but also realizing that getting him to talk about this job, this place, was a battle I was not going to win any time soon. "Fine. How old are you?"

"Twenty-three."

I thought about that for a minute, and when I instinctually calculated the age difference, I froze. Yes, twenty-three was much too old for a seventeen-year-old girl, as I was a minor. *But . . . how old* am *I? What month is it? Hell . . . what year?*

"What's wrong?" Eddie asked, moving the table aside and perching on the edge of my bed, the warmness of his leg against mine sending pulses of electricity through me.

I shook my head from side to side, the reality of my situation crashing over me like tidal waves, one after the next. "It's nothing," I lied.

"You can trust me."

"Can I?"

"Of course."

"Then help me get the hell out of here!" I wailed, tears flowing freely once again.

"Shhh," he said, rubbing my back with his open palm.

"What . . . what month is it?" I asked, my cheeks flushing in embarrassment.

"It's March."

"Is it still 2024?" I asked, realizing that my concept of time was so far gone that years could have passed, and I wouldn't have noticed.

"Yes," he said. "March 12, 2024. Are you all right, Foster?"

"I . . . didn't know how old I was," I admitted, sniffling between words.

"That must be scary as hell."

"It is. If it's March 12 . . . that means I missed my eighteenth birthday," I groaned, peering up at him through my tears. "My birthday was last week. I'm eighteen."

"Come here," Eddie said, moving closer to me and wrapping his arms around my shoulders, pulling me as close to him as my handcuffs allowed. I nuzzled my face against his neck, overwhelmed by how good it felt to be held but still devastated by the thought of my family mourning me and my disappearance on my birthday. "It's going to be okay."

"I wish I could believe you," I admitted, feeling very conflicted. "Why am I here, Eddie? What did I do to deserve this? And why are you being so nice to me? Please, Eddie. I *need* to know."

"Ask me something else. Anything else. Come on—it will take your mind off this," he said, gesturing around my jail cell of a hospital room.

I nodded in agreement, squeezing his hand, and the warmth of his skin on mine sent pulses of reassurance through my entire being, and I knew he was right. Taking my mind off this was the only thing that would get me through. "Do you . . ." I sniffed. "Do you have any brothers or sisters?"

"I have a little brother, Juan."

"How old is Juan?"

"Twelve," he said fondly.

"Twelve is a fun age," I said, thinking of my siblings, whom I missed more than anything in the world. "Do you get along with him?"

"I guess you could say that." He smirked.

"What?" I asked, finding his reaction to my question cute, to say the least.

"I basically help raise him," he said, shuffling the deck and dealing me two more cards.

"Where's your mom and dad?"

Eddie inhaled deeply and exhaled dramatically, and I realized then that I'd hit a nerve, and I silently prayed he would keep talking. He dealt me one nine, himself a two, and me another nine.

"I'll split these," I say with confidence, "and then double."

"I'm taking you to a casino when we're done here." He winked.

"Don't change the subject."

Eddie flipped over four more cards before busting, and I won by a landslide.

"My dad is fine—great, even. He works in construction."

"Your mom?"

"Mom died when I was ten years old," he said, his jaw tightening and his exterior toughening.

"I'm sorry," I said, somewhat regretting my interrogation but at the same time feeling an overwhelming sense of validation because Eddie trusted me enough to confide in me.

"Don't be. It was a long time ago. We're okay."

It was my turn to comfort Eddie. I placed my hand on his and gave it a gentle squeeze before surprising myself with my boldness. I slid my hand up his waist and paused, finding a bit of humor in his shocked expression, but instead of doing anything naughty, like I'm sure he was anticipating, I reached into the inner pocket of his lab coat and retrieved his black Sharpie.

"Here," I whispered while I drew my best attempt at a smiley face on his wrist. "Now, you have to be happy. You have my smile."

"Thank you," Eddie said, his smile softening.

"You thought I was putting the moves on you." I snickered.

"I don't know what you're referring to," Eddie said with a wink and shuffled the deck once more.

"Did your dad ever remarry?"

Eddie's eyebrows rose, and he narrowed his stare. "I don't really want to talk about it."

"So, yes?" I asked, interested in how much he would share with me if I kept pressing him.

"He—" Eddie was interrupted by the jiggling of the doorknob followed by two loud bangs on the door. "Shit," he muttered, gathering the cards from the table, and yelled something in Spanish.

He slid everything back into place and grabbed his clipboard before unlocking the door as I turned onto my side, pretending to be asleep. I couldn't understand what the guard was saying to him, but Eddie didn't seem fazed. He said something back to the guard, appeasing him with whatever he needed to know. But then I heard a voice—*Carmen!*—and excitement shot through my veins like fireworks on the Fourth of July.

"Watch the hands, buddy," she scolded the guard. "These gowns don't close in the back . . . But I think you know that, don't ya? Enjoy the view, but keep 'em where I can see 'em."

I sat up straight in my bed, eyes wide, eager to see my friend. "Carmen," I said with a smile. "Hey."

"Hey, girl," she replied, climbing into her old bed and allowing the guard to cuff her.

The guard muttered something to Eddie in Spanish before closing the door behind himself.

"Where's Maria?" I asked, hoping beyond hope that she was safe.

Carmen glanced from me, to Eddie, and back to me again.

"Oh, he's cool," I said, finding comfort in the realization that I'd started sounding like my old self.

"Weird lab guy is . . . cool?" Carmen asked, confused.

"Eddie," he said with a nod. "Nice to officially meet you."

"Where is Maria?" I asked again, hugging my knees to my chest as they bumped fists. "Is she okay?"

"She *was*," Carmen answered, staring blankly in the distance.

"What do you mean, she *was*?" Eddie asked, as if reading my mind.

"Wait, you speak English?" Carmen asked, eyes wide and nose scrunched in confusion.

"Carmen!" I shrieked. "Answer us. Is Maria . . . Is she okay?"

Carmen exhaled before lying back in her bed and staring at the ceiling. "I don't really know. They hooked her up to all these machines and started taking all these tests. This morning, they started an IV, and they haven't fed her one meal since yesterday."

"When was the last time she ate?" Eddie asked, rising to his feet.

"Yesterday morning. Why?"

"Because it sounds like they're taking her to surgery," Eddie explained, running his fingers over his chin. "That's not good."

"Why not?" I asked, my stomach tightening into a thousand knots. "This is a hospital, right? Could she be sick? Maybe she needs surgery because she's sick."

"Foster," Eddie said, choosing his words carefully. "If Maria is going into surgery . . . it's probably . . ." His voice trailed off as he looked away.

"Oh, come on, Alanna," Carmen hissed. "You haven't figured it out? You're going into nursing school, for heaven's sake."

"Someone just tell me what's going on. Please?"

"This is not a hospital. It's an abandoned warehouse designed to look like a hospital. It's a *clinic*, for the love of God. Open your eyes."

"If Maria is going into surgery, it's to remove an organ," Eddie explained, his tone soft but firm, side-glancing at Carmen like he wants to tell her to shut up.

I don't blame him. Her once-bubbly personality was turning cynical right before my eyes.

"An *organ*? Like, from her body? No . . . you need to stop them." I locked eyes with Eddie as he sat back down on my bed and hugged me once again. Then I made eye contact with Carmen, clearly shocked by our exchange of affection, but I didn't care. "Eddie?" I asked again.

"Your friend Carmen isn't wrong, Foster," he whispered into my ear. "People pay *big* money for blood . . . and for organs."

"It's called organ trafficking," Carmen added, matter-of-factly, "and someone's making big bucks off Maria's body parts as we speak."

"I think . . . I think I'm going to be—" My stomach heaved, and I puked with no warning all over my bed and all over Eddie's white lab coat.

"Foster—"

"No," I choked, shaking my head in embarrassment, bile burning the back of my throat, consumed by thoughts of poor Maria being pulled apart like a turkey on Thanksgiving, and even worse, as panic washed over me.

First was Maria, and it wouldn't be long until I was next.

"Just . . . go away, Eddie," I groaned then heaved my lunch over him again. "Either go away or get us out of here," I sob. "But you can't . . . you can't have it both ways."

Chapter Eighteen

Now (May 2025) Lina

I swipe right on my phone, turning down the many divorced dads and unfaithful spouses who are more eager to get into Emery's pants than a starving man at a Golden Corral, but unfortunately for Penelope, none of them are Jasper.

"Come on!" I shout, dropping my phone on my desk with a thump.

"What's wrong?" Travis asks from his corner of the office. He's been on the phone with hospitals in Mexico all day, only to come up short, and he looks just as frustrated as I am.

"It's Operation Treadmill Temptation and the stupid dating app," I sigh. "None of the horny muscle meatheads are Jasper. And I've already done heated spin twice, yoga three times, and HITT once. I just . . . I'm getting frustrated . . . Sorry I lost my cool."

"I get it," Travis says with an empathetic smile. "I thought I had a lead on a hospital in Tijuana that had a Jane Doe in their care, but she doesn't match Alanna's description. I feel like I'm running in a hamster wheel."

"Have you heard from Jon?" I ask hopefully.

Jon, who had a meeting scheduled with Beatriz Navarro, needed to break the news that no prints were identified on the black wig and also to follow up about the photo I took in the bathroom. Beatriz was overly flustered on the phone earlier due to the fact that two more weddings were crashed in the past two weeks and she made sure to relay that to her father, Tanner, who is not impressed with our ability to solve these crimes.

"Not yet." He shrugs. "I would say no news is good news, but knowing Jon, we would know if he had any news. Besides, facial recognition can take time."

"Agreed," I say, sitting back in my chair and kicking my legs up onto my desk. Normally, I would dress up a bit more for work, but after my heated spin class this morning, it was all I could do to throw on a pair of jean shorts and a tank top, twisting my wet tresses up into a messy bun and calling it a day. "What?" I ask Travis, who's giving my legs a once-over with his eyes.

"Nothing," he says.

"Are my legs bothering you?" I huff, slapping a knee with one palm and wondering why Travis was suddenly getting the brunt of my frustration.

"Not at all." He chuckles. "Your legs look good, Lina. You look good—that's all."

"Thanks," I say, shifting uneasily in my seat, as Travis paying me a compliment is more than awkward, considering we not only dated back in July of 2024, but the sex was mind-blowing, and with things being so good with Jon, I'm surprised that Travis would have the balls to hit on me, if that's even what he's doing. "It must be all the ass kicking I've endured at Desert Fit Performance," I say with a roll of my eyes.

"Must be," he says with a smile.

"I hope that photo comes back with an ID," I say, trying to change the subject.

"You and me both."

I study him for a beat, wondering what's going on in that mind of his. *How crazy must all this be for Travis?* He and I met during the twins' middle school ice cream social and dated for a while until Operation Superglue and Jon Cote consumed my entire being. Travis was very open about wanting a relationship with me. He even went as far as to tell me he wanted himself and his son, Smith, to be family with Max, Lucy, and me. He even proposed we have a child together. *Is it hard for him to watch me with Jon? Has he even met anyone else yet? If he has, would he even tell me about it?*

"How are things with you?" I ask.

"Me?"

"Yes. How are you? Things have been so busy. We haven't caught up in a while."

"Oh, you've been *busy*." He winks, gesturing toward the conference room door, clearly referring to my Oscar-winning sex performance on the table after the meeting with Dean Turner.

"Stop," I warn. "You don't want to piss me off today."

"Oh no?"

"No. I've only had one cup of coffee." As if on cue, Travis's son, Smith, enters the office, carrying a tray of Starbucks coffee. "Oh, thank God," I say. "One of those is for me, right?"

"Yes, Ms. Rivera, Dad told me to get you a Frappuccino."

"I love you," I tell Travis as I retrieve the drink, trying to open the straw faster than my fingers allow, and I breathe a relieved sigh when I'm sipping the frosted beverage. "And it's Lina, Smith. Ms. Rivera is my mother," I say, side smiling at Smith. "I think you've grown two feet since I last saw you," I add.

Travis laughs, and I'm thankful for the break in our awkward conversation. Of course Travis heard Jon and me having sex. He was right outside the door, for heaven's sake. *What did I expect? How did I get to a place where I'm so careless with everyone's feelings?* Travis would have done anything for me. And Jon—all Jon wants to do is move back home. I rub my temples with my fingertips, hoping for some relief as a wave of nausea floods over me, and I make a silent promise to myself to get my life in order. Sure, solving these cases is important, especially Alanna's, but I need to figure out my living situation. I need to figure out how to open myself enough to allow Jon back in, fully this time.

The door to Prickly Pen Investigations swings open, and Travis and I look up in unison, both surprised to see Molly standing in the doorway.

"Molly, hey!" I say with a smile.

"Hi," she says, not appearing as smiley, and I'm pretty sure I know why. "Can we talk?"

"Of course," I say. "Conference room?"

"Let's walk," she says, gesturing to the doorway behind herself.

"Okay," I say, picking up my coffee and logging out of my computer. "I'm sorry," I say before we're even out the door, the dry afternoon desert heat slapping me in the face. "I'm sorry I haven't texted you back."

"You mean, sorry for ghosting me." She snorts.

"That's not what this is, Molly." I stop in my tracks and place a caring hand on her shoulder.

"I thought we were friends. Back when you were Gemma," she starts and stops and starts again. "Back when you were Gemma, you never would have ghosted me. But then again, that was all lies, right?"

"It's complicated, Molly. And I think you know that."

"Friends don't ghost friends," she says, walking down the sidewalk, making me struggle to keep up. "When you told me about Operation Superglue, you . . . you promised things wouldn't change."

"Molly, stop. Please," I say, suddenly feeling overly winded and a bit dizzy. I pause to catch my breath and place my open palm against the cool bricks of a building.

"You good?"

"I don't know," I shake my head in frustration. "My head is spinning. I don't feel well. I'm okay, though."

"Like hell you are," Molly huffs. "I'm calling Jon. Give me your phone."

"No," I insist. "He's on a case. I'm okay. And Molly, I'm really sorry. Things are crazy right now. I'm trying to figure things out with Jon, to be there for the twins, and to write my manuscript, and I'm working three cases. I'm sorry I ghosted you. You're right—it wasn't okay of me."

I rest my back against the building and sip my coffee, suddenly feeling inadequate in every aspect of life. I have no idea what's going on with Molly and Max. I'm falling short as a mom, as a friend, and as a . . . whatever Jon and I are, I'm falling short there, too. I'm no closer to solving any of my cases, and the odds of getting Alanna back are slim to none at this point. *What am I even doing? Is stretching myself too thin starting to affect everyone around me, including Molly?*

"It's okay," Molly says, standing beside me, resting her head on my shoulder. I just miss you. And I was worried you didn't like the idea of Max and me."

I think about that for a beat before resting my head on hers. "It's just complicated," I admit. "Max is my son, and you are my friend. You get it, right? How that can be weird?"

"Yeah," she agrees. "I can see that."

"But it's not that I don't like it. You make him really happy, and I can see that. Just . . . promise me that you will be careful . . ." I say awkwardly, my voice trailing off.

"Dude." Molly laughs. "We aren't sleeping together."

"No?" I ask, trying to sound nonchalant.

"He's totally a virgin." She giggles.

I gag on my coffee, and it all but comes out my nose. "Thank God," I say louder than I mean to.

Molly throws her head back in laughter. "He's a good egg," she says. "You're a really good mom, Lina. I hope you know that."

I pull her close for a tight embrace, needing to hear those words more than she knows. "Thank you," I whisper. "I appreciate you so much, Molly."

"He's in good hands, Mama," she says. "But as your friend, I feel the need to warn you that he isn't going to be a virgin forever, so you'd better get your head out of your ass and prepare yourself. You know, just in case."

I laugh at Molly's joke even though I'm not sure how funny I find it, and as we prepare to continue our stroll, I glance in the window of a skeevy pawn shop, one I've seen before but have never found the need to enter. But something catches my eye. The school logo for Emerson Academy was a hard one to miss, and it stood out against the black fabric of a small duffel bag, a large monogram with a cheer megaphone and the initials AF printed just below the zipper.

"Holy shit," I say, grabbing Molly's wrist and dragging her toward the pawn shop.

"What? Where are we going?"

"Inside," I say, marching toward the register, my stomach turning from the musty stench of old cigar smoke, moldy carpet, and possible cat urine and coming face-to-face with a man who appears to be in his sixties. He is a tall, slender, bald man wearing a white tank top and black sweatpants.

"What can I do for you, ladies?"

"That duffel bag," I say, out of breath, my heart pounding from my chest. "Where did you get that? When did you get that?"

"That old thing?" He snickered. "A couple of homeless guys brought those in back in 2023, made a couple of bucks off it. They had an iPad with them, though. That, they got some money for. But the bag, I could've trashed it . . . was just about to. But I figured maybe I'd put it in the window first. Never know who might be looking for an old bag. It has a teddy bear in it, too, if you're looking for a gift for a small child. It's missing an eyeball, but it has a patch on the eye—"

"Patches," I say, covering my mouth with one hand and turning to Molly. "Alanna's parents, they made a list of everything missing from her room. The duffel bag, the iPad, and Patches the Bear."

"Oh my God," Molly says in disbelief as the man walks toward the window, picks up the bag, unzips it, and removes Patches the Bear.

"Did they bring in anything else?" I ask, grateful for this new evidence but longing for more.

He coughs three times without covering his mouth, and I resist the urge to scold him. "There was uh—" He coughs again and wipes his nose with the back of his hand. "Some clothes, maybe?"

"Maybe?" Molly and I ask in unison.

He gestures toward a bin of clothing, and I cringe at the thought of digging through it.

"Do you have the contact info? For the people who sold it to you?" I ask, my tone urgent but hopeful as Molly digs through the pile of dirty clothes.

"Here!" Molly cheers, holding up a pink and faded Luke Bryan T-shirt. "It has her name on the tag in sharpie."

"No way," I say, grabbing it from Molly in disbelief.

"Way."

"Do you have the contact info for the seller?" I ask again.

"No, but I don't forget a name. One of them called the other Slinky. You don't forget shit like that."

"We will take them," I say. "How much?"

The man reaches into his pocket and pulls out a toothpick. He chews on it for a moment before saying, "Fifty bucks."

"Okay." I shrug, reaching into my purse.

"No way," Molly says, slapping my hand away. "That bag belonged to Alanna Foster, and so did that bear. She was kidnapped by those two douchebags, Ace and Slinky, who you should've reported because her disappearance was all over the news. That makes this police evidence. So you can hand it over to my friend here, or we can come back with the cops. But over my dead body are you taking her money."

"Kidnapped, huh?"

"Yes," I say. "And this is the first lead. I'm sure you wouldn't mind if the cops stop by," I say innocently, studying the rest of his merchandise.

"It's all yours," he says, passing me the duffel bag and the bear.

I'm dialing Jon's number before Molly and I have even exited the store. *Finally. We finally have a lead.*

Chapter Nineteen

NOW (April 2025—One Year Later) ALANNA

In a world full of steel and concrete, Eddie is my only connection to humanity. In the suffocating confines of my hospital room, with nobody by my side but Carmen, the mere thought of him and his daily visits gives me reason to keep going, to not give up. To be honest, my former life feels like a dream. The girl I once was died the night of my abduction. The new Alanna is different. She grew so used to being poked and prodded by needles that if a day goes by with the absence of a blood draw or an IV drip, she feels the absence of a new normal, which is unsettling on so many levels that I can't even begin to process what that means for me and a possibility of a real future.

I didn't want it to be this way. I've wished things could be different. But I need to intentionally forget who I was and who I used to be. Missing my family has become just too hard. Thinking of my parents and how much they've missed me has become too overwhelming. Hoping for freedom, dreaming of breaking free just became too exhausting. Sometimes, it was easier to settle than to fight the inevitable. And in this case, settling means more of Eddie, and I'm fine with that too.

I'm still not sure why Eddie is so invested in my well-being, but I figured out early on that questioning this is no longer an option. The night Maria was taken for her surgery, Eddie promised me that he would take care of Carmen and me. He would make sure we got the best care possible. He just needed me to promise that I would stop asking questions. That night was a turning point, to say the least. When I finally stopped yelling at him and the vomiting subsided, I became upset with him, demanding that he choose to help us escape instead of simply helping us survive. Eddie became flustered and frustrated, a helpless expression encompassing his face. He took my face in his hands, pressing my forehead to his.

"I'm not going to give up on you, Foster," he promised me. "But *please* . . . I'm begging you. If you care about your safety . . . and mine . . . you will stop asking."

"How do I know I can trust you?" I asked between sobs. "You're . . . you're one of *them.*"

"Do you really believe that?" he countered. "After all we've been through?"

I knew the answer to his question before the words even finished leaving his lips. But that week got harder, and things grew worse before they started looking up even in the slightest. Eddie discovered that Maria's surgery had complications, and although she made it through the liver lobectomy and bone marrow harvesting, she had minor postoperative complications, and because of that, her doctors placed her in a medically induced coma on a ventilator. Upon hearing this news, both Carmen and I were inconsolable, but Eddie promised us that she was going to be all right, and for some reason unbeknownst to both of us, we believed him.

"I'll stop asking questions, Eddie," I promised him. "But please . . . I *beg* of you. Promise me . . . if they are going to take me in for surgery, Eddie, promise me you will stop them."

Eddie stared at me, blankly, hesitating for a beat before clenching his fists by his sides, tightening his jaw, and muttering, "I promise, Alanna. I won't let them take you."

"Or Carmen," I added quickly, nodding in the direction of my sleeping roommate.

"I'll try my best to help your friend."

"Please," I begged, my eyes welling with tears. "She's all I have left."

"I'll try my best," he said with an exaggerated exhalation. "But she's not all you have, Foster. You have me. Don't forget that."

And I haven't forgotten it because it became nearly impossible to do so. Eddie's presence was *everywhere.* It was in the way he snuck us our favorite snacks, lotions, ChapSticks, and other toiletries we had been denied for so long. It was in the way he convinced the leaders of the hospital that Carmen and I were not a flight risk and should be moved to a room with a private bathroom, giving us the freedom of showering in private and the luxury of shaving. And months after that, it was in the way he grinned from ear to ear the day he announced that he'd bribed the guards and convinced the staff that for Carmen and I, handcuffs were no longer necessary. And when one nurse became jealous of the way he'd taken an interest in our well-being, he set her up with his friend on a date, which apparently went well, because after that, the same nurse began bringing us hand-me-down clothes, travel-size shampoos, books, and even my favorite—fuzzy socks.

For those reasons alone, I will be forever grateful for Eddie. But the connection we share and his ability to ease my fears and calm my anxieties by simply standing beside me are attributes of our relationship that I can't really put a label on. There are multiple layers to what I feel for Eddie. *Am I in love with him? Am I misplacing feelings of gratitude and confusing the security that came with this savior complex he seems to suffer from? Probably. Is that enough to keep me from falling for him? Absolutely. Not.*

"I'm going to hop in the shower," Carmen says, interrupting my thoughts. She dog-ears her Colleen Hoover book and places it down on her bed.

"How's the book?" I ask.

"You know it's the third time I've read it." She snickers.

"I know. It just feels good to talk about . . . you know . . . other things."

"Yes. It feels terrific talking about something other than organ trafficking and involuntary surgical procedures. But if Lover Boy comes in when I'm in the shower, see if he can hit up the nurses for some new literature. Not that I'm ungrateful or anything."

"He's *not* my lover. Get your head out of the gutter. No more romance novels for you."

"I love you, Alanna, but you're kidding yourself if you don't see it."

"See what?"

"Stop!" she wails, dramatically throwing herself onto her bed, then screams softly into her pillow in frustration. "He likes you," she says. "And you like him."

I cross my arms over the black Nirvana T-shirt I stole from Carmen and shake my head. "It isn't like that."

"Then what is it?"

"I don't know." I shrug because that's true. "I don't know what it is. But I know what it's *not*."

"And what *isn't* it?" she asks, hopping to her feet and reaching for her towel.

"Well," I start, stop, and start again. "We don't kiss . . . or you know . . . or do anything like that."

"You don't kiss . . . *yet*."

"Don't you think it's weird?" I ask, stretching my arms overhead. "That he's helping us?"

Carmen thinks about that for a beat. "Yes. And no." She sighs. "I mean, let's be real. This whole situation is screwed up on a level that neither of us can really wrap our minds around. Maybe just take it one day at a time?"

"I guess. But I can't help feeling like this might be a bit one-sided."

"How so?"

"I do like him, Carmen. A lot," I admit, followed by an exaggerated grunt. "And even with the little bit I know about him, I feel like I know everything about him. And I feel like I would do *anything* to see him, and I would do *anything* for him. That can't be normal."

"Why not? I would have done anything for my boyfriend," she says, her lips forming a small pout.

"I know you would have, and I'm sorry to make you think about him."

"Don't be sorry. This is important. And besides, he's looking for me, I'm sure of it. Now tell me, what is going through that brain of yours? What do you need him to do or say to make you feel that this is real?"

I laugh so hard I choke on my own spit and need a moment to compose myself. "How about get me the hell out of here?" I exclaim louder than I intend. "If roles were reversed, I would be thinking about how to help Eddie."

"And you don't think he's helped us?"

"No," I say, "he's helped us a lot. I just . . ." I can't find the words.

"You want him to rescue you," she says, placing one hand on her hip. "And that's totally okay."

"I guess that's it," I agree. "If Eddie is really one of the good guys, why won't he just take me home?"

As I wipe a tear from the corner of my eye, a knock on the door startles us, and the doorknob turns as Carmen and I lock eyes. Of course, we are both hoping for Eddie, but the truth is that we never really know what to expect. It could be Eddie coming to say hello, bringing us something special . . . or it could be a doctor, guard, or nurse, taking our blood, sticking us with needles, or even worse . . . prepping us for surgery like they did with Maria.

"Hey, ladies," Eddie says with a confident smirk as he enters our room, a duffel bag in hand.

"Hi," we both reply with a relieved sigh.

"You scared the crap out of us," Carmen scolds. "I'm getting in the shower." She winks, mouthing the words *more books* before entering the bathroom and closing the door behind herself, leaving Eddie and I alone for the first time in a long while.

"Hi," I tell him shyly, hugging my sweatpants-covered legs to my chest. "Don't worry about her. She's tired of reading the same book repeatedly. She wants me to ask you for a new one," I add, rolling my eyes and tucking my hair behind my ear.

"I'll see what I can do," he says with a smile before sitting down on the edge of my bed.

"How are you?" he asks, placing a warm hand on my knee and sending invisible shockwaves of electricity through me, and I struggle not to blush, but know I fail miserably.

"I'm . . . I'm okay," I say with a confident smile, resisting the urge to beg him to take me with him, to sneak me out, to tell me why he's helping me, but I bite my tongue because I have a great thing going, and I'm determined not to lose it.

"Good," he says, unzipping his duffel bag with a sneaky grin.

"What did you bring?" I ask, clapping my hands like a kid on Christmas morning.

"Well," he says, "the other night when you were telling me about that bear . . ."

"Patches the Bear?" I ask with a pout, wishing more than anything that I could be five years old again and snuggled up with my favorite stuffed animal.

"Yes, Patches. I can't bring him back to you, but this might bring you some comfort," he says, removing a tiny purple plush bunny from his bag and handing it my way. Its floppy ears are so long that they reach the tips of its toes, and its tiny smile sparks excitement that bursts through me, and I resist the urge to jump for joy. "I've named him already. I hope that's okay."

"Eddie! I love him!" I squeal, tucking him under my chin and squeezing him tightly. "What did you name him?" I giggle, finding it ridiculously adorable that Eddie has not only given me a stuffed bunny but has also taken the time to name him.

"Oh, that was easy." He smirked. "He's the Purple Bunny of Courage."

"I love it," I say, smiling for the first time in what feels like years.

"I knew you would," he says, taking my hand in his, and for the first time, he keeps our fingers interlocked as he rests them on my leg. It's the first time he's done this, but he's acting like it's business as usual.

"Thank you," I say again, my eyes locking on our intertwined fingers. "Eddie," I state boldly, my tone even, "you're holding my hand and touching my leg."

"Is that okay?"

I nod, squeezing his hand tighter. "Yes. It's *really* okay."

"Good," he whispers with a smile. "Because I like you, Foster. A lot."

Heat flushes from my chest up through my neck, turning my cheeks a sunburned red—I'm sure of it. And when he tucks my hair behind my ear, my legs turn to Jell-O, and butterflies invade my insides.

"I . . . I like you too." I smile, struggling to believe that this conversation is happening. I hear the shower turn off, knowing that any moment now, Carmen will re-enter our room, and I want to scream at her, to beg her, even, to please just stay away for one more minute. "Thank you for the Purple Bunny of Courage, Eddie."

"You're very welcome, Foster." Eddie grazes the side of my face with his fingertips, stopping at my chin.

We pause, and as I stare into his dark, mysterious eyes, I relish in the feeling of escape. Looking into Eddie's eyes is not only the gateway to his soul, but it could also be my way out of this prison. It could potentially be my freedom, and as I search and search for answers—answers about who he is, his involvement in all of this, and his feelings for me—I become someone else. I'm no longer a helpless kidnapping victim from Tempe. I am just a girl, a girl who's falling for a boy. So I do what feels right.

When he guides my chin toward his face and pauses briefly, the tension building as my lips wait centimeters from his, I take it all in: the smell of his earthy, rich cologne, the heat from his forehead as it presses to mine, the satisfaction I feel, knowing that he feels the same way. I close my eyes and press my lips gently to his, validating what I know—I am falling in love with him. I am falling in love with Eddie, the lab guy, a mysterious stranger who could very well be treating me this way only to manipulate me, to gain my trust so that I lose the urgency to run away. But that is a risk I'm willing to take. Because if Eddie is my new normal and my days left on the planet are being cut short, I will die a happy lady, knowing I'm falling for Eddie and he's falling for me. And as his lips press to mine, they feel incredibly warm and all-encompassing, so dominant yet so gentle, and I pause there, taking in this blip of happiness. And there it is—my first kiss.

"Did you bring anything fun?" Carmen asks, barging back into the room, still pulling a gray t-shirt over her head, startling both Eddie and me. I rub my face with my palms, unable to hide my love-struck grin. I resist the urge to pull him down onto me and kiss him for real this time and to tell Carmen to take a hike or at least go back inside the bathroom.

"I didn't bring any more books," he admits apologetically then clears his throat. "But I did bring this, he says, removing a stack of magazines from his bag. "Stole them from the waiting room at my brother's dentist appointment," he confesses with a mischievous grin.

He brings his brother to the dentist? How cute is that?

"Sweet!" Carmen shrieks. "Alanna, this is like our first look into the outside world since we arrived here. I don't even know where to start. Should I read them all at once? Should I do one a day? Oh God, I don't know what to do. Tell me, Alanna! Tell me what to do."

"Start with one," I say with a smile, thinking that I should suggest she go read in the bathroom so that Eddie and I can finish what we started, but I could never do that to her, not when she's this excited.

"Good idea," she agrees, opening a copy of *People* and lying down on her bed. "Holy crap!" she shrieks. "Sophia Richie had a baby?"

"No way, really? Let me see."

"Oh, that's from last year. Sorry. I should add that the magazines are very outdated," Eddie said.

"It's fine," I say with a wave of my hand. "It's better than nothing. And it's new to us."

"I've got to take this," Eddie says, gesturing to his cell phone and guiding it to his ear.

He speaks in Spanish so quickly and eagerly that not only do I fail to understand what he's saying, but I'm turned on, surprisingly. But as I watch the smile on Eddie's face fade to a solemn frown, a heavy pit forms in my gut. I've gotten to know Eddie well enough to sense that something isn't quite right. He locks eyes with me, and I strain to read his mind. As he covers my hand with his and gives it a tight squeeze, it confirms what I suspect. Eddie is receiving bad news, and this bad news most definitely has to do with either Carmen or me. And judging by the way he hops to his feet and begins pacing around the room, running a hand through his thick, dark hair, I know that whatever the problem is, whatever news Eddie is receiving, he can do nothing to stop it. I say a silent prayer that I'm right about him and that he can keep his promise. Eddie *promised* he wouldn't let anything bad happen to me. And all I can do now, in this moment, is to hold my purple bunny close to my heart, believing now, more than ever, that it can help me formulate the courage I need to get through whatever darkness lies in my path.

Chapter Twenty

Now (May 2025) Lina

"You sure Ryker doesn't mind staying over again?" Jon asks as he slips out of his T-shirt and slides into bed next to me in nothing but his maroon plaid boxer shorts.

"He said he didn't mind." I shrug, thinking for a beat, wondering if this might be a good time to talk about our living situation, something we've put off for about a month now. The truth is that I *do* want Jon to move back home. I'm very much ready for him to move back home. At first, my concern was for Max and Lucy and their adjustment to our getting back together, but now, I'm balancing a tension with Jon and my friendship with Ryker, which is not traditional at all but is still very important to me.

"Good," Jon says, kissing the top of my head then my cheek. "Because I *really* like our sleepovers."

"I like them too." I smile, rolling onto my side so that we're facing each other as Jon slides down my nightgown's strap, pressing his lips softly to my shoulder. "I do want to talk about things," I say, my voice steady at first, but I become distracted by his kisses, and my words fade in the silence between us.

"Okay," he says, kissing my neck once more then propping himself up on his elbow. "What's going on?"

I gaze into his bluer-than-blue eyes, feeling as if I'm both coming alive and drowning at the same time. "I love you so much," I say with a smile.

"I love you too, babe. You know that."

"I'm . . . ready to talk about it. Moving in together," I say, searching his eyes for a reaction.

"That's awesome." He smiles. "Why do I sense a *but,* though?"

Damn you, private investigators! I scream silently. "Because, Jon. There *is* a but."

"The kids?" he asks, his tone sincere. "I'm sure they'll be open to the idea. They seemed fine at dinner, don't you think?"

"That was my concern at first," I admit. "But I think they are okay. They are *so* in their own worlds half the time, I'm, like, the last of their worries." I chuckle.

"Facts," Jon says, tracing my chin with his index finger, and for a hot minute, I regret starting this conversation, as climbing on top of him and kissing him sounds way more fun. "Then what is it?"

I groan in frustration, rolling onto my back and pressing my palms to my eyes. "Why do I always have to overcomplicate everything?"

"Just talk to me." Jon smiles. "It's me, Lina."

"You're right," I agree. "I'm making things way harder than they need to be."

Jon rolls over on his side and kisses me on the cheek. "Talk to me."

"It's just . . . when we separated . . . and I was a single mom . . . there were certain things about my life I needed to adjust. I was in a really dark place, you know?"

"I know," he sighs, rolling onto his back. "I don't know how else to say sorry—"

"No," I interrupt, holding up a hand. "That's not where I'm going with this."

"It isn't?"

"No. What I'm trying to say is I gained a lot of independence quickly. I had to . . . you know? To . . . well, to survive. I did a *lot* on my own."

"I know you did."

"And of course, I had Daphne, and I had my parents. But the person who supported me the most, the one I couldn't have gotten through it without . . . was—"

"Ryker."

"Yeah. Ryker."

Jon sits up and braces his back against his headboard, gesturing for me to come closer, so I do. I lay my head on his bare chest, the rhythm of his heartbeat comforting me and easing my anxieties. "You love him?"

"Yes," I say with confidence. "He's the best gay best friend a girl could ask for."

"And you're afraid of losing him?"

I contemplate this for a moment, determined to choose my words carefully. "Yes and no. I know that he will always be my best friend. He and I, we just click, you know? Sometimes, he knows how I think better than I do. I can talk to him about anything. He's always there for me. He knows me better than I know myself sometimes. He's . . . he's one of the good ones."

Jon runs his fingers through my hair and hugs me tighter. "You didn't answer my question," he says. "You're just listing things you like about him."

"It's just that . . . I love you so much, but I love *him* so much too. Obviously not in the same way, but in a big enough way that I wonder . . . when you move back home . . ."

"Will there be room for both of us?"

"Yes. I guess that's what I'm asking."

"I think this is one of those things, Lina, that we won't really know how to navigate until we're in the thick of it."

"Good point. I just want to make sure we're on the same page. Ryker is like a brother to me. I need him in my life."

"Come here," he says, pulling me on top of him, straddling my legs around his waist, and pressing the side of my face to his bare chest. "I love you, babe. I'm ready to take that next step and move back home. But you've been through so much, and I'm okay waiting. I'm okay waiting until you sort through whatever you need to do to be ready . . . to be happy. The last thing I want to do here is infiltrate your support system. I'd like to, you know, make it better."

I kiss his chest and sigh. "Could you be any more perfect?"

"I'm far from perfect." He snickers, his chest rising and falling to the beat of his laughter.

"Thank you," I say. "For getting me."

"I can't promise things will be perfect," Jon whispers, his lips tickling my ear. "But we will do the best we can, like we always do. And if having Ryker around makes you happy, it makes me happy too. I mean, it's not like you guys sleep in the same bed or shower together, right?" He laughs.

"No," I say faster than I intend.

Flashbacks of the past ten years shoot through my mind like a movie montage: Ryker and I curled up on the couch with popcorn and beer, watching reruns of *Blue Bloods*. A night, years ago, when he climbed into bed with me, spooning me for an entire night after I woke up in hysterics because of Jon's affair. Ryker, perched on the toilet seat in my bathroom as I listed intricate details of my first date with Travis from behind the shower curtain then launched a handful of shaving cream at his face when he joked about Travis's penis size.

"Of course not," I repeat. "Our relationship might not be traditional, but we have healthy boundaries," I say with hesitation. "For the most part."

"You're so convincing, Lina. You should go to law school."

"Stop." I giggle, punching him playfully. "Ryker and I . . . we will adjust. I just want you home. I *need* you home."

"I think your phone is ringing," Jon says, motioning toward the nightstand on my side of the bed.

"You're right." I prop myself up on one elbow and reach for my vibrating cell as Jon glides his fingers down my body and back up again.

"Is it the kids?" he asks, sensing my concern.

"No, at least I don't think so," I say, scrunching my nose and furrowing my brow. "The number reads +52 with a 664 area code. Think it's spam?"

"Answer it!" Jon orders, his tone full of urgency. "That's Mexico. I'm sure of it."

"Oh my God," I say, swiping the call open and placing the phone on speaker. "This is Lina."

"Is this Prickly Pen Investigations?" the person on the other end of the line asks. It's a man's voice, and although his English is good, his Mexican accent is thick and full of panic and urgency.

"Yes," I say. "Yes, it is." I grip Jon's knee so hard that I'm sure my fingernails will leave a mark. But every ounce of my being, every gut instinct is screaming that this is it: the break we've been waiting for.

"I'm calling from Tijuana, Mexico," the man says. "I'm calling from Secretaría de Seguridad y Protección Ciudadana Municipal."

I glance at Jon in confusion.

"It's the police department," Jon explains, nodding encouragingly.

"I'm Lina," I repeat awkwardly. "I'm here with Detective Jon Cote. Are you calling about Alanna Foster? We are on her case from Tempe, Arizona."

"My name is Detective Silva," he says, speaking slowly and clearly. "I'm part of an undercover operation in Tijuana, and I need your help."

"Yes, of course," I say, leaping to my feet. "Does this have to do with—"

"Yes," he says, finishing my sentence for me, "the social media alert that you advertised. I know where she is, but I am going to need your help. She is in *real* danger, and it is critical that we work quickly to bring her to safety."

"You have our attention, Detective Silva. You have no idea how happy this news makes us," Jon chimes in. "Please tell us . . . How can we help?"

Tears of relief flow from my eyes. We've found her. We've found Alanna Foster. But based on Jon's concerned expression and the panic in our caller's voice, I silently urge myself to pause the celebration. I tell myself our work is just really beginning.

"Alanna is being held at a hidden organ-trafficking clinic in Tijuana, and she has been for quite some time now."

"Organ trafficking?" I shriek, unable to hold back my shock. "What in the actual hell is that?"

Jon presses his finger to his lips, but I don't see how I can be quiet. *Of all the horrible things I pictured happening to that poor girl. Organ trafficking? Really?*

"Please continue," Jon says.

"Alanna has a rare blood type that consists of ABO subtypes. This is probably why, after her abduction, she was sold into organ trafficking."

"OMG. That rare blood type! Like on *The Resident*!" I mouth to Jon. "Remember?"

Jon shakes his head and ignores me. "Is Alanna okay? How do you know she is still at the clinic?"

The officer clears his throat. "My name is Eduardo. I'm an undercover police officer. I've been undercover at the clinic for over two years," he explains. "My team has been trying to take down the organ-trafficking operation but has never been successful. I have obtained a significant amount of evidence, but I haven't been able to identify the leaders behind the operation. The clinic has also received a rather large offer from a client I've yet to identify."

"You're trying to stay under until then," Jon finishes for him. "You can't blow the operation, trying to save her."

"Exactly. My role as an employee at the clinic is the closest we have come to taking these criminals down, but I'm not ready yet. Taking down the clinic is my top priority. But . . . I've . . . I've gotten close with Alanna . . . I am embarrassed to admit that I . . . that we . . . I want to . . . I *need* to help her . . . but we can't blow my cover. Too many lives are at stake."

Holy. Shit. Alanna and this guy . . . Could they be a thing? I couldn't write this stuff if I tried. I press my palms to my eyes, shaking my head, and open them to find Jon looking cool as a cucumber, like he's speaking to Eduardo about a football score. *How can he be so calm? Alanna Foster is a victim of organ trafficking, and we need to help her. Like, yesterday!*

"Copy," Jon says, his tone serious and determined. "I understand. No judgment here. We just want Alanna home, safe and sound. Thank you for keeping an eye on her."

"What can we do?" I ask. "Please, we will do anything."

"Come to Mexico," Eduardo says. "Time is of the essence. You see, I just received word that she is scheduled for surgery in less than forty-eight hours, and we can't let that happen."

"Surgery? What kind of surgery? Like a kidney transplant?" I ask, thinking back to what I learned on TV.

Jon grips my hand in anticipation of what this might mean, and when Eduardo goes silent on the phone and struggles to form his words, we realize that Alanna is not only in grave danger, but Eduardo *loves* her. The romantic in me does cartwheels inside my head.

"Eduardo?" Jon asks.

"Up until now, they have just taken her blood," he says, his words catching in the back of his throat. "Alanna and her roommate have the same rare blood type, which is why they have gone under the radar for the bigger procedures. But now . . . they have a client willing to pay huge money for . . . for a heart. It's looking like they are both a match. And if either of them are . . . Well, I don't need to tell you what that means for one or both."

"We are on our way," Jon says, hopping to his feet and glancing at the time on his cable box. "We will be there by morning. I just need to tie up a few loose ends. And Eduardo? Thank you. Alanna is going to be okay. You have my word."

"Thank you, Detective Cote. Please, call me Eddie."

"Thank you, Eddie. Hang tight. We will call you when we land."

Chapter Twenty-One

Now (May 2025) Alanna

That kiss, though. On one hand, it was everything I needed, but on the other, it was the legit definition of a tease. It was literally the equivalent to taking one little lick of a chocolate-chip-cookie-dough ice cream cone, only to have it ripped out of my hands, leaving me longing for more, with only the slightest bit of aftertaste in my mouth and only a faint memory lingering in my mind as I wondered if and when I would ever get another taste.

I've never felt for anyone the way I've been feeling about Eddie, and even though I've come to the realization that I might never truly know why he's helping me the way he is, I've decided that knowing more right now is just out of the question, and maybe, just maybe, it's time to trust him. But how *do* you trust someone who isn't telling you the complete truth about who they are and their involvement with people who treat you like you're disposable? Like a prisoner? After learning what I have about my current situation, and knowing what I know about Maria's medically induced coma, it's getting increasingly harder to trust anyone that has to do with this new reality.

This kiss was yesterday, and Eddie left in a hurry, clearly panicked by the phone call he received. Most of the afternoon has passed, and he still hasn't returned. Carmen and I have just about given up hope that he might visit us, Carmen hopeful for a new Colleen Hoover novel. But as our door creeps open and we grow excited to see Eddie's boyish grin peek into our room, we both freeze, panic sweeping through us simultaneously. Our visitor isn't Eddie. It's a doctor I've never met before, followed by two nurses who point at our beds and demand, in Spanish, that we return to them, and both Carmen and I are poked and prodded, blood is drawn, IV ports are inserted, and handcuffs are secured.

"Ouch!" Carmen says. "Could you be any rougher?"

Just as quickly as the nurses and doctors arrive, they disappear, leaving Carmen and I both dumbfounded and terrified. When a tear rolls down Carmen's cheek and I ask her what's wrong, she can't speak, but she doesn't have to. I know beyond a shadow of a doubt that this team must have been the same team that came in for Maria. And we all know how well that turned out for her.

Lunchtime has come and gone, and when food never arrives for Carmen and me, that confirms our biggest fears. We are both being prepped for surgery, and the clock is ticking.

"I can't believe we trusted him," she says in frustration with a knowing sigh. Carmen, who didn't speak a word for at least two hours post IV drip, turned on Eddie the moment her stomach growled and it dawned on her that we missed a meal.

"You don't know that," I mutter, rolling onto my side and pulling my knees to my chest, shoving her accusations far from my mind.

"Then where is he?"

I mean, she has a point. Eddie, who visited us daily like clockwork, is a no-show at the exact moment we need him most. But I saw the panic and dread in his eyes when he received that phone call. And he *promised* me he wouldn't let anything happen to us. I trust Eddie more than I have ever trusted anyone. If anything, he was out there getting help. Somehow, some way, he was going to get us out of here. But reasoning with Carmen isn't worth it.

So instead of defending Eddie, I say, "It's going to be okay."

A tear trickles down her face, and she wipes it with the hand that isn't cuffed to her bed. "You don't know that. For all we know, we were given these things," she says, gesturing at her stack of magazines, "as a way to keep us from running away. Eddie used us, Alanna. He gave us a reason to stay . . . a reason to care. Don't you see? We were brainwashed . . . love bombed."

Brainwashed? Love bombed? "No," I argue, shaking my head. "Eddie would never do that." But as the words leave my lips, I realize how passionate I am about Eddie, how much I care about him. Hell, if someone told me to jump in front of a train for him, I probably would. *Am I in love with Eddie?*

Or am I part of a game he's playing? If that's truly the case, this is the second time I've been tricked, the second time I've allowed a guy to manipulate me in exchange for my freedom . . . for my *life.*

"No," I say again but with less confidence and more to myself than Carmen. "You're wrong. Just wait. He's coming back."

"You didn't see her face, Alanna," she says, the tears falling freely now. "You didn't watch as they took Maria away from me. I watched them put her under. I saw them suck the life out of her. We're next. How can you not see that? Are you really so far gone that you forgot about Maria? She's lying somewhere in this hospital in a coma, like a vegetable. And we're next."

I tuck the Purple Bunny of Courage under my chin and pause, unsure of what to say to her, knowing that no matter what, the facts line up, and the truth is her theory makes way more sense than any argument I can come up with. Carmen is stating facts about Maria and actual things that have happened to us, while my words are based solely on emotions and feelings I have for Eddie. But as soon as these thoughts cross my mind, I become angry with myself for believing the lies. There were facts with Eddie too. He didn't just bring me gifts—he brought me hope. And even if he is the evil villain Carmen is painting him to be, even if he was spoiling us just to gain trust, he would never sink to the level of connecting with me emotionally, would he?

"I know him. He's coming back."

"Get your head out of your ass, Alanna!" she exclaims, shaking her head, eyes wide. "Joke's on us. It's over."

"You're wrong," I counter. "Eddie . . . He's different. I can see it in his eyes."

"What you see are lies. A false reality. Just like—"

"Don't say it," I snap more harshly than I intend. "Eddie isn't Lincoln Stone."

"I'm sorry," she starts but stops then starts again because the door to our room creeps open.

I hold my breath and squeeze my eyes shut, praying that when I open them, Eddie will be standing in the entryway—Eddie in his white lab coat and his white toothy charming smile—Eddie, who would meander to my bedside and wrap his arms around me, promising me that it's all going to be all right. But once I shut my eyes, the tears start to fall, and I can't make them stop. Even though I trust Eddie, I'm not one hundred percent sure that even *he* can save me from this. And even if Carmen is wrong about him, it might be too late. And if I open my eyes and it isn't Eddie, I'm not sure I can continue. It may just be time to give up, to gather my blackjack chips and walk away from the table. I know that sometimes, when things aren't going your way, it's time to stop playing the game.

"Alanna," Carmen whispers. "Alanna, open your eyes."

"No!" I wail, pinning the Purple Bunny of Courage between my jaw and my collarbone, my words catching in the back of my throat as my chest heaves uncontrollably with the inconsistency of my rapid breaths.

"Open them," she says again, a softness to her tone.

I muster the courage to pry one eye open. When I do, I see the faint outline of a man's figure through my tears. I open the other and wipe my eyes with my stuffed bunny to see Eddie hovering over me, one arm on each side of my trembling body, his face inches from mine.

"Eddie," I murmur under my breath.

"Hi," he whispers, pressing his lips to my forehead.

I melt and turn my head toward Carmen to study her reaction, wondering if she's still skeptical or if she's back on team Eddie.

"I don't have much time," he says, this time to both Carmen and me.

"No kidding," Carmen huffs. "Clock's ticking, Lover Boy. Hope you have a plan."

"Carmen—" I start.

"No," Eddie says, holding up his hand, and sitting on the edge of my bed. "She has a right to be scared. She has every reason to panic. You are both in real danger."

"Can you get us out of here?" I ask. "Please, Eddie. You promised, remember?"

Eddie plants another kiss on my cheek, and warmth floods over me like sunshine on a cloudy day. "We have a plan."

"We?" Carmen and I ask in unison.

"Yes, *we*," Eddie says, tracing his fingers over my handcuffed wrist.

"Who else is helping you?" I ask, searching his eyes for anything. When he doesn't reply, my blood begins to boil, and I feel something I haven't allowed myself to feel for as long as I can remember: anger. "No more secrets," I demand. "If I'm going to trust you, I need to know *everything*."

"What she says," Carmen says, her tone no-nonsense. "Who are you *really*, and what do you want with her . . . with us?"

"Like I said," he starts. "I don't have a lot of time."

"No," I insist. "If you leave this room without giving us the truth, Eddie. I swear on my life, I'm giving up. It's just not worth it anymore." The action of saying this out loud provides an unexpected sense of relief because at this point, giving up would just make more sense. *It would just be . . . I don't know . . . easier?*

Sadness floods Eddie's expression as he stares up at the ceiling before rubbing his hands over his tired eyes, and Eddie looks like he hasn't slept in days. "Okay," he agrees with a long exhalation, throwing his arms up in defeat. "I'll tell you the truth."

Carmen shifts herself to a seated position while I do the same, allowing Eddie room to sit comfortably on my bed, facing me.

"Are you sure you can handle this?" he asks, his words catching in the back of his throat.

"The truth," I repeat. "*All* of it."

"I'm a cop. I work undercover."

"Shut the hell up!" Carmen gasps. "I didn't see that one coming."

I feel blood flush from my chest up through my face, and I know without a doubt that my cheeks are a sunburn red. And as my brain spins, so does the room, and I suddenly feel faint. I'm not sure why this news catches me off guard in the way it does. Maybe it's because Carmen was right. I mean, it's good news that he's here to help, but in the big scheme of things, Eddie was lying to me. He wasn't who he said he was. But if Eddie is a cop and has other people trying to help him, the smart thing to do is go along with his plan to ensure my survival. I can sort through the emotional baggage later. So I do the only thing I can think of doing.

"Go on," I say with a nod.

"I've been on this case for some time now," he says, his tone even-keeled, "trying to take down this whole operation."

"By *operation*, you mean the organ trafficking?" Carmen asks like she's clarifying the weather forecast or his coffee order, not the kidnapping of innocent people for the removal of their body parts.

"Yes. This hospital is a hidden organ-trafficking clinic. You both have a very rare blood type. Did you know that?"

Carmen shakes her head, and I think about it for a beat.

"I don't think so," I say hesitantly. "But then again, I never needed to know my blood type." I shrug.

"Well, you both have a rare blood type that consists of ABO subtypes," he says, like either of us knows what that means.

"So they've been keeping us here to sell our blood?" I ask.

"Yes. Which is why I was able to bargain with the clinic when it came to keeping you comfortable. You were not a flight risk, and they were able to keep drawing your blood and profiting."

I relax a bit, realizing that Eddie addressed Carmen's earlier accusation. "So, what changed?" I ask, locking eyes with Eddie. "Why are they prepping us for surgery?"

Eddie's jaw tightens, and he shakes his head. "Knowing this isn't going to help anything."

"Yes, it will. I need to know," I demand.

"Look, the longer we sit here, the less of a chance we have of getting out of here in one piece," he says with authority.

"Everything," Carmen reiterates.

"Fine," he huffs, tightening his shoulders and sitting up a bit straighter. "They have a buyer who may be a match."

"A buyer?" I ask, squinting my nose in confusion.

"Someone wants to pay for our insides," Carmen clarifies.

"Yes," Eddie repeats, "but we aren't sure yet if you are a match. The results will be out soon. My plan is to tamper with the lab results, which should be in shortly. My goal is to make it look like neither of you are a match."

"What if that doesn't work?" I ask, panic rushing through my veins.

"We have a plan B. Just promise me you will stay calm. Nobody can know about this."

"If you are who you say you are," Carmen asks, speaking slowly and carefully, "why not just break us out of here?"

Eddie pauses for a beat before nodding his head slowly. "I can't blow my cover," he admits, unable to look me in the eyes.

"So, you *could* get us out of here," Carmen asks, her sass not going unnoticed. "But you won't because you'll blow the entire operation."

My heart sinks when I realize she is right. Eddie is choosing to keep us here because he can't get caught. "Well, that sucks," I mutter under my breath, my optimism deflating like the air being squeezed out of a balloon.

"It does suck," Eddie agrees. "But if I can take these assholes down, we will be saving hundreds of lives. Nobody will ever have to go through this again . . . at least not here, at this facility." Eddie intertwines his fingers through my free hand and squeezes tightly. "I can do this. I know I can. I can save the two of you without compromising my position. Please, trust me."

I study his dark eyes and search for answers. I search so hard that I forget what I'm looking for. When Eddie remains silent and I don't have any more questions because he pretty much covered everything, I pull him close and nuzzle my face against his neck and whisper, "Why me, Eddie? What makes me so special?"

A tear escapes from Eddie's eye and trickles down the side of my cheek. "Eddie?"

"I wish I had an answer for you. The truth is, Alanna, there is no strategic reason or scientific medical explanation for why I want to help you."

"Do better," Carmen insists. "She deserves better."

I side-glance at Carmen and roll my eyes, ready to defend Eddie, who is clearly struggling, and I open my mouth to defend him, but he stops me short.

"Because I'm pretty sure I love you, Alanna."

His words suck the air from my lungs, and I'm left shocked, dumbfounded, and overly validated. "Eddie . . . I—"

But Carmen isn't buying it. "Hold up," she demands, pulling her legs to her chest and shaking her head. "You just walked in here on your secret mission, trying to save the world, and you looked at Alanna and thought, wow . . . I love that girl. She seems like a good one to save."

My eyes widen, and I study Eddie's face as he squints and his features contort in confusion. "It obviously didn't happen like that," he chuckles in amusement.

"Then how did it happen?" she demands.

Eddie glances at his watch and tightens his jaw. He clears his throat once more before closing his eyes tightly. "My mother was abducted when I was a child. She was kidnapped, taken to a clinic like this, and had the same rare blood type the two of you share. She was murdered for her organs. She died because of organ trafficking. So yeah, when you guys arrived, I took a certain interest in your case, and it made me work my ass off to find a way to take these guys down. I hadn't expected . . . I hadn't expected to be so connected to you, Foster. I never intended to get so emotionally attached. And I love you. So, if it's okay with the two of you, I'd like to save your lives now."

Eddie opens his eyes as Carmen slow claps from her side of the room, and judging by the way she lies back, relaxed, eyes focused on the ceiling, I decide his explanation was good enough, and I clear the sadness from my throat.

"I'm so sorry, Eddie," I mutter softly. "I can't even imagine what it must have been like for you." And I am terribly sad for him. For me, my heart is full of happiness because I know Eddie feels the same way for me as I feel about him, but it has also just broken into millions of pieces because of his mother.

"Yeah," he says, shaking away a fallen tear. "It's been tough on my dad and my younger brother, Juan."

He searches my eyes for some sort of reaction or response, and as I struggle to put these feelings into words—the anger, the hurt, the hope—I can't find them. Instead, I stare into his soul, bite my lip, and open my mouth to speak but stop again. I squeeze him tighter, wanting to hold him forever, wanting to take away his pain, wanting him to be mine and only mine.

"Get us out of here," I say through my sobs. "Please, Eddie. I want to go home."

Chapter Twenty-Two

Now (May 2025) Lina

Hope. Optimism. Panic. Fear. Frustration. That is what we served up to Patrick and Laura Foster upon calling them in the middle of the night and informing them that we have both good news and bad news. The good news is, of course, that to our knowledge, Alanna is alive, and we have her location. The bad news is that she has been and continues to be in extreme danger, and the news about her whereabouts needs to stay confidential. The police department in Mexico still didn't know who was behind the organ-trafficking operation, and if the information was placed in the wrong hands, Alanna's rescue mission would be compromised for sure.

Last night, when Jon and I received the phone call from Eddie, relief flooded over me, and for the first time since the start of Operation Superglue, I felt as though I could breathe again. We said a quick goodbye to the twins, leaving them with Ryker, who held me longer than normal, only releasing me when Jon promised him that he would get me home in one piece. We stopped by the Tempe Police Department and signed off on some critical evidence then headed to the office to pick up some files on Alanna's case and meet up with Travis. He had our boarding passes and passports ready, allowing Jon and me to land in Tijuana, Mexico before dawn the next day.

Now, Jon and I sit hand in hand in an un-air-conditioned office at a police station in Mexico, and I cling to the bag of Alanna's belongings like a lifeline with one hand and squeeze Jon's hand with the other. My head pounds from lack of sleep and probably lack of coffee, and I silently curse myself for wearing the jean shorts that buckle tightly against my lower abdomen, regretting the Kit-Kats and peanut butter cups I've grown addicted to in the place of alcohol, and I make a mental note to get back into my gym routine with Ryker when we return home as it has been actual years since I've needed to go up a size, and over my dead body will it start now.

Operation Cactus Blossom

The flight was just long enough for Jon and me to discuss my negotiables and non-negotiables, as Jon called them. Negotiables were what I would be comfortable doing if Eddie asked us to help rescue Alanna. Of course, my response had been that I would obviously do whatever they needed me to do, but Jon quickly reminded me of my diagnosed PTSD from before my divorce and after Operation Superglue and cautioned me to think this through carefully. Although I wasn't able to successfully set these boundaries, I agreed to taking Operation Cactus Blossom one step at a time, and I promised Jon that if things got too overwhelming, I would put myself and our family first. But even as the promise left my lips, I knew I couldn't guarantee such a thing. We needed to rescue Alanna, and I would stop at nothing to bring her home safely. Absolutely. Nothing.

"What time did he say, again?" I asked Jon, leaning my head against his shoulder.

"Noon. He said he would be here by noon."

"It's noon now," I say, gazing at the small cactus on Eddie's desk. It's small and is the base for two beautiful magenta flowers, fully blossomed, and I smile, hopeful that this nightmare will soon be over for Alanna and her family.

I lift my head off Jon's shoulder and wipe the beads of sweat from my forehead with the back of my hand, and my eyes drift around the office with curiosity. The room is modestly sized, with beige walls adorned with posters highlighting community safety tips and a large, colorful map of Mexico pinned up. His desk, a sturdy metal piece showing signs of wear, is cluttered with case files and a couple of framed family photos. One picture is a family photograph. A man and a woman pose in front of their home with two boys, one much older than the other, and the second is a photo of just the woman. Her beauty is timeless, characterized by her expressive almond-shaped eyes, gleaming with kindness and sincerity. Her skin has a warm, sun-kissed glow. Her long dark hair cascades down her back in soft waves, adorned with a single fresh flower adding a touch of natural elegance to her appearance. If I had to guess, I would assume she was my age when this photo was taken, maybe even a bit younger. *Could this be Eddie's mother? His wife? Oh God. Is Eddie having an affair with Alanna?* I gasp and clutch my stomach as a wave of nausea hits me like a ton of bricks, and for a second, I feel as though I'm going to be sick.

"You, okay?" Jon asks. "If this is too much—"

"It's not," I reassure him. "I'm just tired." I lean forward and sip from the bottle of water given to me upon my arrival. "I'll be okay. It's just nerves."

"You promise?"

"I don't even know what I'm promising at this point." I laugh.

"That you will tell me if—"

But his words are interrupted because the door to the office flies open, and a tall, very handsome young man enters the office, closing the door quickly behind himself. I recognize him from the family photo and breathe a sigh of relief that the woman in the photograph must be his mother. I thank my lucky stars that, as far as I know, this man isn't having an affair with my missing teen.

"I'm Eddie," he says, reaching to shake our hands. He wears dark-washed jeans and a black T-shirt, and his handshake is strong and confident.

"I'm Jon, and this is Lina," Jon says.

I study Eddie, realizing he's younger than I assumed he would be. If Eddie was a character in one of my novels, I would describe him as a young Tenoch Huerta, from Max's favorite movie, *Black Panther*. He is tall and athletic, and his smile is so charming and charismatic that I wouldn't blame Alanna—or any female, for that matter—for falling for him. And as he greets us and takes a seat behind his desk, I can't help but question if he's old enough to drink, then I silently scold myself to pay attention because lives are at stake and this isn't fiction.

"Thank you for coming," Eddie says as he opens his laptop and digs through his desk drawer, retrieving a large manila folder. He organizes the documents into piles on his desk. "I usually visit Foster—I mean Alanna and Carmen—by now. I'm sure they're freaking out, given the circumstances."

"Carmen?" I ask.

"Carmen is Alanna's roommate," he clarifies. "She's a twenty-year-old female from California who was lured into human trafficking through a modeling and acting scam. They've become close friends. She had another roommate, Maria, but unfortunately, she hasn't been as lucky as them."

"What does that mean?" I ask, eyes wide, gripping my stomach as it flips once more. "Did she . . . is she . . ." I can't bring myself to say the words, and Jon places a hand on my knee reassuringly.

"She's in a medically induced coma. She's undergone multiple surgeries. We need to extract her as well," he says, speaking quickly and factually with little emotion, the opposite of what he sounded like on the phone when he begged for our help with Alanna.

"Understood," Jon says in his serious voice.

I'm not sure if the reason is that this intel has become so intense and overwhelming, but I find myself staring at Eddie's photographs, convinced that the woman in the photo must be his mother. But then I grow confused because peeking out behind the first framed photograph is another family photo, in which Eddie is older and is standing in front of a desert sunset with a young boy, an adult male, and another woman not featured in any of the other photos. She is tall and slender, with short curly black hair.

"Lina?" Jon asks. "Where did you go?"

"Oh, me?" I ask awkwardly, wiping sweat from my neck and squirming uncomfortably. "I'm great. Don't worry about me." I resist the urge to ask more about Maria and Carmen, stopping myself from going down my usual rabbit hole, which leads to feeling empathy toward their mourning mothers. Instead I say, "I was just admiring your photographs. Is that you?" I ask, pointing to the first family photo.

"That's me, yes," he says, clearing his throat. "That was quite some time ago."

I know Jon is going to kill me with his bare hands if I continue taking this conversation places it shouldn't go, but I can't help it. My author brain is intrigued, and I suddenly have a hunch that Eddie's investment in this undercover operation isn't only about Alanna. "Is that your mom?"

"Lina—" Jon starts.

But Eddie holds up a hand and nods in approval. "Yes, that was my mother, Lupe."

Damnit, Lina, I silently scold myself as Jon kicks my foot softly under the chair. "I'm sorry for being nosy. Forgive me."

"No, no, it's okay," Eddie says, chewing on his bottom lip. "My mother died when I was ten years old."

"I'm so sorry. Was she sick?" I ask, crossing my arms over my chest, feeling incredibly sorry for him.

"She was kidnapped," he says, his eyes shifting to the floor. "She was sold into organ trafficking, and a medical procedure went wrong. She was only thirty-five years old."

I sit up straighter, a bit stunned because Lupe was pretty much my age when she passed away, and I regret my question as soon as I ask it because Eddie is rising from his seat and gripping his family photo like he would give anything to hop into it like Bert in *Mary Poppins* with his chalk drawings. Then he shifts his gaze to the other photo, and I feel even worse when I realize that the woman in the other photo could be a stepmother. So, in true Lina fashion, I do what I do best. I make an awkward situation even more awkward.

"Is that your stepmom?"

Jon looks like he's going to spontaneously combust, but Eddie and I ignore him. "Her?" Eddie asks with a roll of the eyes. "I guess you could call her that. Her name is Rosa. She's dating my father, but they never married. She's a highly respected pediatrician in our community, and my father worships the ground she walks on."

"Why didn't they marry?" I ask Eddie for selfish reasons I'm sure I don't need to explain at this point.

"She's sort of stuck up. There is no doubt in my mind that she loves my father, but there is a part of me who thinks she's too good for him. I . . . I won't bore you with the details, but she and my mother were childhood friends. The fact that Rosa and my father ended up together was a plot twist my brother Juan and I hadn't expected."

"I'm an author," I say, enthusiastically. "I love a good plot twist."

But when Jon and Eddie stare at me blankly, I realize I've reached a point of no return and can't take that last remark back, so I shift in my seat and say,

"Sorry. I'm nervous rambling. How can we help? Whatever you need, I'm here."

"That's good news," Eddie says, placing the photographs back on his bookshelf and sitting in his chair. "Because I *do* need your help. There has been a recent development, and with your help, I believe we can extract the girls and take down the entire operation. It would take a small miracle, but I'm convinced we can do it."

"We are all ears," Jon says, taking out a notebook and a pen as I do the same. "I'm sure we don't have any time to waste," he adds, which stings a bit because it is most definitely directed my way.

"Oh," I say, raising my hand like I did in my Gemma days. "We've named the operation."

Jon's cheeks flush a shade of red, and he bites his lip, clearly annoyed with me. "We don't need to spend time on that," he says, calmer than I expect, considering I've hijacked this meeting in ways I myself never even imagined possible.

"No, it's all right," Eddie says, his accent thick. "I'm curious. What did you name it?"

"Operation Cactus Blossom," I say proudly, gesturing toward the flowering cactus on Eddie's desk.

Jon looks like he wants to crawl under the desk in embarrassment, but the name strikes Eddie in a way I don't expect.

"Because she's brave, strong, and resilient," I explain, biting down on my pen's cap.

"And . . . beautiful," Eddie adds, his tone soft and somewhat vulnerable, and he clears his throat and runs his fingers over his chin before getting it together and continuing. "We will need to execute this in phases," Eddie explains, glancing at his watch and noting the time. "Phase one will include forging the test results. There is a client negotiating over 1.2 million for the heart. I'm going to tamper with the results so both Carmen and Alanna won't be a match, but I need to do it quickly before we are too late."

"I hope that works," I say, jotting down *1.2 million holy shit* on my notepad. "What is phase two?"

"That's where you come in," Eddie says, eyebrows raised.

"Me?"

"Yes, you. Because even if I can eliminate Alanna and Carmen from being a match, I *need* this buyer to come forward. With a transaction like this, the leader of the organization will be revealed, as will the buyer. I will be able to identify the head of the organization, and I will need to evidence the transaction *while* it is going down."

"Okay?" I ask, still not sure what Eddie needs me to do.

"Absolutely not. No way in hell," Jon says, slamming his fist against his notepad and tightening his jaw.

"How do you even know what you're saying no to?" I ask, arms crossed over my chest, cheeks burning. "He hasn't even asked me to do anything yet."

Eddie looks from Jon to me and back again, clearly curious about our banter and the protective way Jon stares me down. "I can give you two a moment if you need it."

"I don't need a moment," I snap. "Please tell me how I can help."

"Unbelievable," Jon says with an overly dramatic exhalation.

I wave him off like an annoying fly and turn toward Eddie. "Please," I say. "At least tell me your plan before counting me out."

"I don't think your dad wants you to—"

"For the love of God, I'm not her dad. I'm her . . ." His voice trails off because trying to define what we are at this point is like trying to explain to my children what life was like before Wi-Fi: impossible.

"It's complicated," I say with a slight roll of the eyes. "Please, Eddie. Tell us your plan."

"There's a shipment arriving this evening."

"A shipment?" I ask.

"Of victims, Lina. There is a shipment of kidnapped humans arriving tonight," Jon hisses.

"Yes. They arrive tonight. It is another group of young females. You see, most of the victims that arrive at the clinic are girls that were targeted for human trafficking but because of their rare blood types end up here."

"You need me to . . ."

"I need you to go under as an organ-trafficking victim, Lina. And I'm going to forge your test results. You will be grouped with Alanna and Carmen. And you—"

"You will be a match, Lina." Jon interrupts, running his fingers through his chin's scruff. "You will go undercover as an organ-trafficking pawn who is a match for the 1.2-million-dollar heart. Isn't that correct, Eddie?"

"Yes, that is accurate," he says, wiping his forehead with the back of a hand. "Once the transaction is complete and we've identified the client and the seller, we can extract you too."

"That's not going to work for us," Jon grunts, arms crossed. "We need another plan. There has to be a way we can get Alanna out of there that doesn't involve trading Alanna for Lina."

"I'll do it," I say, knowing that if I walk away from this, I could never live with myself.

"Like hell you will," Jon counters, standing from his chair and raising his voice. "I almost lost you once, Lina. I'm not sending you in there to some third-world butcher shop. It's *not* happening."

"Do you have a better idea, Jon? Do you? Because I haven't been able to recover from Operation Superglue . . . knowing Alanna was still out there. Knowing I couldn't bring her home to her family. Knowing I could have done better, worked faster. I *need* this, Jon."

Eddie stares awkwardly up at Jon and me, now nose to nose, arms crossed, voices raised. "Why don't I give you two some time," Eddie says, clearing his throat and standing to his feet. "My team is working on swapping out the test results for Alanna and Carmen. Also, I haven't stopped by to visit them yet today. I'm sure they're growing increasingly anxious. I'll be back shortly, and we can devise a strategy then."

"Sounds like a plan," Jon says, not taking his eyes from mine, his face and neck turning various shades of purple as he tightens his jaw. "We will talk about phase two and see if we can come up with something a little less reckless, desperate, suicidal, insane . . ."

"I think he gets it," I say. "Please, take your time," I say, closing my notebook and glaring at Jon while Eddie rises from his chair.

"Copy," Eddie says as he closes his laptop and exits the room.

The door hasn't even closed behind Eddie before Jon leaps to his feet and begins pacing around the office, fists clenched by his sides. "Are you insane?" he asks through gritted teeth.

"I'm sorry," I say, my tone matching his. "I thought we came to Mexico to save Alanna. If you have something else of importance that you need to do, then I'm all for it," I snap as I stand from my chair and face my now very annoyed and irritated ex-husband.

"The answer is no. You are not going to be a match for the buyer's heart."

Heat rises within me as a wildfire spread through my insides. "Contrary to popular belief, Jon Cote," I say, "you're *not* my father. You can't tell me what to do."

"Ha!" He chuckles, shaking his head from side to side, stepping closer to me so our faces are mere centimeters apart. "I may not be your father, but I'm your . . ." His voice trails off because defining our relationship is harder than implementing a plan to rescue Alanna. "I'm your boss," he says when he can't come up with anything else.

"Like hell you are," I say, packing up my belongings, a wave of nausea flooding over me.

"Lina, where are you going?"

"I'm going to find Eddie. I'm going to tell him that I'm all in. And you can kiss my—"

But my words are interrupted because Jon's mouth is pressed against mine and his hands clutch my arms, and I'm no longer in Mexico in Eddie's stuffy and utterly miserable little office. I'm Lina again . . . Jon's Lina. Max and Lucy's mom. Ryker and Daphne's friend. And I surrender to his kiss and the electricity that shoots from his body into mine like cool water on the hottest of days. His lips move from my lips up to my nose, to one cheek then the next, and land on my forehead.

He softly whispers, "*We* can't afford to lose you."

I nod in agreement and whisper back, "Plan B?"

I devour my last bite of nachos and smile approvingly at Eddie's office wall. It took us over two hours, but we devised an extraction plan that doesn't put my life at risk as much as the first plan. We've brainstormed some strategies, and now, it's time to piece the steps together, careful not to miss any.

"I feel good about this," I say confidently to Eddie and Jon.

"Thoughts?" Eddie asks Jon, who is staring at the wall and biting on his pen, his expression no-nonsense and his eyes stern.

"Strategically, it makes sense." Jon looks at me. "If I take *you* out of the equation, I don't have a problem with it."

My heart flutters, and a wave of dread encompasses me. I don't want to worry Jon. And I'm nervous about my role in this too. Obviously, I don't want to put myself in danger. I've never been so aware of my people back home, how much I love them, and how much they love me in return, especially my kids. But I *need* to do this. Rescuing Alanna is nonnegotiable. Also, now that we've diverted to plan B, Jon's involvement is a higher risk than I would like, and because of this, I have to work extra hard to shake off a feeling of dread growing in the pit of my stomach.

"I get it," I tell Jon as I take his hand in mine. "I don't want anything to happen to you either. But we *need* to get Alanna home to Patrick and Laura. It's, like, literally our job."

Jon's face softens, and he nods. "All right, Eddie, let's take this one step at a time. I want to go over everything again in my mind to make sure we haven't missed anything."

Eddie glances at his watch and nods. "My guys are getting a team together. We have roughly an hour before the shipment arrives at the clinic, and we need to beat them by a solid twenty."

"Then let's get to it," I say, leaping to my feet and gripping Jon's hand for dear life, realizing that this is happening, and our little class review here is just to ease our nerves.

"Phase one," Eddie says, his tone reminding me of crime television. "Infiltration. We insert Lina into the clinic during the shipment's arrival with the help of my confidential informant, who will also ensure she remains close by. We good with this?" Eddie asks like he is confirming we're all in agreement that ordering burgers and shakes from Five Guys sounds like a hell of a good plan for dinner.

"Yes," Jon and I agree in unison, and we squeeze our hands together so tight that mine begins to hurt, but I don't pull away.

"And don't forget we have these," Eddie says, gesturing to the three sets of inner earbuds a police officer dropped off just minutes prior.

He hands two to me and two to Jon before retrieving his cell from his desk, sending what appears to be a text, and pausing to read a response before returning his gaze to our tactical board. I take this moment to pull Jon close. I stand, facing him, and wrap my arms around his lower back and nuzzle my cheek to his chest. No words are spoken out loud, but the sincerity of this moment is what we both need. And even though we're both hot and sweaty and my nachos aren't agreeing with me and I'm most likely experiencing some level of caffeine withdrawal, I'm sending him all the silent promises in the world that things are going to be all right.

Just as each beat of Jon's heart reassures me that we'll both make it out of this alive, Eddie says, "Foster's test results have been cleared. She isn't a match for the heart. I couldn't forge Carmen's. I'll explain why later, but plan A is entirely out, and we need to get working . . . We need to get going on plan B. Time is of the essence now even more," he reports, shaking his head and running his fingers anxiously through his hair, and I resist the urge to tell Eddie that this is actually plan C. But I don't because if Eddie wasn't able to tamper with Carmen's results, shit just got real really fast. "Ready to discuss phase two?"

Jon clears his throat and mutters, "Affirmative."

"Yes . . . I mean affirmative," I say, imitating Jon's tone, which, believe it or not, makes him smile.

He kisses my temple and wraps his arm around my shoulder before whispering, "You good?"

I nod my head yes, my eyes stuck to our board.

"Phase two," Eddie says, a bit louder this time, and I can't help but notice that he's growing increasingly more and more serious and revved up as the seconds tick away. "Now that Carmen is a match for the heart, we need to assume that she is already being prepped for surgery," he predicts, wiping his forehead with the back of one hand, and it doesn't take a private investigator—even though I am one—to know that Eddie is very worried about Alanna and probably, even more so, worried about Alanna's response to Carmen being wheeled away into surgery. "In phase two, we allow Carmen's heart transplant surgery to begin. I will perform my usual surgical duties, which consist of standing by and observing the medical equipment and providing the doctors with any necessary data. And just before the surgery begins, I will send a signal to Jon, who will lead the charge past security and into the operating room."

"Copy," Jon says as my stomach tightens because this is the part I like the least.

Jon will be entering the clinic undercover as a criminal attempting to intercept Carmen's heart. He will lead the charge, armed and ready to take down anyone who stands in his way.

"And I'll have my inner ears, right? So, I'll be able to listen in?" I ask, my voice shuddering unexpectedly.

"Yes, ma'am," Eddie says as Jon takes my hand again.

"And now that Carmen is actually going into surgery, this means that Jon will need to take hostages in order to keep Carmen safe."

"Dr. Lopez and me." Eddie nods, still way too chill for the situation. "And when Dr. Lopez hands Carmen over to Jon and his team—because no doubt about it, he will—they will lead Dr. Lopez and me out of the room along with the other medical staff, and the doctor that we have standing by will care for Carmen."

"Right," I say, searching my memory for the details we discussed earlier. "And you will keep your cover so you can hopefully, eventually identify the leader of the clinic, along with the buyer later on."

"Correct," Eddie says. "Our goal is to refrain from using force. But we will if necessary."

"When's the last time you fired a weapon?" I ask Jon in my mom voice, and the death stare he gives me in return is enough to keep me from asking any more questions about that.

Eddie appears to find our banter amusing but continues talking over us regardless. "Jon's team will also extract Maria, who is being kept alive on life support. With that being said, timing and our communication is going to be critical."

"Understood," Jon says.

"Of course," I say, knowing full well that at this point in the operation, my radio will be used only for listening and that once I'm in my room with Alanna, there will be nothing I can do but wait.

"On to secondary extraction," Eddie says, glancing again at his watch. His words pick up speed as he paces around the tiny office. "Jon will lead his team away from the building and toward our safe zone with Carmen and Maria, where we will have a medical team standing by. At this point, another team will simultaneously move to extract Alanna and Lina and lead them to the safe zone as well."

"We'll have our Cactus Blossom," I say, smiling up at Jon with hopeful eyes. "Finally."

"Yes," Eddie says, his eyes glazing over. "We will have our Cactus Blossom."

"And then the final phase," Jon says, keeping his tone businesslike. "The buyer."

"Yes." Eddie breaks free from his daydream. "In the final phase, Jon will interrogate the clinic's staff for the buyer's whereabouts. He will take Carmen's intercepted heart, which is a cow's heart, and once the sale is made, my team will apprehend the buyer, who will then lead us to the ringleader of the organization, completely shutting down the clinic—finally."

"Sounds like a plan," I say through a hopeful smile.

"You sure about this?" Jon asks, pulling me close and tilting my chin up to meet his gaze.

"Operation Cactus Blossom for life," I say in my Gemma voice.

"We'd better get started, then," Eddie says, gathering various items from his desk and adjusting his comm in his ears.

"I almost forgot," I say, reaching under my chair and retrieving the bag of Alanna's things. "Make sure you give this to her after this is over. There is something—or someone, I should say—in here that I'm sure she misses very much."

Eddie opens the bag and pulls out the small stuffed bear with a patch covering one eye, and suddenly, the once-tough exterior of the undercover police officer standing before us shatters, and standing before Jon and me is a scared, broken-hearted, twentysomething man holding the stuffed bear of a woman he loves. "It's Patches," he says, choking back tears. "Patches the Bear."

"When all this is over, you can give it to her," I say optimistically, knowing this whole plan is a long shot and the odds are against us.

Eddie pauses, weighing his options, staring from Jon, to me, and back again. "No," he says, his gaze narrowing, an idea formulating in his mind. "Patches is going in with you. Trust me—you're going to need him."

Chapter Twenty-Three

Now (May 2025) Alanna

At roughly dinner time, the flock of mystery doctors and nurses barges into our room, catching Carmen and me off guard, resulting in sheer panic and a downward spiral of emotions. My blood boils angrily inside me as my heart rate increases and my insides tighten. *Where is Eddie? Was he able to manipulate the results? What is going on? Is this it? Is this how my story ends?* I close my eyes and stiffen my body in anticipation of whatever is coming my way, preparing for the worst as two nurses urgently approach my bed to remove my IV port then—*Wait, what?* They turn and walk away. *Yes!* Eddie did it. He really did it. He was able to fabricate the results so that I wasn't a match. I try to hide my smile, but it's no use. I hug the Purple Bunny of Courage tightly under my chin, and I thank my lucky stars for such a break and commend Eddie, my hero, who promised he would get us out of here. He is staying true to that promise.

"No!" Carmen howls, bursting my balloon of happiness before it can even fully inflate.

I gaze over at Carmen and freeze like a deer in headlights. *No. No, no, no, no, no. What is happening?* "Carmen!" I wail over the chaos of doctors and nurses yelling loudly in Spanish, bossing each other around, and pinning Carmen to her bed against her will. "Carmen!" I yell again, yanking at my handcuffed wrist, needing to get to her, needing to stop them. But I can't. Carmen is the only family I have left, and that family is being violently ripped from me, and there's nothing I can do.

"Alanna!" she screams. "Alanna, help!"

My legs turn to jelly, and my thoughts are scattered and spinning together like an invisible tornado sweeping through my mind at lightning speed. "Carmen!" I cry. "Stop! Please! Don't take her! Leave her alone! Take me!"

But it's no use. Three nurses hold Carmen down on her bed as a doctor injects a syringe of something into her arm, and her eyes meet mine for one last plea. In reality, her eyes interlock with mine for a second at most. But for me, it's a lifetime. The world as I know it comes to a screeching halt, and everything freezes. Carmen is drowning, and I can't save her. Carmen needs me, and I can't help her, and I'm stuck. My stare is stuck to Carmen's like superglue. Then, just like that, her eyes close. The life drains from her fragile body, and she drifts peacefully to sleep.

A guard opens the door, and they wheel her out into the hallway, the door creaking closed with a dramatic bang louder than usual. Then—silence, and I am reminded of a scene from my mother's favorite movie, *Titanic*—when Rose and Jack grip the stern's railing surrounded by chaos and sheer panic, and they both take that ginormous deep breath before heading under the water, and the eerie silence encompasses the big screen because the ship is gone. Just. Gone.

"You're all monsters!" I roar. "I hate you! I hate all of you!" The anger pains pulse through me, the trauma of everything I've endured coming to a head. I scream, and I sob. I pull so hard on my cuffs that my wrist begins to bleed, but I don't care. I feel nothing. I'm done. I quit. I'm giving up. I'm bailing on any hope that I will get out of here. I'm giving up on Eddie. My knight in shining armor has once again turned villain. Eddie *promised*. He promised that he would keep both of us safe, and he didn't keep his promise. Clearly, he tampered with my test results but not Carmen's. Apparently, to Eddie, Carmen wasn't worth saving. He could've saved her, but he chose not to. Eddie is obviously choosing taking down the clinic over saving both Carmen and me. I know, in the depths of my soul, I will never forgive him. So I do nothing else—just scream.

Finally, when my throat hurts from my outburst, and the pain in my wounded wrist becomes too much to bear, I chuck the Purple Bunny of Courage to the other side of the room, silently declare Eddie the devil, roll onto my side, and close my eyes, wishing that they took me instead of Carmen. I will never in a million years recover from this. I'm deciding now is the moment when I quit. I give up. And you know what? I'm fine with that. I have nothing left to live for, anyway.

I don't know how long I've been sleeping, and I don't care. Judging by my growling stomach and full bladder, I can only assume hours have passed. My body is weak from the exhaustion I inflicted upon myself, and I feel like a toddler after a no-nap tantrum, hungover from my outburst but rested against my will. My wrist has been bandaged, and my handcuff has been removed while I snoozed away. I pull myself to a seated position, surprised to see the Purple Bunny of Courage back on my bed, perched innocently by my feet, and I'm startled when I look to my left, where Carmen's bed once was, to find I have a new roommate, which enrages me in a way I can't comprehend. Carmen is *gone*. The existence of this new person in her place confirms it. And it's all Eddie's fault. I will never forgive him, and I decide, for the time being at least, that I will ignore her. What's the use? One of us will probably be dead soon anyway.

So instead of greeting the person in the bed next to me, a pretty woman with olive-colored skin and highlighted brunette hair, I make my way to the bathroom but stop short when I notice my wrist and a Sharpie tattoo that was not there earlier. This is new. It's another heart sketched in black Sharpie, similar to the one I received when I started to connect with Eddie. *Eddie. Why would he take the time for such a grand gesture at a time like this? Is it his way of saying sorry? Does he have a plan? Am I giving up on him too quickly? Or is this the manipulation that Carmen accused him of, his way of pulling me back to him even though he effed up? Is this some sort of toxic emotional cycle: wash, rinse, repeat?*

I exit the restroom and plop back onto my bed, rubbing my injured wrist just as my new roommate rises to her feet and approaches me. Her expression is awkward as hell, and she smiles like she knows me, and for some reason, this lights my defenses on fire, and I freeze, unable to speak, unable to tell her to stand back and stay away, and instead of defending myself like I feel the need to do, my chin begins to quiver, and I freeze, staring blankly at her, allowing tears to flow freely down my cheeks, sitting like a statue.

"Hi," she says, her eyes also welling with tears. She wears the same hospital gown I once wore, but she's acting different, like a mom picking up her child after months of summer camp. She doesn't seem scared, and she doesn't seem afraid. *How can she not be terrified? If she was kidnapped like I was, she would be scared, right?*

"Hi?" I ask more than say as I scooch back into bed, pull my stuffed bunny to my chest, and decide now would be a good time to ignore her. The last thing I need is to get attached to this person, whoever she is.

So I roll onto my side, turning away from her and closing my eyes again. I'm not a rude person by nature, but this lady has no idea what she is in for, and I won't be the person to break the news that her life as she knew it is over. *Nope. Didn't sign up for that.*

"Alanna, right?"

Apparently, this chick didn't get the memo. So I roll over and glare at her, stone cold. With my eyes narrowed, I bite my lip, feeling overly defensive, knowing that no matter what I do now, nothing will bring Carmen back, and for that reason and that reason only, I refuse to participate in this conversation. "No hablo inglés."

Her smile softens. "My name is Lina," she says, placing a gentle hand on my shoulder and ignoring my sorry attempt at Spanish. "I'm here to help."

"Help?" I laugh. "Okay, sure. Like Eddie was going to help Carmen. Make yourself comfy, Lina. You're gonna be here a while."

"No, really," she repeats. "I'm . . . I'm a private investigator," she says, seeming a bit too proud of herself for this situation, and I believe she realizes this because she shakes her head and clears her throat. "I've been hired to find you. I've been looking for you for, like, *ever*."

"Don't screw with me. I've been through enough."

Lina decides it's appropriate to sit on the edge of my bed. I contemplate kicking her but decide against it because something about the way she stares at me and places a gentle hand on my shoulder feels maternal, like how my mom might approach me. This not only catches me off guard, it causes me to cry harder.

"It's okay. I have kids just about your age. Trust me, I wouldn't screw with you."

"You don't look old enough to have teenagers," I say.

Lina seems unfazed by my comment. "Your parents, Patrick and Laura, they're worried about you, Alanna."

I freeze. *How the hell does this woman know my parents?* My stomach flips, and the tears fall even more freely. I chew on my lip so hard that I'm sure it's bleeding, and I realize I've been holding my breath. This must be a trick, and I'm done falling for these false promises. Nobody, not even Eddie is here to help me.

"I said don't screw with me," I repeat through my intense sobs. "Did Eddie send you? He's an effing liar, you know. If he promised you anything, don't believe him."

Lina nods in response. "You're upset with Eddie because your friend was taken away."

Then I realize that not only is this impostor *not* a private investigator, she's also not a kidnapping victim. Paranoia consumes me, and because of this, I've met my limit, so I form my injured hand into a fist and punch my pillow so hard that it shakes my bed. "How do you know that?" I snap. "You're one of *them*, aren't you? Carmen said I couldn't trust him. I should've listened. Maybe if I had listened to her, she would've had a chance. There's nothing you can say to prove to me you are here to help. There is nothing *anyone* can say."

The sides of Lina's mouth curl into a half smile. "He knows you well," she says, her tone even-keeled.

"Excuse me?"

"He thought you might say that."

"Who?"

"Eddie. Hold on a sec," she says, then heads back to her bed, reaches under her pillow, and returns to my bedside with—*No way.* No way in hell is that what I think it is.

"Is that . . ." I start, but I can't finish my sentence because I've ripped Patches the Bear from Lina's grip and pressed him to my face, long animalistic wails escaping from somewhere deep inside me, and I morph into a toddler version of myself, crying into Patches the Bear, a naïve, childish wave of hope washing over me. Maybe, just maybe, this person might be here to help. *But what if Patches is just another decoy?* Those sleazy dudes from the bus stop took all my stuff. But I want to trust Lina. I *need* to trust Lina. What other choice do I have?

"Patches the Bear," Lina says, placing an arm around my shoulders. "You can trust me, Alanna."

"No," I say, gripping him close and shaking my head. "The guys who kidnapped me. They took him. They could have just as easily given him to you."

"Ace and Slinky." She nods. "Those guys are scumbags. They kidnapped me, too, once . . . Long story . . . but I didn't get him from them. They pawned your stuff. I came across Patches at my local pawn shop."

I inhale the smell of cigars, cigarettes, and something else I can't quite make out, and somehow, I start to believe her. "They pawned my *bear*? Seriously?"

"Seriously," she says with a roll of her eyes. "You can trust me."

I want to believe her, but I'm at a loss for words, so we sit in silence until I say, "I was kidnapped. I didn't run away."

"Oh, trust me, I know."

"You do?"

"Yes. And I can't imagine what you've gone through. But Alanna . . . if you can trust me, take one more leap of faith. We will get you out of here."

"Okay," I sniff. "But I'm not leaving here without Carmen and Maria."

"Deal," she says, reaching her hand out to me.

But I can't help myself. I throw my arms around her shoulders and cry into her neck, clinging to her like I would cling to my own mom.

"It's going to be okay, Alanna. It's going to be okay."

Chapter Twenty-Four

Now (May 2025) Lina

A wave of nausea washes over me as I silently scold myself for drinking the tap water upon my arrival to the clinic. How did that slip my mind? I had been traumatized when Charlotte, in the *Sex and the City* movie, opened her mouth in the shower for one brief second in Mexico and ended up shitting her pants in front of Carrie, Samantha, and Miranda. For that reason and that reason alone, I swore off drinking anything but bottled water while traveling *anywhere*. But an upset stomach is the least of my worries. The tension in Eddie's office escalated quickly when Jon became heated over my going undercover as an organ donor, but I couldn't blame him. The three of us agreed that Eddie would do what he could with Alanna and Carmen's results, and we would go from there. Alanna's results were easy to manipulate because although she is a match for the buyer, she has higher sensitization levels, which makes her *less* of a match. Carmen, on the other hand, not only has a compatible blood type but has a better HLA match and lower sensitization levels, which makes her a better donor. Forging those results would be nearly impossible and very risky, which left us with one option and one option only: Carmen.

Eddie knew Alanna would be devastated upon Carmen being taken into surgery, which is why he sent me in with Patches the Bear. He understood her history and trauma enough to know that being reunited with a piece of her former life and childhood would help keep her grounded just enough so that we could pull off the next phase in Operation Cactus Blossom, which is not only significantly more dangerous than we'd originally planned, especially for Carmen, but it also means Jon will need to have a heavier involvement in the operation than intended, and both Jon and I both risking our lives at the same time is unsettling, to say the least.

That is why, before I allowed Eddie's colleague to toss me into a van filled with organ-trafficking victims, I called Ryker and Daphne and made them both promise they would be there for our kids if we didn't make it out of this alive, which is unfortunately a reality that I might not be fully processing, but even still, I refuse to quit until Alanna, Carmen, Maria, and the other victims are reunited with their families.

"How much longer?" Alanna asks as she brings her knees to her chest, squeezing her stuffed bunny and Patches the Bear to her stomach. Her already pale skin is now transparent from lack of sunshine, and I can't look away from her veiny arms, pausing when I notice the scars, scabs, and bruises from what I assume to be her blood draws.

"It should be any minute now," I say, struggling myself. I press my finger to my right earbud and secure the other into Alanna's ear so that she can listen too. The absence of windows and a clock make it difficult to know what time it is, let alone if it is day or night. "If things go as planned, we will be out of here in no time," I say with a comforting smile even though I'm resisting the urge to vomit all over my hospital gown.

Our plan is anything but simple. "Sorry, it's just a lot to remember, and I don't want to screw it up," she confesses.

"Of course," I say, crossing the room and taking a seat on the edge of her bed, pausing for a moment while a stomach pain passes.

"Are you all right?"

"Yeah," I moan. "My stomach is just upset. I drank the water."

"Oh." She nods in understanding. "Yeah, that takes some getting used to, for sure."

"I've been through worse," I wink, glancing around our hospital room, which feels more like a jail cell, and my heart breaks for Alanna and her friends because I can't bear to spend one more minute here, let alone years. The walls are painted a cold, clinical white, lack any decoration, and amplify the sense of isolation. Our beds are narrow and uncomfortable, with thin white sheets, and are pushed against the walls, their metal frames jagged and uninviting, and the buzzing of the fluorescent bulbs, the only light in our room, causes my head to pound and my stomach to churn even more.

"Okay," I say, counting to five, and trying with all my might to appear collected. "We completed phase one, which was forging your test results. We didn't tamper with the results for both you and Carmen because not only would that be way too suspicious, but it prevents Eddie and his team from catching their guy. You understand that now, correct?"

"I guess." She frowns. "It's just . . . poor Carmen." She sniffs. "Why couldn't it have been me?" She wipes a tear from her cheek with the back of her hand and runs her fingers through her tangled blonde hair.

I nod in agreement, resisting the urge to admit that I, too, had offered myself up as organ-donor bait to help shut down the operation, but I decided that detail is unimportant, at least for now. "You're a great friend," I say soothingly. "Yes, Carmen is in danger. And I didn't ask Eddie to explain why he made the choice he made, but I do know that *all* of our lives are in danger, his included."

"That doesn't help." She chuckles nervously.

"It's the truth," I say firmly. "So, phase one is complete. Phase two is where it gets more difficult. Carmen is prepped for surgery, and Eddie is standing by as he normally would in case the team has questions about the medical equipment or data he's compiled on the client's case, which puts him in the perfect spot to not only watch over Carmen, but also to act as the victim when Jon arrives. His cue to Jon to move in will be *'Todo se ve bien aquí,'* which means 'Everything looks good here.' It's what he would typically say during this sort of situation."

"I'm glad Eddie will be watching over Carmen."

I nod as I imagine animal claws ripping apart my insides, and I resist the urge to run to the restroom. "Right before the doctor operates, Jon and a team of police officers will infiltrate the clinic. They will be undercover, and it will appear to be a raid, an attack on the organ donor for the rare heart. During the attack, Eddie will act as a victim of the invasion, and he will be treated by Jon's team like he is part of the hospital staff."

"Will . . . will Jon hurt him?" She asks for the millionth time, and I keep my patience in check, realizing this poor girl is terrified and has been through hell and back again, and the least I can do is repeat myself.

"Jon will be armed, but the team plans on operating peacefully, only using force if necessary. So Eddie should be fine."

"Okay," she says, squeezing her eyes shut, pressing her fingers to her earpiece, and nodding.

"Jon will be leading the charge and will demand, upon taking over the clinic, that the surgery stop immediately, that he is here for the heart, and that he isn't taking no for an answer. He will instruct Dr. Lopez and his team to back off and allow his surgeon to take over. He will tell them that as long as the doctor hands over the two bodies he's here to intercept, nobody will get hurt. His cue that everything has gone smoothly will be when he says, 'Dr. Serrano will take it from here,' and that will be our cue to sit against the wall to the left side of the door."

"Dr. Serrano will take it from here," Alanna says with a nod. "Does Jon speak Spanish?" she asks.

"No," I say, realizing that none of us thought about this major detail. "I'm sure Eddie will help translate if necessary."

"I hope you're right, Lina."

"You and me both." I squeeze her hand. "And while the team is distracted in the operating room on the north side of the building," I say, pointing north, "Eddie's team will target the south side of the building and come for us, while Jon meets with the buyer and the police take down the buyer during the exchange. Does that make sense?"

"Yes," she says with hesitation. "I'm just still confused. Without the heart, Eddie won't have his buyer."

"That's correct, which is why Jon and the team will have the other heart, remember?"

"Oh yeah." She chuckles. "Sorry. It's just a lot. I forgot about the cow's heart."

"Jon and his team will apprehend the doctors and the clinic staff, and the police will take them out the south side of the building after our release. Jon will accompany the surgeon and will take the cow's heart with Eddie for transport, where they will complete the transaction and take down the operation. When this is complete Jon will say, 'Mission accomplished.'"

Alanna is quiet for a moment before muttering, "That's a lot. And Carmen will be under anesthesia, and Maria is still in a medically induced coma. Will they be okay?"

This is the first time Alanna has asked this question, and for the life of me, I have no idea how to respond. So instead, I take her hand in mine and smile at her just as I would if I was comforting Lucy. "I know Eddie will take good care of them," I say. "But you and I need to be ready to go."

"I'm *so* ready," she says, smiling for the first time since I met her, and although she presents as a battered victim who's been living a nightmare for the last two years, I can't help but admire how stunningly beautiful she remains. She truly is my Cactus Blossom, and I'm ready to get her the hell out of here.

"*So* ready," I repeat. "And you remember the code names I told you about and the cue for us to be ready?"

"Carmen is Desert Rose," she says with a smile, "and Maria is Desert Moon."

"And me?" I ask, giggling to ease Alanna's anxiety but also because I forced Jon to name me against his will.

"Prickly Pear," she says, with a raise of her eyebrows. "But I still don't get it. Why is that your name?"

"It's kind of a long story." I chuckle. "And our cue? Our way for Jon to tell us that the team is coming for us?"

"He's going to say, 'Dr. Serrano will take it from here.'"

"That's right. Good job."

"My code name, Cactus Blossom. You came up with it?"

Heat rises to my cheeks, and I nod. "Yes, I did. Talking with your parents, your friends, and your teachers . . . they all said the same things about you."

"What did they say?" she asks, shifting awkwardly on the edge of the bed.

"They all knew with one hundred percent certainty that you were a survivor. They all knew you would have the courage and the strength to survive any situation, but they also described you as one of the kindest and most loving girls they had the pleasure of knowing. They *all* knew you were special, and so did I. Jon and I were not stopping until you were safe."

"Thank you," she says, wiping a tear from her eye. "I had some really great friends."

"You still do," I reminded her.

"Hank and Bill, they are going to kill me for not telling them about Lincoln."

"They are going to be happy you're all right."

"You don't know my friend, Hank," she says, rolling her eyes and shaking her head. She pulls her bare knees to her chest and squeezes them. "He's gonna be pissed."

I think about Hank Gallagher for a beat, and I wonder just how much needs to be shared with Alanna, especially in this moment, because the first time I met Penelope Gallagher was at swimming lessons when Hank and Bill were three years old. It feels like yesterday that Hank was a chunky little toddler with a shaggy head of ginger hair and ginormous orange arm floaties. Aside from that, when I was undercover as Gemma Mendoza, it was Hank that I flirted with to get intel on the missing girls. That's interesting, considering the night Hank talked about Alanna, he emphasized her connection with Zach the quarterback. He hadn't gone into detail about him and Alanna being as close as she is mentioning. It's a lot to take in, for sure, and as I study Alanna and her anxious demeanor, I decide that the less she knows at this point, the better.

So instead of explaining that I do know Hank, that I hit on him when I was undercover as a high school senior, and that his mother hired us to prove that her husband is having an affair at the gym, I simply smile and say, "Your friends and family miss you. They love you, and they want you to come home."

This brings tears to her eyes, and she stifles a choked sob before nodding. "I know. Thank you. It's just crazy to think that I might be going home."

"Look at me, Alanna. You *are* going home."

"So much could go wrong," she sobs. "And . . ." She mutters a quiet, "Never mind."

"What? What is it?" I ask, placing a gentle hand on her shoulder.

"It's nothing," she says, wiping her tears with Patches the Bear.

"Listen," I say, like I'm comforting one of my children. "I've been through trauma, and it was nothing like you experienced. *When* you go home, you're going to need to get someone to help you through this. You're going to have to be open about what you're feeling. And that starts here and now, with me."

"This room. It's all I know. I'm . . . I'm scared."

"Of course you are. You've been gone two years. But this room, these walls . . . they aren't your home."

"Carmen . . . and Eddie. I don't know if I can leave them. They've been my family for so long."

I tuck a strand of tangled blond tresses behind her ear and pull her close in a motherly embrace. "It's going to get better," I say. Even though my experiences have been different, I know what it's like to be this terrified about merging the past with the present. "Every day will get better."

"Thank—" Alanna starts, but her words are cut short as Jon's voice pierces our ears and her breath catches in the back of her throat as we realize this is game on.

Alanna rises to her feet and crosses to the other side of the room, returning with a canvas tote. "This is Carmen's. She loves books," she says, removing a stack of Colleen Hoover novels and placing them on her bed. "I'm sure she won't mind if I use it," she says, as she dumps out the books and tucks her bunny and Patches the Bear inside the bag and studies the room. "I don't think there's anything else I want to take with me," She shrugs.

"I don't blame you," I say with a smile, which makes her laugh.

"Do you think . . . Do you think Jon and his team are here yet?"

"I don't know," I say because I don't. "All we can do . . ." My voice trails off because there is really nothing to do.

"All we can do is wait," she says. "Actually, hold on a sec." She smiles, digging a hand between the bed frame and the mattress to retrieve a deck of cards. "Ever play blackjack?"

After ten rounds of blackjack and three rounds of vomiting, we've listened in to our comms long enough to hear that Carmen has been prepped for surgery and Jon is standing by for Eddie's signal. To kill time, I've told Alanna the story of Operation Superglue and our rescue mission to save her, Chloe, and Teresa. I shared with her my undercover assignment as a high school student and even went into detail about how it rekindled my relationship with Jon. Alanna had listened, intrigued by my efforts to bring her home safely. And now, we sit hand in hand on Alanna's bed, and we pray that both Jon and Eddie will be okay. It's taking a long time—maybe too long—and my worry for my ex-husband far exceeds any fear I have for myself, because so much could have gone wrong.

Then we hear it. *"Todo se ve bien aquí,"* Eddie says, and we both jolt upright, our eyes wide and gazes locked.

"It's happening," Alanna gasps. She leaps to her feet, the deck of playing cards scattering around us, and she immediately scrambles around on the concrete floor, desperate to collect each and every one.

"Alanna, it's okay," I say, another wave of nausea taking my breath away, and I wonder how in the actual hell I have anything left to puke up.

"No," she says, her tone serious. "I'm not leaving them behind."

Alanna slips each playing card eagerly into her tote bag like she's scooping up millions of dollars, and my heart breaks for her and what she's been through, but my knees grow weak in anticipation of our jail break, and I make it to the bathroom just before vomiting one more time.

"Are you okay?"

"Yes," I call back although I'm not so sure, and I begin to wonder if the nachos I ate in Eddie's office might have given me some kind of food poisoning. "Be ready," I instruct as I secure my earpiece back in place, eagerly awaiting Jon's cue, wondering what on earth could be taking so long. If Carmen was prepped for surgery, Jon should be inside the clinic, and it should be go time. *So where is he?*

Then we hear it: one gunshot then another, followed by the blast of an alarm.

"Oh God!" Alanna wails, her eyes widening in shock and her face contorting into a frantic, almost wild look. Her pupils dilate, absorbing every flicker of the harsh fluorescent light overhead, and I resist the urge to puke again. Another gunshot sounds, and I react. I grab her by the wrist, and we scamper together toward the door. I jiggle the door handle, confirming what I assumed—locked from the outside. I hear shouting, mostly Spanish, the sounds of feet against the concrete, echoing in the hallway, then the power is cut, and we are in complete darkness.

"What do we do, Lina?" Alanna whispers, her voice trembling.

That's a freaking good question. Our plan was simple enough, but the truth is there's no way of knowing what's happening on the other side of the door. It could be Jon and Eddie's team coming to our rescue, or things could have taken a turn for the worse, and Alanna and I could be in danger. If that's the case, I don't even want to think about what that means for Jon. *My Jon. Oh God. What if something happened to Jon?*

Panic sweeps over me as the room spins, and I turn and vomit on the concrete floor as it all comes back to me: the metal baseball bat to my head during Operation Superglue, being tossed into that stupid pest control van and hauled away to the abandoned warehouse, Owen's sneaker as it kicked me repeatedly in the gut the night I found Jon cheating on me at the frat house, and suddenly, I can't breathe. I'm having a panic attack and can't do anything to stop it.

"I . . . I don't know," I choke, holding onto Alanna with one hand and pressing my radio comm with the other.

The silence is even more frightening than the gunshots we heard earlier and Alanna squeezes my hand as we nuzzle together against the wall, sheer terror racing through our veins as we worry about not only ourselves but also the two men that we love more than life itself.

"We should go help," she says, narrowing her gaze and rising to her feet.

"Get down," I say. "You aren't going to help. We aren't armed."

"Eddie," she whimpers. "What if something happened to him?"

My stomach pains take my breath away, and I resist the urge to vomit again. Not knowing what is happening is a level of torture I never experienced. Alanna was right—it would be easier to be out there, risking our lives.

"Code red!" Jon barks into his radio, and as relieved as I am to hear his voice, this is terrible news for our operation.

"Code red?" Alanna asks, eyes wide and face contorted. "That wasn't in the plan."

"No, it wasn't," I admit as the room spins again.

"Target down," Eddie says into my earpiece.

Alanna bursts into tears, surely relieved to hear his voice and feeling just as terrified and helpless as I do.

Our doorknob jiggles, and Alanna screams. I cover her mouth with my trembling hand as my stomach aches and now my head pounds, and I am again consumed by thoughts of the past: Jon's naked body as he hovered over Hilary, her fingers pressed firmly over his infinity tattoo, the smell of the underground homeless camp, the pest control van. *That freaking pest control van.*

Get it together, I scold myself.

I yank Alanna by the wrist and guide her into the small bathroom and shut the door behind us, and we both climb into the shower, and I wrap Alanna in my arms, hovering over her, protecting her like a mama bird sits on her babies in a nest, promising myself that no matter what happens, I will protect her like she is my own child.

But I don't have to.

Jon says, "Desert Rose and Desert Moon Secure."

Eddie follows with an intense "Hang tight, Cactus Blossom. I didn't forget about you."

Alanna cries harder, and I squeeze her tighter. "Are you okay?" I ask, unable to think of anything else to say.

"Yes . . . no . . . I love him, Lina. I can't leave him."

"One thing at a time," I say because that is the only way I am currently surviving this mission—literally one thing at a time.

"On my way to meet the buyer," Jon says, tossing our code out the window, which feels reassuring because he must have everything under control if he can speak freely. *But what could have gone wrong?*

As if reading my mind, Jon says, "Interference. It's handled. Eddie, I'm going to need the medical team to the operating room."

"What does that mean?" I ask Alanna, wondering who could've put a wedge in what felt like our perfectly devised plan.

"I don't know." She sniffs. "It's so dark, and I'm so scared. And you're right, I want to go home. I need to go home," she whimpers.

"Stay put," Jon repeats.

The door to our room explodes with a gigantic *bang,* and I hover over Alanna, protecting her with everything I have, then the shower curtain is thrust open, and we are greeted by a male and a female police officer, dressed in street clothes. They flash their badges at me and gesture for us to follow, and we do. Alanna stops by her bed to grab her tote bag, and I can't help but notice she pauses to take one final glance around the room she has called home for so long.

"Come on," I say, taking her hand in mine. "Let's go home."

"Time to go!" one of the cops warns through a thick Mexican accent.

Alanna takes my hand, and we run, my legs weak beneath me, but even still, I run faster than I have in my entire life. Alanna grips me with one hand and her tote bag with the other. The female cop leads the charge, and the male officer follows behind. As we run through the white-walled halls, the concrete floor rough and cool under my feet, I wonder how many victims are behind each door, and I pray to everything I believe in that we are able to save them.

Then we are led outside, and the strong burst of sunlight burns Alanna's eyes so badly that it stops her short in her tracks. "Oh God," she wails, covering her eyes. "It hurts. It hurts so bad."

"Here," the male cop says, placing a pair of sunglasses on her small, pale face. "Officer Silva said you might be needing these."

"He was right," she agrees as we begin running again, this time hot, gravelly terrain burning my feet as we sprint to safety.

We are out of breath as we approach the safe zone. Police cars and ambulances flank the edge of a parking lot, and we're guided toward an ambulance and medical team. I wrap my arms around my chest, suddenly aware that I'm wearing only a transparent hospital gown, and as if reading my mind, a team member drapes a thin blanket over my shoulders. I nod in thanks, securing my earpiece in my ear as I prop myself up against the side of the ambulance, the intensity of the operation catching up to me, and I steady myself in anticipation of what happens next.

I'm relieved when Eddie's fellow officer states, "Prickly Pear and Cactus Blossom marked safe."

Then I lean against the back of the ambulance and vomit on the paramedic's feet.

Twenty minutes have passed, but it feels like decades when the police, who have been standing by, receive some sort of intel and they race off in their cars at lightning speed, sirens blazing.

Jon reports, "Mission accomplished."

Alanna and I crumble to the ground in relief because our men are okay, because we get to run from this nightmare, and most of all, because we took down a major organ-trafficking operation and are watching in awe as victim after victim is guided to safety.

"It's over," I say, rubbing Alanna's back. "We did it."

"It's over?" Alanna asks, peering up at me with tears in her eyes. "I get to go home?"

"You get to go home," I say, my smile the biggest it's been in years, and I feel like the weight of the world has been lifted off my shoulders.

"Where are Carmen and Maria?" Alanna asks for the millionth time.

"They went directly to a hospital," I remind her.

"Oh yeah. Sorry."

"Don't be. You've been through a lot," I say reassuringly.

"Look!" Alanna says, her smile beaming, and I don't need to look up to know that Eddie must be approaching us as we sit, perched on the side of the ambulance. But when I look up, I'm overly relieved to see not only Eddie, but also Jon approaching. Both look like they've been through the wringer, but they seem okay nevertheless.

"Jon!" I scream, louder than I mean to, and I leap to my feet, dropping my blanket to the ground, and I bolt to my ex-husband in nothing but a hospital gown. Jon, *my Jon,* is running toward me, and I sprint to him, my arms extended. When he's close enough, I leap up into his arms, wrapping my legs around his waist and flood his face with kisses. Only then do I notice his cheeks are also covered in tears. "We did it!" I say, nuzzling my face into his neck. "We found Alanna."

"We sure did," he says, pulling back and studying me. "You're something else, Lina Rivera."

I clear my throat. "Lina Rivera . . ."

"For the love of God. You're something else, Lina Rivera, private eye."

"That's right," I say and kiss his nose, then his forehead. "But that's Prickly Pear to you."

"Well, you're *my* Prickly Pear. And I'm never letting you go again."

"Please don't," I say, bringing my feet back to the ground and turning to see Eddie and Alanna in a soft embrace by the ambulance. "She really loves him," I tell Jon. "She doesn't want to leave him."

"She's been through a lot."

"I know. But . . . she's going to be okay. Our Cactus Blossom is as strong as they come," I say as a wave of nausea sweeps over me and I grip my stomach.

"You okay?"

"I'm fine. I drank the water, and I've been paying for it."

"Ouch," Jon says, rubbing my lower back.

"So, what happened in there?" I ask, not taking my eyes off Eddie and Alanna as we walk back toward the ambulance. "Eddie doesn't look like he's celebrating." I notice his body language as Alanna seems to be consoling him. "Something bad happened, didn't it? Is it one of the girls?"

"No, the girls are going to be okay, as far as I can tell. But yeah, it wasn't pretty."

"What happened?"

"Well, we weren't the only ones looking to intercept Carmen's heart."

"Shut up," I say, eyes wide and stopping in my tracks. "Who showed up?"

"It turns out that Maria's father also hired a private investigator."

"Oh wow," I say, bringing a surprised hand to my chest, remembering what Alanna had said about Maria's father. "Was he the buyer?"

"No . . . he wasn't the buyer. But he did hijack the buyer's car and almost killed him. He interrogated him until there was almost nothing left of him," he said, shaking his head in disgust.

"The PI? Or her father?"

"Both," Jon says, biting his lower lip. "But I probably would've done the same if someone messed with you or Lucy."

"Facts. Is that what the gunshot was?"

"Yeah. I shot the other PI in the leg."

"You what?" I gasped. "Jon Cote!"

"He showed up at the same time as we did. I had no choice. I didn't know at the time he was on the same mission as us. I just thought he wanted the heart. I did what I thought was right in the moment."

"Can you get in trouble?" I ask, picturing Jon in a Mexican prison.

"Nah," he said. "We just took down one of the biggest organ-trafficking operations in the country. I'll have paperwork up the ass, but that's about it," he chuckles.

"If you shot the PI, then how did you find the buyer?"

"Maria's dad."

"He's here?"

"He's here. He's at the hospital with Maria now."

"You're amazing," I say and kiss his chin. "But . . . why does Eddie look like someone died? I feel like this is all good news."

Jon pauses and looks down at his feet before making eye contact with me again. "Because," he says then clears his throat and exhales deeply. "The ringleader of the operation showed up, and I shot her in the ass."

"Wait . . . *her*? Who did you shoot?"

"Remember those family pictures you were so obsessed with in Eddie's office?"

"Yeah," I say, my head beginning to spin.

"Remember Eddie's stepmother, Rosa?"

"Yeah?"

"Let's just say she will be in prison for the rest of her life."

"She's the—"

"She's the clinic's ringleader."

My shoulders stiffen. "No way."

"Way."

"But that means . . . if she's . . . Holy shit . . ." I'm at a loss for words, which is a rare occurrence itself.

"There is a very strong possibility she has a *lot* to do with the death of Eddie's mother."

Chapter Twenty-Five

Now (May 2025) Alanna

When I was younger, my mom and her sister organized family movie nights with reruns of their favorite eighties movies. They never seemed to tire of one in particular, *Flight of the Navigator*, which of course was lucky for me. While most kids my age were viewing *Sesame Street* or *Blue's Clues*, I had the privilege of watching young David Freeman navigate life after he mysteriously falls into a ravine and loses consciousness, later awaking to discover that eight years have passed and the world continued on without him, but he hadn't aged or matured one bit.

In the movie, David was taken to NASA, where scientists discovered that his brain charts and brain waves showed evidence that David had been to space, and they later find his spacecraft. It's a cool movie—for 1986—but I won't bore you with more details. However, I am going on record that I've never, in my entire existence, been able to relate to a movie character as much as I can relate to David Freeman. Not only have I been poked and prodded and treated like a piece of meat for the past two years, but life as I knew it has continued without me, and facing this reality head-on is going to be even harder than the kidnapping itself.

As I lie here scooping up the last bits of my cherry Jell-O in a hospital bed back home in Phoenix, Arizona, I can't help but appreciate the facility and the fact that it isn't a prison, and the nurses and doctors have been very attentive. I also appreciate the fact that Jon and Lina made sure I was settled prior to seeing a doctor for Lina, who just couldn't seem to shake whatever virus she must've picked up in Mexico. Jon has checked on me periodically, and he informed me just under half an hour ago that my parents are on their way and are beyond excited to see me. I am, of course, excited to see them, too, but I can't lose this feeling, this nails-on-a-chalkboard sensation that I am being thrust back into my former world just like David when he returned to space, and not only am I sure to be the center of attention—Jon told me to keep the news turned off and that reporters have surrounded the building—but I'm going to be forced to navigate this new reality while somehow missing the people who have become family: Carmen, Maria, and Eddie.

Eddie. Eddie is now and will forever be my hero. If not for Eddie reaching out to Jon and Lina, I wouldn't be alive today, and that is a fact. I will never forget what it felt like to run safely out of the clinic, hand in hand with Lina, knowing Eddie would be waiting for me on the other side. Of course, I will always be indebted to Jon and Lina, the team of private investigators that didn't quit until I was brought to safety. But Eddie will always have a piece of my heart.

Saying goodbye to him was the hardest thing I ever had to do. It just doesn't seem fair that I survived everything I'd endured, only to fall in love then have him ripped away from me so suddenly, especially since he was slapped in the face with the reality that his father's girlfriend, Rosa, was the ringleader of the organ-trafficking clinic this whole time. That most likely means his mother's relationship with Rosa was the reason she was murdered for her organs. Eddie, being Eddie, stayed strong for me, though. When I pushed for details and asked him questions about what was next for his family, based on this information, he gently explained that we would have more time in the future to discuss this and focused on saying our goodbyes. But I couldn't shake the devastation I felt for him. A woman who had been present in his life for so long was responsible for so much of his heartache, and she had done so without even stepping a foot inside the clinic until the day I was rescued. I suppose Eddie dodged quite the bullet because if you think about it, she would have recognized him immediately, which would have blown his cover in a second.

Goodbye. My knotted stomach tightens as I remember the torture and devastation of saying goodbye to Eddie, a man I'm convinced is the love of my life. Lina had all but ripped us apart at the airport when the time came to board our plane, promising me that it wouldn't be the last time I would be with him if it was meant to be, and I cried on Lina's shoulder for the entire flight home until we landed. Then Lina surprised me with a phone call from my mom and dad.

Hearing Patrick and Laura's voices shifted something inside me and awakened a piece of me I'd put to rest during my time at the clinic. It was like talking to a ghost, except *I* was the ghost. And although their efforts were obvious and they attempted to remain calm, it was nearly impossible. Dad cried more than Mom, and even though I could tell they had so many questions for me, they refrained from asking them, somewhat for my benefit and somewhat for theirs.

Soon after that phone call, somewhere in the Phoenix airport, my nervous system decided that now would be a good time to shut down, and that speaking words of any kind was not part of my skill set for the foreseeable future. I want to talk—really, I do—but it just isn't happening. The doctor explained to Jon and me that it is very common after trauma for the body to react in this fashion. This disassociation and emotional overload has caused my body to need a break, but surely with the right help, I will be myself in no time.

So now, as I sit here in my hospital bed, tracing the sharpie heart on my wrist, totally lovesick, totally grateful that not only have I been rescued, but so have Carmen and Maria, I squeeze Patches the Bear and the Purple Bunny of Courage to my aching heart and inhale deeply in anticipation of being reunited with my parents. *What will it be like? Will they be angry with me? Have they changed?* Surely, I've changed. Even having showered a little over an hour ago, I have no doubt in my mind that my appearance will be shocking to them. It certainly was for me. There were no mirrors at the clinic, and my first glimpse of myself had taken my breath away. To say I am pale is an understatement. My skin is such a ghostly white that my blue veins decorate my arms and legs like tattoos, which wouldn't be so bad, but scars, scabs, and bruises speckle my skin in every place imaginable, and I know this is going to be overly difficult for my parents to come face-to-face with.

A knock on the door startles me, and Jon enters first. With one hand on his hip and the other on the hospital room door, he says with a smile, "Hey, Alanna. You have a couple of visitors. They are dying to see you."

A smile forms across my face before I even think to make it, which is a sensation I haven't experienced in years. The butterflies in my stomach intensify as my heart rate increases.

"You ready?"

I grin and nod my head, desperate to find the words, and when they don't come naturally, I sit up straighter and nod again.

"Pumpkin," my mom says, choking on the word.

She bursts into tears upon entering, and the moment I lay eyes on her, I'm five years old again, and I, too, burst into tears. She seems smaller than I remember. Her once blonder than blond hair is gray at the roots, something she never would have allowed before, and it isn't curly and perky like it used to be but instead slicked back into a low bun. She leaps toward me with her arms extended, and before I can even process what's happening, I am in her arms, surrendering to the familiarity of her embrace, and she's flooding my cheeks with tearful kisses.

"My baby," she cries, "my baby," and squeezes me tightly. She pulls back and studies me in disbelief, touching my cheeks with her trembling fingers before pulling me close once more.

I start to wonder where my father is, but I no sooner complete this thought than I hear, "There she is, there's my girl," and I peek over my mother's shoulder to see my father, Patrick, approaching my bed as well.

No words can explain what a relief it is to see my father approaching me, dressed in his park ranger uniform, looking just as I left him. Well, maybe he has a little less hair, but other than that, he's just normal—just Dad.

"Daddy," I whisper through my tears, relief flooding over me that my words have resurfaced, my throat crackly and sore. "Daddy. I'm *so* sorry."

Then my sobs increase, and so do my mother's. She sits beside me, rubbing my back with one hand and rubbing my leg with the other while my dad scoops me up in his arms and pulls me in for a huge bear hug. As I press my tear-streaked face to his and feel the warmth of his skin against mine and inhale his familiar woodsy scent, I'm instantly transformed back into Alanna Foster, a teenage girl from Tempe, Arizona, daughter of Patrick and Laura—not Alanna Foster, the girl who shamed her parents; not Alanna Foster, the victim; but Alanna Foster, the luckiest girl in the world with parents who never quit. They never gave up on me. They knew I was out there, and they found me. And I know in this instant that no matter where I go in life, whatever comes next for me in this chapter, I will always be forever grateful for a second chance at *this* life. And I make a quiet promise to them in my mind that *they* are my home. Whatever twists and turns come my way in the future, I will never betray them ever again.

Two hours have passed since I was reunited with Mom and Dad. I have to admit they are doing a great job keeping our conversation light. When Dad asked me if I needed anything from him, I requested root beer so we could play blackjack. When Mom suggested checking the hospital gift shop for a deck of cards, I pulled out the deck Eddie gave me and smiled, remaining silent as I slapped the deck of cards onto the bedside table. This caused Dad to lose it once more, apologizing for his emotions over and over again.

While Dad retrieved the root beer, Mom set up my cell phone, an old one that belonged to Eliza prior to hers being upgraded, and the first thing I did upon receiving it was to create a contact for Eddie with the phone number from the business card he stuck in my pocket at the airport, and even though I still wasn't up to speaking, I smiled the biggest smile and gave my mom the biggest hug, whispering a scratchy "Thank you."

I would wait until I was alone to text Eddie my number, and I embraced this alone time with my mom, gesturing for her to sit with me on my bed.

"Hank and Bill are wondering if they can stop by," she said, kissing my forehead softly. "Would that be okay? The boys have been so incredibly worried about you. He and Zack never gave up on you."

Hank. Zack. Bill. These names sound foreign, like characters from a story I read in another life. They had been my friends, my *best* friends. *So why didn't I think about them more while I was away?* Emotions flood my soul, and I burst into tears once more.

"It's okay," she says, rubbing my lower back and squeezing my knee. "It's too soon. I'll tell them it's too soon."

But it's not that I don't want to see my friends. I *do* want to see them. *So, what is my problem? Am I embarrassed about what I did? Am I embarrassed about what I look like? Is it because I don't feel like myself? Yes, that must be it.* Sure, I feel like the new Alanna, the one who survived an organ-trafficking kidnapping, but I don't feel like the old Alanna, the senior at Emerson, captain of the cheer team, recipient of a full ride to nursing school, and my stomach groans in agony as I realized I will never be her again, no matter how hard I want to be.

"Too soon," I agree with a nod, collapsing against my mother's chest, soaking her blouse with my tears.

"I wish I could take away your pain," she whimpers, holding me tighter. "I can't imagine what you've been through, and we don't have to talk about it yet. The hospital has arranged for a social worker to come this afternoon, and I already have a call into a highly reputable therapist in our area, but baby girl, if there is anything you need, anything at all I can do for you, just say the word, and I will make it happen."

I pull back, my eyes interlocking with hers, and I can tell she means this. And although I'm sure she's referring to a phone call to a friend, my favorite ice cream, or a potential day of pampering, I can think of one thing and only one thing that I need, and I know this in the deepest part of my heart.

"Anything?" I ask, biting down on an ice chip and allowing the coolness to soothe my throat.

"What is it, sweetheart?"

I swallow and clear my throat because she really needs to hear what I'm about to say. There's no room for error here because every part of me knows my only hope to ever finding my way back to who I *used* to be is going to require putting myself back together piece by piece, and one component of the new me is necessary, and I refuse to live without it. Even though I've been rescued, even though I am home, I am no longer complete—not without *him.*

"Please," I beg, gripping her wrists tightly and staring into her soul. "Eddie. I need Eddie. Please, Mommy, please," I repeat wrapping my arms around her shoulders and sobbing into the nook of her neck. "Please, Mommy," I repeat. "Eddie."

"The detective?" she asks, drawing back, obviously surprised, and I realize that Jon and Lina really did mean what they said when they promised they would only share relevant details with my parents.

"Yes." I nod unapologetically.

"He's the one who rescued you." She nods. "That makes sense," she says, clearly justifying the idea that I've somehow confused my feelings of gratitude for a detective who saved my life. Of course, she would think this. Any mother would. I can't blame her for not understanding what I've been through. Maybe it's unrealistic to expect her to wrap her mind around the bond I've formed with Eddie over the years. I'm still trying to figure it out, and I *lived* it.

"Yes," I say with a smile then sip my water and clear my throat. "But that's not why. I'm in love with him, Mom," I whisper, holding up my wrist and showing her the Sharpie tattoo. "He's in love with me too."

"We sure do have a lot to talk about," she says, her mouth forming a soft smile.

"Yeah. Yeah, we do."

"Who's ready for some blackjack?" my dad asks, his overly elated voice breaking our silence like a baseball piercing a closed window.

"I am," I say, cheerfully.

"Hey!" he exclaims. "Look who found her voice!"

And *this*. I couldn't have said it better myself. I may have gone through hell and back . . . but if nothing else, I, Alanna Foster, have found my voice. And I don't intend to shut up anytime soon.

Chapter Twenty-Six

Now (May 2025) Lina

"Dude. I can't take my eyes off you for one effing second. We *have* to stop meeting like this."

"Ryker," I say, unexpected emotions flooding over me, and I can't tell if the cause is exhaustion or relief, but either way, I burst into tears and extend my arms to my best friend like I'm drowning and he's my only lifeline.

"Did I say something wrong?" he asks as he approaches my hospital bed and perches next to me, draping an arm over my shoulder and pulling me close, chuckling with amusement over my outburst.

"Not at all." I laugh nervously, reaching for a tissue and dabbing my eyes. "I guess I'm just . . . relieved. Relieved to see you."

"Yeah, I get this reaction from all the ladies. You're not the first, and you most definitely won't be the last."

"Yeah, okay, Ry."

"What's with all this?" he asks, gesturing to my IV fluids, puke bucket, and open can of ginger ale.

"Who even knows?" I huff, bringing my soda to my lips. "Maybe I'm dehydrated. I've been sick since I drank the water in Mexico."

"Dude! You drank the water in Mexico? Don't you remember that scene from—"

"Yeah, yeah, yeah. I know. Trust me, that scene was downplayed. No way that chick only shit herself once."

"Point taken," he says with a nod. "You really think that's all this is?"

"Yeah . . . unless maybe it's a virus or some sort of infection, but I never had a fever."

"Can I get you anything? Where's Jon?"

I pull my knees to my chest and squeeze them tightly, a wave of nausea flooding over me and taking my breath away. "At some point, I need coffee.

But right now, I'm just waiting to talk to the doctor. They said just clear fluids for now. I asked them to put caffeine in my IV, and they didn't think it was very funny."

"Assholes. That's hilarious."

"Right?"

"And Jon?"

"He's with Alanna. She's reuniting with her parents as we speak," I say, clearly conflicted that I can't be there to witness their reunion, but I'm also very happy for her and so proud of us for finding her. The short time I got to know Alanna validated what I somehow always knew. She is a very special girl, and the idea that I was able to bring her home is exciting on a level I've never experienced, and I suddenly realize why Jon does what he does for a living. It's surprisingly gratifying to make a difference in this world.

"Congratulations," Ryker says, kissing my forehead. "You did it, Lina Rivera, private eye. You found your Cactus Blossom."

"I did, didn't I?" I say, returning his high five. "Now, I just need to get the hell out of here. I want to see my kids, and we have *so* much work to do on the other cases." I cringe, thinking of the missed calls and texts from Penelope, wondering how on earth Travis wasn't able to pick up the slack on either of my cases while I was away, as we still have our wedding-crashers case to sort through. *What the hell has he been doing?*

"You'll get it done. You always do."

"Mr. and Mrs. Cote?" A female doctor asks, who could double as Robin Williams's character, Mrs. Doubtfire, as she all but skips through my door, laptop in one hand, adjusting her thick black-rimmed glasses over her dramatically large nose with the other.

"Oh, this isn't—"

"That's me," Ryker lies, charming Dr. Doubtfire with his Abercrombie-model glistening white teeth, which seem to sparkle as he presents his commanding, firm handshake. "Jon Cote, private eye."

"Seriously?" I whisper through gritted teeth.

"You must be so proud of your wife," she says, flopping down on a stool and rolling to my bedside.

"Oh yes," Ryker agrees, taking my hand in his and kissing it, causing me to erupt in a fit of laughter. "I'm so proud of my *wife*. You should have seen her in action. A cross between Jennifer Garner in *Alias* and Angelina Jolie in *Tomb Raider*. I didn't think we were going to make it out of there alive," he says, pretending to sob into his T-shirt sleeve. "But Lina, she was so . . . so heroic. At one point, there was a gunshot-and-ninja-knife situation all at the same time."

I stare at him wide-eyed, loving him more than I ever have, for taking my mind off everything, but also wondering what the hell a gunshot-and-ninja-knife situation might entail. "I can't take all the credit," I say. "Jon's just being humble. He handled the, uh, ninja-knife situation as well."

"Well, either way," she says, clicking away on her laptop, "you two are all over the news."

Ryker freezes, realizing his cover has been blown. If she's seen the news, then she's seen the photo of Jon and I, and Ryker is *not* Jon.

"He's my best friend. He's family. Can he stay?" I blurt, my words jumbling together and my cheeks flushing from embarrassment.

"Sorry," Ryker says though he's clearly not, because his smile is only bigger than before.

"He can stay." She says, nodding, with hesitation in her voice. "But you should know your labs are back, and if you do want some privacy, I'm sure your—"

"Ryker," he says. "I'm her Ryker."

"Right. I'm sure your Ryker wouldn't mind waiting in the hall?"

My smile turns downward faster than that of a child dropping an ice cream cone, and I realize that something isn't right—no, something is terribly wrong. *What the hell did I pick up in Mexico? Am I dying?* That's it. I'm dying. It's cancer. It must be cancer. *Oh God, what am I going to tell the kids? Jon? Or worse, did I get some sort of mosquito-borne illness?*

"Don't panic," she says, scooching closer and placing a caring hand over mine.

"He can stay. What's wrong with me?"

"Yeah. What she said," Ryker says, eyes narrowing, moving closer. "Is she going to be all right?"

"Oh yes," she smiles, reassuringly. "Your wife—your *best* friend," she revises with a wink, "will be feeling *much, much* better around late December, early January."

I stare at her like she's talking some sort of foreign language because she's making zero sense. *I drank the water in Mexico. Why would it take that long to feel better?* I side-glance at Ryker, who looks just as confused as me, and Dr. Doubtfire waits for a reaction that we fail to deliver.

"I'm sorry, Doctor . . ."

"Doctor Porter."

"Doctor Porter, I'm not following. Can you be a bit more specific?"

"Yes, of course, dear. You've been through so much. Your scattered thoughts are probably flying through that mind of yours at a million miles per hour. Am I right or am I right? I apologize for not being clearer. You're *pregnant,* dear. Of course, we will need to do an ultrasound to confirm dates, but you are very much pregnant."

Ryker bites his lip and turns a ghostly white, while I leap to my feet, almost knocking Dr. Doubtfire off her stool, and she wobbles like Humpty Dumpty, unsteady on his fairy-tale wall.

"Nope," I insist. "There has been some sort of mistake. I'm not pregnant. I'm thirty-five—"

"You're thirty-six," Ryker says.

"That . . . that's irrelevant," I hiss, swatting his hand away.

"Clearly, this news comes as a surprise," she says, rubbing the back of her neck with her open palm.

"You think?" I snap. "I can't be pregnant. I'm divorced."

"Divorced sperm don't discriminate," Ryker mutters, then pretends to dodge a punch to his face.

"You have the wrong chart or file thingy there. I'm not pregnant. You see, I have teenagers. I can't be pregnant. Those labs belong to someone else. *Anyone* else."

"My . . . file . . . thingy . . . is not incorrect. You, Lina Rivera, are pregnant. Now, I want to run some more tests and check on a few things. Would you like me to speak with your husband?"

"No. We are not speaking to my husband. Because I'm not pregnant."

"When was the date of your last menstrual period?" she asks, looking up from the laptop screen, raising one brow, and in this moment, I know she's right. *Shit, shit, shit, shit.*

"I'm in menopause."

"Really?" she asks, sticking her nose up at me like every doctor before her. "What makes you think this?"

"Well last fall, I was having *really* bad hot flashes and mood swings. But they did get better."

"Alcohol use?"

"Excuse me?"

"Sometimes with patients, alcohol use and hot flashes go hand in hand. For me, it was tequila."

Damn you, tequila, I say silently. "I haven't had a drink in months. I had multiple concussions, and the doctors encouraged me to quit."

"And did you?"

"Yes, *unfortunately.*"

Ryker stifles a laugh, but Dr. Doubtfire remains serious as can be.

"And the hot flashes?" she asks. "Once the drinking stopped?"

"They stopped," I say, choosing my words carefully, wondering why I hadn't picked up on the fact that my hot flashes were alcohol induced. "But I skip cycles. I haven't had my . . ." My voice trails off because I have set the volleyball in the air perfectly for her to say:

"Because you're pregnant. Let me give you a moment to process this," she suggests, rising to her feet and placing a gentle hand on my shoulder. "Take this one minute at a time," she says, unable to leave my room fast enough, leaving Ryker and me staring at each other in shock.

"I'm not pregnant," I tell Ryker as though this is somehow his fault.

"Okay," he says, taking his hand in mine and shrugging. "You're not pregnant."

I rest my head on his shoulder, squeezing his hand more tightly, my mind a foggy haze processing some thoughts and swatting others away. "I'm not pregnant."

"Okay," he says, kissing my forehead.

A tear rolls down my cheek, and I place my hand on my abdomen. *Jon and I were careful, weren't we? We mostly used condoms except . . . Oh God . . . Except for . . .*

"It was the office sex, wasn't it?" Ryker declares so that I don't have to.

"Yup."

"You're *so* pregnant."

"I'm *so* pregnant."

"You're *so* screwed."

"I'm so freaking screwed." I sniff. "Ryker?"

"Yeah?"

"Don't tell Jon."

"Who's Jon?"

"Ryker?"

"Yeah."

"Don't leave this room."

"I gotcha."

"Ry?"

"Yeah?"

I look up at him with tears in my eyes, and I squeeze his hand so tightly that I'm sure I've cut off his circulation. "I love you."

"I love you too. It's going to be okay."

I nod in agreement, still unsure that his words hold any amount of truth. The fact is that this is the worst-case scenario for my relationship with Jon. Just when we get our fresh start and I start trusting him again—just when we get to have the life we've been waiting to live, history repeats itself, and we're going to have to start over. I couldn't write this stuff if I tried. Two stupid twenty somethings have sex on their first date, and *bam*, pregnant with twins. Then, after years of separation, they begin to rekindle what they tried to start once before, and *bam*, pregnant again.

But am I giving Jon enough credit? He's different now, isn't he? We've both grown so much since then. We've been through so much together. Maybe this time will be different.

"Yeah," I say. "It will be okay," I whisper, lying down on my side and overly grateful when he curls up behind me, spooning me, just as he did those first nights after I left my husband.

"You're too tall for this bed," I say, noticing how his feet are wedged uncomfortably between the end of the mattress and the plastic footboard.

"Nah," he says, kissing my neck and holding me close. "Lina?"

"Yeah?" I ask, reaching for his hand.

"Didn't anyone ever teach you about birth control?"

"Ryker?"

"Yeah?"

"Didn't anyone ever teach you about *not* being a dick?"

"You know you love me."

"I do love you. But please, for the love of God. Stop talking."

Chapter Twenty-Seven

Now (June 2025) Alanna

Three days have passed since I was discharged from the hospital and five since I saw my parents for the first time. Reuniting with my siblings, Eliza and Chris, was both overwhelmingly awesome and incredibly devastating at the same time. They've both grown a lot, and seeing this was total validation of everything I'd missed: Christmas, birthdays, Chris's eighth-grade graduation, Eliza's braces, and countless other milestones I can't even begin to wrap my mind around. And even though my family has been nothing but supportive, leaving the safety and security of my childhood bedroom has been quite a feat, to say the least.

My mother kept her promise. After speaking with my father, they both agreed that if seeing Eddie would make me happy and help my recovery, they would do everything they could to bring him here, to visit me. But that, unfortunately, is not in the cards because Eddie can't leave Mexico until Rosa's case is closed and the organ-trafficking ring is completely shut down. I don't blame him, but the ache I have for him in my soul is like nothing I've ever experienced.

After a knock at my bedroom door, my mother enters my room. "Good morning, pumpkin," she sings. She brushes my hair away from my eyes and plants a soft kiss on my forehead.

"Good morning, Mom," I say. *But is it good?* I ask myself. There is so much evil outside these bedroom walls. So many horrible things can happen if you make one stupid mistake. *How good of a morning can it possibly be if this world is filled with so many bad things?*

"I'm thinking that today might be a good day for you to shower up, get dressed, and come downstairs. What do you think about that?"

It's such a small request but at the same time *so* big. I stare up at her, eyes wide, wondering why my leaving this room is so important to her. She should be happy I'm here, snuggled up in my bed with Patches and the Purple Bunny of Courage. Nobody can hurt me here.

"I think I'm good," I say with confidence. "I'm fine here. Right?" I ask without even meaning to.

"Your friends are coming to visit you today," she says, speaking with intention. "Would you like them to visit you here? Or downstairs?"

I bolt upright in my bed, shaking my head in confusion. "My friends? Mom, what did you do?"

"I didn't do anything." She shrugs. "Hank organized it. They are home from school for the summer, and they want to come see you."

"They?" I ask, rubbing my eyes and collecting my hair into a messy bun.

"Hank, Bill, and Zack."

"I don't even know what schools they go to," I say with a muffled laugh. "Don't you see, Mom? I'm not the same girl I used to be. I'm different. I've changed."

These words sting her soul, and her eyes well with tears, and I immediately feel remorse.

"I'm sorry," I say, because I truly am. "Don't you see it, though? This is . . . It's just too hard."

"You are a brave girl, Alanna. And we start counseling tomorrow morning, and I'm sure your therapist will be a huge help. But until then, I need you to get out of bed. I need you to shower. And I need you to put on clothes. You still haven't worn anything but . . . but those," she says, gesturing to Carmen's Nirvana T-shirt and the gray shorts I lived in for a year's time.

"I don't expect you to understand," I say, chewing on my bottom lip and fighting back tears.

"That's fair," she says softly. "Because I will never understand what it is like to go through what you went through. Just as you will never understand what it was like for me," she counters, choking back a sob.

"Mommy," I say, my voice breaking as I reach for her. "I'm so sorry."

"Don't be sorry. Just be . . . just be Alanna. Can you do that? Can you just be the strong, sassy, beautiful, talented girl I raised?"

I think about this for a beat, knowing that, deep down, I don't know if I will ever find that girl again. But for my mother, the woman I put through hell and back for two years . . . I muster up a somewhat convincing "Okay" before pulling the covers off my legs and rising to my feet.

"Thank you," she says, genuinely grateful. "I'll turn the shower on. You pick something from your closet."

"Okay," I say, approaching my closet, a door I haven't opened since the day I ran away. And as I place my hand on the doorknob, that night flashes before my eyes, and I resist the urge to run back to bed, but Mom returns with a hopeful smile.

"Did you pick something?"

"Maybe . . . maybe you can do it," I suggest. "Maybe you can pick my outfit."

Mom's eyes light up like I've informed her she's won the lottery. "Yes! Oh . . . sure . . . yes!" she exclaims, eager to fling open my closet door and search through my clothes.

"Thank you for keeping my room the same, Mom. It's like all of this has just been here . . . waiting for me," I say, knowing this will make her happy.

"I wouldn't have it any other way," she says, handing me my favorite jean shorts and a pink crop top. "Do you . . . Do you think . . ."

I finish the sentence for her. "Will they still fit?" I ask, wondering the same thing as I've lost an insane amount of weight since I left home, which is shocking since I was just sitting around for two years. "I guess we will see. If not, I can borrow something from Eliza."

Mom nods, and I am sure she's thinking the same thing I am. An almost twenty-year-old female borrowing her ten-year-old sister's clothes is a heavy pill to swallow.

"It is what it is," she concludes. "And this is a fabulous reason to go shopping."

"Right," I say, planting a kiss on her cheek even though the idea of going shopping is overwhelming in a way I can't quite comprehend. So, instead, I ask, "What's for breakfast?"

"You tell me."

"Waffles?"

"Chocolate chip?"

"OMG, ye-e-esss."

"Chocolate chip waffles coming right up," she says like nothing has changed.

And with that, I turn from my bedroom and make my way into the already running shower, and I pause, overwhelmed in a way I can't quite put into words. *It's just a shower, Alanna!* I scream silently. *How can a bathroom and a shower cause me to feel like an intruder in my own home, like I just don't belong here?* This room is too big and is equipped with all these toiletries and cosmetics, and I can't help but wonder why anyone would need all this stuff. *And why in the actual hell I would give anything to shower in the tiny jail cell of a hospital room with the men's body wash that Eddie snuck in for Carmen and me? Why would I rather be a prisoner in a life-threatening organ-trafficking clinic than climb into a shower I've used for sixteen years of my life?* I can't help but think, *Eddie. It's Eddie I miss, right?* Because any other reason would be way too sad to say out loud. I couldn't possibly miss that life. *Could I? Get it together, Alanna,* I beg myself. I survived a kidnapping, I dodged a fatal heart transplant, and I fell in love with an undercover detective. Surely, I can climb into my shower and bathe. So I do.

"Your turn," Hank says to me with a wide, goofy, grin, one I'm so overly grateful to see before me that I can't help but fixate on it for seconds longer than appropriate.

"Sorry. Spaced it," I say, reaching for an Uno card, flipping over a green number three, and keeping it in my hand.

"Dude, don't be sorry," he says, taking the next card. "Bill, get your nose outta your phone, and pick up a card. Damn, man, can't you two focus long enough to play a game of Uno with our girl?"

"Sorry," Zack says, brushing his shaggy blond hair from his eyes. "Texting my guy, James, about a rager downtown tonight."

I study Zack and Bill, realizing that they look the same as before I left, surprisingly. They were both high school athletes who have continued to play sports in college. Hank is the one who's changed the most. Hank, who I had known since grade school, was always as tall as his brother, Bill, but never built like an athlete. Hank was apparently recruited for swim team his freshman year. Physical education was a requirement for his school, and when the PE teacher saw his butterfly stroke, he cornered him by the indoor pool and requested his presence at tryouts. Because of this, Hank has blossomed into a version of himself I don't yet know. His chest and shoulders are bigger and broader. His biceps are defined, and his leg muscles are somewhat bulky, making him look more like his twin brother, Bill.

"My turn again," I apologize again. *Really . . . Uno*? I get it—they're trying to have fun with me in a lighthearted way, probably per my mother's request, but really, they're avoiding the elephant in the room—*me*.

"No worries," Hank says again, pulling his next card, a reverse card, and sending it back to me.

"Where's the party?" Bill asks.

"Downtown Tempe," Zack says, and my stomach turns as I picture the bus stop, the place where my nightmare began, and I let out an unintentional yelp that sounds like a mix between a barking puppy and an angry cat.

"You, okay?" Hank asks, leaping to his feet.

I nod and wave it off as nothing, but I know I've been made. "No, it's fine, really," I say with a smile as the three of them stare at me, trying like hell to find the right words.

But really, what words are there? My lower lip begins to tremble, and I fight back the tears because I *hate* this. I hate what happened to me, and I hate that I miss Eddie, but more than anything, I miss being normal. And as a tear escapes my eye, I brush it away and I realize I'm not going to get through this new phase of my life by trying to get back to the person I used to be, just as I didn't survive the past two years in organ trafficking being *that* girl either. *And if that's the case, who should I be?*

I close my eyes and search my mind for some sort of direction. Maybe I need an alter ego, someone I can become just until I'm strong enough to be *her* again—someone I know well enough to *play*, you know, like portraying a character in a movie. I inhale deeply then exhale a long breath, knowing right away whose persona I will be taking on. It's time for the guys to meet one of my favorite people on the planet, Carmen. So, I open my eyes and scan the eyes of my friends, three boys—scratch that, three men, because they are men now—and I become her.

"Are you three morons going to sit there and gawk at me all afternoon?"

"Huh?" Hank asks, jolting upright like I've slapped him in the face. Bill sits in silence, and Zack lets out a loud and exaggerated snort.

"You heard me," I smile slyly, just as Carmen would. I slap my deck of cards down on the coffee table and say, "Uno? Really? You haven't seen me since 2023, and you want to play Uno?"

"I . . . thought it would be nice," Hank replies hesitantly.

"Nice? I've been a prisoner for two years locked up in a hospital room. The only thing I could do for fun was play cards. So why in the actual hell do you think playing cards would be fun?"

"Your mom said—"

"Screw what my mom said. We all know you have questions for me. I was sold into organ trafficking, for heaven's sake. If you didn't have questions for me, that would be effed up. Enough of *this*," I say, gesturing to my circle of friends. "I'm opening the room up for questions."

"You're what?" Zack asks, clearly confused.

"You get one hour," I say, gesturing to the clock on our cable box. "One hour to ask me anything you want. From how I got kidnapped, where they took me, who I met . . . anything. And then, after that, we never talk about it again. Deal?"

"Deal," they say in unison.

"And what is said here stays here," I say, pointing at them like they're three children being warned to behave.

"So," I say, flicking my hair over one shoulder just as Carmen would, "who wants to go first? Time's a-ticking, and I've already lost two years, so don't keep a girl waiting. That would just be plain rude. And if you want to know the juicy deets, I'd start by asking who put this heart on my wrist in Sharpie and why it's the most important thing to me in the world."

Chapter Twenty-Eight

Now (June 2025) Lina

"Working on Penelope's case?" Jon asks, rising from his office sofa and making his way toward my desk.

"What's that?" I ask, sounding way too guilty, closing the search browser on my computer and sitting up a little too straight.

"What are you working on?" Jon repeats, rubbing my shoulders and kissing the base of my neck. I pull away, side-glancing at Travis, who is typing away on his computer keyboard.

"Just research," I say. "For my book." As soon as the lie escapes my lips, I feel guilty.

"Nice," Jon says. "Can't wait to read it."

"You don't read my books." I chuckle.

"It's never too late to start. Hey, I was thinking. Want to have dinner tonight? We haven't gone out since Mexico."

"I'm hanging with Daph tonight," I say, tucking a loose strand of hair behind my ear.

"Okay," he says, clearly disappointed. "Tomorrow night?"

I hesitate for a beat, my insides feeling all sorts of guilty. "Play it by ear?" I ask with a hopeful smile. "I'm swamped. I missed my writing deadline because of Mexico."

"Sure," he says, reaching for his keys. "I'm heading to Starbucks. Anyone want anything?"

I'd kill for a coffee, but I've already had one today, and if I order decaf, Jon will know something is up. "My stomach isn't great," I lied. "Thank you, though."

"Right," Jon nods. "Sorry, babe. I forgot that you're still all messed up from the giardiasis. My bad."

I'm an asshole, I cry silently as I cringe, recalling how I forced Ryker to search bacterial infections picked up in Mexico so that I would have a cover. "Don't be sorry. I'm sure it will be better soon."

He closes the door behind himself, and I continue my internet search as I'm determined to put the fact that I am pregnant out of my mind, and because of this, I've become obsessed with Alanna's case again. Yes, we found her, but I can't shake one very important question: How did the kidnappers and traffickers know that Alanna had a rare blood type? Alanna mentioned that her blood wasn't drawn *until* she was at the clinic. They had to have known her blood type prior to that. My initial thoughts are that this ring of organ trafficking is so highly sophisticated that they were able to hack into medical records. I've been searching all day, looking into closed cases, trying to find a pattern that relates to Alanna's situation, and I've come up short.

Aside from that, Jon is all over me, wanting time alone. I know damn well he wants to finish our conversation about him moving back home, and now, more than ever, I'm not ready for that to happen. I've been avoiding him like the plague. Hell, I've even been avoiding my kids somewhat. I can't look anyone in the eye, and Ryker being the only one who knows is like a ticking time bomb—Ryker and secrets don't go hand in hand.

Dinner with Daphne will be a good thing. She's always been very grounding when I'm in crisis, which happens to be quite often.

"How's it going on the wedding-crasher case?" I ask Travis.

"Why are you ghosting Cote?" he replies, way too matter-of-fact.

"Excuse me?" I gasp. "I'm not ghosting anyone. In case you don't remember, I was fake kidnapped into organ trafficking, and I rescued Alanna from the clinic. There were gunshots, by the way. And I'm fine, thanks for asking."

"I know you're fine. That's why I haven't asked. But man, way to be defensive," he calls out before running one hand over the dark defined skin of his beautifully sculpted bicep, and I shake my head from side to side, angry with myself for being so transfixed by the body parts that attract me to him. "But it's also a fact that the way you're treating Jon is how you treated me . . . when we were dating."

"I didn't ghost you."

"Yeah, you did. Look, all I'm saying is if you don't want to see him anymore, just tell him that. You guys have been through so much together that you owe him that much. You owe him the truth."

"I *want* to see him. Jon and me, we're fan-freaking-tastic. Like I said, I'm swamped. I've got two kids, a book deadline, and two open cases. Which is why I'm curious, Travis, how it's going with the wedding crasher case."

"Ghosting," he repeats with a wink. "You're a heartbreaker, Lina Rivera."

Is Travis . . . Is he flirting? I roll my eyes and mouth a solid "Whatever" before typing into my search engine, "how many weeks pregnant will I start to show." I find that it might be sooner since I was already pregnant once, which infuriates me.

"I've been working that case hard. I have a few interesting leads," Travis says like he wasn't just busting my balls. "While you were in Mexico, there were more robberies and an increase in stolen items. We've got to get this job done," he sighs. "When Jon gets back, I'll share more."

"Fine," I huff.

"Fine," he repeats, matching my tone. "I'm here for you if you . . . if you need anything."

"What's that supposed to mean? Why would I need anything?"

"Lina," he says, standing from his chair and walking toward me. When I click out of my web browser, he catches the response, and I silently beg him to let me off the hook. "I don't know what's going on with you, but I *know* you," he says, taking a seat on the edge of my desk. "I was there, remember? When you were kidnapped from the bus stop, when you were held underground, when you were saved from the warehouse."

"I remember," I say rubbing my arm. "You were there when you tackled me to the ground and broke my arm," I add.

"Let bygones be bygones." He smirks. "But I was also there when you were trying to start something with me. We were never able to because you were juggling everything, trying to save the world. Whatever this is, girl, talk to Jon about it. He's a good man. He deserves the truth."

"Okay, Travis Mullins, private eye. If you're that good, what secret am I keeping?" I challenge.

"Well, I never said you have an actual secret, but thank you. Now, I know you have something going on." He laughs.

"You know what I mean," I say trying to be chill. "What am I keeping from Jon?"

"Well, it's obvious you've got some major PTSD going on. Who wouldn't?" Travis crosses one leg over the other and rubs his chin's scruff with his thumb and forefinger.

I have to look away from his hips because I remember all too clearly how they move, and those days are gone. *Lina! Those days are gone!*

"And knowing you," he continues, "You're still looking into Alanna's case. Because let's face it, there are loose ends."

"Maybe," I say faster than I intend. "Does that mean you are looking into it too? Because there are *so* many unanswered questions."

"And of course," he says, smiling even bigger. "Jon wants to move back in. And knowing you, you are avoiding that conversation for sure. Because you have commitment issues. Especially when it comes to Jon Cote."

"You're annoying," I say through clenched teeth while raising one brow. "So, what if you're right? Are you going to tell my boss-slash-ex-husband-slash-boyfriend-slash-baby daddy that I'm being *bad*?" I cringe because I didn't mean for this to sound flirty, but oh boy does it ever, and this causes heat to rise through my chest and neck, and I know damn well I'm blushing.

"I didn't say anything about being *bad*, Lina. But like I said, he's a good man. And he loves you. I respect the dude."

"I know," I say, moving my gaze to the floor. "I respect the dude too. I would never hurt Jon."

"And I've been there. You're not an easy woman to get over. Trust me. I work on it every . . . damn . . . day."

"Travis—"

"Conversation over," he says with a charismatic grin. "Let's just try to keep our workplace friendly, shall we?"

"Of course," I agree. "And Travis?"

"Yeah?"

"I'm sorry I hurt you."

"I know. Now, honestly. Why don't you want coffee? I've never heard you turn down coffee."

"Enough!" I say, crumpling up a piece of notebook paper. I whip it at his head but miss by a long shot. "I have work to do." And with that, I reopen Google and search "how much coffee can I consume while pregnant."

"He did *not* say that!" Daphne exclaims as we make our way to our table at our favorite Mexican restaurant.

"Oh, he sure did," I say, gathering my hair over one shoulder and hopping up onto my seat across from her. "Travis said *all* of that."

"I need a drink after that story," she chuckles. "You having a margarita?"

"I wish," I whine. "Still no drinking. You know, the concussion."

"You care if I have one? It's been a day."

"Of course not," I say although I would commit murder for a margarita.

Daphne orders her drink, and I order a ginger ale, the only thing that seems to calm my nausea, and we order some chips, salsa, and guac to start. Daphne is in the middle of blabbing on about her workday with a twenty something new hire who thinks she runs the world—and Daphne's company—and contemplating if she should order a burrito or a burrito bowl when I blurt, "I'm pregnant," and she almost falls off her seat.

"I'm sorry . . . I think I've lost my hearing. I thought you just said you're pregnant."

"I am," I say, banging my fist down on the table and causing the table next to us to stare. "Sorry," I tell them with a shrug. "Long day."

"How?"

"How what?"

"How are you pregnant?"

"Come on, Daph. We are far from sex ed."

"You know what I mean!" she bellows, and her blond curly messy bun bounces to the beat of her inability to process this information. "Is it Jon's?"

"Of course it's Jon's!" I holler back, pounding my fist to the table once more, again causing a scene then mouthing an apology to a couple on the other side of us who appear to be on a first date. "Who else's would it be?" I ask defensively.

"Well, I hadn't thought that far. Sorry, I'm surprised . . . shocked, even. How far along are you? Does Jon know?"

"It's okay," I say then bite into a chip and rinse it down with my soda. "I had an ultrasound. I'm roughly nine weeks along. Thank God, there's only one baby this time. And no, Jon doesn't know." I cringe, wishing I could take back that one comment. I love both my kids. Of course I'm thankful for both Max and Lucy, but I'm so incredibly thankful for just one more . . . not two more.

"You haven't told him? Why wouldn't you tell him? I thought you guys are good?" She waves our waitress down for another drink before adding, "You got an ultrasound without Jon?"

"Stop judging me," I whine.

"I'm not judging. Just trying to figure out why on earth you would be avoiding this conversation with the one person who could help you through it the best."

She's right. I know she's right.

So I sigh and say, "The ultrasound was at the hospital when I was admitted post-Mexico. I thought I had some sort of illness from drinking the water in Mexico or some sort of infection."

"But you did. You told me you had . . . oh."

"That wasn't true."

"Apparently not," she says with an annoyed raise of her brow.

"I needed a cover," I explained, placing my hand on hers. "You were with my kids when I told you that."

"Who else knows?"

"Ryker."

"Of course, Ryker," she says, her face forming an expression I'm not familiar with.

"Are you . . . are you jealous of Ryker?"

"Of course not. You know it's not like that. I'm not like that. I'm just surprised. Anyways, enough about me. Are you okay?"

"Not really. I don't know what to do."

She stares at me mid-bite before asking, "What do you mean, you don't know what to do?"

"I'm having the baby," I say, faster than intended. "It's just . . . it's so hard, Daph. Jon and I, we were just getting to a good place . . . and history repeats itself once again!"

"History?" she asks, confused.

"You know. I got pregnant with twins on our first date. We never really got a chance to be just us. Right before Mexico, we talked about him moving back home. I was so excited to move forward with him. I was ready . . . like ready . . . for a fresh start with him."

"And now you can't have that?" she asks, genuinely confused.

"No," I say with a sorrowful sigh. "I've been through this before. I'm going to be huge *again*," I say, gesturing toward my midsection. "I'm going to have to give birth, *again*. And I'm going to have to raise this baby—"

"This time will be different," she interrupts.

"How do you know that?"

"Because *you* are different. *Jon* is different. You guys were babies when you had babies. Maybe instead of thinking about this like an ending, you think about it as a new beginning . . . you know, a second chance?"

"I'm not following."

"You and Jon didn't get to raise the twins together. But this time . . ." She smiles optimistically. "This time, you get that chance."

I dab my tears with my napkin and thank her for being such a wonderful friend. "I love you," I say through my tears. "You always know what to say. You always know how to make things better."

Our waitress approaches the table with Daphne's margarita, and she takes it from her, sipping it before the glass touches the table, then she orders herself a burrito bowl. As I'm in the middle of ordering myself plain rice with another round of chips, Daphne blurts, "I'm leaving Mal. I hired a divorce lawyer, and the papers are being drawn up as we speak."

My gaze locks onto hers, and I'm so shocked that I forget to order another ginger ale. Our waitress has a better poker face than I do, and she smiles happily, turns, and hurries away.

"Your face, Lina," Daphne scolds. "It has subtitles."

"I'm so sorry," I say. "Now, it's my turn to be surprised. I had no idea you and Mal were in a bad place."

"Oh, come on," she says, waving me off. "He was never home, and you know it."

"You *liked* that he traveled so much. At least, that's what you told me."

"It's just not working, Lina."

"Did you try couples counseling?"

"Nope," she says, biting into the last chip and sipping the rest of her drink.

"Why not? Don't you want to fix it?"

"Of course I want to fix it. It's my marriage. Let's talk about something else."

"No!" I say, pounding my fist against the table, this time unapologetically. "I'm your best friend. I was your maid of honor. We are talking about this, and we are talking *now*."

"But you're the one with the news tonight. You're the one with the crisis. This can wait."

"No, no, this can't wait. And I'm always in crisis." I smile.

"Truth."

"Now start from the beginning, young lady," I say like I'm talking to my teenagers. "And don't leave anything out."

"It's a long story, Lina."

"No story is too long when it comes to you, Daphne. Please, spill it."

Chapter Twenty-Nine

Now (June 2025) Alanna

Two days have passed since I opened up to Bill, Hank, and Zack about my kidnapping experience. Some of their questions were easy to answer: the surface-level questions about my living conditions, meals, and how I occupied my time. Answering the trickier questions involved reliving my Snapchat romance with Lincoln Stone, which was the most embarrassing of all. Talking about Maria, Carmen, and Eddie had been the easiest, especially Eddie.

Eddie. Just thinking about him brings an involuntary smile to my face but also causes my heart to ache. I feel like I haven't seen him in years even though we've FaceTimed multiple times since I've returned home. Our conversations have been light, focusing mainly on Rosa's case and the trafficking operation, always followed by him needing reassurance that I'm doing all right, then ending with me all but begging to see him again. I've considered returning to Mexico to see him, but I'm sure my parents would never agree to that in a thousand years.

I've taken to my new Carmen persona, and I'm eager to see her again too. Now that my new cell phone is up and running with new and restricted social media accounts—I've closed my others because I became somewhat famous upon being rescued—I've searched for both Carmen and Maria, and so far, I've come up short. Eddie assured me they were both alive and well and had spent time in a hospital in Mexico before being reunited with their families, and he told me to hang tight because he would find a way for me to get into contact with both. For now, acting like Carmen is helping tremendously, and I approached this concept with my new therapist, Evelyn, a super sweet woman in her early seventies who lets me pet her lapdog during our sessions. Evelyn was supportive of this idea but cautioned me to break free of it as soon as possible, as finding my true and authentic self was of the utmost importance. But she could appreciate, after all I went through, that I might need to utilize a tool like this until I was back on my feet.

Now, as I lie on my couch, sipping my lemonade, curled up with my two favorite stuffed animals and clutching Carmen's T-shirt like a child might hold a security blanket, engrossed in the episodes of *OBX* I've missed while I was away, I realize that for the first time since my return, I've become comfortable in my own home again. This is good, considering this will be my first full day home alone. Eliza and Chris are at summer camp until at least five in the evening, Dad works until three, and Mom is on a flight and will return home tomorrow. Currently, it's only noon, which means I have the house to myself for the day, and I consider the possibility of taking Hank up on his offer to go out some time and grab lunch and a movie. As if reading my mind, my phone flashes with a text message from Hank.

Hank: *Hey. Can I come by?*
Alanna: *Sure. It's just me and Netflix. BTW season three of OBX was fire.*
Hank: *I didn't watch it.*
Alanna: *Why not?*
Hank: *Um, it was our thing. And you were gone.*

I cringe at Hank's text, reminded once again that my actions had hurt those around me, and I shake off the feelings of guilt and shame, both of which were addressed with Evelyn at our session. *Everyone makes mistakes. This was a huge consequence for one mistake. It wasn't my fault.*

Alanna: *Gotcha. Well, you missed out. It was awesome. I didn't think it was possible for John B to be any hotter.*
Hank: *Yeah, for a dude, he's pretty dope. I'll be by in ten.*
Alanna: *Kk*

I consider getting up off the couch and checking my reflection, seeing that I'm having company, but the truth is that, after my time away, I've become less focused on my appearance, less superficial. Besides, if Eddie could fall for me in a hospital gown with my ass sticking out half the time, I could chill with Hank in my comfy clothes, which my mom had been happy to buy for me at Target. Allowing her to pick out my outfits made her the happiest I've seen her in a lifetime.

I check my messages for anything from Eddie but come up short, so instead, I hit play on Netflix and study John B and his chiseled abs while sipping my lemonade and crunching on my peanut butter cups until I hear a knock on the door and freeze. Of course I know Hank is coming over, but my brain seems to think I'm in danger. My knee trembles, and my legs grow weak. At another knock, I struggle to find my voice. Of course it's Hank. *But what if it isn't?* Anyone could be on the other side of that door. One false move, and my life as I know it could be over . . . again.

"Alanna? I'm here."

"Who is it?" I ask, my voice shaky.

"It's Hank."

"Just a minute," I say, trying to sound chill but failing miserably. I hop up from the couch, my bare feet cool against the tiled kitchen floor, and make my way to the front door and unlock it, then greeting Hank with a faux enthusiastic smile. "Hi," I say, falling into his arms, relief flooding over me as I silently remind myself that I'm not in danger, that I was never in danger.

"You good?" he asks, pulling back from our embrace and studying me intently.

"Yeah. I'm good. Just got a little nervous."

"Nervous answering the door?"

"Yup. Don't worry, my therapist thinks that with time, I won't be so effed up," I say, welcoming him inside. "Want some lemonade?"

"I'll take a water, thanks."

"Sure," I say, opening the fridge and retrieving a bottled water for Hank.

The food and beverage selection in my family's fridge continues to overwhelm me. *Why, exactly, do we need Smart Water, generic store-brand bottled water, Hint water, and multiple different flavors of seltzer water? Why not just have water? And why does this annoy me?*

"Pick a water," I grunt. "Too many choices."

Hank finds this funny and reaches over me to grab a Hint water. "This stuff is lit," he says as he unscrews the cap then sips it eagerly.

"What in the actual hell is Hint water, anyways?"

"It's water that smells like a flavor but tastes like water."

I stare at him blankly. "I don't get it."

"Try it," he says, offering it up.

"I'm good with my lemonade, thank you." I smile. "It's juice from a lemon that smells and tastes like lemons," I say, sass intended. "Want me to start season three over?" I ask, leading Hank to my spot back on the couch. "I'm sorry, I hadn't realized that you had . . . waited . . . you know . . . for me . . ." My voice trails off because I can't tell if Hank waited for my return or assumed I was dead.

Judging by his silence, neither does he. "No, it's okay," he says. "I'm not really up for TV today."

We flop onto the couch, and I squeeze Carmen's shirt to my chest, realizing for the first time that Hank doesn't look great. His freckled face appears pale and haggard, and his shaggy ginger hair is disheveled. His ocean-blue eyes are tinted pink as though he's been crying.

"Hey," I say, taking his hand in mine. "What's going on?"

Hank slumps forward and shakes his head. "I can't bug you with this," he says with a sigh. "I'm supposed to be cheering you up."

"I was kidnapped and held prisoner in a hospital. I'm not dead," I say with a laugh, as though this is a normal statement to make. "Hit me with it."

"Ugh. It's . . . it's my mom and dad," he says, running his fingers through his hair in frustration. "They aren't good."

"Penelope and Jasper?" I gasp. "They're, like . . ."

"The perfect couple, I know. Which is why this sucks so bad."

"What happened?"

"Nothing *happened*. I can just sense something isn't okay."

"Have they been fighting?"

"No, not really. But I can just tell something is off. I love my mom and dad, Alanna. Growing up, my friend's parents seemed to separate or divorce all around me, and it was always one of my biggest fears."

"You think . . . You think they're getting divorced?"

"I don't know what to think. All I can tell you is that something is wrong. They aren't screaming at each other or anything like that. They just aren't *them*."

I nod in understanding because Hank has always had a sensitive side. If something was going on with Jasper and Penelope, Hank would surely be the one to notice. "What does Bill think?"

"Ah, Bill." Hank snickers. "Bill likes to live in a state of denial."

"How so?"

"He thinks my mom is going through a midlife crisis."

"Is she even forty yet?"

"Basically. I think she's, like, thirty-seven."

"Kind of young for that, don't you think?"

"Maybe? Bill says that it's because they are empty nesters now. You know, with us being at school, it's just her and my dad. Before she had us, she had this huge career teaching middle school history, and she quit to raise us, but even then, she was *so* involved at Emerson. She basically ran the place as a volunteer. Bill thinks she's struggling now that the world doesn't revolve around us."

"I remember her involvement at Emerson," I say, remembering Mrs. Gallagher fondly. "She used to bring really fun snacks to field day."

"Right?" he exclaims. "Those little fruit kabob sticks. That woman sure loves her Pinterest."

"Well, maybe Will is onto something," I suggest. "It sounds like your mom could be going through something."

"Maybe." He nods with trepidation. "I feel like it shouldn't be bothering me this much. I'm almost twenty years old. It's not like I'm a little kid."

"Hey," I say sternly, "You're entitled to your feelings. I'm sure they're just going through a rough patch."

"You're probably right," he says, smiling for the first time since his arrival.

"Hey," I say, suddenly eager to cheer him up, "let's get out of here. Want to do lunch? It will be my first field trip out since my return home, so I get to pick the place."

"But what about Netflix?" he jokes.

"Oh, John B will be fine." I laugh. "Just give me a minute to change." I'm suddenly excited to run upstairs and choose a new outfit. "The remote is there if you—" but my words are interrupted by a soft knock on the front door, and I freeze.

"You expecting someone?"

"No," I say, rubbing my arms and grabbing his hand.

"You all right?"

"No," I admit. "I think I'm scared of strangers."

"I don't think anyone would blame you if you were," he says, biting his lower lip and tightening his jaw. "Maybe it's just Amazon or FedEx."

"Maybe," I agree as we hear another knock.

"Come on," Hank says, taking my hand in his, and I grip it tightly, his skin warming mine. "We'll open it together."

"Okay. Let's do it. But if it's a bad guy, I'm running."

"You can't fool me, Alanna Foster. I know you're a badass."

I smile as Hank and I approach the front door, and he places one hand on the doorknob and grips mine with the other.

"You ready?"

"Ready," I say.

Hank thrusts the door open, and I turn my body toward the kitchen, squinting my eyes closed and pressing myself firmly against Hank's side.

"Hi," Hank says, and I can tell instantly that Hank doesn't know the person outside. "Can we help you?"

"I'm here to see—"

That's all I need to hear. I would recognize that thick, gravelly, sexy-as-hell Mexican accent anywhere.

"Eddie!" I scream. My knees turn to Jell-O, and I brace Hank for support. "Eddie, is it really you?"

"It's, uh, really me," he says, looking from Hank to me and back to Hank, pausing for a beat to focus on Hank's hand holding mine.

"You're really here?" I shriek, ignoring the awkwardness of the moment.

"I am," he says with a smile. "It's over. Rosa's trial is on, and the trafficking operation . . . It's gone. Everyone has been released. I wanted to tell you in person," he says, lowering his eyes to the ground. "I wanted to surprise you."

I release Hank's hand, which drops dramatically to his side with a thud louder than necessary, and I leap into Eddie's arms, wrapping my legs around his waist and flooding his face with kisses while inhaling his sweet, familiar scent. "Thank you!" I squeal. "Thank you for coming here. Thank you for telling me in person. And thank you for helping everyone at that clinic . . . You really are my hero."

Eddie places me securely on the ground, clearly happy to see me but, even more importantly, looking like he wants answers. *Answers about . . . Hank? Oh God. What that must have looked like: Hank and I, answering the door like that?* Of course, this would be upsetting to Eddie.

"Eddie," I say, my smile the biggest it's been since my return home. "Eddie, this is my friend, Hank. Hank, this is Eddie, you know, the guy I told you about," I say, gesturing to the heart on my wrist.

"I've heard a lot about you," Hank says, shaking Eddie's hand. "Thank you for what you did. We missed our girl." *Our girl? What the hell, Hank?*

"She's an easy one to miss," Eddie says, planting a kiss on my cheek and grabbing my hand somewhat possessively. *Are they . . . Are they being territorial? Dear Lord, like I need this in my life right now.*

"Come in," I say to them both. "I can't believe you're here. How did you get my address? I mean, you are a detective, so . . ."

"Your mom gave it to me."

"My mom?"

"She reached out to me at the station. She said you really wanted me here," he says, placing a kiss on my forehead, his eyes locked on Hank's.

"Yes! I did . . . I do!" I shriek, hugging him close to me, feeling like myself again, feeling whole.

"Good. I'm glad," he says with a relieved sigh. "At first, I thought . . ." His voice trails off as he sizes up Hank once again.

"Hank? God, no." I laugh nervously. "He was just . . . I was just . . . and the knock at the door . . . it was just . . ."

"I was *just* leaving," Hank says through clenched teeth.

"Hank, no! Lunch, remember?"

"Rain check. No biggie. Thanks for hanging."

"Hank, wait," I say, wrapping my arms around his shoulders and whispering, "It's going to be okay, I promise. Your parents will work it out."

"Yeah, yeah, of course. Have fun, you two lovebirds." Hank winks.

"Nice meeting you, man," Eddie says, patting him on the shoulder before he exits the house, then for the first time outside the clinic, Eddie and I are completely alone.

"I really can't believe it!" I squeal. "I missed you so much," I say, pressing my lips to his, longer this time, then pulling back only to smile up at him. "I want to hear everything," I say, guiding him to my living room.

"Oh, you will," he says with a mischievous grin. "Because you're stuck with me for the weekend."

"You're staying? Yes!" I say, jumping up and down like the twelve-year-old version of myself.

"Nope, you're coming with me," he says, his smile growing wider.

"What?" I ask, confusion sweeping over me. "Back to Mexico?"

"No." He chuckles, reaching into his wallet and retrieving a hotel key. "You and me, penthouse suite, Skyline Vista Resort and Spa, two nights. Just you and me."

Holy. Freaking. Shit. I'm speechless. I feel like I'm dreaming. I *must* be dreaming. Because if I had one wish in the whole world, it would be to spend time alone with this man, and honestly it wouldn't matter where. *But the Skyline Vista?* I'd only been there once for a wedding because people like me don't spend time at places like that, or at least they didn't in my former life.

"I . . . um . . . holy shit, Eddie," I say. "I just made it out of my bedroom for the first time a few days ago. My clothes are from Target, and I get scared shitless when the doorbell rings."

"Yes," he agrees. "Your mother filled me in. She was describing a different Alanna Foster from the one I knew back in Mexico. The Foster I knew wasn't afraid to get the door."

"I know," I admit with a frown. "It's just different, being back here, you know?

"I know. Which is why your mom is agreeing to a little getaway."

"I'm sorry, what? Now you're telling jokes. There is no way my mother would agree to this. Or my father, for that matter."

"Oh yeah? Go check her bedroom closet. She packed you a suitcase and left you a note."

"She . . . she what?"

"Go on. Go see for yourself. I already checked us into our room. So, you can either stand here in the kitchen arguing with me, or you can go grab your stuff, and we can hit the road."

"Give me ten minutes," I say with a smile, shocked beyond belief that my mom was backing this plan, but readier than ever to bust out of here with Eddie, *my* Eddie. For the first time in as long as I can remember, I'm happy—truly and honestly happy—because not only am I convinced that this man is the love of my life, but my mother also has my back, and this grand gesture is more than I could have ever asked for, in my past or present life, and for the first time in a long time, I know I'm going to be okay.

Now . . . how exactly do I tell Eddie I'm a virgin? For the past fifty-five minutes, we've been lying poolside, getting lathered up with essential oils by Brad and Stanley, massage therapists with the strongest but gentlest hands on the planet, and I know, in just a few short minutes, Eddie and I will be alone—in the *penthouse* suite of the Skyline Vista—and I'm willing to bet my life that Eddie isn't looking to play blackjack and drink root beer.

I was barely seventeen when I was kidnapped, and even though I'm a grown-ass adult, I still feel like a sixteen-year-old girl on the inside as the only relationship I had prior to my experience in Mexico was with Lincoln Stone, and we all know how that turned out. But I've never been with a guy, like *never,* and up until now, I've felt I could talk to Eddie about anything, but this statement is not correct because I can't talk about this. It's *very* embarrassing, and uncertainty washes over me like tidal waves because I'm not sure I *want* to be with a man in that way yet. *Will Eddie stick around once I confess this?*

So, as Brad and Stanley bid us farewell, leaving us by our private pool, naked, covered only by thin white sheets, I turn my head toward Eddie and smile my biggest smile and say, "Hi."

"Hi." He smiles back. "How was your massage?"

"Amazing," I say, pulling up to a seated position, taking care to cover myself with my sheet. "That was my first massage, ever."

"For real?" he asks, wrapping his sheet around his waist and approaching me.

"For real."

"First hotel on my own too," I say with pride.

"Wow, a day of firsts for Foster," Eddie says, kissing my cheek then my forehead. "It's so nice to see you smile," he says.

"*You* make me smile," I say, pressing my lips to his and opening my mouth for a kiss, a *real* kiss, like the one we shared when Carmen was showering, and time was our enemy. And as Eddie's tongue traces my teeth and tangles with my own tongue, a soft moan escapes me, and I shudder with embarrassment.

"What's wrong?" Eddie asks, rubbing my oily arms with his palms.

"It's nothing." I blush.

"Oh, it's *something*." he winks. "I know you, Foster."

"I've been . . . We've both been through a lot," I say with confidence because we have.

"Yes, we have," he agrees.

I realize now that we haven't talked about his mother's involvement with Rosa, and I'm sure this has been devastating for him to process, and for a moment, I think about suggesting we get dressed and go to dinner so that we can talk. But Eddie and I have done our share of talking since we first met. There has been lots and lots of talking. And even though I'm scared to death and nervous and excited on so many levels, I want Eddie. I need Eddie. And even though I'm still a teenager at heart, I've grown up. *And if I want to express my love to this man, I should be able to, right?* But in the same breath, I know I'm not ready. I've spent so many minutes regretting one, single, decision. I'm just not ready to make the wrong one again.

"I . . . I need to tell you something," I say, taking his face in my hands and kissing his nose.

"Anything," he whispers, moving his mouth to my ear and nibbling on it gently, causing me to gasp.

"Oh God," I moan, falling against him and almost dropping my bedsheet.

"What do you need to tell me, Foster?" he asks, tracing my jaw with his pointer finger and grazing his lips over mine, creating *too* much space between us, bringing them closer, and pulling away again, making me feel like I'm on fire, making me want him more.

"*God,* Eddie," I say, cringing in frustration.

"What is it?" He asks, pressing my forehead to his.

"I've never done this before," I say, my voice cracking a bit because he's now tracing the curve of my neck, and his fingers against my oily skin feel very, very good.

"I know. You told me this was your first massage," he jokes.

I'm thankful for the playful banter. "Not the massage." I punch him playfully. "Eddie, I'm a virgin."

"You're assuming we are having sex," he says, kissing my neck then my shoulder as he very carefully slides the sheet off my shoulder and kisses farther down my arm.

"It's a safe assumption to make."

"I'm not going to even *think* of doing anything you aren't ready for, let alone pressuring you."

"I want to, really I do," I say, my words jumbling together. "I *really* want to," I say, slower and more confidently this time. "I just . . . It's just . . . Eddie, that kiss we shared at the clinic? That was my first kiss. It was the . . . You're the only one . . ." My cheeks flush. "I just don't think I'm ready. But Eddie . . . you need to know if I were going to do that with anyone, I would obviously want it to be with you."

"Foster," Eddie whispers, his words tickling the inside of my ear. "You call the shots, okay? I only want you doing what makes you feel comfortable. This is about you. You deserve to feel . . . good. You deserve to feel . . . incredible. I watched you suffer for far too long. I want to make you feel so . . . so . . . good," he says, his tone deep and seductive.

"You make me feel incredible," I admit, bashfully.

"Good. So even if this is all we do tonight, I'm okay with that. I could kiss you forever."

I press his lips to mine once more for another kiss, and this one sends electric shocks through my body. "I could kiss you forever too," I gasp.

"But if that kiss in the hospital was your first kiss *ever*, I'm pretty sure you're a natural."

I chuckle at this as I grip the back of his head and guide my lips toward his once again. With the smell of eucalyptus and lavender permeating my senses and the comfort of Eddie's body this close, the enormous feeling of security that he brings to my entire self just by being *him* takes over, and I become someone else entirely. "I want to go inside," I say.

Eddie secures his sheet over his waist then wraps mine under my armpits, covering me like I might wear a bath towel, then he picks me up like a groom carrying a bride over a threshold, and I'm overwhelmed with joy, anticipation, and most of all love—love for Eddie and the man he is. Feeling secure in his arms as he carries me inside our suite, I relish in the pure joy of feeling safe as he carries me past the designer kitchen and into our prestigious bedroom and places me gently in a seated position on the king bed.

"You're so beautiful, Foster," he says, tracing his finger over my bare shoulder and sending goosebumps down my spine. "So breathtaking."

"No," I shake my head and laugh self-consciously "Thank you, Eddie, but I'm anything but breathtaking," I say, lowering the sheet to reveal my veiny scarred arm and gesturing toward my scrawny figure. "Please, Eddie. I want to be with you, but I want you to be honest with me. Don't be saying things just to make me feel good. You've *always* been honest with me, and that's why . . ."

"That's why what?"

"No." I shake my head and bite my lip, angry with myself for being too open too soon, and I pull the sheet higher up over my chest, not even wanting to look at the ugliness of my body.

Eddie tilts my chin up toward him with one finger and pleads with his eyes. "That's why what?" he repeats, and my heart races faster than an Olympic track athlete's.

"It's why I love you."

"I love you, too, Foster. And I mean it when I say it," he says, removing the sheet once again. "You are stunning," he whispers with authority, guiding me onto my back and towering over me. "Your neck is perfect. Your skin, Foster. It's so . . ." He groans. "So soft." He presses his lips to my neck and kisses it all over.

I decide I might pass out from the adrenaline rushing through me.

"Your arms," he says, extending one of my arms toward him before moving his mouth over my oily skin. "Your arms are perfect. Your scars are beautiful. They are battle wounds, Foster, and you are a survivor," he says, kissing my upper arm and my elbow then moving down to my forearm.

Pulsating waves of electricity rush through my entire body, and I've forgotten my name.

"And these veins you speak about," he says, tracing his mouth over my deep-blue veins, "they are perfect too. Because the blood that travels through these veins is rare, in case you didn't know. And that blood pumps from the most loving heart I've ever known. And *that* makes you perfect. You are perfect to me, Foster. More than perfect," he says, moving his mouth back to my chest and kissing down toward my breasts, and I gasp as he cups one with a hand and presses his lips to the other.

"Eddie," I moan, silently surrendering to him, allowing his words to become the truth. "Yes," I gasp, giving in to him, believing him, loving him, and feeling beautiful.

"Is this okay?" he asks, gliding gently to my other breast and kissing that too.

"Uh-huh," I whimper beneath him. "More than okay. Please don't stop," I beg because I've never felt anything so wonderful.

"It feels good?"

"Yes."

"You will only feel good now, baby. I promise."

Baby. Eddie called me baby. I allow his words to spiral through my brain at lightning speed, unable to process his promises, unable to fully understand what is happening to me. *I've never. Felt. This. Good.* "I like when you call me that." I smile as Eddie guides me onto my back and kisses my abdomen, and I run my fingers through his hair.

"Your body is perfect, baby. But so is your heart. Your soul. And I love you."

"I love you so much," I say, gripping his strong, muscular arms, my fingers feeling tiny against them as Eddie continues kissing my chest and traces my abdomen with the tips of his fingers, my oily body responding easily. "Yes," I whisper, overwhelmed with feeling something good, something that other people my age have probably experienced long ago. Now, it will be mine to experience too, and the fact it's with someone like Eddie makes me happy on a level I can't even comprehend, and I stop trying because Eddie has kissed one of my legs and is tracing his fingers over the other, and I'm pretty sure this is all it's going to take to put me over the edge. Just having him touch me is enough, but in the same breath, it's not. I feel a burning desire for more—so much more.

"Are you okay?" he asks, lying down beside me and kissing over my belly button.

"Yes." I smile. "Thank you. I'm really okay," I say, reaching for the bedsheet around his waist and untying it as heat rises to my cheeks because not only is his body even more perfect than I imagined it would be, I've never seen a naked man in real life, and as my eyes drop to his groin, I am both turned on and a little shocked, which brings a smile to his face, and I know he's enjoying my reaction a little too much. "Stop," I say playfully. "Don't make fun of me."

"I'm not making fun of you. I'm smiling because you . . . you make me happy."

"Clearly," I snicker.

"Enough of that," he says, taking my hand and placing it against himself.

I gasp at this new overwhelming feeling, and when his body responds to my touch, I'm gone. "Eddie," I gasp.

"Yes," he says, guiding my hand over him, teaching me what to do, and tracing up my leg and between my thighs with the other. He stops in a place no man has touched me, ever, and he presses down with a firmness I don't expect, and I can't take it anymore.

"Eddie! Oh my God," I cry as he caresses me gently then firmly and gently again, and it takes only seconds for my body to explode from his touch. I think my insides must have burst out of me as relief floods through my veins and I lie there in shock, pressing my palms to my eyes.

"Are you all right?"

"All right?" I laugh, rubbing my eyes. "Whatever that was, you can feel free to do it again whenever you want."

Chapter Thirty

Now (June 2025) Lina

The only thing worse than going undercover as twenty-year-old Emery Shaw to prove a husband's infidelity is going undercover as twenty-year-old Emery Shaw to prove a husband's infidelity while pregnant. But there's no rest for the weary, especially when the target is on the move. And in this case, my target is Jasper Gallagher, husband to Penelope Gallagher and father to twins Bill and Hank. Ironically enough, just this morning, I was going to call a meeting with Jon and Penelope to inform her that we didn't have any leads on Jasper, but he pinged me under the username GymCasualJ on the dating app and requested a hookup just moments before I dialed the phone. Of course, any sleazy creep could go by the name GymCasualJ, but the idiot was stupid enough to use a profile pic. Of course, this app request is enough proof for Penelope, but I promised her I would do this right, so therefore, I will.

So, here I am on a scorching-hot summer day an hour north of Tempe, Arizona, preparing to meet Jasper Gallagher at his requested location, the Red Rock Motor Inn, a sketchy motel just minutes away from Desert Fit Performance, and it doesn't take a rocket scientist to figure out that if Jasper is cheating, which he clearly is, this is where he's been doing said cheating. The plan is simple. Aside from the screenshots I've already taken, I will take one final screenshot after informing Jasper of my arrival, under the username ShawPower, a name obviously created by Ryker and Daphne, which is a story for another day.

After I obtain Jasper's location, Jon, who will be standing by in the parking lot, will snap photos for evidence. Then, upon meeting with Jasper, I'll get him talking about the hookup app, lure him in until he confesses, and get out of there without allowing the creep to lay a finger on me.

I pull into the parking lot of the Red Rock Motor Inn in my rental car, waving to Jon in my rearview mirror, thankful he will be in the parking lot while I'm inside, but a bit annoyed he doesn't trust me to get this job done myself and further annoyed that he wouldn't let me take my own car.

"Everyone needs backup," he'd insisted before kissing me on the cheek. "Even a badass like yourself. And even idiots like Jasper can trace plates these days."

My belly flips as I think of Jon and how great he has been since our return from Mexico. Only days have passed since Travis's third degree at Prickly Pen Investigations, and the more I think about Travis and his accusations, the angrier I get, but I can't tell if it's Travis I'm angry with or myself.

ShawPower: *I'm here. Where should I meet you?*
GymCasualJ: *Room 323, first floor around the side of the building. Park there.*

I cringe, wondering why Jasper cares where I park, and I voice dial Jon before following the instructions, and he answers on literally half a ring.

"Hey, babe. You good?"

"Great," I say, because I am. "After what we went through in Mexico, this is nothing."

"Never let your guard down," he warns. "Remember, you never know what you're walking into. Every situation has potential for danger."

"Copy that," I say, placing a hand on my belly and inhaling deeply, knowing full well that Jon would never allow this to continue if he knew of my—our—pregnancy. "I'm heading around the side of the building. Room 323. He wants me to park in front of the room."

"Of course he does. He wants to make sure you're alone."

"But I'm not alone."

"Right." Jon laughs. "It's going to be a bitch for me to get the photos I need because of where the room is positioned. Jasper isn't an idiot."

"Well, clearly, he's done this before."

"Exactly."

"Okay, Officer Cote," I sing. "See you on the flip side."

"Hey, Lina, wait."

"What's up?" I ask, clearly annoyed.

"Are we good?"

I hesitate for a moment, cursing his timing. "Why wouldn't we be?" I ask, hoping my deflection is enough for now.

"You've just seemed off. And I know this is an infidelity case, and I'm just hoping—"

"No, not at all," I say reassuringly. That's history," I say because at this point, it sort of is. I've moved on to bigger and better things like infectious viruses from Mexico and hidden pregnancy. "We good," I say, mimicking Max.

"Okay, just promise me you'll be careful."

"I promise," I say to appease him, but the truth is I want to be done with this mission just so I can put Jasper and Penelope behind me, help Travis catch the wedding crashers, write my book, and figure out how the kidnappers knew Alanna had an unusual blood type. God, it's no wonder I'm exhausted.

I hang up with Jon, screenshot my convo with Jasper and send it to Jon, then I delete the screenshot from my phone just as Jon suggested. "Okay, you sleazy bastard," I whisper under my breath. "Today's the day you're going down," I grunt as I tuck my cell phone into my shorts pocket.

Next, I adjust my black tube top, thankful I chose something loose and not revealing, considering I'm already feeling bloated and swollen and I'm still so early, according to my ultrasound. I shrug off this thought and try harder to get into character as a college student, Emery Shaw. For whatever reason, I find that pulling my brunette tresses up into a higher ponytail and chewing on a piece of Trident gum puts me into character better, so I go with it. I hop out of my car and head toward Room 323, scanning my surroundings for anything out of the ordinary, click Record on my audio recording app, and knock three times on the door. I take a few steps back when Jasper opens it, just as Jon instructed, and I position myself innocently enough, for Jon to capture the perfect money shot.

"Hey," I say, twirling my ponytail between my thumb and pointer finger, feeling overly empowered because just by standing here, I'm ruining this man's life and giving Penelope the validation she deserves. "I'm Emery."

Jasper looks older than I remember, which irks me in ways I least expect, considering I'm playing the role of a young college student and he's in his mid-forties. His hairline recedes upward, creating a widening at the tip of his forehead, and his hair is way thinner than in his photograph, and I can't help but wonder what's keeping him from shaving it entirely.

"GymCasualJ, I assume." I giggle, cocking my head to the side and looking him up and down. "Or did I knock on the wrong door?"

"No." He clears his throat and wipes his palms on the front of his Under Armour tank top, and for someone who claims to frequent the gym like he does, he does not have the body to back that up. "Not the wrong door. Come on in," he says, peering over my shoulder longer than normal as I enter the musty, dim motel room consisting of only one double bed clothed in a comforter that belongs somewhere back in 1990 and looks like it hasn't been washed since then, either. To my left is a small bathroom that smells as though the plumbing has become an issue, and I can't help but think, *Damn, Jasper. I'm returning from an organ-trafficking clinic in Mexico that was more appealing than this. Women really meet you here? What is wrong with people?*

"Looks like my dorm room," I joke.

Jasper doesn't laugh. Instead, he sits on the edge of his bed and rests his hands on his knees and sits in silence, like he's waiting for something, and if this dip weed thinks this is how this is going to go down, he's got another thing coming.

"So, I have to confess," I say, thinking on the fly and making sure I obtain the necessary evidence in my recording. "This gym app thing, it's new. I've never done it before."

"No?" he asks, running one hand over his face and back to his knee.

"Nope, never. Have you?"

"Have I used the app?"

"Yeah, like, before me?" I ask, chewing my gum faster now, hoping to get what I need and get out of here because it's becoming harder to breathe as the air conditioner is also from 1990 and sounds like a freight train.

"Why do you want to know?" he demands.

Okay, Jasper, I'll play your stupid game. Sitting on this bed is the absolute last thing I want to do, but I do it for the case. I flop down beside him so our shoulders are roughly an inch apart, and I rest my chin on my hand, tilting my head toward him again. "I guess this whole app thing made me curious."

"Curious?"

"Yeah, well . . . I found out about it at the *gym*, so I assumed it had to do with, you know . . . fitness. But yet, here we are. Just you and me, in a *motel* room. I mean, clearly, I misunderstood." I chuckle.

"You thought we were going to be . . . working out?" he asks, furrowing his brow and scrunching his nose so tightly it falls into his face.

"What did you think was going to happen?" I ask innocently as Jasper turns colors before my eyes. "I mean, you're old enough to be my father," I say, my tone even-keeled. "You do know that, right?"

"Listen," he says, clearing his throat. "I don't know what game you're playing, but the meetup app is very clear. If this is some sort of prank—"

"Not a prank. Like I said. Just curious," I say, placing a hand on his sweaty knee and batting my eyelashes. "I did the meeting up. I just want to know what you're, you know, expecting from me."

"Well, usually," Jasper says, clearing his throat again, "I meet women here, and we . . . you know, are intimate."

"You hook up," I say for clarification. "You meet women here, and you have sex with them. Is that what you want from me?" I ask, dragging a finger down his arm and scooting closer.

"If you're up for it," he says, his confidence increasing.

"Got it," I say, because I totally do. "Sorry," I say with a shrug, "I was looking for a gym buddy. You know," I say, giving his flimsy bicep an annoying squeeze, "someone to get buff with. If I want to *hook up*, I'll do it with someone my age. Don't you think that's a good idea?"

"Wait," he says, leaping to his feet and showing me the door.

I pause, my hand on the doorknob, and turn towards a man I once respected, but now can't even look in the eyes. "Yeah?"

"You look . . .you look familiar. Do I . . .do I know you?"

Shit. I feel the heat rise to my cheeks as I turn the doorknob, eager to leave this sketchy hotel and leave Jasper behind. "Nope."

Jasper squeezes by me and props the door open with his foot and I take this opportunity to push it open further with my heel before planting a kiss on his cheek and whispering, "You might know my mom? She's more your *age*. Best of luck with your next hookup, sir." I wink before getting into my rental car and closing the door behind me, waving goodbye to a man who must be wondering what just happened and who also probably needs a *really* cold shower.

Chapter Thirty-One

Now (June 2025) Alanna

I will always remember my weekend with Eddie as the best two nights of my life. We didn't get out of bed much—no complaints here—and we talked even more than we did at the clinic. Eddie trusted me with information and details about his family that he's never trusted anyone with, and I shared what my plans had been for college and that I've found they've changed since I returned home. I decided, just over the past couple of days, that I was eager to do something with my life that would help prevent other women from going through what I went through. I'm not sure what that looks like yet, but I know where to start. Rather, I know *who* to start with.

So, as I enter the office of Prickly Pen Investigations, the home of Jon Cote and Lina Rivera, two of the people I owe my life to, I'm both eager to be reunited with my new friend, Lina, and also hopeful that this private practice might have space for someone like me. Of course, I don't have the necessary schooling to lead an actual investigation, but Eddie did some research, and in the state of Arizona, I can act as an apprentice to any of the PIs in the office. I'm hopeful that Jon and Lina are open to the idea of my coming on board because I won't rest until this sort of criminal activity is stopped, and that will only happen one case at a time. So I want to be part of *that* statistic.

The door to the office jingles as we enter, and I'm not sure what I expect Jon and Lina's office to look like, but I do know I don't expect it to look like *this*. Natural light floods the room, and a large glass sign that reads Prickly Pen Investigations hangs on the wall, along with a white leather sectional in the corner and three sets of glass desks and white leather office chairs. It is much cleaner than I expected, and I can sense Lina's touch as cacti in various shapes and sizes have been placed strategically around the office with large magenta cactus blossoms. I smile fondly, remembering my code name, Cactus Blossom.

"Can I help you?" Lina asks, poking her head out from the conference room, and when she sees Eddie and me, her face turns from serious and businesslike to excited like a teenager seeing her best friend. "Hi!" she whispers, waving like a child waving to a parent. "One minute," she says, holding up one finger. "Have a seat." She gestures toward the sofa. "Make a coffee, or grab a water. I should be done in roughly ten minutes. You look great!" She adds before closing the door behind herself, heading back into what I assume to be a conference room.

"I look great," I sing to Eddie.

He kisses my cheek and leads me to the couch. "That's because you do," he agrees, placing a hand on my sun-kissed leg. "That dress is perfect. I knew it would be."

"You didn't have to buy it for me."

"Yes, I did," he argues. "It was made for you."

"Well, heck, if a white Gucci sundress from a hotel gift shop was made for me, you shouldn't have had to pay for it," I snicker, punching him playfully in the side.

"Anything that makes you smile like that needs to be yours," he says, his tone smooth and accent thick.

"I don't want this time with you to be over," I say, squeezing his hand in mine. "I want you to stay."

"We will cross that bridge when we come to it," he says.

I know he's right, but losing Eddie would be like losing an actual piece of myself, which almost happened, so I know what that might feel like. I scroll through my phone and answer my mother's latest text, thanking her again for allowing me to spend the weekend with Eddie and once again telling her how much I love her.

Mom: *I'm so glad you had fun and you are feeling better.*
Alanna: *So much better. Wait until you see how tan I am.*
Mom: *When do I get to meet him?*
Alanna: *Eddie?*
Mom: *No, the Easter Bunny. Yes, Eddie. Daddy and I want to meet him.*

Alanna: *He got a room at the Horizon Palms for the next couple of days. It's a little bit more in budget, LOL.*

Mom: *Dinner tonight? Our house?*

Alanna: *I'll check with him and let you know. Thanks again, Mom. I love you.*

"So," I say with a sigh, stretching my arms overhead. "How do you feel about meeting the parents?"

"Whose parents?" Eddie asks with a sneaky wink.

"Mine, silly," I say with a nudge. "They want you to come to dinner tonight. I mean, we *are* dressed for it," I say, gesturing to my white dress and his tan khakis with a white button-down linen shirt.

"Our resort wear is on point," he agrees. "Sure, why not? Do you think you can come back with me afterwards?" he asks, kissing the top of my head. "A night without you just seems so . . . unfair."

"The past nineteen years without you seem just as unfair," I counter, kissing him on the lips and pulling back with a smile. "If there is a silver lining to getting kidnapped into organ trafficking, you're it," I say, tapping his nose with my finger then kissing his cheek.

If Lina doesn't come out of there soon, I'm going to end up climbing on top of him, because if I've learned anything about myself over the past forty-eight hours, it's that when it comes to Eddie, I have zero restraint, and he unleashed a part of me I hadn't known existed. "I'm going to rip that shirt off of you if they don't come back in five minutes."

"Don't tease me, Foster," Eddie warns. "I would want nothing more."

My phone buzzes as I receive a text message from Hank, who finally responded to my message from two days prior, when I had asked him if he was okay.

Hank: *I'm good. Party at Zack's tonight. You game?*

Alanna: *I'm sorry, I just made dinner plans. My parents want to meet Eddie.*

Hank:

What is up with him? I scream silently. Hank was never this weird before I left, but then again, I never had a boyfriend. This is the first time in all the years I've known the twins that I've been in any sort of relationship. Of course Hank wouldn't know how to act, especially knowing that, while I was away, I was falling for anyone, let alone a man as handsome and charming as Eddie.

"We will be in touch," Lina says as the conference room opens and she steps out, followed by Jon and another man I have yet to meet.

He's tall, too, maybe even taller than Jon, which feels hard to do, and he's both muscular and attractive, and the turquoise short-sleeved button-down shirt he wears creates a charming contrast against his dark skin.

"Take care," the man says to a woman exiting the conference room behind them, and my eyeballs almost pop out of my sockets as my jaw drops to the floor when I recognize her.

Mrs. Gallagher? I put the pieces together faster than humanly possible. Hank was concerned about his parent's relationship, and now Penelope Gallagher is hiring private investigators. *Could Hank be right?* I squeeze Eddie's hand and turn my head away from Mrs. Gallagher.

"I know her," I whisper scream. "What do I do?"

"Act natural," he advises. "Show Jon and Lina you can be professional."

"How the hell do I do that? It's my best friend's mother. You know, the guy from the other day?"

"Territorial redheaded kid with attitude. Yeah, I remember him. He most definitely wants to be more than your friend, Foster."

"He's fine," I insist, waving him off. "He's upset because his parents aren't getting along."

"Just be yourself, but don't act surprised to see her. Pretend you're just running into her at the bank or something."

"I don't go to the bank."

"You know what I mean."

I tuck a strand of blond hair over my shoulder and turn towards Jon, Lina, Mrs. Gallagher, and New Guy.

"Have a good day, Penelope," Lina says, opening the door for Mrs. Gallagher, and a wave of relief washes over me as she exits the office without recognizing me, thank God. "Alanna!" Lina shrieks as soon as the coast is clear and her client has left the building. "How nice of you to drop by. This is such a nice surprise," she sings.

"It's so nice to see you too," I say, wrapping her in a tight embrace.

"You look stunning," she says, pulling back and looking me up and down.

"You do too," I say, studying her black pencil skirt and white blouse. Something about her is different, for sure, and I chalk it up to having spent only a short amount of time with her, during which she was puking her guts out in a hospital gown and rescuing me.

"Freedom looks good on the two of you," Eddie jokes, hugging Lina and shaking Jon's hand.

"Eddie and Alanna, this is Travis Mullins," Jon says, making proper introductions. "Come on in." He gestures toward the conference room, so we follow him into a what looks to be a completely new and renovated conference room, and I take a seat at the long wooden table, next to Eddie.

"Didn't know you were in town, Eddie," Lina says with a smile. "You two couldn't stay away from each other, could you?" she winks.

"No," I say, taking Eddie's hand in mine. "But you know what that's like, right? You and Jon are inseparable."

"Those two lovebirds can't keep their hands off one another," Travis says, crossing his arms and winking at Lina, who shifts a bit uncomfortably in her seat.

I make a mental note to check in with her to make sure she's doing okay, because it's very clear to me that she isn't.

"Don't you know it," Jon says, and again, I sense a little something that wasn't quite there during my rescue mission. "So, what brings you two crazy kids into Prickly Pen Investigations?"

I sit a bit straighter in my chair and grip Eddie's hand for support. "Well," I start, getting my words sorted out, "My plan before . . . well . . . everything, was to go to nursing school after high school. After going through what I went through in Mexico, I've decided to change that plan."

"What do you have in mind?" Lina asks.

"Well, I'm not really sure yet," I admit with a smile and a nervous giggle. "But what I do know is I want to make a difference. I want to figure out what happened to me, you know? Not because I need closure or anything like that. I want to stop it from happening to other people. I don't really know how to do that except . . . maybe . . . I could become one of *you*," I say, gesturing across the table towards Travis, Jon, and Lina. "Maybe I could intern or apprentice with you. If I could make a difference in even one life like you have all made in mine, I would be happy with that."

The room is silent for a moment before Lina says, "Jon was a cop prior to becoming a PI, but Travis and I . . . we became involved with this practice because of you, Alanna. Of course, Jon is the boss, and he makes all the *big* and *important* decisions around here," she says, rolling her eyes to further emphasize the words, "but you have my vote for sure."

"We would love to have you join our team, Alanna," Jon says, smirking at Lina and shaking his head in amusement at her sarcasm.

"I agree," Travis says. "I'm happy you're home safely. And I'm happy I'm not the new guy anymore." He winks, and my cheeks flush as I wonder if he can read minds.

"Thank you!" I shriek pumping my fists in the air. "I won't let you down. If there is any way I could start by looking into how the kidnappers knew my blood type, I'd love to start there. If that's okay with you."

"I can help head that up," Lina chimes in before I can even finish asking my entire question. "Jon," she says, turning toward him, "there are so many loose ends to Alanna's case. I'd also like to look back into the pest control van."

"Pest control van?"

"Super Scorpion Pest Removal," Travis clarifies. "That van transported Lina and one other missing girl to the abandoned warehouse during our first rescue mission."

"Operation Superglue," Lina clarifies.

I leap from my seat and pause momentarily as a wave of panic sweeps over me, and I break out into a panicked sweat as I'm faced with a major flashback: a black van with green lettering, and I remember it clear as day.

Super Scorpion Pest Removal was the last thing I remember before being blindfolded and shoved into the van by Emmett.

"Foster..." Eddie says like he's been repeating my name for hours. "Foster, are you okay?"

"Holy crap," I say, shooting my eyes open and realizing I'm lying on the conference room floor. "What happened?"

"You passed out," Eddie explains. "Are you hurt?" he asks, kissing my forehead and searching my eyes for some sort of explanation.

I reach for Eddie, and he helps me to a seated position, and I'm thankful for the cushion of conference room carpet. "Nothing hurts," I say, reaching for the water Lina has offered me. "This is so embarrassing." I wipe a tear from my eye.

"We're family here," Jon says, and I can tell that melts Lina's heart. "Nothing to be embarrassed about."

"Thank you," Eddie says, before helping me to my feet and hugging me longer than usual. "Maybe, Foster... Maybe this is too much too soon."

"No," I insist, shaking my head. "I need this. I need to help."

"I understand where she's coming from. I think... I think she can do this. I can help her," Lina insists.

Eddie runs his hands over his eyes and stares up at the ceiling in frustration. "If that's the case, I'd like to stay too. I don't know how that will work on my end," he says, searching the team for answers, "but for the time being, I'd like to help too. And that way, I can keep an eye on my girl."

"Eddie," I say, leaning my head on his shoulder, the idea of him staying making me the happiest girl alive.

"Of course," Jon agrees. "You're always welcome here."

"Why did you react to the news about the pest control van in that way?" Travis asks, chewing on his pen.

"Oh," I say, taken back to my flashback as I ignore a chill that raced up my spine. "I've been in that van. It transported me from the underground camp to the abandoned warehouse where they held me for, like, ever."

"You were right under our noses the whole time," Jon says. "I can't believe you were right under our noses. Okay, we need to bring this evidence to the Tempe police," Jon tells Travis. "We'll follow up on this first thing tomorrow. Now that we've closed Penelope's case, we need to focus on the wedding crashers."

"Please speak correctly," Lina adds. "Treadmill Temptation and Project I Do."

"Code names." Eddie chuckles. "You will have to get us up to speed."

"Of course. Two of you have plans tonight?"

"My parents are having Eddie over for dinner," I say, a bit disappointed but also eager for an emotional break. "Not for another couple of hours, though."

"Do you have to go anywhere beforehand?" Lina asks.

"No, we're between hotels. We just left the Skyline, and we're staying at the Horizon Palms until we figure out our plan."

"That's plenty of time," Jon says with a nod.

"Wait," Travis says, holding up his hand to get our attention. "Horizon Palms in Scottsdale?"

"Yes," Eddie replies.

"There's a wedding set to happen there one week from today. And if I'm right, Horizon Palms is the next targeted venue. How long do you plan on staying there?"

"My plans are pretty much up in the air," Eddie says, winking at me with a shrug. "As long as my bank account allows."

"Let's brief them on Project I Do," Jon says. "I have an idea. Eddie and Alanna might be just who we need."

Chapter Thirty-Two

Now (June 2025) Lina

"Well, that's what I call things going full circle," Jon says with a smile while we wave goodbye to Eddie and Alanna as they exit Prickly Pen Investigations, off to dinner with Alanna's parents.

"Seriously," I agree. "Our cactus is truly *blossoming*," I say, proud of myself for being so poetic.

"One week," Travis says, closing his laptop and gathering his keys. We're going to catch those wedding-crashing assholes."

"Sure are," Jon agrees.

"Have a good night," Travis says, hooking his bag over his shoulder and nodding to Jon and me.

"Where are you heading? Hot date?" Jon asks.

"Something like that," Travis winks. "Good night, you two," he says, giving me a once over that says, *Figure this out*.

I turn from Travis and gather my own things from my desk, my head spinning from this day. This incredibly long day started with a counseling session of my own where my therapist betrayed me by encouraging me to share my news with Jon, followed by presenting Penelope with the news of her scumbag husband's affairs, and ending with the happy but emotional visit with Alanna and Eddie. Man oh man, what I would give for a margarita, and as I rub the base of my neck with my palm and Jon comes up from behind me, I know damn well this day isn't over yet.

"Hey," I say with a smile. "Nice way to end the day, huh?"

"You got your happily ever after with Alanna's case," he says, kissing the back of my neck. "We're looking into your pest control van and Alanna's blood-type data breach, *and* Project I Do is under control."

"Yeah," I say with a yawn. "Now, I just need to get a handle on my book."

"You submitted your manuscript this morning. I heard you tell Ryker when he called to tell you that he and Alex went out."

"Oh," I say, forgetting that Jon knew I submitted the manuscript to my editor. "The kids—"

"The kids are both at sleepovers. I heard you telling Daphne that when she called to tell you that she and Mal met with their divorce lawyer."

"Oh."

"What's going on, babe? Why are you avoiding me?"

A wave of sadness encompasses me as I burst out into tears and begin ugly crying. "I'm sorry," I say. "I'm a horrible person, and you have every right to hate me," I wail.

"What is going on?" he asks, taking my hand and leading me to the white sectional, and I sit beside him and sob all over his black T-shirt. "You've been a complete disaster since Mexico. Do you still not feel well? Was it too much for you? I knew it was too much—"

"It wasn't too much!" I snap, surprising us both, but as much as I don't want to share this news with him, as much as the idea of raising another baby terrifies me, having Jon think that Operation Cactus Blossom was too much for me hits worse than all that put together.

"Then what is it?" he asks, taking my hand and bringing it to his lips. His kiss feels extremely good, and all I want is for things to be normal again, like they were before Mexico. We were in such a great, great place.

"Jon," I say, my voice weaker than ever, and as I lock my stare with his baby blues, I know this will be a defining moment for us.

Sure, we've been through a lot together, but we've never been through "I'm pregnant with your kid, and I lied to you about it." Jon is either going to embrace this like Daphne claims he will, or he's going to shut down. Either way, this isn't my news to carry alone anymore.

"What is it? You can tell me anything. I love you, Lina."

"Jon," I say, wiping a tear from my eye, "I lied to you."

"Huh?" He pulls away, tightening his jaw. "What did you lie about?"

"In Mexico when I was sick . . . I didn't have a bacterial infection."

"Wait, what? Oh God, are you all right?" he asks, clearly alarmed. "Are you okay? Is it something . . . Is it something worse?"

His panic-stricken face melts my heart, and I'm reminded what a sweet, sweet man he is. "I'm okay," I say. "But I *did* lie to you, and you have every right to be mad at me." I sniff.

"What did you lie about, then?"

"Jon, I didn't get sick from drinking the water. I'm sick from the office sex," I say, tripping over my words and slapping my palm to my forehead. *What in the actual hell did I just say? Sick from the office sex?*

"Holy effing shit," Jon says, locking eyes with mine, and in this moment, I'm glad he's an intelligent human who speaks Lina. "You're . . . You're . . ." His bottom lip begins to quiver, and he closes his eyes, inhaling deeply.

"Jon, I'm pregnant."

His eyes shoot open and he asks, "Is it mine?"

"Um, of course it's yours," I say, breaking into tearful laughter. "I don't have office sex with just *anyone*."

"Good to know," he says, wiping a tear from my eye. "Why didn't you tell me? This news, Lina, it's great news."

"It is?" I ask, throwing my arms around his neck and flooding the collar of his shirt with tears of relief.

"Of course it is. Lina, we are having a baby!" he exclaims cheerfully. "How could this be anything but great news?"

"Because," I whimper, "the last time we were just starting out, we got pregnant. Now, we have our second chance, and I'm pregnant again," I wail, throwing my arms over my head dramatically.

"Nothing has to change," he says reassuringly. "We are still *us*, Lina. And sure, we've had really big bumps in the road, but we are going to be okay."

"Well, I'm glad you feel that way because I'm going to have a *really* big bump," I say, gesturing to my abdomen.

"It's not twins again, is it?" Jon asks, wide-eyed.

"No, thank God."

"Seriously."

"So . . . you're happy?" I ask. "Like, really happy?"

"I couldn't be happier, Lina. With the twins, I missed out on a lot. The idea of getting to do this with you, together, makes me the happiest man in the world."

"You have no idea how happy I am to hear you say that."

"No more lies, okay? Lies are what got us in trouble the first time. Promise me, no matter what the news is, no matter how bad it is, we go through it together." He places a gentle palm to my belly, making me burst out into tears once more.

"I promise," I say pressing his palm against me. "And I'm sorry. I freaked out. Will you move back home, Jon?" I ask, my eyes pleading with him. "We miss you. *All* of us," I say, gesturing toward his palm on my stomach.

"You don't have to ask me twice," he says with a smile. "How far along are you?"

"Roughly nine weeks," I say. "When you were with the Fosters at the hospital, they did an ultrasound," I confess.

Jon processes this news by tightening his jaw and nodding his head. "You're healthy, and the baby is healthy? Because honestly, Lina, that's all that matters to me."

"Yes," I smile.

Jon sighs a relieved sigh, and we share a silent moment together on our white sectional in the office of Prickly Pen Investigations, and I take a moment to think about all we've been through and how much we have to look forward to, moving forward. Then I say, "We have to tell Max and Lucy."

"No, Lina. We *get* to tell Max and Lucy."

"That's right," I agree, wondering when Jon became the optimist. "We *get* to tell them."

"Our family is growing," he says proudly.

"Our family is growing," I repeat with a smile.

"I knew something was up when you turned down coffee."

"Oh, I know. You're a smart man, Jon Cote. And I am so incredibly in love with you."

"I love you too," Jon says. "Let's continue celebrating this miracle at home . . . It's been a day."

"My home or your home?" I ask, genuinely confused.

"Let me swing by my apartment, and I'll meet you at the house," Jon says, rising to his feet.

"Sounds like a plan." I reach for my phone and check my texts, and my heart stops beating for a solid minute as a heat wave flushes from my chest to my neck, lighting my face on fire. "Jon," I gasp. "Look at these text messages."

I pass my phone to Jon, pressing my hand to my pounding heart, wondering who on earth would write something like this. It's from a phone number that very much looks like spam, but still.

Jon reads the message aloud and with each word becomes more and more enraged: "'You bitch. Tell your private investigator boyfriend that his next assignment is going to be to locate your body. Because when I get my hands on you, I'm going to rip you into a million pieces and scatter your remains all over the state of Arizona. You're as good as dead.'"

"It's got to be Jasper," I say, my knees growing weak and trembling. *How have I been so naïve?* Of course Jasper is going to be angry with me. *Why haven't I prepared myself better for the idea he would want some sort of revenge?*

"You're staying with me tonight," Jon insists. "We will trace this number in the morning."

"What a dick," I say, rising to my feet and holding onto Jon for support. "We were having a nice moment."

"We still are," he says placing one hand behind my back. "Unfortunately, this is part of the job. Just try not to get too worked up."

"And he called you my *boyfriend*," I add, wiping my tears with my blouse sleeve and rolling my eyes, ignoring Jon and his advice.

"I'm not your boyfriend?" Jon asks, trying to calm me with humor.

"You're many things, Jon Cote. But you are *not just* my boyfriend. But I think you know that."

Jon snickers at my remark, although at this point, I'm not entirely sure why it's funny, and my heart stops beating as Jon reaches for the doorknob just as a sharp knock on the other side of the door stops us short.

"Holy shit!" I exclaim, gripping Jon's arm tightly and shoving him in front of me. "Who do you think it is?" I whisper. "Jasper? Good as *dead*!"

Jon glances toward the corner of the office and his safe, and I know we're both thinking the same thing. *Jon's gun.* "Who is it?" he demands, backing away from the door and gesturing for me to move aside, so I do. "I said, who's there?"

"Tanner Navarro," a man responds in a heavy Spanish accent.

"Mr. Navarro?" I mouth to Jon, wondering why Tanner Navarro couldn't pick up the phone like everyone else but instead found it necessary to come to PPI after hours.

"Just a second," Jon says, unlocking and opening the door, revealing Mr. Navarro himself.

I must admit he is much shorter and older than I expected, as Jon hovers over him by at least a foot, and his thinning salt-and-pepper hair, receding hairline, tight, dark-washed jeans, and pointy penny loafers—which probably cost more than my monthly mortgage—confirm this.

"Hello, Mr. Cote," Tanner says, entering our office as if he owns it or at least plans to at some point. "We need to talk," he barks, looking me up and down and plopping down on the white sofa, crossing one skinny-jeaned leg over the other.

"Of course," Jon says with a confident nod before taking my hand and whispering, "You all right?"

"I'm good," I smile, clasping my fingers through Jon's and taking a seat on the sectional next to Jon and across from Mr. Navarro.

"What can we do for you?"

Mr. Navarro seems to find this question hilarious because he erupts into a fit of laughter. "What you can do for me," he says, the volume of his voice increasing tremendously and his cheeks flushing a fiery red. "What you can do for me is please do what I hired you to do. Find the scumbags that are stealing from me and my guests. That's what I need you to do."

"I understand your frustration—"

"Like hell you do," he huffs.

Jon releases my hand from his and runs his fingers over his chin's scruff, and I place my hand on my belly because I suddenly feel a need to puke, and a wave of dizziness washes over me, and I let out a soft groan.

"Lina," Jon says, placing a hand on my back. "Are you okay?"

"I'm okay. It's fine," I say, but I'm not sure if I am. Between coming clean about the pregnancy, Jasper's threatening text, and now Tanner bursting in like this, I'm experiencing some sort of anxiety attack. "I think I just need some water."

"Excuse me, please," Jon says, voice filled with authority as he rises to his feet and heads towards the conference room, leaving me with Mr. Navarro. I lean my head back and close my eyes, breathing in through my nose and out through my mouth just as Ryker taught me in a training session, but calming down is becoming increasingly difficult. *First off, who the hell sent me those nasty messages? It had to be Jasper. Of course it was Jasper. And now, this?*

"Listen," Jon says, returning with a bottle of water and handing it to me. "With all due respect, Mr. Navarro, this isn't how we operate here at PPI. Barging in here after ten o'clock at night and barking orders at us like this—it's unacceptable."

Get him, Jon. I silently cheer as I open my water bottle and gulp the chilled water eagerly.

"You have to understand—"

"No," Jon says, wiping the sweat from his palms on his jeans then sticking them in his pockets. "I don't have to understand. *You* have to understand."

"I understand that I'm a paying customer and other cases have taken priority," he says, his eyes falling on me, and at this moment, Jon and I both know that he's referring to Operation Cactus Blossom, and he's insinuating that we have placed his case on the back burner, and he isn't really wrong.

But Jon doesn't bat an eyelash. He simply shrugs and says, "My other cases are not your concern."

"They are when mine is being ignored."

"Okay, sure," Jon starts. "*I've* been a bit tied up, but I've had my best guy on your case, and he's made your wedding crashers *his* top priority."

"Well, your best guy isn't cutting it," he argues, hopping to his feet and tilting his head upward to make eye contact with Jon. "And your *guy*, Travis?"

"What about Travis?" Jon asks, inching closer to Tanner as I imagine steam shooting from his ears like an angry cartoon character.

"You say he's making my case top priority." Tanner's accent is thick, and he laughs. "You know who he's making top priority? My daughter, Beatriz."

Holy shit! Travis and Beatriz? How has he kept this from us? Why would he keep this from us? Wait, am I . . . am I jealous? Beatriz is stunning and can pass for a young Jennifer Lopez. I could say her skin is perfect, but that would be an understatement, and I would kill for her long legs. Forget her long legs—I'd kill for her boobs, fake or not. With this thought, I squirm in my seat, unsure what do to with my hands, so I remove my scrunchie from my wrist and gather my hair behind my neck in a low ponytail. Jon, however, seems unfazed, and I can't help but wonder if he knew about this new development in Travis's life.

Jon tightens his jaw and rubs the back of his neck with his palm. "Travis and his personal life are not my concern nor yours," he says with confidence.

"That may be true," Tanner counters, crossing his arms over his chest. "But as far as I'm concerned, you've done nothing. I've hired you to catch the wedding crashers . . . and alas!" he says, throwing his arms overhead. "No wedding crashers!"

"Okay, enough of this," I say in my mom voice, like I'm breaking up a fight between Max and Lucy. "Sit down, both of you," I demand firmly, and to my surprise and amusement, they comply. I look from Jon to Tanner and back to Jon. "Everyone take a deep breath. We both want the same thing. Now, Mr. Navarro," I say in my most businesslike tone I can muster up, "You will be happy to know that *Travis*," I say, unsure why I am putting so much emphasis on my ex-boyfriend's name and still trying to shake the image of Beatriz riding Travis's hips because Travis and his hips—*Stop it!* I beg myself. "Travis has some great . . ." I say, shoving away the image of Travis and his dark eyes as they stared into my soul and his hands as he gripped my waist and moved me in ways I will never forget until the day I die. "Travis has some great *leads*. And we just met as a team about your case, and we have a plan. It's a solid plan at that, right, Jon?"

"Yes," Jon says, pressing his palms to his eyes and inhaling deeply before exhaling. "And I would be happy to meet with you about that plan. But storming in here like this? It can't happen."

"My apologies," Tanner mumbles so quietly that I wonder if he really spoke. "There has been a new development, and the reputation of my hotels is at stake."

"What sort of development?" Jon asks as I sigh in relief that the two men have calmed the hell down.

"Brides have started canceling their weddings. Word is getting out about the wedding crashers, and they don't want to put their friends and families at risk."

"The Wellington wedding," Jon says, his voice full of hesitation. "The one set for one week from today?"

"Canceled."

"Oh no," I gasp. "We were going to attend that wedding. We had it all figured out."

"Well," you're going to need a new plan. "As of right now, they have canceled. There are currently no more weddings on the calendar until August."

"Shit," Jon says. "How will we catch the wedding crashers if there's no wedding to crash?"

"My thoughts entirely," Tanner agrees, shaking his head in defeat. "Your leads," Tanner asks, making eye contact with me. "Are they decent?"

"Well, yes," I start, but I stop, wondering what is okay to share and what isn't, and Jon nods in encouragement. "Travis has narrowed down a pattern and was convinced that the Wellington wedding was the next target. We know it is a male and female operating together, and we *had* a plan on how to catch them at *that* wedding. But without a wedding," I sigh, "there is no plan."

"What was your plan?"

I look toward Jon and beg him with my eyes to take over the conversation, so he does.

"We have two new team members staying at the hotel over the long term. They were going to act as our boots on the ground at the resort, leading up the wedding. They were going to gather intel and see what they could do from behind the scenes, you know, bachelor and bachelorette parties, that sort of thing. Travis has identified a pattern for the robberies that take place during the wedding, like when things begin to go missing, when security is cut, power outages, that sort of thing. And this time, we were going to use trackers on the wedding gifts." Jon pauses for a beat before adding, "This wedding was going to be all hands on deck. We were . . . We were ready to take them down. I even have Scottsdale PD ready."

"Trackers on the gifts. That's good thinking."

"That's all Travis," Jon says with confidence. "He's been working hard on this. He's even noticed some consistencies with some of the wedding vendors. Did you know that three of the crashed weddings have employees who have confessed to working with individuals they had never met before?"

"It's because the crashers wear disguises," I add.

Tanner thinks about this for a beat. "I need to catch them. It's the only way. We can afford to cancel some events. It isn't finances that are my concern. My reputation is of the utmost importance. My guests need to feel safe. No guests . . . no hotel. You see?"

"Understood," Jon says. "But how do we catch the crashers without a wedding?"

We sit in silence for minutes that feel like hours, my brain spinning with ideas all the while, like how my mind works when I write. *If this were a novel and my characters needed to solve this crime, what would they do?* Then I have an idea, and I press my fingers to my temples and squint my eyes, searching my mind for the pros and cons of my plan prior to presenting it to the two men. Because it's either the best idea I've ever had or the worst, and I'm unable to predict what Jon will think, let alone Tanner Navarro.

"Hey," I say, nudging Jon with my elbow, making a face similar to Jon's when he has an idea, the same expression he made when presenting me with Operation Superglue last fall. "Hear me out," I say with a smirk.

Jon smiles at me in amusement and asks, "Hear what out?"

"I have an idea."

"Okay," Jon says. "Out with it."

"Mr. Navarro," I say, clearing my throat and leaning forward to rest my chin on my hands. "If I'm hearing you correctly, you are saying that when it comes to catching the wedding crashers, your budget isn't a concern, correct?"

"Correct."

"What if I told you that we have enough people and resources to stage a wedding at your hotel? You wouldn't need to do a thing except provide us with the venue," I say, then bite down on my lower lip and count to five, unsure if I've just said the smartest thing in the world or the silliest. "I mean, it's probably more complicated than I'm making it—"

"Lina," Jon says, reaching for my hand and squeezing it tightly. "That could work."

"It could?" I ask, trying to hide my surprise but failing miserably. "We'll have to figure out the details, and someone would have to pretend to get married. I'm not sure who would agree to that . . ." I say, my words flying out of my mouth at lightning speed then drifting away into thin air.

"I don't care how you do it," Tanner says, standing to his feet. "I don't care if you marry Gordon Ramsay and Mister Rogers. Just marry *someone*, and catch those criminals."

"Oh . . . okay," I agree, unable to picture Gordon Ramsay and Mister Rogers having a conversation, let alone a relationship. "You've got it. Even if we hire actors, you will have your wedding."

"Beatriz will reach out to you with details, but the venue is yours."

"Thank you," I say, standing and reaching out to Tanner's extended hand for a handshake so firm that it hurts.

"I'll let Scottsdale PD know the new plan," Jon says. "You will have your wedding, and we will catch your bad guys," Jon says with a confident smile. "You have my word."

Chapter Thirty-Three

Now (June 2025) Alanna

Eddie and I planned a relaxing Saturday poolside in an effort to scope out the scene for the upcoming wedding-crashing extravaganza. Those plans changed quickly, however, when Jon called Eddie late last night and explained the situation. Apparently, Tanner Navarro has lost all faith in Prickly Pen Investigations because the wedding we were assigned to infiltrate was canceled, and we haven't been kept in the loop as far as what our next steps might be. However, we would be finding out soon enough because as Eddie holds the conference room door open for me at PPI, I sense that the team is no-nonsense and they mean business, for sure.

The original plan was for me to be planted as an undercover agent smack-dab in the middle of the prestigious wedding of Ivy Wellington, daughter of Robert Wellington, an up-and-coming politician in the state of Arizona, to Richard Prince, a prestigious and reputable trial lawyer from Phoenix, Arizona, at none other than the glamorous Horizon Palms resort and hotel. I even had the coolest undercover name—Cynthia Brodrick, friend of the bride—and Eddie took on the identity of Mario Delgado, college friend of the groom, and our first assignment was to join the wedding party for drinks poolside prior to getting ready for the big day.

The problem with our plan, however, was that not only was the wedding canceled, but Tanner Navarro became furious when Ivy and Robert canceled their wedding. At first, there was a misunderstanding. Tanner assumed the wedding had been called off because of PPI and our involvement with targeting their particular event. But the truth was that Ivy was beside herself at the thought of her friends and family being at risk during their wedding celebration, and I don't blame her. Tanner became furious with Jon, accusing him of not making his case a priority, and because of this, Jon and Lina have decided to take some drastic measures, even going so far as hosting a fake wedding.

Lo and behold, Tanner was not only on board with this plan but agreed to pay for this fake wedding in an effort to put an end to the robberies. I'm curious to learn what our plan will be.

So now, instead of sipping virgin strawberry daiquiris with the love of my life by the pool and reminiscing on what a success dinner with my parents was, I'm taking a seat at the conference table between Eddie and Travis and across from Jon and Lina, and the tension in this room is so thick and heavy that it feels like I'm moving through honey. Every movement and every thought is slow and filled with such effort that I'm tired just sitting here.

"Good, you're here," Jon says, sipping the last of his black iced coffee and slamming it down with such energy I can only assume it's not his first of the day. He means business and is focused, and I realize that, until now, I've seen only a couple sides of him—valiant rescuer and compassionate confidant—not Jon Cote, private eye. And in this case, he's my *boss*, and I'm suddenly intimidated. As if reading my mind, Eddie reaches under the table, takes my hand in his, and gives it a soft squeeze, and I nod in thanks.

"Good to be here," Eddie says, winking at me, then opens his laptop.

"I need more coffee already," Lina says with a sigh, and I can tell by the dark circles under her eyes that she and Jon most likely pulled an all-nighter.

"Okay, team, we have lots to do and no time to waste," Jon says, opening his own computer. "I'm going to catch up Eddie and Alanna, and then, Travis, the floor is yours."

"Got it, boss," Travis says, typing away on his laptop.

"As you know," Jon starts, "last night, Tanner Navarro paid us a visit. He's unhappy and rightfully so. As of now, his properties have been robbed a total of six times in three months, with a total of at least a hundred and fifty thousand dollars between missing items and legal fees, and that cost is only climbing. And most importantly, Mr. Navarro, who has trusted us with this case, has his reputation on the line. Couples have started canceling their weddings, and even business events have been postponed. Bottom line, guys, we need to catch these crashers, and we need to do it *yesterday*."

"Copy," Eddie says, somehow able to take notes on his computer while not breaking eye contact with Jon.

"We had a plan, as you know, to take them down at the upcoming wedding on Friday night, but that wedding has been canceled. And since we need a wedding to catch the crashers, we need to stage a wedding of our own."

I narrow my eyes in concentration to follow what Jon means, but I'm coming up short. *How do we stage a wedding? Like, host a wedding that isn't real? And if we can pull that off, how do we trick the crashers? Won't they know something is up?* I raise a nervous hand like I'm a student back in class at Emerson.

"How do we stage a wedding?" I ask, my voice barely above a whisper. "Won't the wedding crashers know the bride and groom aren't the Wellingtons?"

"Great question," Jon says, cracking a smile for the first time this afternoon. "Lina and I have that covered. With the help of Ivy and Robert, we were able to update their home page on theknot.com where they explain that their wedding has been postponed for the time being, and we've created our own site for the new wedding . . . *your* wedding," he says, locking eyes with me and smiling wide, like he's just informed me I'm the next contestant on *The Price is Right*.

"Her wedding?" Eddie asks, sitting up a bit taller, whereas I have lost the ability to speak words.

"Yes," Jon says. "Don't worry, it won't be an official ceremony. But it makes sense and here's why. Alanna is all over the news, and everyone knows of her kidnapping and her rescue, and as of last night, after our social media updates and press releases, America now knows of Eddie too. So, when there was a last-minute cancellation at one of the swankiest hotels in Arizona, you Eddie, proposed to Alanna, and she said yes."

Eddie and I stare at Jon as if he's gone totally nuts, and although I'm completely aware that this plan is absolutely genius, I can't help but wonder if Eddie will be angry with Jon and Lina for violating his privacy. *What gives Jon the right to tell our story to the world? Shouldn't that be up to me and Eddie?* I side-glance at Eddie, his eyes narrowed, typing away on his keyboard and taking notes like he's in history class. *How is he not bothered by this? Hell, shouldn't I be bothered by this?* On the other hand, I owe Jon and

Lina my life. If they need something from Eddie and I, well, I'm going to give them what they need.

"Copy," Eddie says again, as he continues typing.

"Alanna?" Jon asks. "Do you understand?"

"Me?" My cheeks flush, and my throat is dry. "I think so?"

Eddie turns to me and nods confidently. "It's an undercover assignment," he says reassuringly. "I'm an undercover groom, and you're an undercover bride. Don't let the emotion in," Eddie says, making me cringe with the unfamiliarity of his tone.

"Okay . . . it's just . . . everyone knows about us. You're okay with that?"

"Yes, I am."

"How?" I ask rubbing my arms. "Our story . . . it's personal."

"It's for the job, Foster. Whatever Jon and Lina need."

"Okay, then," I say, sitting up a bit straighter, feelings of anxiety washing over me. "If that's what they need, then that's what we do."

"Thank you," Jon says, clearing his throat. "The wedding will be Friday night. Your jobs are simple. Get the word out to your friends and family. We need to fill the venue and make it seem legit."

"Wait," I say, a soft laugh escaping. "Do I tell them it's a fake wedding?"

"They need to think it's real. That's the only way this will work," Jon says, like he's simply asking me to invite some friends for dinner. "Afterwards, you can disclose whatever you would like, but for the time being . . . yes. They will believe the wedding is real."

"I—"

"We will figure out those details later," Eddie says, placing a caring hand on my leg. "Let's let Jon finish briefing."

"Okay," I say, wondering how on earth I'm going to pitch this to Patrick and Laura when I swore I would never lie to them again, and I realize I can't do it. I can't lie to my parents, even if it means blowing this entire operation. "I'm okay with relatives and friends not knowing the truth," I say firmly, surprising myself. "But my parents, they need to know the truth." *Oh God . . . I silently freak out. What am I doing? I have the opportunity to go undercover with a real PI firm, and I'm blowing it, like really blowing it.*

The room falls silent for what feels like hours before Lina says, "Of course. Patrick and Laura *should* know the truth. They are your parents. That's fine, right, Jon?" she tells him more than asks, and I breathe a relieved sigh.

"Yes, of course. Now, let's talk logistics. Eddie and Alanna are our bride and groom, and Lina is going to take care of outfitting you and your wedding party."

"My wedding party?"

"Yes. Please make a list, both of you. This needs to be as realistic as possible."

"Copy that," Eddie says, and I want to shake him for staying this calm and unfazed.

"Yeah, uh . . . copy that," I agree.

"Lina's friend Daphne is a designer, so outfitting your wedding party will be easy. Her mother, Celeste, will be making your cake," Jon says, smiling toward Lina.

"Hope you like prickly pear," Lina adds.

"I . . . uh . . . yes, I do," I say because I do.

"Good," Jon says. "The venue is taking care of basics: bartender, servers, cocktail hour, and food, and Lina's friend Ryker will be your fake justice of the peace. Our children and Travis's son will also be attending, along with Max's girlfriend, Molly. They will oversee the gift table and guest book and serve as an extra set of eyes."

"Going on record that I am not fully on board with this," Lina adds with a roll of her eyes.

"There's nothing to worry about," Travis counters. "These wedding crashers have shown no sign of violence."

"Yet," she argues.

"It's fine," Jon says, making me imagine they didn't land on this decision easily.

"That leaves music," Jon says. "We need a band or a DJ."

"Actually," Travis chimes in, rubbing the base of his neck, "there is something you should know." When the room falls silent, he says, "I've got that covered."

"You know a DJ?" Jon asks, eyebrows raised.

"No. But I am one."

"Excuse me?" Lina snorts. "You *are* one?"

"Yes. And since I've been covering the past three weddings, I've . . . you know . . ."

"You've been the DJ?" Jon roars.

"Don't judge me."

"Fine," Jon huffs. "You can DJ. That leaves me and Lina. Now, Lina has already had face time with our suspect, so she needs to hang back with me on security. Okay, Travis, or should I say DJ Travis . . . you're up."

I look from Travis to Jon and back again, unable to fully comprehend what's happening, and I want more than anything to whisk Eddie away back to our bubble of happiness, back to our hotel room, where it was just he and I. But as I study him as he eagerly takes notes, eyes glued to Travis as he briefs the team on his findings, I realize his commitment to this case isn't only about catching the wedding crashers. It also involves his gratitude toward this team and their rescue mission to save *me*. And if I know Eddie like I think I do, he's also thinking about the bigger picture. I'm pretty sure he's concocting a plan of his own, one that involves staying here with me and not going back to Mexico, and I hope beyond hope that he finds a way. Because losing Eddie is not an option, and I'm willing to do whatever it takes to ensure that I will never need to know life without him ever again.

Chapter Thirty-Four

Now (June 2025) Lina

After a mere three days since the team met at Prickly Pen Investigations with the goal of revamping our original schematics for Project I Do, to say we've crushed this wedding-planning extravaganza would be an understatement. So far, Alanna and Eddie have filled in Patrick and Laura on their plan, and surprisingly, they are one hundred percent on board and have already begun rallying friends and family for Alanna's big day. It seems the Fosters are so incredibly grateful to Jon and I for bringing her home that they wouldn't think twice about helping us, resulting in Daphne whisking Alanna and her bridesmaids away for dress fittings, trial hair appointments with Alex, and a meeting with my mother, Celeste, for the cake—paid in full by Tanner Navarro, a man who, in his desperation to save his hotel's reputation, hasn't batted an eyelash as he pays for every expense imaginable.

At first, choosing a wedding party was challenging for Alanna. Her sister, Eliza, would be her maid of honor, and her brother, Christopher, would be included on the groom's side of the wedding party. And although she would've preferred a smaller wedding party, considering she currently didn't have many close friends, Tanner insisted that this wedding needed to be monumental and luxurious, attracting the most attention possible . . . and by that, he meant the *wedding party* needed to be larger, more monumental, and more luxurious. Jon had suggested including Max and Lucy in the wedding party or even seeking out cousins and old friends of Alanna and Eddie, but this became frustrating for Alanna, causing her to become overly emotional, overwhelmed, and withdrawn about the wedding, and considering the circumstances, none of us blamed her. So, imagine how grateful she was to Eddie when he suggested they try to locate Carmen and Maria for the big day, and although this was the epitome of short notice, Alanna agreed, and Daphne has chosen bridesmaid dresses based on Alanna's size, as all three girls lost a significant amount of weight during their time in Mexico. If all goes according to plan, Carmen and Maria will wear light-pink sheath dresses with side ruching, and her sister will wear the same in magenta.

Now, as Daphne and I leave Desert Blossom Floral Arrangements, we can check bouquets and centerpieces off the list as well, as Alanna and her bridesmaids will be carrying bouquets of succulents and desert roses, and her centerpieces will consist of hibiscus and agave, complimenting Alanna's chosen color scheme. Of course, some are concerned that Eddie and Alanna might not be able to find Carmen and Maria in time, and the idea that both girls will be able to travel so soon after their rescue is a huge gamble, so in true Jon and Lina fashion, we've come up with a solid plan B.

As if reading my mind, Daphne asks, "Any word from the team about the bridesmaids?"

I hold the door open for her as we exit the florist and are smacked in the face by the excruciatingly hot summer desert air. I wipe the beads of sweat from my forehead with the back of a hand after unlocking my car's door. "Not yet," I sigh.

"You do realize this wedding is in three days?" Daphne reminds me as she climbs into the passenger seat and I start my car, cranking the AC to high on max speed.

"Thanks for the reminder, Daph." I don't attempt to hide my frustration in the slightest, as Mr. Navarro has called me twice already in anticipation of the possibility of two more organ-trafficking survivors being included in the ceremony, as their involvement would surely attract even more attention to the hotel, and therefore less attention would be placed on the wedding crashers and his falling reputation.

"Anytime. That's what I'm here for."

"Don't worry about it, really," I say as I navigate my way out of the parking lot and follow my GPS, which leads us back toward Prickly Pen Investigations, where Daphne's car is parked. "I have a meeting with the team when we get back to the office. If we haven't confirmed their involvement by then, we'll go to plan B."

"You're really okay with the kids being at the wedding?"

"Honestly, I'd rather have Max, Lucy, Molly, and Smith *in* the wedding. It somehow feels safer than having them man the gift table and the guest book."

"Nobody wants the guest-book job."

I chuckle at this because if we do revert to plan B, Daphne will oversee the guest book. But she doesn't need to know that just yet. "Right," I say. "I'm not worried about it, though. If anyone can locate these girls, we can."

"Did you end up finding someone to act as your fake justice of the peace?"

"Oh yes," I say, side-glancing at her with a smile.

"Don't tell me . . . Ryker?"

"Yup."

"How in the actual hell did you get him to agree to *that?*"

"Honestly, it wasn't really that hard."

"Lina. This is me. I know the two of you."

I sigh, remembering that Daphne knows me better than I know myself. "You got me." I chuckle. "He gets permanent residency in our guest room whenever he wants, even once Jon moves back in."

"That's it? That seems like a win-win for everyone . . . Well, everyone except Jon."

"Well, yes," I start but stop as I merge on to the highway, stifling a laugh as I recall Jon's face as Ryker listed his demands.

"Oh, gosh. This is going to be good, isn't it?"

"Yup," I smile. "Jon had to agree with binging all thirteen seasons of *Blue Bloods* with Ryker."

"Stop it right now!" Daphne shrieks, slapping her open palm to my dashboard while belly laughing. "I have to say, that is genius."

"Sure is," I agree.

"Sounds like *someone* may be feeling threatened by the return of Jon Cote."

"Possibly," I reply, even though I know deep down she is right. "You know, Daph, you can come hang with us anytime you want, too."

"Uh," she says, her smile turning downward as she adjusts her blonde curls into a perky ponytail atop her head. "This is where you ask me more about my divorce?"

"Yes, actually it is," I say firmly. Even though we talked about it at the surface level at dinner, we never really got to the bottom of anything, and I still have what feels like a million questions for her. "What the heck happened, Daph? I feel like this was so . . . out of nowhere."

Daphne turns from me and stares out the window, and I know her well enough to predict she will change the subject, so I'm unfazed when she says, "That's a story for another day. What time do the guys have their tux fitting tonight?"

"Stop. What happened?"

"Dude," she whines. "I don't know, okay? It just isn't working."

"Did he meet someone else? Did you?"

"You really think if that were the case, you wouldn't know about it?"

"Maybe. You don't talk to me about your marriage."

"Things change. People change. End of story," she huffs.

I side-glance at her before pulling our car along the road's curb in front of PPI, knowing it's time to leave well enough alone and Daphne will talk to me when she is ready. "Well, I'm here for you when you're ready." I sigh. "Just know I'm here for you."

"Duh."

I shake my head and try and to hide my worry for Daphne. She's always there for me but seldom lets me be there for her in return.

"Seriously. I love you," I say.

"I love you too," she says, climbing out of the car and closing the door behind herself, obviously ready to end this conversation. "Keep me posted about the meeting," she says as I approach the sidewalk, arms open for an embrace, and she welcomes this eagerly. "Hey." She pulls back and studies me with concern. "Any more sketchy texts from Jasper?"

I contemplate lying to her as I don't need her worrying about me, with everything she has going on with Mal. But I can't lie to my best friend. I'm just not wired that way. "Yes, but Jon plans on paying him a visit sooner than later, so please don't worry."

"I'll stop worrying about *you* when you stop worrying about *me*."

"So . . . never, then?"

"Never."

"Love you, Daph," I call to her as she's walking toward her car, and I turn and enter PPI, where Travis sits at his desk sporting a tighter-than-usual tank top, and I scold myself for looking twice as Jon paces back and forth around the office, with Alanna and Eddie seated on our white sectional, wearing smiles larger than the state of Arizona, and I know without a doubt the news about Carmen and Maria is good.

"Are they coming?" I mouth to Alanna, who nods in return, her eyes beaming with joy.

"Yes," she whispers, giving me a thumbs up and planting a huge kiss on Eddie's cheek.

"Awesome!" I whisper back before dropping my purse at my desk and gathering materials in preparation for our meeting, which starts in just a few minutes. I retrieve my phone from my purse and prepare to text Tanner but become distracted when I see a text from Lucy.

Lucy: *My friend needs to know if I can go to that Darcy Blue Boots concert.*
Lina: *When is it?*
Lucy: *It isn't until February, but Mom, she's my fav! I'm like low-key dying to see her live. Please? I'll do extra chores for a year.*

I think about this for a beat, doing the math in my mind, and become overwhelmed with both excitement and dread as I realize Lucy will more than likely have a new baby brother or sister by that time, and I find myself *low-key dying* as well, but I can't find a single reason why Lucy should miss her favorite country artist, so I agree.

Lina: *Okay. We will talk details later, but yes, you can go.*

I toss my phone onto my desk, and it lands with a louder thud than intended, and I shake off the uneasy feeling that forms in the pit of my gut and I can't help but wonder if I'm nervous about my daughter attending her first concert, about becoming a mom again, or both.

"Sounds excellent. Thank you so much," Jon says into his phone. "We look forward to your arrival. Yes, that is correct—your hotel and air fare are paid in full. Yes, that is correct—no expenses. Thank you. We appreciate it so much. Alanna is thrilled," he says as he hangs up the phone and pumps his fist in the air before turning to Alanna and Eddie and announcing, "Your friends arrive tomorrow night."

"Thank you!" Alanna shrieks. "You have no idea what this means."

"I'm pretty sure I have an idea," he replies, his smile genuine. "Come on," he says, gesturing toward the conference room. "We have work to do."

Later that evening, after we brief the team on our plan for Alanna and Eddie's fake wedding and update Tanner on the arrival of Carmen and Maria, everyone leaves the office except for Travis and me. Jon was eager to begin packing up his apartment, so he instructed us to work on finding a lead on Alanna's case. We still have no idea how the kidnappers knew of her rare blood type, and the time is approaching nine thirty, and we don't have much to go on. I become increasingly frustrated, and Travis begins to notice.

"You okay over there?" Travis asks me from his desk.

"Me? Yeah, of course," I say, my tone rather unconvincing.

"Any more texts from Jasper?"

"I blocked the number . . . for now," I say as I return to an article about a group of people kidnapped for their organs in 2015, and I find that the authorities were unable to fully understand why those individuals were targeted. "Hey," I said, glancing up at Travis, who's kicked his feet up onto his desk and is stretching his arms overhead, his black tank showing off his defined arm muscles, no doubt on purpose. "Every case I study involving organ trafficking talks about HIPAA violation or insider information. Let's be honest, Travis. It had to have been Dean Turner, right?"

Travis bites down on his pen, nodding in agreement. "I've been thinking the same thing. Dean Turner is our guy for sure. Think about it, Lina. He wasn't honest with us at first about any of it until we really pushed him."

"We need another visit with him."

"I agree. Let's get past Friday, and we'll tackle it then."

"Yeah, that and the pest control van," I add.

"Well, that lead was handed over to Tempe PD."

"Wonderful," I say with a roll of my eyes, remembering how frustrating it was to get them to pay attention to the lead the first time around.

"You have enough on your plate with Friday night coming up. Take this one day at a time."

"You're right," I agree, rubbing my tired eyes. "There is a *lot* going on. I'm just thankful this isn't *my* fake wedding." I chuckle. "If I hadn't encountered one of the crashers in the bathroom that night, it would be Jon and I up there for sure."

"And that would be a bad thing?" Travis asks.

"Excuse me?"

"Marrying Jon. Wouldn't that be a good thing?"

Oh no, no, no, Travis. We aren't going here, I counter silently, simply shrugging and ignoring his question and asking, "How's Beatriz?"

"Feisty tonight," he says through gritted teeth, and I can tell I've managed to get under his skin or shut him down—I can't tell which. "He's going to ask you to marry him again, you know."

Under his skin, for sure, I decide. "Oh yeah?" I ask, pretending to be unfazed when that couldn't be further from the truth. I am very much fazed.

Why on earth would Travis, my ex-boyfriend and co-worker, find it appropriate to talk with me about my possible remarriage? I want to change the subject—really, I do—but I'm suddenly curious. *Does Travis know about my pregnancy?* So far, the only people who know are Ryker, Daphne, and Jon. Hell, I haven't even told Max, Lucy, or my parents yet. *There's no way Jon confided in him, right?* I gulp, a wave of nausea flooding over me as I recall part of the reason my relationship with Travis didn't work out. Sure, there were many reasons, but our last argument had been about starting a family.

He'd been set on the idea of my twins and his son becoming one big happy family, *Brady Bunch* style. He even went as far as suggesting *we* have a baby together, and I immediately shut that down, insisting that no way, no how could I ever start over again at this point.

"What makes you say that? Did he say something to you, Travis?"

"I can just tell," he says with a shrug.

I give him my best evil eye and cross my arms over my chest. "Out with it," I demand in my best mom voice.

"It's nothing, really," he says, returning to his computer.

I stand and walk toward his desk, ready to fight it out of him if necessary. "What did he say?" I whine, like a middle school girl begging for information about her crush. "Tell me!" I say, poking him playfully in the chest.

Travis finds this funny and raises his eyebrow in amusement. "He may have mentioned that it was silly we were having a fake wedding when the two of you could have easily had a real one."

"What?" I say, scrunching my nose in disgust. "Jon wouldn't say that."

"Well, he did."

I investigate his facial features, convinced Travis knows about my pregnancy but still refusing to show my cards. "When?"

"This morning. Over coffee."

Coffee! "I'm sorry, I guess I didn't realize you are in a bromance with Jon," I say, rolling my eyes and sitting on the edge of his desk, my mind working in overdrive, striving to synthesize an appropriate name for Travis and Jon combined, and I stifle a laugh as I mutter, "Travon. It has a nice ring to it, don't you think?"

"It isn't a bromance," he says through his laughter, "but that's cute."

"Well, are you like . . . friends now?"

"Why do you care so much, Lina?"

"I just do, okay? Besides, you and I . . . we dated . . . and now that Jon and I are back together . . . I guess it's just a weird dynamic." *Admit it, Lina,* I think. *It's a weird love triangle. That's what it is. A love triangle.*

"Dated. That's what you call what we had?" He looks sad, which makes me feel bad.

"Enough with the labels," I say with a shrug.

"Says the woman who just named Jon and me *Travon*."

"Seriously, though, why do you care? Some things are personal, you know? Between me and Jon."

"So, you're afraid we are trading insider information about you."

"Maybe. So what if I am?"

"This is kind of fun, watching you squirm."

"I'm not squirming."

"Yes, you are. Very much so . . . I'm just curious, are you more worried that I will share things with Jon about you and me? Or are you worried he's talking to me about you?"

This guy has some nerve, and I've just about had it with him. "Neither," I say, stepping closer, not backing down from what feels like an intense staring contest. I can feel the heat flush from my chest and the fire rising to my cheeks, and I can't tell if I'm frustrated with Travis or if I'm liking this playful banter. "There are just some things that are shared with two people when they *date* that doesn't need to be repeated once they are no longer in said relationship," I say, images of Travis sex flashing through my mind, and I'm blushing. "I—"

"Come on, Lina, we're friends, you and me. And . . . I won't tell Jon about our mind-blowing connection or the fact you admitted I was the best sex of your life . . . not him."

Did he just say that? I can't believe he just said that. I take a couple of steps backward, unable to fully speak, his eyes still locked on mine. *Is Travis flirting? Yes, Lina, of course he's flirting. Or is he just trying to establish some common ground?* Either way, I'm done with this conversation, and I'm sure my facial expressions and body language are signaling as much.

"I'm going to call it a night," I say, trying to sound chill, gathering my things as quickly as humanly possible.

"Lina—"

"No," I say, through nervous laughter. "This conversation is finished. I really don't have anything more to say to you right now."

"I didn't mean to be inappropriate."

"Well, you failed. Try harder, Travis. You were *very* inappropriate. And if you still have feelings for me, then we need to have a serious conversation."

Travis stands up and rushes toward me, urgency in his eyes. "I'm sorry, Lina. You're right. This is a lot to navigate. And I did have huge feelings for you. But I don't anymore. Seriously, we're good. I was just playing around. I'm sorry."

I stare at him, tears burning behind my eyelids, feeling both vulnerable and angry simultaneously. *How dare he throw my words and my feelings in my face in that way? Yes, the sex was great, but to bring that up now . . .*

"Well, I'm glad you're sorry, because that was mean. And if Jon ever found out I said that, he would be hurt. Really, really hurt. So please, never repeat anything like that ever again."

"I won't," he says, reaching for a hug.

Instead of reciprocating, I grab my purse and turn away, backing up toward the door.

"I'm sorry, Lina."

"Good. Because, Travis . . . I'm pregnant. Jon and I are having a baby," I add, turning toward the door and exiting our office, not looking back once but only imagining the look of shock on Travis's face. I know that I probably shattered his heart into a million pieces, but in this moment, I couldn't care less. But in the words of my best friend, Daphne . . . that is a story for another day.

Chapter Thirty-Five

Now (June 2025) Alanna

Carmen and Maria will arrive at the airport at eight in the evening, which is why I'm shocked beyond belief when Eddie suggests a quick detour to Camelback Mountain, insisting he can't pass up an opportunity to do a bit of sightseeing prior to the wedding chaos.

"They arrive in less than two hours," I say, gawking at him like he's completely lost his mind.

"That's plenty of time," he insists. "Besides, once the three of you are reunited, you're sure to be inseparable."

"I'm not ditching you for my friends," I joke, leaning my head on his arm as he turns toward the mountain. "I'm just excited to see them. You, Maria, and Carmen . . . You were my family, you know?"

"Correction. We are your family," he says, kissing the top of my head while keeping his eyes on the road. "Come on. It will be good for you. These past couple of days . . ." His voice trails off because no words can describe how chaotic the past couple of days were.

"Nuts," I sigh. "The last couple of days have been insane," I say, visions of dress fittings, shoe shopping, hair and makeup trials, seating charts, and everything in between flashing through my mind at lightning speed. One week ago, I wouldn't have known one thing about weddings. Now, I could plan one in my sleep.

Only thirty minutes later, Eddie and I have parked the car and walked a short distance on a hiking trail, stopping to view the city of Phoenix from a lookout point as the Arizona sunset takes my breath away. We stand, hand in hand, gazing out at the horizon, the sky canvased with various shades of pink, orange, yellow, and even wisps of blue, and even though I've grown up here, it continues to take my breath away. The shadows of rocky outcrops and cacti flank our path, and as the sun continues its descent, a crisp chill forms in the air, causing me to rub my arms and nuzzle up to Eddie.

"Cold?" he asks, his tone sincere.

"A little," I admit.

"Let me warm you up," he says, pulling me close and swallowing my body with his embrace.

I lean into him, nuzzling my cheek against his T-shirt, his heart beating against my ear as he grips my waist, pulling me closer then running his fingers along the small of my lower back.

"That better?"

"Yes," I whisper, inhaling deeply, capturing the scent of his favorite cologne. I've always appreciated his scent but have only recently learned the brand is Armani Code. That, combined with his Nivea men's deodorant and the natural essence of his sun-kissed skin creates a fragrance that I would pay *anything* to bottle up and keep with me forever because I love this man so, so, much. Sometimes, it literally pains me to think our time together might be limited, and the idea is enough to send me spiraling, which was one of the reasons I've struggled this week. I mean sure, recovering from my experience in Mexico would take time. And planning a fake wedding when your social circle is nonexistent can be overwhelming. But the idea of Eddie going back to Mexico and leaving me behind is enough to make me want to scream and even, possibly, miss being held captive at the clinic, because at least back then, Eddie and I were together.

"Good," he says, pulling me closer and tilting my chin up toward him and drawing me in for a kiss.

I want to stay in this moment forever, but I gently pull away to say a soft "I love you." I whisper it into his chest before looking up at him and locking eyes. "I mean it, Eddie. You're . . . you're the love of my life."

He doesn't respond to this with words but instead with his eyes. They become softer but more serious; like he's trying to solve a challenging puzzle, but specks of joy sparkle from his pupils, and the sides of his lips form a soft smile. Before I can comprehend what is happening, Eddie is down on one knee, extending a small black velvet box that he has yet to open.

"Eddie?" I ask, slapping my hands to my cheeks, my eyes welling with tears. "What are you doing?"

Eddie takes my hand in his and presses my fingers to his lips. They feel warm against the cool desert breeze that kisses the back of my neck and sends a slight chill through me. "Before I met you, Foster, I was . . . I was in a very dark place, completely consumed with only solving my mother's murder . . . It encompassed . . . well, everything . . . It was the only thing that mattered to me. It was all I cared about . . . and it didn't bring out the best in me. Not one bit."

"It's okay—"

"It wasn't okay then. But it is now," he says, placing my palm to his cheek. "My days were the darkest," he whispered, his words catching in the back of his throat. "And even though you showed up in my life during one of *your* darkest times . . . you still managed to be my light."

I wipe my tears away with my free hand, but Eddie doesn't let go of my other, and as I try to process what he's saying, relief washes over me, and surges of certainty electrocute me from the inside out.

"Do you have any idea how it feels to be thankful we met, Foster? It's like I'm thanking God for your kidnapping. I'm grateful you were sold into organ trafficking. It's all so . . . surreal and twisted—"

"It's not." I smile softly. "Eddie, it's all *okay*," I say reassuringly, my eyes glued to that freaking box, wishing I had the power to see right through it. The hope I'm beginning to feel for him and the anticipation for what might be happening is overwhelming, causing me to feel every emotion on the planet, and I'm unable to hide my smile any longer. "What are you trying to say?" I ask between laughs.

"Seriously, Foster." Eddie chuckles, his accent thick. "Let me get this out, will you?"

"Okay," I say, jumping up and down, tiny, unplanned giggles escaping from somewhere I haven't known existed, because I know deep down the next few moments are going to change my life.

"I may have saved you," he says between sniffles, "But Alanna Foster . . . *you* rescued *me*. And there is nobody in the entire world I would care to spend the rest of my life with. Would you please do me this honor and make me the happiest man in the world? Would you be my wife?"

And with this, Eddie snaps open the jeweler's box to reveal a diamond engagement ring. A simple gold band supports a small but dazzling diamond, and my knees grow weak, and my heart flutters with excitement. I can't contain my happiness, and I decide in that moment I don't need to. I let out a loud shriek as I release my hand from his grip and leap into his arms.

"Yes! I holler. "Yes, yes, yes . . ."

Eddie is removing the ring from the box and is sliding it onto my finger, and although it's two sizes too big, it's the most perfect thing in the world. "It's beautiful," I say through my tears.

"Really? Yes? Yes, you will marry me?"

"Yes! I will marry you! Of course I will marry you," I say, tears flowing freely down my cheeks as I fiddle with the ring.

"It's too big, isn't it?"

"That's an easy fix," I say, removing it from my ring finger and securing it around my thumb.

"We will get it fixed," he says, shaking his head, his smile the biggest I've ever seen.

"You can't have it back," I joked. "I'll go with you to have it resized because I'm never taking it off . . . ever."

"It was my mother's ring," he says, pressing it to his lips, his eyes locked on mine.

"Oh Eddie," I gasp. "Thank you."

"It arrived last night," he says with a smirk. "My father brought it with him."

"Your father is here?" I ask, eyes wide.

"And my brother," he adds. "You think they would miss our wedding?"

Then it hits me. Eddie and I are getting married *tomorrow*. *Heck, why wouldn't we?*

"Tomorrow night? We're doing this tomorrow night?" I ask, jumping up and down like a child who's been given the promise of Disneyland.

"If you want to," Eddie says with a shrug.

"I can't think of one single reason why not," I say, because I can't. "Wait," I say, staring up at him in disbelief. "Does this mean you can stay here? With me?"

"I met with a lawyer this morning," Eddie says. "Our marriage will help, of course, but I'm not guaranteed a green card just yet."

"But you can stay . . . at least for now?"

"Yes. And I know I don't need to explain this to you, Foster, but I'm not doing this . . . you know, proposing to you, so I can stay in the States."

"You're right, Eddie, you don't need to explain that to me. I know you love me. And I trust you."

"I love you more than anything, Foster."

"I love you too!" I shriek. "OMG, I need to tell my mom and dad," I say, reaching in my purse for my phone.

"Of course," he laughs. "You can tell them . . . but they already know."

"They do?"

"You think I wouldn't ask your dad for his blessing? He is one hundred percent on board."

"I . . . I feel like I'm dreaming."

Eddie dips me for the most passionate kiss we've shared thus far. "You're not dreaming. You are very much awake, and from this day forward, I promise to make you the happiest woman on earth. I love you, Foster."

"Not for long," I say, pulling away. "Tomorrow, I'll become Alanna Silva. You can't call me Foster anymore," I tease playfully.

"That turns me on," he says, kissing me again and gliding his fingers under my shirt and around the waistband of my jeans. "But I'll never stop calling you Foster. Come here," he says, kissing me again.

"Nope. Time to go the airport." I snicker. "My bridesmaids are arriving shortly. You, Mr. Silva, are going to have to wait until our wedding night," I say with a wink.

But Eddie remains serious as he pulls me closer for one more kiss. "I would wait forever for you," he says, his jaw tightening and eyes narrowing.

"I know," I say, because I do.

Stacy Lee

I know it sounds crazy, rushing our wedding and getting engaged after such a short time in the *real* world, but it isn't. For the first time in a long time, I see a light at the end of the tunnel. And I'm ready to move forward with my new life, a future made possible only because of the pain and suffering I endured over the past two years, but hey, you know what they say. What doesn't kill you makes you stronger. And I, Alanna Foster, would do it all over again if it meant landing in the arms of my prince, Eddie Silva and I'm ready for my happily ever after, just as soon as I pick up my girls from the airport.

Chapter Thirty-Six

Now (June 2025) Lina

"Thank you," I tell Travis as he holds the conference door open for me at PPI.

"This better be good," I say with a slight roll of my eyes. "Jon and I had plans with the kids tonight." I glance over my shoulder for Jon, who is still parking his car and not inside the office yet, which leaves me alone with Travis Mullins for the first time since I dropped the pregnancy bomb on him.

"*Oh*, it is. I had meetings this morning with a few of the brides who fell victim to our crashers, and my findings will change how we approach tomorrow," Travis says, stepping closer to me, causing my arm to brush against his then placing a hand on my shoulder and invading my personal space by at least three inappropriate inches.

"What are you doing, Travis?"

"Listen . . . I want to apologize for the other night. I was out of line and, if I'm being honest, a little jealous."

I study his expression, which seems sincere enough, and I say, "Yeah. You were. Very much out of line."

"I'm sorry for that."

"Thank you," I say, pushing past him and taking my usual spot at our conference room table. "And I'm sorry, too, for dumping that news on you in that way, like that. I should've been more sensitive about it."

"Nah, don't worry about me. I'll be all right," he winks. "We good?"

"Yeah," I say, exhaling longer and deeper than I intend. "We were going to tell the kids tonight."

"About the pregnancy?"

"Yeah. We had dinner reservations down the street."

"That sucks. I'm sorry. But I promise this will be worth it. Breakthrough in the wedding-crasher case—timing couldn't be better."

"Can't wait to hear about it. It's just that . . . I wanted to tell Max and Lucy prior to the wedding tomorrow night, you know? *People* are starting to know, and I don't want them to hear it from anyone but us."

"And by *people*, you mean . . ."

"I mean *you*."

"I didn't say anything, and I won't."

"Okay, good, because Smith and the twins have been hanging out quite a bit."

"Copy that."

"Copy what?" Jon asks, making his way toward the table and dropping his computer bag on his chair before kissing my cheek.

"Travis has me on the edge of my seat," I say quickly. "He says we have a major breakthrough for tomorrow's wedding."

"That's the word on the street," Jon agrees. "Oh, before I forget, though, Lina . . . You need to tell Ryker that he isn't the justice of the peace anymore."

"Wait . . . what . . . why not?" I ask, picturing Ryker and how crushed he will be to learn all his practicing will be for nothing. "He's going to be so bummed," I whine but then check myself because I can become too defensive over Ryker, so I decide to dial it back a notch or two. I relax my shoulders and tuck a strand of hair behind my ear before asking, "Does this have to do with Travis and his wedding-crasher breakthrough?"

"Actually, no. You know just as much as I do," Jon says, taking a seat beside me. "This has to do with our bride and groom."

I stiffen, thinking of Alanna and Eddie, and become nervous that something has happened to one of them. *Did Eddie have to leave and go back home?* If that's the case, Alanna is sure to be devastated. *Did Alanna decide she wouldn't be able to go through with the faux ceremony?* That would be a worse scenario, as closing this case is *necessary*. Not only do we need to get Tanner Navarro off our backs, but we can't work on the end of Alanna's case until this is behind us.

"What happened?" I ask, running my hands over my tired eyes. "Please don't let it be bad news."

"Oh, on the contrary, Lina Rivera, private eye." Jon winks, placing a hand on my shoulder. "Eddie proposed. They are *really* getting married tomorrow. But don't worry, Navarro hooked them up with his go-to JP. We are good to go."

I jolt upright, praying that Jon is being serious, because honestly, I couldn't think of a happier ending than Alanna and Eddie getting married, and I *am* an author, after all. "OMG, for real?"

"Get the eff out of here," Travis says, stretching his arms overhead. "You serious, man?"

"Very serious," Jon says, then twists open his bottled water and gulps half of it. "He proposed last night on Camelback Mountain."

"That's *so sweet*!" I shriek, gushing over the idea of Eddie proposing in such a romantic way.

The two men shrug, unable to relate. "Yeah," Jon says, clearing his throat. "My proposal was better," he says with a wink, but very quickly switches to a frown, as he realizes he's crossed an unsaid boundary.

We *never* talk about our past, even the good times, and I can't help but notice Travis sitting on the edge of his seat, looking from Jon to me and back to Jon again, and if the guy could've broken out popcorn and Twizzlers, he would have, and I imagine the potential movie trailer flashing through his mind. *Ladies and gentlemen, Jon Cote has just mentioned the proposal . . . A snapshot from their former lives when they were . . . wait for it . . . happy! What will Lina do?*

"I'm sorry—"

"No." I smile, tilting my head just a bit to reassure him. "You're right. You nailed that proposal. I mean, who wouldn't want to be proposed to via Frappuccino? It's every girl's dream, for sure."

Travis sits back in his seat and crosses his arms before opening his laptop and removing his notebook from his bag, while the sides of Jon's mouth turn back to a smile.

"Really?" Jon asks.

The three of us know damn well that he isn't asking for validation that his proposal was better. What he's really asking is *Did we really get here? To a place where we can remember our marriage fondly?* And the answer to this is yes.

"Really," I say, taking his hand in mine. "And I'm happy for them, Alanna and Eddie. They are adorable together."

"Me too," Jon agrees.

"I think it's rather fast, if you ask me," Travis chimes in. "Didn't they just meet?"

Says the guy who wanted to be my baby daddy after dating a few months, I want to bark, but I don't. "I mean, these circumstances are far from conventional . . . She was kidnapped into organ trafficking and held captive in a sketchy hospital, and they had all that time together—"

"I get it," he says, his voice increasing in volume. "Let's get down to business. We have a big day tomorrow. I just hope that we don't let our *emotions* get in the way of execution now that we know this wedding is for real."

I feel heat rise inside, and my cheeks burn. "I'll keep my *emotions* out of it, Travis," I spit back. "As long as you promise not to let your *performance* interfere," I say, in reference to the fact he is the wedding's DJ, which, in my opinion, is rather unnecessary.

"Oh, I think we *both* know that my *performance* has never and will never be an issue."

"Um, can someone please tell me what is going on here?" Jon asks, his tone calm and professional. "Is there something going on with you guys? Do we need to clear the air? I'd hate to have whatever this is"—he gestures to Travis then back to me—"interfere with our investigation."

I lock eyes with Travis, giving him a moment to decide how much of this he wishes to share with Jon, as I, myself, am trying to figure it out too. And when he says nothing and I'm left with the ball in my court, I decide that honesty with Jon Cote is the only avenue I'm interested in, especially if we're really going to do this—and by *this*, I mean being a couple.

"Travis knows," I sigh. "About the baby."

The shock on Jon's face speaks volumes, and when he narrows his gaze and runs his fingers over his chin's scruff, I realize he's putting the pieces together as to why Travis would be projecting his jealousy onto this situation.

"And this is making the two of you fight like nine-year-olds out at recess because why, exactly?"

I rub my hands over my arms and glance up at Travis, who shifts in his seat. I want to say it's because Travis is eager to start a family or because Travis has yet to find someone he connects with, or even because Travis is mourning the loss of his own marriage, but I can't. I can't lie to Jon, and he deserves to know the truth.

"Since Travis needs to grow a pair, I'll be the one to say it," I say, my words jumbling together, which makes it hard to understand me clearly. "Obviously, you know that we have a history," I say, turning away from Travis and making eye contact with Jon.

"A history." Travis chuckles. "You were my girlfriend. Why can't you just say that?"

"I was his girlfriend," I say, like Lucy might respond to me when she's frustrated with the world and in need of a punching bag. "And he wanted more than I was willing to give."

"She didn't want a baby with *me*. Now, can we please get back to this?" he asks, gesturing to his notes.

"This wasn't planned!" I say, leaping to my feet and gesturing to my midsection.

"It's pretty simple, Lina," Travis counters, rising to his feet as well.

Now, it's Jon's turn to break out the popcorn and candy. *Ladies and gentlemen, what will happen next? Will Travis admit that he is never and was never over Lina?*

"Damn, guys, haven't you heard of birth control? It wasn't an issue with us—"

"Okay," Jon says, leaping to his feet. "That's enough. Travis, Lina never meant to hurt you, and we didn't plan on this, but we are very happy about it. And need I remind you that when I hired you at PPI, you promised me that your *history* wouldn't be an issue? And honestly, man, talk to her like that again, and you're going to have issues of your own—me."

I want him *now*, like sex-on-the-conference-room-table bad, and I watch the two men, arms crossed, eyes locked, tension building. *Who will throw the first punch? Will it be the honorable Jon, protector of Lina, or egotistical Travis, the man who never stopped loving her?*

"I'm sorry," Travis huffs. "That was out of line, and I'm sorry. Really. The both of you don't deserve this . . . You've both been through enough."

"Thank you," we say in unison as we sit back down, and I wipe the beads of sweat from the back of my neck.

"Good," Jon says. "Let's take five and get back to work."

"Sounds good to me," I say as I stand to my feet and head toward the restroom, eager to move forward with these two but feeling suddenly pessimistic that just five minutes might not be enough either to bury what was destroyed between Travis and me or to dismantle this love triangle that I hadn't admitted to myself really existed until now.

Less than ten minutes later, Travis has begun revealing his findings, and he's correct. The developments in Project I Do are not only game-changing, but they affirm that his assumptions about the wedding crashers are completely spot on. And as he speaks about the timeline he's created for the crashed weddings, he's overly eager to flip over photographs from said weddings, and those photographs prove that our crashers changed disguises multiple times, which we had assumed but hadn't been sure of.

"So, as we talked about yesterday," Travis explains, "the police were unable to identify our female suspect with the photograph Lina took in the bathroom."

"Yes, I know," I sigh. "Sorry, I'm a rookie."

"It's more than okay," Jon says, kissing my hand. "You did great."

"But, with these photographs, we are hoping we can have an ID on them by tomorrow morning. But, either way, as you can see, we have our first shots of our male suspect. This first one was taken at the wedding of Jennifer Hannaford. She and her husband were the couple who were robbed of their wedding bands."

"Hannaford? Like the store?" I ask, eyebrows raised.

Travis stares me down like he may just break my arm again. "Yes, like the store," he says and exhales deeply. "They have searched and searched through their wedding videos and photographs, but these came from the most unexpected place."

I study a photograph of the female suspect, confirming that this was the wigged woman from the bathroom, but in this picture, she has black curly hair, clearly another wig, and she's dressed in black pants with a white blouse and is carrying a clipboard. She's pressing an earpiece to her ear and appears to be acting like an event coordinator. The photo has been taken at the oddest angle, almost like the photographer was seated and pointing the camera upward.

"What?" I gasp. "She's obviously posing as a wedding coordinator of some sort. But she must have managed to avoid every security camera, right?"

"Correct."

"Who took it, then?" Jon asks, holding the photograph closer for better inspection.

"These particular photos were taken by the ring bearer, on our flower girl's cell phone."

"What?" I gasp. "How old are they?"

"Young Devon Hannaford is the groom's nephew, and he may have just helped us solve our first crime at the ripe young age of three."

"Three?" I ask, belly laughing. "What was he even doing with the phone?"

"His nine-year-old sister, Grace, gave it to him to keep him busy while they waited their turn down the aisle. He had grown overtired and fussy, so she gave it to him as a distraction."

"Nine-year-olds with cell phones?" Jon sighs, clearly thinking with his dad brain.

"I thought the same thing," Travis snickered. "But it really *isn't* a phone, more like an iPod . . . but it does take photos. That's why nobody thought to look there."

"Who did, then?" I ask, giggling to myself over a three-year-old coming up with more leads than me.

"When I questioned Jennifer about the missing rings, she was sure they made it to the ring pillow. She was frustrated with herself for putting them there and not letting the best man hold them. Because of this, they were overly careful to be sure and place the rings on the pillow right before the ceremony. It made sense that whoever grabbed the rings had access to Grace and Devon moments before the ceremony."

"And with everyone focusing on the bride . . ."

"Nobody noticed that the wedding coordinator didn't belong."

"Bitch!" I say, suddenly angry. "You know what's worse than taking candy from a baby?"

"Taking wedding rings," Jon finishes for me.

"Okay," I say, clearly impressed with Travis and his findings. "What else you got?"

"These are from Phoenix's wedding," Travis says, clearing his throat as he places two pictures in front of Jon and me. The first is of a tall man with blond hair and an athletic build, wearing a security guard uniform, and the second is the selfie of Ryker and me.

"Why is my selfie with Ryker important?"

"Look behind you," Travis says, his tone firm and serious.

Behind Ryker and me stands our female suspect, only this time she's wearing her natural blond hair in a low bun, and she's dressed as a waitress.

"What?" I gasp. "That's her!"

"Where did you get this?" Jon asks, studying them closely then looking at me with a raised brow.

I think back to the day of Phoenix's wedding and search my brain for any memory of her reception. Ryker and I had our eyes open, for sure, and we were so distracted, searching for anything out of the ordinary, that I don't remember the cocktail hour or dinner too much, but from what I could remember, she would have blended in for sure. I sigh in frustration.

"They were for the guests to take photos. I can't believe I didn't think of this before."

"Apparently, Phoenix had disposable cameras on her tables?" Travis asks more than tells me, and my heart sinks to the bottom of my stomach as I remember the moment I took a selfie with Ryker. *How did I miss this? Was I so consumed with talking to Ryker that I let her slip right through my fingers?*

If I'd remembered this minor detail, we would've had these photos back in May.

"Yes, she did," I groan, rubbing my tired eyes. "I'm sorry. I knew about these cameras."

"Clearly," Travis mumbles. "Would you like this? It's a great picture of you two—"

"It's all right," Jon says. "The most important thing is that we have the photos now. And judging by the time stamp on the pictures, these were taken moments before the security footage was cut and the power went off."

I side glance at Travis for reassurance that I didn't screw everything up but come up short. "Right," I say, determined to move on. "And when I saw her in the bathroom, she was changing into her third disguise with her black bob. Probably just acting like a typical guest."

"Correct," Travis agrees. "And last but not least," he says, slapping the last photo down in front of us with pride, "our male suspect, dressed in all black, carrying wedding gifts to what I assume to be the bridal suite. Time stamped post power outage."

"And you found this one . . ."

"It turned up with the other camera photos. I assume a drunken wedding guest started snapping random pictures. I don't have any other working theories."

"Well, I'm glad they did. And hopefully, tomorrow night will go off without any glitches and we can move on from this," I say.

"Okay," Jon says, pulling up his laptop. "Let's get these images sent out to the rest of the team. Tomorrow night, these two scumbags are going down."

"Copy that, boss," I wink, squeezing Jon's hand.

"I hope you're right," Travis sighs. "I would really like to put this behind me."

I nod, making a silent promise to myself that no matter how wonderful it is to see Alanna and Eddie get their happily ever after, I can keep it together and stay focused enough to do my job. Because now, more than ever, not only do I have something to prove to Travis Mullins, but even more importantly, I have something worth proving to myself.

Chapter Thirty-Seven

Now (June 2025) Alanna

The arrival of Carmen and Maria was a reunion I will never forget. Maria arrived first by a mere fifteen minutes, followed by Carmen, and watching them both run toward me, dressed in their own street clothes instead of our hospital attire, was enough to put me in tears. But when I showed them my engagement ring and witnessed the look of happiness in Carmen's eyes, I really lost it. The three of us being together again, no longer in danger, made me the happiest girl in the world.

Well, I thought nothing could make me happier. But this very moment as I walk, arms locked between my father and mother, toward my fiancé, Eddie, whose eyes have welled with tears as he studies me, I now realize that I really am the luckiest girl alive. I'm about to marry Eddie Silva. I take my eyes off him momentarily, only to admire the Arizona landscape and the stunning sunset that acts as a backdrop over the picturesque desert oasis, and I feel like a princess as I parade past friends and family, all of us nestled between towering saguaro cacti and rugged rock formations, with the warm hues of the desert sands stretching out under a brilliant blue sky, and as the sun sets, the sky takes on soft pink and magenta tones, matching Carmen, Maria, and Eliza's tea-length dresses and their bouquets of succulents and desert blossoms.

My bridesmaids dab their eyes with handkerchiefs as they study me intently, and as I glance around our venue and the guests as they meet my stare, I realize there isn't a dry eye in the house. *Who would blame them?* This isn't a typical wedding—it's a horror movie turned fairy tale, and I suddenly feel overwhelmingly grateful for Jon and Lina pulling this off for Eddie and me. Of course, they will be busy locating the wedding crashers with the police standing by, but for now, in my mind, it's just Eddie and I, the only two people on earth.

"Who gives this woman to this man?" the JP asks.

"Me," my father says, tears streaming down his cheeks. "Her mother and I do."

They both kiss my cheeks and guide me toward Eddie, and I take his hand in mine as Carmen adjusts the train of my strapless A-line wedding gown, Maria takes my bouquet, and I stare into the eyes of Eddie, the love of my life. I met the man in the worst possible way, but regardless, he has made me the happiest woman in the world. It's now clear to me that Eddie loves me in the absolute best possible way you can love a person. He loves *me* for *me*, and clearly, he always will.

The ceremony moves quickly, as Tanner Navarro requested, and as Eddie and I begin our vows to each other, I notice Lina and Jon out of the corner of my eye and follow their gaze to a woman in a curly black wig who paces around the venue with a clipboard, and I know without a shadow of a doubt she's our suspect. But, as we'd all agreed on, we needed to catch them in action, so we couldn't act too soon. The worst-case scenario would be apprehending the suspects with too little evidence. But as I promised my mother that morning, I would fully appreciate my wedding day as my special day, and I would leave the investigation to the team. So, as we prepare to exchange vows, I do just that.

Eddie takes my hands in his, and when our eyes connect, he feels like the only person in the world because a world with just him would be simply *enough*. Eddie had volunteered to go first, and I didn't mind as public speaking has never been my thing.

"Foster," he says, smile beaming, and I'm beyond thankful that he's chosen his nickname for me instead of my full name, and I am already done.

Carmen hands me a handkerchief, and I release one of Eddie's hands to dab my eyes.

"Foster," he starts again, giving my hand a gentle squeeze, and I quickly gaze over his shoulder to his father and brother, who are also overly emotional because when two people get married because one is a rescued kidnapping victim, it's sure to be an emotional roller coaster. "My mother used to have a favorite expression," he says, his accent thick and his words catching in the back of his throat.

"It's okay," I whisper because it is.

"My mother used to have a way of putting things in perspective," he says, starting again. "When I was a young boy, my parents used to take us to the ocean. Memories at the beach with her are some of my happiest memories," he explains, tears flowing freely. "One vacation, the weather was *almost* perfect. We had roughly five straight days of sunshine and little to no rain or even humidity, and I had told her, during those days, how much peace I found in the sea. We stood there, hand in hand, she and I, studying the tide rolling in and then back out again, collecting seashells, and swimming the day away. However, on our last day, a storm was on its way, the rain began to fall, and it wouldn't stop. I had become frustrated with our situation because I knew our time at the beach was ending, and I was devastated we couldn't enjoy the ocean like we had the previous days. But my mother was a smart woman, and she never let a learning opportunity pass," he says, smiling up at the painted sky as if looking toward his mother as his father places a caring arm on his shoulder. "She took me down to the water, even in the rain," he says through his tears. "And she said, '*Look*, Eduardo. This is the *same* beach. This is the *same* ocean. It hasn't changed. Yes, there is rain, but the sea, it has not changed.' She told me that when you love something, truly love it for what it is, you will be able to appreciate it for what it is, not what you want it to be . . . even in the poorest circumstances . . . even in the storm."

"Oh, Eddie," I whisper, pressing his hand to my mouth and kissing it softly, wishing I could take away his pain and wishing I could stop his tears, and for a moment, I forget that we're standing in front of hundreds of our closest friends and family and two criminals who are about to get what they deserve.

"When I met you, Foster, we were both in one *ugly* storm. I was prisoner to the pain of losing my mother, and you were . . . well, you were an actual prisoner. There was no sunshine, there was no freedom. Hell, before you met me, there was no deodorant," he winks, and we pause to wait for a few laughs to subside. "But we fell in love. We fell in love inside the eye of a storm. And now that we are both free from our prisons and the sun has started to shine, we get to love one another in the happy times too. But just know, Alanna Foster, I will always be here for you, and I will always appreciate you for who you are, even through the storms. Because that, my darling, is the greatest lesson she ever taught me. And I can't wait to spend the rest of my life with you, through every season, in any kind of weather."

It isn't time for applause yet, but some of our family and friends miss that memo, and the cheering and clapping begins, and I inhale deeply because I'm not out of the woods yet. It's my turn, and I'm so nervous that my palms sweat and my throat goes dry. I close my eyes and pretend that just the two of us are standing here, under the Arizona sunset, which gives me the courage to speak.

"Eddie," I say, sniffling back my tears. "When I met you, I legit thought I was going to die." I pause because the notion that we made it out of Mexico alive is still very difficult to process, and for a moment, I feel like I need to sit down. My words have become stuck inside my body, begging to break free, but I can't find them. Then Carmen hands her flowers to Maria and places a hand on my shoulder, and comfort washes over me as I find the courage to continue.

"They gave me the name Cactus Blossom," I say and clear my throat. "Because of my resiliency and determination to survive. And when I met you, Eddie, I was weak, and there were times, especially when my friends were in danger, that I didn't want to continue. But then . . . you brought me root beer and playing cards," I say, making eye contact with my dad, who wipes tears from his eyes. "I knew then that I was going to be all right. Because even if I didn't have my freedom, and even if my life was at stake every single day, I had you. I had you to sneak in surprises. I had you to make me laugh. And even when things became really bad, I had you in my dreams. And even though what happened to me was absolute rock bottom and I will regret the decision I made to betray my parents and their trust for as long as I live, I will always be grateful that the experience led me to you. You are my family, Eddie Silva. And I can't wait to live happily ever after with you, my hero, the love of my life . . . my *everything*."

Again, the crowd cheers before it is time, but I'm pretty sure that, given the circumstances, we get a free pass on wedding etiquette. But once we exchange wedding bands and the JP announces, "You may now kiss the bride," the guests erupt with cheers as if we've just won the Super Bowl, and Eddie dips me down for a long, passionate kiss. I know in this moment that we have our happily ever after, and this is only the beginning for Eddie and me, now husband and wife. And as we march down the aisle hand in hand, not only am I ready to begin our future together, but I'm also ready to help Jon and Lina take down the wedding crashers. They saved my life. And for that, I will be forever grateful.

Chapter Thirty-Eight

Now (June 2025) Lina

"I still have eyes on her," I say into my mouthpiece to Jon, referring to our female suspect, who has scurried about during the entire ceremony with her iPad and clipboard, impersonating a wedding coordinator, and even though I literally *hate* her for distracting me from the most beautiful wedding ceremony I've ever been a part of, I must admit that she's very convincing. "She's dressed as a waitress now. Blond bun. Do you still have eyes on him?" I ask, referring to the male suspect.

"Yes, I do. He's still acting as security."

"Watch them closely," Travis advises in my ear.

Now that cocktail hour is over, things will start to build momentum. I nod over at Travis, who's behind his DJ booth, but I'm struggling to take him seriously.

I make my way over to the gift table and the guest book, where Max, Lucy, Smith, and Molly are gathered. "You guys clean up nicely," I say, kissing Max on the cheek.

"Thanks, Mom. You don't look so bad yourself," he says with a smile.

I adjust the straps of my black halter dress and say, "This old thing? Thank you. You guys holding up okay?" I ask, looking from him to Molly.

"Yes, except I miss you, Lina," Molly whines, pulling me close to her in an embrace. "Seriously, when this is over, we need to hang."

"Yes," I tell her. "Yes, we do. Although you and Max have been seeing a lot of each other," I say, raising my brows in approval.

"Enough, Mom. Aren't you supposed to be catching bad guys or something?" Lucy asks.

"Oh wow, thanks, Lucy. I almost forgot that I'm trying to track down two serial wedding crashers. Thank you for that."

"I can't believe my dad is a DJ," Smith says, shaking his head in awe. "I would've lost a bet on that one."

"He's actually doing a great job," I admit although it pains me to do so.

"How much longer do we need to stand here?" Lucy asks. "I'm starving."

"Actually, you're good to go," I say. "Dad and I have eyes on the gifts now, and we need to give the crashers an opportunity to steal them," I say like I'm explaining rain is in the forecast but nobody should worry.

The kids stare at me like I have three heads before leaving their station and finding their tables, and I do a double take. *Does Smith have his arm around Lucy's waist?* The idea of Travis's son dating my daughter is way too overwhelming for this instant, so I file it away in the stuff-I-will-figure-out-later folder in my mind. Because right now, I have a job to do.

"If we're right," Travis says in my earpiece, "the power will be cut shortly after dinner is served, and the female suspect will change disguises. Remember, we don't want to call in the cops too soon. It's imperative we allow them to continue with their plans, and we *can't* look suspicious."

"Hey, Travis," I reply. "How many times are you going to tell me not to act suspicious? Because I know math isn't really my thing, but I think we're at a possible twenty times today."

"Then make it twenty-one. We can't blow this."

"Enough, you two," Jon scolds over the radio. "Just be ready."

"Copy," Travis and I say in unison.

"Ready for the toast, Travis?" Jon asks, his tone no-nonsense.

"At this time, we ask for everyone to take their seats," Travis says from the DJ booth. "The father of the bride would like to make a toast."

Guests file inside, taking their seats at their perfectly decorated tables, and I scan the room for the female suspect, as Jon and Travis have made her my responsibility, and over my dead body will I lose her. But with that being said, I'm pretty sure I've lost her.

"Damn," I whisper under my breath. "Where did you go?"

I scan the room for her but come up short, realizing that Travis, Jon, and especially Tanner Navarro will burn me at the stake if I screw this up, and just as Patrick Foster takes the mic from Travis, I feel two hands grab my waist, and I shriek, startling the guests at the table next to me.

"Ryker," I say, "don't do that."

"Sorry," he says, spinning me around and pulling me close for a quick hug. "You look stunning, as always."

"Thanks," I say as Patrick begins his toast. "I can't find *her*." My heart rate is increasing. "I had one job," I whine.

"Who?" He shrugs playfully.

"You know *who*."

"We still don't have a name for her?"

"Nope. Facial recognition should be in soon, but not yet. As for now, she goes by the name *female suspect*."

"Blond hair? Red lipstick? Waiting tables?"

"Yes! Where?" I ask, following Ryker's stare and breathing a sigh of relief when I spot her busing one of the tables closest to the bathroom. "Thank you," I say, resting my head on his chest.

"That's what I'm here for," he says with a smile. "So, what happens now?"

"Now," I whisper, "we wait for Patrick to finish his toast and for dinner to be served. That's when the female suspect will change into her wedding-guest disguise and her accomplice will cut the power so she can start stealing shit."

"Okay, then," he chuckles. "I'll make sure to keep my shit close by."

"Good idea. Please tell me you got the steak this time."

"Obvi."

"Good. Where are you seated?"

"With the kids and Daphne. You do realize you put Daph and me at the kid's table."

"Sorry, Ry. It is what it is. At least you have Alex. He did such a nice job with Alanna's hair and makeup. She looks stunning."

"Yeah, he's pretty great."

Alanna's father pauses to wipe his tears with a handkerchief, and the room goes so silent that I swear I can hear Alanna's tears hit her cheeks. "And just when I thought I had lost my daughter forever," he says between sobs, "she has not only returned to us, but I have also gained a son. Cheers! To Eddie and Alanna!"

The room erupts in celebration as glasses clink, and Eddie and Alanna, seated at their sweetheart table at the front of the room, kiss, and the guests cheer even louder.

"I remember your toast at Daphne's wedding," Ryker whispers, wrapping an arm around my waist.

"That was *so* long ago," I say because it was.

"You totally hit on me."

"Yeah. I did, didn't I? That was before I knew you were gay." I shrugged. "I'm worried about Daphne," I say, following the female suspect around the room with my stare.

"Why, what's going on?"

"She says her and Mal are getting a divorce."

"What? That's so . . ."

"Sudden, right? I mean Daphne doesn't share much about their relationship—that's just how she is. But it's like she doesn't even want to try. It doesn't sound like anything big happened. I just wish she would talk to me."

"Interesting," Ryker says. "Maybe I'll chat with her during dinner."

"Don't tell her I said anything."

"I won't."

"And I think there may be something going on with Lucy and Smith," I say, crinkling my nose in disgust.

"Why the face? We like Smith, don't we?"

"Smith is great. It's his dad I can't stand right now," I admit, watching the suspect like a lifeguard keeping eyes on the ocean.

"What's going on with Travis? I thought you two were good."

"We need to catch up," I say, realizing I never talked to Ryker about my recent Travis encounter. My phone buzzes, and I swipe it open, wondering who could possibly be texting me. Everyone I know is here.

Unknown Number: *Great move, sending your cop boyfriend to bully me, bitch. You can block my number, but you can't block me.*

My legs grow wobbly, and my stomach flips as I shove my phone inside my clutch, but nothing gets by Ryker.

"What is it?" he asks, placing a gentle hand on my shoulder. "What's going on? You literally just changed colors."

"Work stuff," I say. "I can't really talk about it," I lie. "Confidential."

I can tell I've hurt his feelings, but I don't want to worry him with this. Jon has it under control, and we're filing for a restraining order against Jasper Gallagher first thing on Monday morning. Jon paid a visit to Jasper, who denied sending the threatening texts, but it's as clear as ever that he was lying through his teeth.

"Okay," Ryker says, clearly disappointed. "I'm going to go eat that steak. Good luck," he says and kisses my cheek before making his way to the table where my kids and their dates converse with Daphne.

I quickly find the female suspect, who's making her way toward the bathroom, red bag slung over her shoulder. "She's heading to the bathroom," I say into my earpiece.

Travis is swaying to the beat of his dinner music, and he presses his ear and says, "Copy."

"Copy," Jon adds. "I have eyes on the male suspect, heading upstairs toward the offices, just as we expected. Remember, let them cut the power, and *don't* go after them. Cops are standing by, and the gifts have trackers. The *worst thing*, I repeat, the *worst thing* we can do is get in the way."

"And don't act sus," I add.

"PD just texted. We have possible IDs on our suspects. Saffron Price, twenty-five years old, and her brother Landon Price, age twenty-nine. No record or documentation of them since 2013. Last anyone has seen of them was when they ran from foster care back in Andover, Massachusetts. Looks like they've been on the road since."

I think about that for a beat and suddenly feel sad for them. If they were in foster care, that would mean something had happened to their parents. 2013 made that a long time to be hiding out. No wonder they've been making a living this way.

"Take the emotion out of it, Lina," Travis warns in my ear. "I see you feeling all sorts of bad for them. Just remember, the lady stole a wedding band from the pillow of a three-year-old boy."

"Copy," I say, standing up taller and gluing my eyes to the bathroom door just as the room goes dark and the guests gasp.

"There will be a two-minute delay before the generator kicks in," Jon explains. "Watch for her, guys."

I turn my cell phone's flashlight on just as a few other wedding guests have done and scan the room for Saffron, who at this point should be clothed in her third outfit and sporting a black bob. "There you are," I whisper as I watch her move from table to table, grabbing anything and everything she can get her hands on, and I can't for the life of me realize how this has been able to go on without anyone noticing her. *Sure, she's quick, but really? Taking an old lady's clutch purse from right under her nose? And that man's watch? And . . . good God, the JP's wallet?*

"Power is coming back on," Jon says, his phrases short and to the point. "Landon is heading to the bridal suite. I'm trailing him now."

"Be careful," I say.

"Copy."

I watch Saffron as she slings her now rather full purse over her shoulder and leaves the reception hall, possibly heading toward the bridal suite, and I realize this is it. I need to follow her without being noticed. She did, after all, see me in the bathroom that day. So, I glance at Ryker and Daphne's table, and they seem to be doing all right, along with the kids, and I follow Saffron, making sure that I'm keeping a safe distance from her, just in case she turns around, and I place my cell phone to my ear, pretending to get a phone call, just as Jon had instructed.

I exit the reception hall, phone to my ear, head down, and follow Saffron up a spiral staircase, my heart pounding against my chest and my adrenaline flowing, and I kick my shoes off, leaving them behind, just in case I need to run. *Please, God, don't make me run,* I beg as I've had way too much water to drink, and I will surely pee—everywhere. "Staircase," I whisper into my earpiece. "She's heading toward the bridal suite."

"Stay there," Jon whispers. "They're both in there now, loading the gifts into a large black box . . . Looks like something that would be used for music equipment."

"Copy," I say, leaning against the staircase's wall, realizing that if they have a box that big they will take the elevator down and I should go unnoticed.

"Will they take the elevator?" I whisper, feeling like a child playing hide and seek. But Jon doesn't answer. "Jon?" I ask again.

"Cote?" Travis asks, "Are you good?"

"Jon?" I ask, louder this time.

"Don't go after him, Lina," Travis orders.

"He's not answering me. Something is wrong."

"Lina, you're pregnant. Don't be an idiot."

Screw it, I think, running up the stairs toward the bridal suite, taking them two at a time, clutching my purse against me, and praying Jon is okay. I realize that this pregnancy is taking more of a toll on my body than I realize, as I feel as though I may pass out from climbing the stairs. As I turn the corner toward the bridal suite, I make eye contact with Jon, who has his hands in the air in surrender to Landon and Saffron, who have their backs toward me. Landon has Jon pinned up against the wall, holding him by the throat.

"I said, are you a cop or not?" Landon demands.

"Nope. Not a cop," Jon says. "I told you already . . . I'm a friend of the bride."

"He's lying," Saffron insists. "Don't you watch the news? He's the cop that rescued the bride from Mexico."

"He's a private investigator, not a cop," I laugh, awkwardly and loudly.

The two of them start, and I'm pretty sure Jon wants to kill me himself, based on the way he glares at me, his eyes full of worry, and when Landon turns around and I see he's holding a knife, I see that his reasoning is sort of valid.

"Who are you?" Landon demands, extending the knife toward me.

"I've met you before," Saffron insists. "You were at another wedding—"

"Yes," I say, impressing myself with the steadiness of my voice. "Phoenix's wedding. You were her nanny, right?" I ask, smiling. "What's with the knife?" I press my finger to my earpiece. "Why would you need a weapon in the bridal suite?" I ask innocently, warning Travis that we need backup. "Actually, why would you need to be up here in the first place?" I demand.

"We work here," Saffron says, and I realize that my playing dumb might be working. "We're moving the gifts downstairs for the bride."

"And why are you holding a knife to my . . . to my . . . boyfriend's . . . to my ex-husband's . . . to *his* throat?" I ask, frustrated with myself for choosing now to struggle with the nonexistent label for Jon and me. "I sent him up here because the *moron* forgot to put cash in the card," I say, emphasizing *moron* and reaching into my purse for a wad of cash. "See," I say, holding the cash out to Saffron. "We were going to get our card out of the box. Can you imagine opening an empty card on your wedding day? I mean, especially from two people who went through the trouble of rescuing them from organ trafficking, wouldn't you think they would at least put *something* in the card?"

"Is she telling the truth?" Landon asks Jon and backs away, lowering the knife to his side.

"She is," Jon says, brushing off his dress pants and straightening his tie. "I am a PI, but I took the night off. I'm not looking for anyone in particular . . . just my dignity," he says, staring at the cash in my open hand. "I forgot to put the money in the card." He laughs. "But it's been a week. Can't win 'em all."

"I'll take the cash," Saffron says, like she would be doing me the biggest favor in the world. "I'll just put it with the gifts. You can tell . . . the bride that it's in the box."

"Perfect," I say, studying her black bob, impressed she got another one so quickly after having to ditch her first one. "Come on, Jon, let's go. I don't want to miss the cake." I look from Jon to Landon then to Saffron and back to Jon, hopeful that this is working and that our backup is on the way and I reach for Jon's hand, and when it's securely in mine, I feel like I can breathe again. "It's prickly pear," I say with a smile. "The cake . . . My mother made it. Make sure you try some." I wink before turning and walking away.

Jon and I turn the corner and head down the stairs as Jon says, "They're in the elevator."

"Copy," Travis says into his earpiece. "I called PD. They're waiting. You two had me scared for a minute."

Jon and I stand, backs against the wall, out of sight from the elevator door, and when it dings and the doors open, I hear the rolling of the box.

Saffron says, "That was close, I told you this one was too risky."

"We did what we had to do," Landon says. "Like we always do."

I lock eyes with Jon and listen as the door to the hotel is kicked open, then Jon says, "Wait for it . . ."

"Scottsdale PD! Put your hands where we can see them!" a police officer hollers. After a commotion, he continues, "You are under arrest. You have the right to remain silent. Anything you say or do can be used against you in a court of law . . ."

"Are you all right?" Jon asks, looking me up and down like I was physically attacked.

"I'm all right." I giggle. "But are you?"

"Thanks to you." He smiles. "You crushed it back there," he says, bringing my hand to his lips and guiding me toward the reception hall. "I don't know what I would do without you."

"Facts," I say as he holds the door open for me. "Now about that cake . . ."

Chapter Thirty-Nine

Now (June 2025) Alanna

"We did it," I tell Eddie with a smile. I'm curled up beside him in the king bed of our bridal suite, wearing the white nightgown Carmen and Maria purchased as a gift for my wedding night, but it isn't much of a nightgown. It's more like fancy underwear I've only seen on models in magazines until now.

"Are you referring to our marriage or the undercover takedown of the wedding crashers?" he asks, kissing the top of my head.

"Both," I say with confidence. "Both are pretty wonderful." I climb on top of him and straddle his waist, kissing his bare chest. "And now that you're my husband . . . and I'm your wife," I say, my tone seductive as I lift my nightgown over my head. "I thought . . ." My voice trails off into the darkness of our room.

"We don't have to if you aren't ready, Foster," Eddie whispers. "I told you I don't want to rush you. You've been through so much."

"You also told me that you wanted to make me feel *good*," I say. "This will make me feel good, won't it Eddie?" I ask innocently.

"You're too much," he chuckles, pulling me down on top of him and squeezing me tightly. "Yes, it will, but like I said, we have forever, right?"

I adjust myself on top of him and tease him with my hips, feeling him harden against my thighs. "Yes, we have forever. But there is no time like the present. Besides, Eddie. Those vows. You're lucky I didn't jump you right there at the altar," I say, working my body over his, pleased with how he responds. "And I love you, so there's that."

"I love you so much," he moans, reaching toward my breasts and cupping them in his hands.

My body responds to his touch quickly. "Eddie," I gasp. "I want to be with you. I want you to make love to me. Please?"

Eddie rolls me onto my back and rolls onto his side, flooding my face with kisses. "Are you sure?" he asks, his breath heavy and his hands eager as he traces down my abdomen and between my thighs, as if reading my mind, pausing in the exact place I need him to.

It hasn't been long since we started doing this, and he already knows me in this way, better than I know myself, and as he presses against me, I gasp in surprise as unexpected surges race through me.

"Yes!" I gasp. "Oh God," I moan, my chest rising and my back arching as he continues touching me, bringing his lips to mine and swallowing my gasps with his mouth. "Please," I beg.

"All right," he says, rolling over onto his other side and digging through the hotel's nightstand.

I'm thankful he's so responsible, as I'm not on any sort of birth control, and he knows this. Eddie climbs into bed and rolls onto his back, positioning me over him, and without breaking eye contact with me, caresses me between my thighs before guiding himself against my entrance and pressing gently into me, easing his way inside little by little, reading my facial expressions with each movement, slowing down when I grimace and pushing deeper when I relax.

"Okay?" he asks repeatedly.

"Yes." I nod. "Keep going."

And he does. With one final thrust, Eddie is inside me, and I feel complete and whole in a way I've never experienced. Eddie moves beneath me with ease, gripping my waist with one hand and one breast with the other. He guides me over him like we've done this before, and even though it's new and I'm a tiny bit scared, it's *Eddie*, and that's what makes this perfect in every way possible.

"I love you," I say, over and over again, and my words begin to match our movements. With every thrust and every touch, every feeling of pleasure and every new feeling, I cry, "I love you," until my words become louder and so passionate that I don't recognize my own voice. "Yes, Eddie! I love you, Eddie!" I cry out as he thrusts his hips faster beneath me, and his movements become more and more desperate. And when his body responds to mine and he collapses back against the larger-than-life bed, I collapse on top of him lifelessly, feeling more relief than I ever have in my entire life.

"I love you, Alanna Foster," he whispers in my ear.

"I love you more than life," I say because I do.

Eddie rolls me off him, and we lie there, side by side, staring into each other's eyes, simply taking each other in. "So, what did you think?" he asks, smiling slyly.

"What do I think?" I giggle. "About what?"

"Oh, come on," he says, tracing my jaw with his finger. "Sex. What do you think?"

I giggle squeamishly and laugh a nervous laugh. "I don't have an opinion about sex," I say firmly. "Because I've never had *just* sex."

Eddie stares at me in confusion. "I beg to differ."

"I've never had sex," I say, kissing his lips then pulling back gently. "Because I just made love to a man I want to be with forever. I just made love to you, my *husband*. And I may be new to this, but I have a feeling there's a really big difference."

"Okay," he chuckles. "So, what did you think about *making love* to me, Foster?"

"It was . . . it was simply amazing," I say because it was. "I do have one very important question for you though," I say, dabbing his nose and kissing his cheek.

"What's that?" he asks, the sides of his smile curling up as he eagerly awaits my question.

"Can we do it again? Because wow, Eddie. Just . . . wow."

"I told you I would make you feel good, Foster," he says, his words tickling my ear as he kisses my lips, my chin, my neck, and my abdomen. He continues between my legs, kissing me softly then firmly, and softly again, reaching his hands up to meet mine and gripping them tightly. Then he climbs back on top of me and presses his forehead to mine, allowing me to feel so connected that I'm almost speechless—almost.

"Eddie?" I say, my voice growing weak and full of desperation.

"Yeah?"

"There is a solid chance," I gasp, "that I'm never leaving this bed. Ever."

"Copy that, Foster. Copy. That."

Chapter Forty

Now (June 2025) Lina

Less than twenty-four hours have passed since Eddie and Alanna's wedding and the takedown of Saffron and Landon. Tanner Navarro couldn't be happier with the execution of Project I Do, and we received word that every single missing item has been accounted for, and Navarro's hotels were back in the headlines for positive reasons. The first is the mere fact of the glorious wedding of a recently rescued organ-trafficking victim and the police officer that helped rescue her, and the second is that Prickly Pen Investigations came through once again, rescuing the Navarro hotels and the missing valuables.

As for Saffron and Landon, well, their story isn't as happy, and I can't help but feel bad for them both, as they were in foster care due to a house fire that killed both parents when they were younger. They were on the run since then because they stole their foster father's car to head west and have survived solely on criminal activities. Maybe it's because I'm a mom, or maybe it's simply because I have a soul—either way, I'm keeping them in my prayers because no children should have to survive in that way, but then again, the chick robbed a three-year-old. So, there's that.

Jon and I have agreed to meet with the kids for lunch tomorrow to break the news about the new baby, which will be a relief because I've already started to show, and I have chosen, against Jon's advice, to work late at the office this evening.

"I don't want you there by yourself," he said. "The restraining order against Jasper won't be processed until Monday, and those texts are just . . . They're scary, Lina." I understood where he was coming from, but everything I need to work on Alanna's blood type case is here at PPI, and we have another online meeting with Dean Turner on Monday afternoon, and I *need* to be ready. We are *so* incredibly close to completely solving Alanna's case, and I just know that this is linked to the pest control van. Whoever sold out Alanna for her rare blood will be directly connected to the pest control van. I just know it in my gut. Besides, it would be silly for Jasper to come at me here at the office. I have the doors locked and the alarm set, so to say I'm not worried is an understatement.

I stretch my arms over my head and glance at the clock on our wall, which reads ten in the evening, and I sigh, desperately wanting to stay and work longer, but I had promised Jon I would stay no later than 10:00 p.m.

Lina: *Wrapping it up now. I'll be at your place in fifteen.*
Jon: *Perfect, I'll be waiting. Just packed my last box.*

I smile, giddy with excitement that Jon will be moving home tomorrow, and although I still have my hesitations and reservations about how certain things will work out, I know he's meant to be with us in our home, and I can't contain my smile as I place one hand on my belly and become excited for the first time, like really excited by the idea of Jon and I raising this baby together.

Lina: *How are things at the house?*
Ryker: *Great. Tell my homeboy Jon that I have the pilot of Blue Bloods loaded on Netflix and ready to go for him tomorrow.*
Lina: *LMAO. You got it. Smith and Molly still over?*
Ryker: *Yes, ma'am. And your motherly instinct . . . Spot on. They are definitely a "thing" or whatever the kids are calling it these days.*
Lina: *TY. I'll talk to her tomorrow.*

I stand from my chair and gather my things before heading to the alarm pad to cancel the alarm for *stay*, preparing to set it for *away*, and I unlock the office door. But as I return to the keypad to reset the alarm, I notice my car keys are still on my desk, and I grunt in frustration, turning from the door and making my way to my desk. I retrieve my keys, realizing that I haven't powered down my computer, so I take a second to do so, and as I do, something catches my eye on the whiteboard behind my desk. It's a photograph of Dean Turner, with lines drawn to the photographs of each missing girl and a diagram to the right of that one with the faces of Ace and Slinky. *Where did they go, anyways?* I think to myself as I realize they just sort of left the picture, and we're unsure of their whereabouts. They're flying very much under the radar in this investigation. *Could they be linked to the pest control van?*

I slide open my desk drawer and remove a whiteboard marker to write *pest control van?* Then I add *access to medical history?* But the second I write this, it hits me like a ton of bricks because I recall my first undercover day as Gemma: the stress of trying to fit in and the agitating fluorescent lights in chem lab and how I was overly grateful that the school nurse had my migraine medicine if I needed it. *The school nurse. If the nurse had my medication, what else had she known about me?* I also think back to the year I was a chaperone for Max and Lucy's kindergarten field trip, and within just my group of children, I had one bee allergy, one peanut allergy, and one diabetic. I was given an entire folder of information for these children, and I was only responsible for them for one afternoon. *Would the nurse be aware if a student had a rare blood type? But even more importantly, over the course of Alanna's schooling, who else could have been privy to such information?*

Lina: *I think I have a lead. Be there soon.*

I hold my phone in my left hand, and with my right I scribble *school nurse?* under Dean Turner's photo and stare in awe as I'm certain I've found our missing puzzle piece. I never met the school nurse, but I imagine it would have to have been someone in the medical field. As I trace a finger slowly from Dean Turner's mug shot and drag it down to the words I've just scribbled, a hand forcefully grips my wrist, and I freeze, stunned. I hadn't heard anyone enter the office, but I had been deep in thought and overly focused, and I *had* unlocked the door and turned off the alarm—*Nice one, Lina.*

"Hand me your phone. Slowly. And if you're lucky, you will make it out of this alive."

This can't really be happening, can it? But as the hand grips my wrist tighter and I struggle to process what's happening, all I can think is *Jasper*, and I instantly regret my involvement with his infidelity case. I *really* regret it.

"Let go of me," I say, my tone firm, squeezing my phone tightly.

"Hand it over now, bitch!" the man orders, this time gripping my neck with his other hand and pulling me away from the whiteboard and spinning me around so that I come face-to-face with a person I least expect.

What in the actual hell? "Hank?" I mouth more than say. "Hank," I finally manage, my words stifled by my lack of oxygen. "What the hell are you doing?"

"Sit," he demands, guiding me down to my chair, and I plop into my seat with a thump as he rips my phone from my grip. He towers over me, pressing down on my shoulders so hard that my lower back begins to ache.

"Stop," I beg. "Please, Hank."

"*Don't* say my name," he growls as his pale and freckled face grows red with anger. "You," he hisses, "need to stop making a fool of my family!" His mouth is inches from my face.

"I . . . I'm sorry," I say, fear ripping through my core, and my heart rate increases by the second.

I'm instantly taken back to the night at the frat house when Jon's frat brother attacked me and the night I was kidnapped from the bus stop in Tempe, the same week that Travis accidentally broke my arm. As my breathing grows heavier, I'm convinced I'm going to die right here at my desk in the office of Prickly Pen Investigations. I hold my hands up to make him go away, but he doesn't. Instead, he moves closer.

"I'm so, so, sorry."

"For what part?" he roars. "Pretending to be into me at Zack's party last year? Do you know how effed up it was that I thought I was trying to get with someone my age, and I was hitting on . . . hitting on *you*?"

Oops . . . forgot about that part. When I was undercover as Gemma Mendoza, I flirted with Hank in an effort to get intel on the missing girls. I suppose I underestimated the impact that left on Hank Gallagher, and I cringe, realizing that although I apologized to his mother, Penelope, I never actually apologized to him.

"I'm so sorry," I repeat. "I was . . . I was undercover. I was trying to find the missing girls." I think about that for a beat and remember that Hank and Alanna had been close, but I only became aware of that when Alanna told me. *Why hadn't Hank told me they were best friends, as Alanna had indicated?* "I was trying to find Alanna, Hank."

"Don't say her name!" He hisses, pounding his fist on my desk, and I choose to burst into tears. "Don't cry!" he says, pointing a finger to my face. "Don't you dare cry."

"I said I was sorry, Hank. Please let me go. We can sit and talk about this."

"Talk about what? Talk about how you set up my dad? I heard that recording, you know. You basically seduced him."

I open my mouth to defend our investigation, but I decide there's no point in doing so. Hank is clearly hurting, and he has pinned me as the bad guy, probably because accepting that his father was cheating on his mother is simply too much to process, too much to bear.

"I'm sorry I hurt you. Just please, try to understand, I was just doing my job. I was hired to find the girls, and then I was hired . . . I was hired by your mom."

"Well, I'm just doing my job when I do this," he growls, raising his fist to my face.

"I'm pregnant," I yelp. "Please." I sob. "Don't hurt me."

Hank's face freezes, and he drops his fist to his side. "Sure, like I believe a word you say," he says, shaking his head in disbelief. "You do *lie* for a living."

"Listen," I say, tears flowing freely, placing a hand to my cramping abdomen. "You are going to turn around and walk out of here, and we are going to pretend this never happened."

"Like hell we are."

"Hank—"

"I said don't say my name!" he yells even louder this time, and my only hope is the sketchy pawn shop guy who lives above his store might possibly hear him, because nobody is looking for me—nobody except Jon. *How long has it been since I sent that text? At least thirty minutes. Will Jon come looking for me? Please, Jon,* I think, but I'm caught off guard as another shooting pain rips through my gut, and I can't tell if my stomach is cramping up because I'm being literally attacked or if something could be wrong with my baby.

"I need to get to the hospital." My tone is even-keeled and somehow calm. "Something is wrong with the baby," I say, begging with my eyes. "Please."

"Why should I help you? The only thing you did was ruin my life, and you don't know a thing about me or my family."

"That's not true," I say, locking eyes with him. "I've known you for a long time."

"No, you haven't."

"Yes, I have. We took a swim class once, the twins and I . . . and your mom and dad were there with you and Bill."

At this, he freezes, and maybe he's either going to punch me or crumple to the floor in a ball of tears. "He was?"

"He was. My own husband wasn't there because he had to work. But your dad was there. He's a good man. He's a good man who made a horrible mistake," I say because I mean it. If nothing else, I've had my share of lessons in forgiveness. "And I found Alanna, didn't I? I brought her home safe and sound," I say, both hands on my belly.

"I wish you hadn't. She isn't the same person, and she's with *him* now."

"You weren't at the wedding," I say, realizing this for the first time.

"Nope."

"You love her, don't you?"

"Shut up!" he roars, pounding his fists on my desk, which makes me cry harder.

"Please stop," I beg. Then I remember the pepper spray Jon stuck in my purse when I insisted on working late even though Jasper had been sending nasty texts, and I consider reaching for it, but the thought of pepper spraying someone's kid in the eyeballs makes me cry even harder. "Those texts were from you, not your dad," I say, my voice catching in my throat. "You're upset with me because I'm the one who found evidence on your dad."

"You set him up," he barks.

I stare at my purse and consider reaching for it. But just as I do, a shadow moves by the office door, and I see him. *Jon.* I quickly bring my eyes back toward Hank as Jon pushes open the door slowly, carefully not to jingle to bells, and as he closes it softly behind himself, he puts one finger over his lips. "Please, Hank," I beg. "I need to get to the hospital. I really think something is wrong with my baby," I say again, this time for Jon.

When I glance up, I see his expression switch from calm to pure rage as he leaps forward and tackles poor Hank Gallagher to the ground.

"Get the cuffs, Lina," Jon says.

I do, scurrying over toward the other side of the office and returning with the cuffs Jon keeps by his desk.

"Dial 911," Jon says. "Tell them what happened . . . and if you were being serious about the baby . . . tell them you need an ambulance," he says, pressing down on Hank forcefully as he says this. "You are going to live to regret this, you little—"

"Stop," I say to Jon as the 911 responder answers the phone. I explain the situation, and she instructs me to stay on the line. "He's just a kid," I tell Jon.

"He's a punk kid," Jon hisses, removing his phone from his pocket.

"Who are you calling?" Hank asks, his once-intimidating voice now shaking like a leaf.

"Who else? Your mother."

"Please," he begs. "Don't call my mom."

"Telling jokes now, kid? You really screwed this one up," he says, heat rising to his cheeks.

I watch as Penelope's child rolls around like a fish out of water, begging Jon to let him go, and my heart shatters into a million pieces as I realize that we can do everything we can to raise good kids, but even the good ones make life-altering mistakes. And if I hadn't realized this with the abductions of Alanna, Chloe, and Teresa, I sure as hell am realizing it now. So I do the only thing I can think to do. I sit on the ground beside Jon and Hank, and I place a motherly hand to Hank's back, and I rub it gently like I would for Max.

"It's going to be okay," I whisper because that's what I would want another parent to do for me. *In the end, isn't that really what all this has been about for me, anyhow?* "It's all going to be okay."

Chapter Forty-One

Now (June 2025) Alanna

"I'm so sorry this happened, Lina," I say, wiping a tear from my cheek.

"It's okay," she says from her hospital bed although I don't really believe her. "Can you believe I'm pregnant?" She chuckles, gesturing toward a monitor at her bedside. "My kids don't even know yet, so shhh," she says with a wink.

"I won't say anything. So, when you were puking your guts out in Mexico . . .?"

"Pregnant."

"Wow."

"Consider this your friendly reminder to use birth control," she says with a smile.

"Noted. When Jon called Eddie to tell him what happened, it felt so . . . surreal. I know Hank is going through a hard time, but I never knew he was capable of doing something so horrible." I grimace, thinking of Hank breaking into PPI and attacking Lina, and the thought of that makes me start to cry again. "I just want all of this to be over," I say, biting down on my lip and clenching my fists.

"It will be soon," she says.

"How long are they keeping you here?" I ask, glancing around the hospital room, feeling like the walls are going to close in around me, and I realize that I may now have a fear of hospitals.

"Just another couple of hours," she smiles. "The baby looks good. I had a little bit of bleeding, but that can be normal. They just want to be sure. Where is Eddie now?"

"He's with Jon, talking about your lead. So, you think the school nurse may have outed my rare blood type?" I ask, thinking of Mrs. Small and her caring smile and tenderhearted personality, unable to believe that she might've had a part in all of this, and my instinct says no. "I just don't see it." I shrug. "But I guess you never—"

"Mom!" Lucy shrieks, bursting through the door, followed by Max, Jon, Lucy, and Eddie. Lucy throws her arms around Lina and sobs into her neck. "Are you okay?"

"You told them?" Lina scolds Jon.

"I'm sorry, babe," he says, taking his hand in hers. "It's sort of all over social media."

"How?" she gasps.

"Word gets out fast around here," Max says, kissing his mom on the cheek. "I hear you have something to tell us," he says, studying the monitor wrapped around Lina's abdomen.

"Lina!" Daphne gasps as she enters the room, followed by Ryker, who looks like he's been crying a lot.

"I'm okay, you guys," Lina smiles. "It's the middle of the night. Doesn't anyone sleep anymore?"

"Um, not when there's an emergency, and not when it comes to you," Ryker says as Molly and Smith enter behind him and Lina's hospital room is now filled to the max.

"Hey, guys," Lina says with a raise of an eyebrow.

"So, you had something to tell us," Lucy says, studying her mother in anticipation.

"Lina!" Travis says as he squeezes in beside Smith. "Are you all right?"

I laugh to myself, as Lina can't seem to catch her breath, and as I study her with her friends and family, I make a promise to myself to surround myself with people like this, people who will show up for me in the middle of the night simply because they love me. "She's going to be okay," I say so that she doesn't have to say it again.

"How's the—" Travis starts, but Jon holds his hand up to stop him.

"Lina and I were just going to tell the kids our news," Jon explains.

"We're having a baby," Lina says, smile beaming. "Max and Lucy, you're going to have a baby brother or sister," she says, her eyes welling with happy tears.

"Get the eff out of here," Max says, eyes wide and mouth agape.

"A baby!" Lucy shrieks. "Yes! I've always wanted a sister. Please let it be a sister."

"It's not a dog, Lucy," Max huffs. "This is, like, an actual human being that is going to grow up to be, like, a person."

"Yes, it is." Jon chuckles.

"I think," I say with a smile, "the word they are looking for is *congratulations*. Really, congratulations, guys. You really deserve this," I say, taking Eddie's hand in mine. "We are so happy for you." And I smile to myself as my eyes scan the crowd, which consists of Jon and Lina's friends and family, and I'm once again overwhelmed with emotion because I want *this*. This is what I want for Eddie and me. Then my thoughts come to an abrupt halt because I realize we already have it. I've had the love and support of my family this entire time. And now, I'm ready to embrace it.

An hour later, Eddie and I are back in our hotel room and back in bed, my new favorite place in the world, and as I nuzzle my head against his chest and inhale his sweet scent, I am very thankful that Lina is all right and really happy the baby is going to be okay. But I can't help thinking about Hank. *How could he do something so horrible? And even more importantly, how could I have missed this?*

As if reading my mind, Eddie asks, "You doing okay? I know you and Hank are close."

"Were close," I say. "Hank and I were close. I don't know if I can forgive him for this one."

"It's a tough one," Eddie agrees.

"Lina said something that didn't sit well with me," I say, looking up at Eddie in the darkness of the night. "She said that when she was undercover as Gemma, she asked Hank about me, and he never admitted we were close. Why do you think that is?"

Eddie thinks about that for a beat. "I'm not sure. Could be a lot of reasons," he says with a sigh. "It sounds like he's in love with you, Foster. Maybe it was just too much for him to talk about."

"Maybe," I agree. "But you don't think . . . you don't think that he was involved in it somehow?"

"What makes you say that?"

"Well, I just don't see poor Mrs. Small as a threat, for starters," I say, thinking about the accusation that the school nurse disclosed my blood type.

"And you think Hank would?"

"I don't think it's that black-and-white," I say, considering this as I trace Eddie's chest with my pointer finger. "I'll talk to them about it tomorrow. We have that meeting with Dean Turner, right?"

"Right," Eddie says. "Want to get some sleep?"

"I don't know," I say, kissing his chest and his abdomen then reaching my hands on either side of his face and drawing him close for a passionate kiss. "It's really hard to sleep when we can be doing this instead."

"Yes," he says, pulling me on top of him and gripping my waist in his hands. "I have a feeling I'm not going to be getting much sleep in my near future," he says, his accent thick.

I pull my shirt over my head and toss it to the side. "We have the rest of our lives to sleep. Make love to me, *husband*."

"Ohhh, say it again." He chuckles.

"Husband," I say as I roll onto my back and pull him on top of me, and my laughter is muffled by his kiss.

And we don't sleep one wink, but it is pretty freaking awesome, and dare I say—I'm one happy woman.

Chapter Forty-Two

Now (June 2025) Lina

"We have five minutes until our call with Turner," Jon says as he stands at the front of the conference room table and addresses Travis, Eddie, Alanna, and me. "Let's work this theory once more."

"Here's what we know," I say, rising to my feet. "Turner *had* to have found out about Alanna's blood type from someone at Emerson. My theory was the school nurse, Mrs. Small, could have disclosed this to Turner or maybe even anyone else during Alanna's time at Emerson. That will be nearly impossible to pinpoint on our own. We'll need Turner to confirm this. If we can get that, we can take down whoever did this and prevent them from wreaking havoc on another family. Also, it could bring us one step closer to figuring out the pest control van and their involvement."

"Good," Jon says. "Anyone else have anything to add?"

"I do," Alanna says. "I know Mrs. Small, and I don't think she would have hurt me intentionally."

"That's a good point, Alanna," Jon says, running his fingers over his chin's scruff. "But with that being said, can you think of anyone who would have? Hurt you on purpose?"

"No." She sighs. "I can't."

"Okay," Jon says, "let's get ready." He turns on the TV and clicks a few buttons, and there sits Dean Turner in his prison garb, looking worse than last time.

"Ten minutes," a guard barks.

"That's all we need. Thank you," Jon replies.

"Where's my daughter?" Turner hisses. "You promised me a visit from Molly."

"Yeah, about that." Jon sighs. "I can't force her to see you. I tried, but she isn't interested."

"Enough," he says, slamming his fist. "I'm done with you."

"She's dating my son, remember?" I say, just as Jon and I rehearsed.

"Your son?" he asks, narrowing his gaze and clearly not liking this idea.

"Yes, my son, Max. They have been together for quite some time now."

"I thought you were bullshitting me," Turner admits.

"Nope. No cap," I say.

"Dear Lord," Travis groans.

"They've been together a while now," I repeat with a shrug.

"Is that true?"

"It is," I say, staring into the camera and making my way closer to the TV. "And Max is a great kid, a great kid who listens to his mother." I shrug. "I bet Max would take Molly to visit you."

"Okay, Rivera, what do you want?" Turner huffs.

"First," I say, as Jon had earlier instructed, "Slinky and Ace. Where are they now?"

"That's what this is about?" he cackles. "Those two morons got the hell out of dodge last year. Probably in Mexico somewhere."

I look to Jon who shrugs and nods, encouraging me to move on, clearly not wanting to waste any more time talking about two men who were clearly Turner's pawns and nothing more.

"Alanna Foster has a rare blood type," I say, crossing my arms over my chest. "It is our assumption that you knew this when you sold her soul to the highest bidder."

"Thanks for that," Alanna mutters under her breath, too softly for him to hear her but validating enough, I'm sure.

"I wasn't aware," Turner says, glancing from Alanna to me.

"Okay, then," I say with a slight shrug. "I guess we're done here. I won't be asking Max—"

"Wait," he interrupts.

"I'm all ears," I say, a soft smile forming as I bite my lip in satisfaction.

"To be clear, you think I informed Alanna's kidnappers about her rare blood type?"

"Yes," we all say in unison.

Turner's mouth morphs into a demonic smirk. "No comment."

"Dean Turner I—" Travis starts but stops because the villainous belly laugh that erupts from the depths of his monstrous soul catches him off guard.

"Then no Molly," I boldly state. "I think we are done here," I say, rising to my feet. "And I can't wait to share what I learned about your wife's affair with the ladies at the next fundraiser meeting."

"Does she *ever* shut up?" Dean Turner asks, and I can't tell who he's asking but when Travis snorts because he has the emotional intelligence of a sixteen-year-old boy I decide I'd like to punch him, but instead I settle for kicking him in the shin underneath the table with my strappy work shoe.

"Ouch!" Travis cries out, biting down on his lip and clutching his shin.

I raise my brows and shrug as if to say 'you deserve it' because he did. "No," I say, gathering my hair over my shoulder. "I don't shut up. Ever."

"And she's an author," Jon adds. "I'm sure she would tell your story quite nicely."

"That's a great idea! What do you think Turner? Want to collab on a memoir? We could title it—"

"You have my attention," he interrupts, biting down on his bottom lip and running his fingers over his beard.

"Two minutes," the guard states with authority.

"Spill it Turner," Jon demands, as we all lean forward, holding our breath in anticipation of what we might be about to learn from the devil himself.

"If I tell you, you need to *promise* I can have a visit with my daughter."

"You have our word," Jon says because Molly agreed to this if he provided us with the information we're looking for.

"That little redheaded twerp, Henry Gallagher. He told me."

The room falls silent and I side glance at Alanna who has just turned a sickly shade of green and muffles a soft, "no," with a shake of her head as Eddie wraps his arm around her shoulder and pulls her close.

"Hank Gallagher?" I ask, finally finding my words, my mind blown over such a coincidence. *But was it a coincidence?* I'd just asked myself why it was that Hank hadn't told me about his relationship with Alanna. It was actually possible that Hank was hiding something. I glance over at Alanna, who is gripping Eddie for dear life.

"Hank didn't know about my blood type," Alanna argues. "*I* didn't even know about my blood type."

"I don't believe you," I say to Dean Turner. "If you're going to make things up—"

"One minute," the guard announces.

"Hank's mother, Penelope," Turner says, leaning in and raising his brow, "was *very* involved at Emerson, as you probably recall. She chaperoned her share of field trips and was privy to confidential information."

"That's true," Alanna and I say at the same time.

"She learned of Alanna's rare blood type during her involvement at the school and mentioned it to Hank, who had a strong interest in genetics and biomedical studies at the time. Hank had approached his teacher with the information because he wanted to write his senior thesis on the topic. The teacher came to me to ask permission, and I turned her down as it was an obvious privacy violation. But even still . . . that's how the information came about."

Holy shit! I scream silently. Hank gave Turner the information about Alanna's blood type without even meaning to. Of course he would feel guilty once Turner was convicted and it was revealed that Alanna was kidnapped for that very reason.

"Poor Hank," Alanna whimpers into Eddie's shirtsleeve. "He must feel so terrible."

"It was an accident," Eddie says. "We'll make sure he knows that."

"And you," I start but stop, placing one hand to my racing heart and the other to my belly. "You just couldn't resist sharing this information with a human trafficking gang?"

"We've been over this," he says, turning multiple shades of red. "They had my son. I did what I needed to do for my family—"

I flinch, and the way the screen goes dark and our call ends so abruptly shakes me to the core.

"No!" I wail.

"It's okay," Jon says, rubbing my back. "You did great."

"I didn't ask about the Pest Control Van," I say, shaking my head from side to side, and wiping an unexpected tear from my eye as Eddie and Alanna rise to their feet and exit the office, explaining that Alanna needs some air and I don't blame her. A parent volunteer at Emerson Academy privy to confidential information that, because she shared it with her son on a whim because of his interest in science, was the reason Alanna Foster was kidnapped into organ trafficking. *Like, for real?* I couldn't make this stuff up if I tried.

"It's okay," Jon says again. "Like I said, the police have that lead. Besides, isn't it safe to say that whoever was driving that van was just another creep involved in Turner's plan?"

I think about this for a minute, and I wonder if Jon might be right. Why am I so obsessed with solving this piece of the puzzle? Am I simply thinking about it from an emotional lens because *I* was transported in that van? Could it be because in the back of my mind, I am convinced that the first day Super Scorpion Pest Removal showed up at my house they were somewhat interested in my own daughter? Is this why I want to take them down? Or could there be more?

"I agree with Lina," Travis says, surprising both Jon and me.

"You do?" I ask, unable to hold back my surprise.

"I do. Sure, their involvement is most likely connected Orson Turner and Operation Superglue, but what if there is more to it? When they showed up at Lina's house they were more interested in her age than they were in actual pest removal."

"That's right," I agree. "What if they are part of a bigger operation?"

"They could be," Jon sighs. "But like I said—"

"What if Lucy had answered the door," I say, my words jumbling together in a panicked cluster. "What if aside from the Dean and Operation Superglue . . .what if this is another way these assholes to case neighborhoods and target women?"

Jon runs his fingers over his chin and thinks about this for a beat and I realize I've left him speechless. "I'm sorry," he says with a sigh. "I guess this whole time I've assumed you've been so consumed with the vans because of your own kidnapping. But yeah, when you put it that way, we may be on to something. I just wish there was more we could do."

I think about this and wonder if Jon might be right. If we've already handed this lead over to the police, is there really any more we can do? But as soon as the thought crosses my mind, I have my answer. Because if there is anything I've learned during this experience is that there is always something we can do. And as I study Jon and recognize the wheels turning in his mind, I know that for now, I've done enough. Because now that Jon has this idea in his mind, I know that he won't stop until we are able to get to the bottom of it. And for now, that needs to be good enough for me. And as I smile at Travis, who nods back at me in approval before closing his laptop and scooping up his paperwork, I finally feel the validation I've been waiting for. Because Jon Cote of Prickly Pen Investigations is on the case. But that of course, is a story for another day.

Later that night, Jon has moved in back home, and all is right with the world. That is, until we inform him that our *Blue Bloods* marathon is about to begin in the living room, and Ryker is waiting.

"You promised," I said, kissing him playfully on the cheek. "Turn that frown upside down."

"I know. I just *really* wanted to get you alone tonight," he whined.

"And you will. I promised Ryker one episode, and then you are all mine," I say with a smile. "Come on, everyone is in the living room."

"Everyone?"

"Yeah. Ryker, Daphne, and the kids," I say. "And . . . Molly and Smith."

"Seriously?"

"Seriously. Sorry, Officer Cote, I'm a package deal now."

"We are going to need a bigger house, aren't we?"

"Probably," I say, gesturing to my midsection and smiling playfully. "How about we take this one day at a time? And by *this,* I mean you and me."

"As long as my minutes are filled with you, Lina Rivera, I'm a happy man."

"I love you so much," I say, taking his hand in mine and leading him downstairs.

"Love you more," he replies as we make our way to the living room. "To infinity."

"Ready?" Ryker asks, remote in hand, popcorn on lap.

"Ready," Jon says, high-fiving Ryker and sitting on the end of the couch, leaving me with room to nuzzle in between Jon and Ryker. Ryker passes me the popcorn, and I hold it on my lap as season one of *Blue Bloods* begins. An overwhelming sense of happiness washes over me, and I can't tell if it's simply because I have everyone together, because of the notion that there's space in my life for both Jon and Ryker, or because of the closure I've finally received from Operation Superglue, but I, Lina Rivera, private eye, finally feel a sense of closure that I have been craving for over a decade.

"Hey," I whisper to Jon.

"No talking," Ryker says.

"Sorry," I say before leaning in again to whisper in Jon's ear. "Hey," I repeat.

"Trying to get me killed?" He smirks, looking toward Ryker. "That man is serious about Donnie Wahlberg."

"I can hear you," Ryker says between handfuls of popcorn.

"Sorry," I say again but continue to ignore him.

"Jon?"

"Yeah?"

"I'm happy you're home."

"I'm happy to be home. Now, let me watch some *Blue Bloods*, will you? I've been looking forward to this all day," he says with a wink.

"Like hell you have," I say, nuzzling up to his arm and resting my head on his shoulder.

I study Molly as she snuggles against Max, and I watch Lucy as she shyly reaches for Smith's hand. Then I place my free hand on my belly and can't help but wonder what the new addition to our family might bring, and I decide that I'm grateful for the unprotected office sex because Jon and I are going to be *parents* again—a second chance at this thing we call life. *And what's so bad about second chances anyways?* I'm ready. Ready to settle down with Jon and rebuild what we started— our family. I'm eager to spend time with my children and focus on my friendships with Ryker, Daphne, and Molly. Yes, I am ready for things to calm down a bit. Operation Superglue and Operation Cactus Blossom have been closed out, for the most part, and finally, after all this time things are starting to calm down. Yes, taking a little break will be just what I need.

"You good?" Ryker asks, between bits of popcorn.

"Huh?" I ask, not realizing how deeply I was zoning out.

"You, okay?" Jon asks, and I realize both men are staring at me with concern.

"Yes," I say, smiling at them both. "I'm great," I say, because I am.

But just as I lean my head on Jon's shoulder, and reach my hand into my popcorn bucket, my thoughts drift to the pest control van, Ace, Slinky, and other possible loose ends and I can't help but wonder if I could be doing *more*. More to stop the evil in the world. More to protect my own children, and I realize in this moment, that I am not going to be keeping things quiet anytime soon. I, Lina Rivera, Private Eye, will not stop—ever. In fact, I might just be getting warmed up.

Epilogue

February 2026 (8 Months Later)

The Midst of the Storm

Within the thirsty sea of sands,
A cactus blossom in cruel hands.
Resilient, strong, she never bends,
But with his touch her spirit mends.

In the darkest night, in fear's tight hold,
The truth unknown each promise gold.
Threatened by hope, longing to shine
In the midst of storm, their hearts align.

Love blooms in places unexpected,
A heart once guarded, now connected.
In desert winds, he finds her way,
A silver line on the darkest day.

The fading sunset calls to all,
In calm or rage, we rise, we fall.
But can we see, in tempest's might,
The beauty in each other's light?

She rises tall, with gratitude,
Appreciating life's vastitude.
For every mistake, a new life's begun,
Love is a gamble—this time they've won.

The audience claps and cheers as Alanna finishes reading an excerpt from her new book, a novel she wrote about her experience in organ trafficking—with my help, of course—as part of the campaign she's started with Carmen and Maria to help stop human trafficking and raise mental health awareness. As I waddle over to her, nine months pregnant and ready to pop, I couldn't be prouder.

Eddie wraps her up in the biggest of hugs, and the two of them rush over to Jon and me.

"You did great," I say, because she did.

"Thank you," Alanna replies. "I couldn't have done any of this without you."

"*You* did this," I reply, and this is a conversation we have often. "Your story is helping people. This is just what you wanted!"

"Yes, and also, we have news," Alanna says, looking from Eddie back to Jon and me.

"My green card," Eddie says proudly. "It was finalized today."

"Yes!" Jon says, high-fiving and hugging him. "That's good because I like having you around. You're an excellent detective."

"Back at you," Eddie says, patting Jon on the back.

"Speaking of which," Eddie says, leaning closer to Jon and me. "A friend of mine called me this morning about a cactus heist. Have you heard of it? A fifty foot, 150-year-old saguaro uprooted in plain daylight from a state park, for starters."

"Wow, that's something else. Look into it, and bring it to the team on Monday?"

"Sounds good, boss. Will do."

"For now," Jon says, rubbing my enormous belly, "my wife is eating for two, and she's overdue and starving. Anyone up for Italian?"

"That sounds amazing," I say, because it sounds *really* amazing, and I'm already planning to order the chicken parm with extra spaghetti.

But my thoughts are cut short because my phone rings and Lucy is calling, and she never calls; she just texts.

"It's Lucy," I say, concern washing over me. I put the phone on speaker and hold it up so Jon can hear. "Lucy? What's going on? Everything okay?"

"Mom!" she wails. "Mom, did you hear?"

"Hear what?" I ask, locking eyes with Jon. "Lucy, hear what?"

"What is it, baby girl?" Jon asks as Alanna and Eddie lean in, clearly worried about our daughter.

"Darcy Blue Boots, you know, my favorite country artist?"

"Of course we know who she is," I say, as it seems Darcy's concert is the only thing on Lucy's mind these days. "What is it? Was the show canceled?" I pout, disappointed for Lucy. "I'm sorry, girly, I know you've been looking forward to the show for quite some time now."

"Yes, it's canceled. But that's not all of it."

"What is it, then?" Jon asks, rubbing my back with the palm of his hand.

"She's missing."

"Missing?" I asked, struggling to process this information.

"Yes, they think she was kidnapped," Lucy sobs. "You can help her, right? You can find Darcy?"

"That's really not how this works, baby—" Jon begins.

But I'm hormonal, and my daughter is hysterical, and I refuse to accept this as an answer, so I give my husband the death stare and tell him with my eyes that he is fixing this.

"Please, Daddy. If anyone can find her, you and mom can."

"I'll see what I can do," Jon says with a sigh. "But it doesn't really work like that—"

"Thank you, Daddy. You will find her. I know you will," she says before hanging up the phone and leaving the four of us standing in a circle in the Emerson Academy auditorium, wondering what the hell we just got ourselves into. But we don't have time to overthink Darcy and her blue boots because I'm caught off guard by immense pressure in my belly followed by unexpected cramping as my water breaks over Eddie's very expensive custom-made brown leather boots!

"Oh God!" I shriek. "My water . . . I just . . . I'm so sorry, Eddie!" I wail.

"It's okay," he says reassuringly.

"Is that . . .? Did that . . .?" Jon asks, clearly going into panic mode.

"It's my water. It broke," I say, gripping Jon's wrist.

Of course, Jon wouldn't know what water breaking looks like because he was on the job when my water broke with the twins, and I was all alone in his apartment, and for a moment, a weird wave of excitement washes over me as amniotic fluid surrounds Eddie, Alanna, Jon, and me. Jon missed my water breaking for the twins, but this time, he's sliding around in it, trying to get a grip on the fact that he's going to be a dad again and very soon. And as Eddie runs to get the car and I waddle to the parking lot arm in arm with Jon and Alanna, I'm overwhelmed with joy. This time *will* be different for Jon and me. Because this time, he will be present in our lives, and I know beyond a shadow of a doubt that this time, we will get it right.

Until next time, Lina Rivera, private eye, signing off.

Operation Cactus Blossom for Life.

About the Author

Stacy Lee, the acclaimed author of the best-selling *Nubble Light* series on Amazon, is eagerly diving into her new venture—the captivating *Prickly Pen Investigations* series with Speaking Volumes Publishing.

A proud New Englander through and through, Stacy calls New Hampshire her home, where she resides with her endlessly supportive husband, two exceptional teenagers, and two cherished rescue pups.

Stacy's creative pursuits extend beyond the written page. Alongside her compelling fiction, she's currently engrossed in crafting a thrilling TV series based on the Prickly Pen Investigations, diving into the dynamic world of television production. Stacy's enthusiasm for storytelling spans her written works and her dedication to scriptwriting, where she eagerly collaborates within the vibrant and ever-evolving landscape of the entertainment industry.

Upcoming New Release!

STACY LEE

OPERATION DESERT BLUES
Prickly Pen Investigations
Book Three

Get ready for another thrilling ride with the Prickly Pen Investigations team! From one sticky situation to another prickly one, the team is back at it—stronger than ever.

This time, Jon and Lina are chasing a large reward for the return of missing country artist Darcy "Blue" Blaze, a sensation known for her talent and signature thigh-high blue suede boots. They find themselves navigating a maze of Darcy's past, filled with betrayed friends, a possible affair, a super stalker, and multiple enemies, making it nearly impossible to know where to begin—all while under the watchful eyes of the public.

Grab your Starbucks and reach for that popcorn, ladies and gentlemen, because Jon and Lina are back with more comedic drama and chaos than ever...

**For more information
visit:** www.SpeakingVolumes.us

Now Available!

STACY LEE'S

OPERATION SUPERGLUE
Prickly Pen Investigations
Book One

**For more information
visit:** www.SpeakingVolumes.us

Now Available!

EM TEMPLIN

THE SAPPHIRE GHOST
The Seriphin Ghosts
Book One

**For more information
visit: www.SpeakingVolumes.us**

www.ingramcontent.com/pod-product-compliance
Lightning Source LLC
LaVergne TN
LVHW041655060526
838201LV00043B/445